a place for for unicorns

NICOLA LINDSAY

D1385744

POOLBEG

Published 2002
Poolbeg Press Ltd.
123 Grange Hill, Baldoyle,
Dublin 13, Ireland
Email: poolbeg@poolbeg.com

© Nicola Lindsay

The moral right of the author has been asserted.

Copyright for typesetting, layout, design
© Poolbeg Group Services Ltd.

1 3 5 7 9 10 8 6 4 2

A catalogue record for this book is available from the British Library.

ISBN 1 84223 100 6

Cover designed by Slatter-Anderson
Typeset by Patricia Hope in Goudy 11/15
Printed by Cox and Wyman

www.poolbeg.com

About the Author

A latecomer to writing, in her early fifties, Nicola Lindsay had a collection of poetry and a book for children published before turning to novel-writing. Her novel, *Diving through Clouds*, was published by Poolbeg in November 2001. She is often heard reading her work on RTE's *Sunday Miscellany* and enjoys the challenge of writing material for workshops, revues, songs, radio scripts and magazine articles.

She firmly believes that diversity is the spice of life and has discovered that life gets better and better – if you give it the chance.

Acknowledgements

To all at Poolbeg for their interest, enthusiasm and professionalism and who made this book possible.

Also affectionate thanks to Charles, without whose loving support and encouragement it would have been very difficult for me to actually get down to it and write for seven hours a day!

For my daughters, Rebecca, Francesca and Alexandra with my fondest love.

The Unicorn

This is the creature there has never been.
They never knew it, and yet, none the less,
They loved the way it moved, its suppleness,
Its neck, its very gaze, mild and serene.
Not there, because they loved it, it behaved
As though it were. They always left some space
And in that clear, unpeopled space they saved
It lightly reared its head, with scarce a trace
Of not being there. They fed it, not with corn
But only with the possibility of being.
And that was able to confer such strength,
Its brow put forth a horn. One horn.
Whitely it stole up to a maid, to be
Within the silver mirror and in her.

Rainer Maria Rilke
From 'SONNETS TO ORPHEUS', Second part.

Chapter One

Anna woke sweating and terrified. Over the past few weeks, her dreams seemed to have become more vividly alarming. The sense of being lost in unrecognisable surroundings with no way of extricating herself had been so real, the following morning was tainted by their memory.

But this latest dream was different. Her father had been standing at the top of a long flight of stairs, calling her. His face looked as though he were in pain as he pleaded for her to come to him. Not only was she unable to move but also she was being slowly sucked under by some force or thing she could not see.

She sat up in the bed and stared around her. For a moment, she couldn't remember where she was. The only thing she was sure of was that she desperately wanted her father – not the one in her dream but the familiar, smiling man who knew how to comfort her when she was afraid. "It's all right, Annie. There's nothing to worry about," he would say, putting an arm around her and giving her a kiss on the top of her head. And suddenly, there *was* nothing to worry about.

As she sat, rigid in the tangle of sheets, her head cleared and she remembered where she was; an exile in a strange house, in a strange country, hundreds of miles away from him and all the things that were ordinary and understood.

The tall, louvred shutters let in a faint glimmer of light from the house opposite and the smells of the town filtered into the stuffy bedroom on the hot, night air. Smells that were alien to the eight-year-old child, brought up in middle-class England in the late nineteen-sixties. She could not name them. There was the faint whiff of bad drains mixed with the scent of sizzling olive oil, garlic and aromatic herbs from the Mediterranean, which she had not smelt before. It was tangy and exotic – and somehow exciting.

The sounds from the street below were different too. She had never heard trams or the angry, wasp-like sound of the speeding Vespas and Lambrettas as they wove their way determinedly through the clogged evening traffic. Somewhere in the background, car horns blared impatiently.

She and her mother had arrived in Pisa two days earlier. Anna was still finding it difficult to grasp the fact that her father would not be joining them for their Italian 'holiday', as her mother insisted on calling it. He had been left behind, in disgrace in Cambridge. Anna felt a sharp pang of homesickness, of wanting to be with him, sitting close to him, he with his arm around her. She could imagine his smell, of aftershave and cigarettes, of gin and of the peppermints he used to suck to try and conceal the fact of his drinking from her mother. Anna always knew when he had 'imbibed a little too much', as he jokingly put it and she would wait anxiously for the inevitable angry criticism from her mother, who thought his behaviour shameful. Each time it happened, it seemed to Anna that her mother became more cold towards her husband and each time it ended in increasingly violent confrontation.

One evening, only a week ago, Anna had been in her room, reading, when her father returned home and she heard their voices in the room below as the inevitable argument gathered momentum. She had held her hands over her ears and tried unsuccessfully to concentrate on her book. Then, everything became very quiet. A little while later, the front door slammed and she ran to the window.

Her father, carrying a small holdall, was walking over to his car. He looked tired and strained. As he started up the engine, he peered out through the windscreen, looking up at her window. He waved and gave her a small, deprecating smile, as though to say, 'I know. I'm sorry'.

That night, she cried herself to sleep.

And now, they were so far away, in a country peopled by dark-haired, olive-skinned beings, whose breath smelt and who spoke a language Anna could not understand. These noisy strangers seemed on the verge of warfare most of the time, so loud and excited were their voices. One minute, all-out war seemed to have been declared. Then suddenly, they would start to embrace one another with enthusiasm, wreathed in smiles. Even the men kissed each other. She had observed their antics with surprised interest, tinged with apprehension.

A sudden noise from the street below made her jump. She strained to hear if her mother was coming up the curving, stone staircase, her high heels clicking on the steps. But all she heard was the sound of distant animated conversation and laughter as a downstairs door was opened and then silence when it was closed again.

She sat, knees drawn up to her chin in the almost dark room, listening, willing her mother to come. Why did she have to spend so much time at the dinner table she wondered.

Rosalind spoke Italian almost as fast as the rest of them but with a gentler intonation and a touch of English reserve that they seemed to find charming. The child thought how strange it was that her mother had changed so much in just two days. The angry, bitter woman had been left behind in England. Now, her beautiful mother seemed to relax and blend in with these people, as though this were where she really belonged.

Anna suddenly froze. It had started again – the high-pitched mosquito whine, circling her bed, full of malice. She could imagine the creature poised, waiting to dive down and feed on her flesh, to pierce her skin and suck her blood. She desperately tried to pinpoint where the small enemy lurked. After attempting to cover herself with the sheet, leaving no possible point of entry, she started to feel as though she was suffocating and re-emerged, hot and disorientated.

There was a rustle of silk and the smell of gardenias. The light was switched on and her mother stood by the bed. Rosalind, perfumed and fresh, in spite of the heat, looked down at her sweaty-faced daughter who was large-eyed with misery and close to tears. There was a tiny hesitation, a hint of impatience before she sat down at the end of the bed.

"What's the matter, Anna?"

Anna looked up at her. She suddenly felt that her fears of being eaten alive by a giant mosquito would seem ridiculous to her self-possessed mother, who was not equipped with much imagination or patience.

She took a deep breath.

"There's a mosquito and it won't go away," she said, as calmly as she could manage.

Her mother disentangled her daughter's hand from her arm and got up from the bed.

"Is that all? Well, we'll just have to deal with him, won't we?"

Rosalind walked briskly into the adjoining bathroom. When Anna had first seen it, she considered it the height of luxury with its curving, ornate taps and sunken bath with wine-coloured marble from ceiling to floor. She had not known that people had bathrooms like this. She wondered if there were other ones as large and as beautiful in the rest of the house or whether she had been given it as a treat, because she was a guest.

"Come on, Anna! Show me where this dreadful mosquito is," her mother said, coming back into the bedroom, swishing a hand towel backwards and forwards in a menacing fashion.

Together they tracked down the insect, which Anna thought looked very much less alarming in the lamplight than it had sounded in the dark. She was almost disappointed. Rosalind gave chase around the room and was so energetic in her pursuit that Anna started to thoroughly enjoy the scene and encouraged her with cries of, "It's over there! No, above you! Look! It's hiding in the corner!"

Eventually, it was all over and a small, telltale smear of blood streaked the wall above her bed and also, she noted regretfully, the beautiful, cream towel that her mother dropped with a careless flourish onto the chair.

"Now! Enough of this nonsense! It's time you were asleep."

"Can I have the light on? Please?"

"Don't be ridiculous! That will only encourage the little brutes to come in their thousands and then you will have so many holes in you that you will end up looking like one of those smelly cheeses in Mr Brewer's shop!"

Anna giggled, then her face became serious again. She suddenly had a mental picture of hordes of ravening, blood-hungry mosquitos, queuing up outside her window, ready to launch an attack. She could imagine that awful whine, multiplied by a thousand.

"Will you stay with me for a bit?"

Again, the child noticed the fleeting but often seen look of irritation on her mother's face. Anna knew that Rosalind would rather be downstairs with the others but she wanted her to herself, even if only for a little while.

Her mother perched on the edge of the bed, as though she were a bird poised for flight.

"Well, what do you want to talk about?"

"Tell me about the place you said we were going to tomorrow."

"Tirrenia. I told you. It's got a nice sandy beach with pretty little wooden chalets and we will have a picnic there with the others. You'll love it." Rosalind got up, smoothing back her hair. "Now, for goodness' sake. Tuck down and go to sleep. I must go downstairs. They will be wondering what on earth has happened to me. There's no need for you to look like a wet weekend." She paused and looked at her daughter intently. "You know, Anna, I don't know how long we are going to be staying here but it could be for quite a while. So, buck up and start enjoying it."

Anna's heart sank. She thought of her father and wondered what he was doing at that precise moment. He would be lonely at home without her to read to when he got back from the office.

Rosalind leaned over and brushed Anna's cheek with her lips.

"Goodnight. See you in the morning."

The bedside lamp was switched off with a brisk click and she was gone, leaving a faint trace of perfume in the darkened room. The girl listened to her fading footsteps as she descended the stairs and then the sound of a door closing.

Anna lay for some time without moving, relieved that there were no sounds of any kind inside the bedroom. She thought of Tirrenia and tried to conjure up a picture of how it would be, splashing in a sea that was not freezingly cold like back at home.

Promising herself that she would 'start enjoying it', as

7

she had been instructed by her mother, she turned onto her side with a sigh. Involuntarily, her thumb crept up to her mouth as she fell asleep.

* * *

In the elegant dining-room downstairs, the men at the dinner table watched admiringly as Rosalind entertained them with amusing stories about a mad aunt of her husband's, her expressive face animated and slightly flushed from the wine. Her green eyes sparkled attractively in the candlelight. Speaking Italian almost masked the malicious edge that was invariably present when she described anyone who showed affection for the absent David.

Chapter Two

Rosalind Armitage stretched her long, elegant arms above her head and yawned. She moved slowly towards the shuttered windows of her bedroom, aware of a feeling of nausea, a reminder that she had drunk a little too much the night before. She had enjoyed herself in that beautiful dining-room, well aware that she was the centre of attention as she regaled them with amusing stories of her husband's demented aunt.

Her slight headache became more noticeable as she pushed the shutters aside, stepping quickly back from the bright morning sunlight.

She was angry and her anger – as it usually did – made her feel aggressive. She was angry with her mismatched husband, left behind at home and getting up to God knows what with some trollop he had met through his work or whom he had just picked up. He was notorious for giving lifts to nubile blondes at bus stops. She was angry that it had not been possible to leave her daughter with her husband and that the child seemed to go out of her way to be unattractive and unremarkable. And Rosalind was angry that she felt like a poor relative staying in this fine house that she would have liked for herself.

Frederica had always been a generous friend, right from the time they had first met at the expensive boarding-school which Rosalind's parents had barely been able to afford. Both Frederica and Roberto, her darkly handsome husband, had been kindness itself since she and Anna had arrived in Pisa. Kind, and yet with an aloofness in the way they had asked after the missing David, whom they privately remembered as an entertaining and agreeable man. It was as though they thought that leaving one's husband after only ten years of marriage was a sign of a badly ordered existence – and not quite 'comme il faut'.

Roberto's mother, the formidable Contessa, had been completely civil and correct with Rosalind but there was more than a touch of frost in her cultured voice every time she spoke to her. She seemed not to want to enter into any unnecessary dialogue with the Englishwoman. Rosalind knew perfectly well that she was being put in her place and did not like the feeling. Especially as her place, in the Contessa's eyes, seemed to merit little attention at the bottom of the heap.

La Contessa came from an old, aristocratic family and she talked, using the seductive French 'r', as did many of the Italian upper classes, including Roberto. Somehow, Rosalind only found it irritating when his mother spoke in this way. The Englishwoman made sure she rolled her own 'r's with gusto.

She held a dress up at arm's length. What would look fetching for a day at the beach? Roberto and his younger brother, Carlo, would be accompanying them, also Frederica and her sister, Chiara, with her fiancé Gianni.

Chiara was musical, artistic, very beautiful and obviously radiantly in love with Gianni. She gave off a sense of wellbeing that made Rosalind feel sour with envy.

She tossed the dress onto the bed and pulled another garment from the wardrobe.

There was a discreet knock on the bedroom door.

"*Pronto?*"

"*Signora, la prima colazione l'aspetta,*" the cheerful voice of Gina, the housekeeper, sang out.

"*Sì, sì. Grazie, Gina. Vengo subito.*"

Rosalind sighed. The last thing she felt like was a polite breakfast presided over by Roberto's bloody mother.

She remembered Anna and the nonsense of the night before. I suppose the wretched child is fast asleep now that it's time to get up, she thought irritably. How free David was, unencumbered by an over-sensitive small daughter. He was able to suit his day to his whims. Even his work as a solicitor was arranged around his lunching at the club or attending an auction or race meeting. He juggled his clients around his social calendar in such a cheerfully charming manner that none of them seemed to mind.

'Why is life so unfair?' she asked herself, spraying her neck and wrists with a liberal quantity of '*Joy*', which she knew she could not afford to replace when it ran out.

* * *

11

Anna had been awoken by Gina, with a wide smile and a loud "Isa nice day. Plenty sun, plenty hota!"

On Anna's arrival in the house, she had immediately taken a liking to short, plump Gina with her friendly manner and her delightful way of talking English, lingering on each consonant and with 'A's thrown into every and any available gap. They had already had several misunderstandings, which had ended in a lot of laughter and hand-flapping, shoulder-shrugging and eyes to Heaven on the part of the housekeeper.

Gina came from a tiny village in Sicily and her family was large and poor – a grinding poverty, unguessed by the child. To Anna, she always seemed cheerful, making jokes and flirting with Alfredo, the gardener. She refused to dwell on life's difficulties and if Gina had been asked about the problems of living under the watchful eyes of the Mafia, she would roll her own eyes and laugh, saying, "*Che Mafia?*"

* * *

The child sat quietly at the breakfast table, watching and listening – trying to make sense of the conversation going on around her. Gina loaded her plate with a crusty roll and butter, apricots that were still warm from the tree and figs and cherries. A glass of freshly squeezed orange juice stood in front of her. The delicious aroma of expensive coffee filled the air.

La Contessa was seated at the head of the table, drinking from a wafer-thin cup of palest rose. From time to time, her glance touched on Anna without interest as she discussed plans for the day with Roberto. However, halfway through the meal, she inclined her head slightly in the child's direction.

"Is your mother coming down to join us for breakfast?" she asked pointedly, in almost accentless English.

"Yes. . . I think so." Anna felt crumbs of bread sticking in her throat. She swallowed hard. "Though she usually has hers in bed . . . at home."

There was a silence and La Contessa glanced over to Roberto at the other end of the table. She raised her eyebrows a fraction. Anna felt that she had said the wrong thing but was not sure why. She squirmed in her seat and slid a little lower in the chair, trying to make herself look less obvious.

Just then, Rosalind entered the room and all eyes turned towards her. She was looking a little pale and there were slight smudges under her eyes. She was wearing a clinging, apple-green dress that crossed over in front, accentuating and flattering her figure and the effect was extremely appealing. She knew her appearance was appreciatively noted by all the men at the table. She also saw how cool was the regard of the dark brown eyes of the woman at the other end.

"I'm so sorry to be late," she said airily. "Good morning, Anna." This greeting to her daughter was almost an afterthought. Rosalind slid gracefully into her chair, unfolded the heavy linen napkin on her side plate and turned her attention to Roberto.

While the adults talked, Anna finished her breakfast. Then she sat, gazing around at the room. She rested her head against the back of her chair and looked up at the painted ceiling, where a cluster of rose-pink cherubs cavorted amidst a fruit salad of peaches and dew-bejewelled grapes. The child had never seen anything quite like it before, certainly not on a ceiling. She wondered how difficult it had been for the artist to avoid getting paint in his eyes while he was working and whether it would not have been easier for him to have chosen to decorate the walls instead.

"Would you like to leave the table, Anna?" asked Frederica.

"Oh, yes, please," said Anna, gratefully. "May I go and see Gina?"

Frederica nodded. She smiled as Anna left the room and turned to Rosalind. "I think Anna has found herself a friend."

Rosalind did not hear her. She was now talking to the Contessa's younger son. He was gazing into her green eyes with rapt attention.

Anna made her way along the corridor towards the kitchen. She liked the sound her sandals made on the stone floor and the feeling of being bare-legged, wearing only a thin cotton dress. Already, the morning was hot and airless inside the house.

Timidly, she pushed open the door and saw two figures standing in the glare of sunlight at a further door that opened into the courtyard beyond. The woman was leaning against the man, cradled in his arms. He had his cheek against her neck and his hands cupped her large breasts. He was talking in a low voice.

Anna knew instinctively that her mother would not approve of what he was doing but she thought they looked very comfortable, standing so close to each other like that and the way the man held the woman was gentle. She had never seen her parents standing like that together, so close and happy-looking. The girl suddenly realised the woman was Gina. She was not sure if she should make her presence known or not and was on the point of retreating when Gina turned and saw her.

"Ah, isa Anna, Alfredo. Look, Anna hasa come to visit."

Anna loved the way Gina pronounced her name, lingering on the 'n' of Anna, making it sound so much more interesting and musical than it ever had before.

Alfredo reluctantly relinquished his hold on Gina and moved away from her. He winked at Anna and ran a dusty, brown hand through his thick black hair.

"*Buon giorno, Signorina!*"

She felt that he was gently teasing her but decided that she did not mind – and she liked being called Signorina.

Gina beamed at her.

"Isa good, the breakfast?"

"Yes, thank you, Gina. It was lovely – especially the apricots."

"You want to come and picka the cherries with Gina?"

Anna's face lit up.

"Oh yes. I'd like that."

Gina scooped up a large wicker basket from under the enormous, wooden kitchen table and beckoned to her. Then she turned towards Alfredo, who stood by the open

15

door, watching her, and said something quickly, making shooing movements with her free hand as though she were chasing out an errant chicken that had strayed indoors. Then she made as though to offer the child her hand but thought better of it. This young girl was so unlike any eight-year-olds she had ever known – so solitary and contained. Gina had noticed how her mother showed no interest in her.

As they went outside, the woman thought of her own, mostly happy childhood. They had gone without material things but they had never lacked love and attention from their parents. She remembered her father, teasing her mother as he sat at the table with a glass of wine and how they had all touched and hugged and cried and laughed together and, most of all, she remembered how they had cared for one another. She longed to hug this little one and make her become more alive and animated.

Gina led the way, under the lemon-scented mimosa and the wisteria with its contorted trunk that looked to Anna as though it was almost alive, climbing the walls, holding on to the old house in a sinuous grip like some monstrous serpent. She admired the carpet of delicate lilac petals under her feet. It made her think of the confetti she had seen being thrown at the wedding she and her father had accidentally come across one day when they walked past the little church near their home.

Contentedly, she followed Gina through the archway into the garden beyond. There were several fruit trees and espaliered peaches growing against the old stone walls that enclosed the property. Anna walked silently, taking in her surroundings with interest, soaking up the hot sunshine, inhaling the unknown scents of the garden. She liked the cool sound of the splashing fountain, its rim encrusted with fossils, some serpentine, some cigar-shaped, some round. She stopped for a moment to trace them lightly with her finger. The granite felt slightly rough and was warm to the touch.

Alfredo was hoeing in the shade of some large fig trees, positioning himself so that he had a clear view of Gina as she placed a small wooden ladder at the base of a heavily laden cherry tree.

"You come picka the cherries?"

Anna went over to the tree. With a polite smile, she refused the outstretched hand the other offered her.

"It's all right, Gina. I can manage. I will be nine in two weeks, you know."

"Nine! That isa very big. Soon I think you will be *elegantissima* lady, like-a your mamma, no?"

Anna did not reply but climbed carefully up the first few rungs of the ladder. She had no intention of growing up to be like her mother but neither did she want to offend Gina by saying so.

The fruit hung in clusters around her, the leaves making a shady canopy, flecked with narrow streaks of sunlight. The cherries were so dark that they looked almost black and their skins were shiny and smooth. They seemed unreal, too perfect to be true when she thought of the dusty, dull red, bruised fruit she had seen in the market at home. These made you want to cram them into your mouth; she could imagine how juicy they would be. She called down to Gina, who was methodically picking fruit from the lower branches.

"Is it all right if I eat some?"

"*Sì, sì, certo*. Eat, eat," came the cheerful response from below. "Then you help Gina make the pasta. *Sì?*"

"*Sì*," said Anna, solemnly.

When Gina decided they had picked enough and that Anna had probably eaten more than was perhaps wise, they started back towards the house. They were just about to go through the archway when Rosalind appeared from the other side. She looked annoyed.

"Anna, what *are* you doing? You were supposed to be getting ready to go to the beach," she said accusingly.

Anna moved closer to Gina's flank.

"I want to stay. Please? I'm going to help Gina make pasta. Please let me stay."

"You really are strange, Anna. Most children would jump at the idea of a day at the sea. Anyway, you'll only get in Gina's way."

Gina rested one hand lightly on Anna's shoulder.

"No, *Signora*. Anna can stay witha Gina. *Niente problema, Signora.*"

Rosalind looked at Anna's stained mouth and hands and then flashed a brilliant smile at the woman. She knew that Gina did not like her. She could feel the unspoken criticism, which showed itself only in the other woman's large, dark eyes.

"Oh, very well. I suppose it will be all right. Are you quite sure, Anna?"

Anna had never been more sure. She nodded. "Yes, thank you."

18

"Well, be good and do as Gina tells you." She was already turning away from them as she spoke. "*Ciao*, Gina."

"*Arrivederla, Signora,*" came the dry response from Gina as she watched the slim figure hurrying back to the house, eager to get on with the day ahead without her small daughter. The woman looked down at Anna with a broad grin. "We have good a day – Anna and Gina. *Sì?*" she said, in a conspiratorial voice.

"*Sì*," replied Anna again but, this time, with an answering smile.

* * *

Anna did indeed have a good day. Together, they washed the fruit, removing the stalks and leaves. Some of the cherries were simmered in a copper pan. Then pastry was rolled out and tarts made, decorated with shapes that Anna cut out – stars, flowers, and animals – all much admired by Gina.

"*Che bello!*" she exclaimed, clapping her hands together, when Anna shyly showed her the assortment of shapes scattered on the flour-covered table.

The child watched as the woman rolled out the pasta mix until it was paper-thin, rolling and cutting with the lightning movements of many years' practice. Fresh vegetables were chopped, ready to be added to the minestrone for the evening meal.

It was very hot and they drank iced lemonade. Anna was asked by Gina to take a glass out to the sweating Alfredo, who thanked her gravely, treating her in a way that made her feel grown up.

Paola, the skinny young maid who made the beds and scrubbed the floors, joined them for lunch. It was one of the nicest meals Anna could remember having eaten. They sat at the large kitchen table and she slipped off her sandals so that her feet rested on the cool flagstones as she watched the others laughing and talking. They encouraged her to eat as much as she was able and tempted her into tasting a slice of the fat garlic salami and the strange, round, white cheese that Gina kept in a bowl of water.

In the middle of the laughter and conversation, Anna suddenly thought of her father and an ache that was almost more than she could stand spread across her chest.

Gina noticed her withdrawn expression and was immediately full of concern.

"Anna! *Che cos'è?*"

"I'm sorry Gina . . . I . . ." Anna halted, her face stiff with tension.

"Anna isa tired, no? *Una piccola siesta*, you like?"

The child scrambled thankfully from her chair and, picking up her shoes, fled from the room. As the door closed behind her, Paola looked at Gina.

"*Poverina!*"

"*Sì,*" agreed Gina, quietly, "*è vero. Poverina.*"

Chapter Three

"It is a nice day," Anna enunciated, carefully.

"Ita isa nice-a day."

"No, Gina. It is a nice day."

"That isa what I say! Isa nice-a day," protested the other, laughing at the look of concentration on her young tutor's face.

Anna was starting to think that although she might succeed in teaching Gina new vocabulary, she was not going to succeed when it came to a new style of delivery. She leaned back against the warm, stone wall, her face dappled by the sunlight that filtered through the feathery leaves of the mimosa and watched the woman as she expertly topped and tailed a bowlful of green beans. Gina looked up at her and smiled.

"Gina not speaka good the English."

"Oh, no! You speak very well," Anna reassured her hastily. "It's just that you sound rather . . ."

"*Italiana*, no?" suggested Gina, with an amused smile.

"A bit. But if we go on practising, you *will* get better."

"*Certo, carina!*"

Their lesson was interrupted by the Contessa's bell. Gina stood up, hastily poking back strands of her long dark hair into the carefully arranged coil on top of her head and vanished indoors.

* * *

The Contessa never came into the kitchen, leaving the domestic arrangements to Frederica and Gina. The elderly woman spent much of her time in her dead husband's study, reading and writing letters or listening to music on the old-fashioned radio in its heavy, wooden case. Occasionally, in the afternoons, she would order the car and visit old friends to take tea.

She had been a talented cellist before she married. She was also a knowledgeable botanist and fluent in several European languages. As a young woman, Malvina was a restrained, private individual. Then she had met and fallen in love with the Count and slowly she had changed and become not so inhibited, less cool in her manner – for a while.

Until she discovered that he had been keeping a mistress for many years. Although aware it was considered '*de rigueur*' by many of her husband's friends, somehow she had thought that he would never need to stray and that she would be able to give him all the intellectual stimulation and feminine companionship he required. It was a blow to her self-confidence to discover his infidelity and she was deeply hurt. The thought of making a scene and confronting him was distasteful and unthinkable. So, she had suffered the indignity of his betrayal with fortitude and in silence.

It had been something of an embarrassment to find herself pregnant with Carlo so late in her marriage, fourteen years after the birth of Roberto. But then, the Count had been a passionate man with a charming and persuasive way that she found irresistible, even after the disappointments of many years of marriage.

The Contessa was now sixty-four and nineteen-year-old Carlo with all his *joie de vivre* was sometimes a little hard to take but he reminded her so much of her dead husband. He had the same rare gift of making women feel special and interesting. She found it easy to forgive him his wild behaviour. The woman would look into his handsome face and see the man she married so many years before.

She was not at all happy about the arrival of the two newcomers – the unwanted child, whose presence she found strangely disturbing and her insouciant mother, for whom the Contessa had no time. She had seen that type before, all vivacious and fun-loving with no idea of self-discipline. She was sure that Rosalind took pleasure in not playing by the rules. If Roberto were to be believed, the woman planned a long stay and seemed untroubled by any thoughts of her abandoned husband or what the future held for herself and her young daughter.

* * *

As the days passed, Anna missed her father less acutely

although she thought of him every night before she fell asleep. She wondered why he had not written to her as he had promised but she managed to convince herself that he was probably too busy. After all, she reasoned, he had to look after himself as well as going to the office. She was sure he would write, when he had time.

Also, her phobia of mosquitos was diminishing and, aided and abetted by a laughing Gina, they had done to death dozens of them in their regular evening forays before she went to bed.

Anna's mother seemed content to spend her days in excursions to art galleries and shopping sprees with Frederica and, sometimes, a somewhat unwilling Chiara. The evenings were full of dinner parties or sorties to the theatre.

To Rosalind, it was like rainfall after an interminable drought. This was what life should be like, she thought: exciting, varied, smart and fast-moving. She revelled in the attention she attracted and could not get enough of it. The Englishwoman was much in demand by Frederica and Roberto's friends. Her fine looks and excellent dress sense, fluent Italian and instinctive appreciation of beauty and quality and of the good things in life, stood to her advantage. The fact she had left her husband behind in England also intrigued them.

* * *

Early one evening, after a sultry, overcast day, which had made even the sunny Gina a little out of sorts, Rosalind snapped at Anna in front of the others, making her young

24

daughter flush with resentment. Her action had given rise
to a sudden, awkward pause in the general conversation.
The woman immediately regretted her ill temper, blaming
it on the weather and an incipient headache. She retired
to her room to lie down and rest before the evening party,
which was to be given by a friend of Roberto's in an old
palazzo, hidden away in the hills several miles from the
town.

Rosalind was particularly annoyed with Anna, who had
inadvertently embarrassed her that morning. Gina had
been unable to look after the child and a reluctant
Rosalind took her to visit the *Banca d'Italia*, where she had
been invited to take coffee with Gianni and see his smart
office, much to the displeasure of Chiara who had been
unable to join them.

Anna fidgeted about, finally upsetting her glass of
orange juice onto the beautiful carpet, causing her mother
to slap her and speak in a sharp, scolding voice. Rosalind
knew immediately that this behaviour of hers had ruined
the image of the unflustered, cool, slightly vulnerable
creature that she wished to portray to the man sitting
opposite her. The whole thing had been unsatisfactory and,
in spite of Gianni's protestations that no damage had been
done, she cut short the visit.

Holding Anna's hand in a vice-like grip, they had
emerged into the heavy midday heat. As they made their
way down the wide steps that swept up to the bank's
imposing entrance, the skirt of Anna's dress was caught in
an eddy of air, causing it to float upwards to reveal a total
lack of any form of undergarment. Rosalind was mortified

by the scandalised stares from a couple of well-dressed elderly ladies and the look of intense interest from a small boy sitting astride a red tricycle in the company of his smart, uniformed nanny.

She gave Anna's arm a particularly sharp tug, causing her to stumble on the bottom step.

"Good God! I thought at least you knew how to get dressed properly. Or are you just trying to embarrass me?"

"What's the matter?"

"What do you mean what's the matter? You're not wearing any knickers."

"Oh, I forgot."

"How *could* you forget?"

Anna did not answer. She was puzzled, as she so often was, by the strength of Rosalind's reaction to something that seemed unimportant. In the rush to get down to see Gina that morning, she had forgotten to put on her knickers – that was all. She had not done it on purpose to annoy her mother.

The journey back to the house was fast and furious, with Anna more or less frogmarched along the baking pavements. There was a smell of freshly roasted coffee in the air. The child looked longingly at the people who sat in the shade of the striped café awnings, eating mouth-watering, bite-size confections called *dolci*, sipping cool drinks and enjoying ice creams which Anna knew from experience were delicious. She also knew that this was not the right time to request either a cool drink or an ice cream from her furious mother.

* * *

That afternoon, Anna considered it might be prudent to make herself scarce until it was time for the evening meal. She lay on her bed, feeling limp and bored. It was oppressively hot. Little beads of sweat gathered on her forehead and upper lip and her dark brown hair felt damp where it touched her neck and temples.

She closed her eyes and imagined herself walking with her father in the small park near their house in Cambridge. She remembered the walks they had taken the previous autumn when drifts of crisp, russet leaves crunched under their feet as they circled the small pond, counting the ducks.

On one occasion, her kite had become entangled in the branches of a large chestnut tree and her father had climbed up to rescue it, showering her with conkers as he clambered awkwardly down, teasing her and laughing.

"Annie! You'd better let me fly it – or I'll spend the rest of the day up a tree like a squirrel!"

The memory brought back the ache that had been absent for a while.

Anna dragged herself back to the present. She rolled slowly off the bed and padded across the room in her bare feet, pushing open the dark green shutters and stepping out onto the warm, iron balcony.

Down below, the street was less noisy now. There was a lull in the traffic and most of the people seemed to have gone home to prepare the evening meal before re-emerging for the obligatory *passeggiata*. She had watched them the previous day, fascinated, as whole families, smartly dressed, strolled along the paths in the nearby park, greeting and being greeted. To her, the sense of leisurely enjoyment in looking and being looked at was a new phenomenon. At home, you walked quickly from A to B. Usually, you walked fast so that you kept yourself warm.

Heat still spiralled up from the ground, even though the sun had set. Peering over the edge of the balcony, she could see into the house opposite. Lights had been turned on and she watched as a maid set places around a large, oval dining-room table dressed with flowers and candles. Anna thought how lovely it looked and wondered if the people who lived in the house were happy.

Sounds of laughter made her glance up. She could see two faces looking down at her from the open, arcaded top floor opposite. The girls seemed to be about her own age, perhaps a little older. There was an animated conversation going on between them. Anna wondered if she dare venture a greeting in her newly acquired, but limited Italian.

She took a deep breath.

"*Buona sera!*" she shouted up to them, giving a small, uncertain wave.

She waited, clutching the balcony rail, head tilted back, hoping that she would understand their response.

The girls immediately stopped talking and observed her in silence. Then the taller of the two, slowly and deliberately, stuck out her tongue. The heads withdrew and she again heard their laughter but this time it sounded mocking as it bounced back and forth between the two buildings.

Anna quickly stepped back into the shadow of the window. She was pretty sure she had used the correct greeting. Perhaps she had sounded too English, she thought, wistfully.

She made her way slowly to the bathroom to wash her hands and face in cold water before going downstairs.

Outside, the first grumble of thunder could be heard in the distance and the air felt thick and difficult to breathe. Clouds sagged, like overfilled eiderdowns above the dusty buildings and the failing light was an unhealthy shade of lilac-grey.

* * *

Cautiously, Anna peeped into the dining-room. Paola was placing dishes of almost transparent prosciutto and delicate, half-moons of melon, plates of cheeses and crisp rolls onto the lace-covered table. A light snack for the adults before they left for the party.

The maid looked up and smiled at her. She pointed in the direction of the kitchen.

"*Gina è nella cucina.*"

Anna noticed that half-circles of sweat darkened the girl's uniform under each arm and that her upper lip, which was covered in a fine black down, was also damp with perspiration.

"*Grazie, Paola,*" she replied, carefully.

She made her way along the high, domed passage, towards the heavy door that opened onto her favourite room in the house.

Alfredo was already sitting at the table, devouring large mouthfuls of Gina's delicious, home-made soup.

"*Ecco la bella Signorina!*" he said, pulling out the chair beside him and patting the seat.

"Whata you like, *cara?*" asked Gina, knowing what the answer would be.

"*Prosciutto e melone, per favore,*" said Anna, naming her favourite dish.

"*Brava! Anna sa parlare molto bene l'Italiano, no?*" Gina demanded of Alfredo, who nodded, his mouth too full to speak.

He watched the skinny, brown-eyed girl who could almost be Italian herself, as she sat beside him, napkin on her lap. He noted how she ate – tidily breaking the bread over the plate so that there would be no crumbs left lying on the table. He thought there was something very appealing about this young one who made so few demands on others and seemed content to read by herself for hours. She obviously enjoyed being with Gina. He had observed the bond that had grown between her and Anna and he liked to see the child responding to the woman's kindness and affection. He was pretty certain she smiled more than she used to. He wiped his forehead with the back of his hand.

"*Mamma mia! Che caldo!*" he complained.

Anna twisted round in Gina's direction.

"What is *caldo*, Gina?"

"*Caldo vuol dire* hota, *cara.*"

"Oh, hot."

"*Sì!* Hota," confirmed Gina, as she sat heavily down opposite Anna. "*Fa troppo caldo.* Isa too hota," she added firmly, mopping her own forehead with the corner of her apron.

* * *

After supper, Anna watched as the adults prepared to leave for the distant party. The women looked lovely in their silk and chiffon dresses, so cool and elegant, as if unaffected by the heavy, moisture-laden air. She thought Roberto and Gianni looked handsome in their evening clothes and even wild Carlo was looking tidier and smarter than usual. He caught sight of her.

"*Signorina!* I am the only man with no lady. You are not coming with me to the ball?" he teased loudly, bowing low in her direction.

Anna blushed as the rest of the party turned to look at her. She wished they wouldn't. She gave Carlo a stern look.

"I'm not old enough to go."

"No, you most certainly are not!" Her mother's voice sounded irritated.

Rosalind was looking particularly attractive in a dress of deep blue with a long string of pearls wrapped around her slim neck. Anna knew that they had belonged to her father's mother.

"Come here, Anna."

The child hesitated and then, seeing the familiar look of impatience in the green eyes, moved slowly over to her. She could smell her perfume. It was not the one she usually wore and it had a musky edge to it that Anna disliked. She took an involuntary step back and waited.

"Now, be good, Anna, and make sure to be in bed by nine o'clock at the latest."

Rosalind looked down at her daughter and wondered, fleetingly, why she felt no affection for or interest in the solemn, pale-faced child. She herself had never been kissed or cuddled by her own mother, whom she recalled as having been quite happy to make the necessary sacrifices in order to send her daughter away to school and out from under her feet. When Rosalind had become attractive, she remembered her mother had used her as a sort of theatrical prop to be flaunted in front of other mothers with ugly daughters.

Anna shifted from one foot to the other, wondering how long it would be before she could make her escape.

"Can I go now?"

"Yes, of course. Go!"

Rosalind turned back to the others, full of pleasurable anticipation at the thought of the evening ahead. She smiled at Gianni as he courteously offered his arm and led her out to the waiting car.

She was to travel with Frederica and Roberto, while Chiara would accompany Gianni in his beautiful, new Lancia. Carlo insisted in driving himself in his Alfa Romeo, complaining that the other's driving was too sedate for his liking and he would make it to the Leopardi's well before the rest of them.

The Contessa stood at the foot of the stairs, watching. She looked formidable and detached from the flurry of activity going on around her. The sombre black dress she wore accentuated the pallor of her proud face with its dark, hooded eyes. Earlier, Anna noticed that she also gave no sign of suffering from the evening heat.

The woman had observed the brief exchange between Rosalind and her daughter and felt a twinge of guilt that she had not made more of an effort to make the child's stay a more pleasant one. But, she reasoned, if Anna became too settled and content, the mother might be tempted into prolonging their stay for an unacceptable length of time. She noticed that, before the doors closed behind the partygoers, Anna had slipped quietly back to the kitchen, apparently relieved to be out of sight of Rosalind.

Now alone in the large entrance hall, the Contessa turned, a poker-straight figure, and made her way slowly up the stairs towards her husband's study.

The lights on the walls and the chandelier flickered briefly as another rumble of thunder shook the now dark sky, rattling the crystal drops so they tinkled slightly.

Chapter Four

The storm broke with an intensity that took Anna by surprise. Usually, she quite enjoyed them – the way the lightning lit up the surroundings, suddenly making her world into a black and white photograph. She liked counting the seconds between flash and crash, the way her father had taught her, to see if it were coming nearer or was in retreat.

The wind slammed against the door into the garden and made the old wisteria's branches squeak protestingly against the shutters. Then the rain started. She thought it was as if someone had turned on a giant tap in the sky and she listened to the drops bouncing and dancing crazily against the windows and the stone paving outside.

After a flash of lightning that seemed to sizzle in the air directly above the house, followed by a loud thunderclap that made the plates rattle on the kitchen dresser, the lights went out.

"*Jesu Maria!*" moaned Paola, crossing herself then cowering back in her chair again with her hands over her ears in a vain attempt to block out the noise. She was no lover of storms. Her family came from a small fishing village south of Naples and they had lost menfolk on nights such as this. She knew only too well the grief and poverty that resulted from their loss.

* * *

Carrying a heavy, iron candelabra, Gina walked swiftly along the passage to the study, shielding the flames with her hand. She knocked on the door and entered.

For a moment she thought that the room was empty and then a flash of lightning lit up the tall, gaunt figure of the Contessa, standing by one of the long windows that opened onto the balcony overlooking the garden. She was gazing out at the tormented night sky. Gina was struck by how tired she looked – tired and dispirited – as though the old lady had aged without her noticing. Perhaps it was the harsh, white light from the storm that showed up the bone structure under the thinning, fragile skin, making her look suddenly vulnerable and perhaps even approachable.

She carefully placed the candelabra on the desktop and then looked questioningly at the immobile figure by the window. Gina wished she could somehow communicate to her employer that she knew and shared something of the worries that must be occupying the other's mind, worries about her beloved younger son driving too fast on flooded roads, for example. Instead, she remained silent. She had not been in the Contessa's employment for seven years without learning that you behaved inappropriately at your peril. That lady had the ability to shrivel you with one penetrating look.

"*Grazie, Gina,*" came the measured voice, gently dismissing her.

After the housekeeper had left the room, the Contessa resumed her train of thought. She was concerned on several fronts. She feared for Carlo's safety. He had a reckless streak that had not been inherited from herself or her husband. He liked nothing better than to race his car against others on the road, taking terrible risks and she knew that high winds and torrential rain would only add to his sense of excitement. She wished now that she had insisted he travel with Roberto or Gianni. Foolishly, she had allowed him to talk her into doing what he wanted – just like his father.

She was anxious too for Frederica's lovely younger sister, Chiara, and for Gianni. The Contessa had seen the look in Rosalind's eyes when he accompanied her out to the car, how her long fingers with their scarlet nails had wrapped themselves around his arm and the way she had walked, her hip lightly touching his, looking up into his face and laughing provocatively. He had been unaware of the anger in Chiara's face as he solicitously helped Rosalind into Roberto's car. The Contessa knew that neither of them would be a match for the manipulative Englishwoman if she decided to entrap Gianni.

Gazing out into the temporary darkness, she sighed. It was time to speak to Roberto and insist the woman be encouraged to leave. It was a pity that the child had such a mother as a role model. Although, she had to admit, from the little she had seen of the girl, she was coming to the conclusion that Anna was of a higher calibre than her parent. There was a quiet seriousness about her that was charming in one so young and also a certain gentle quality. The Contessa wondered if Anna perhaps took after her missing father.

* * *

"Anna, *cara*, isa time to go to bed. You not frightened of thisa . . ," Gina struggled for the right word.

"Storm, Gina? No, I'm not frightened. Will the others be all right? Only, Carlo told me that the party was quite a long way from the town."

"*Sì, sì*. All is good. Nota to worry, *cara*." Gina's tone was more confident that she felt.

They both jumped as the door was flung open with a crash and a dripping Alfredo burst into the room. His hands were grazed from struggling with the loosened shutters and his shirt was plastered to his back and arms. His hair hung down in front of his eyes, dripping rivulets of water onto his chest.

"*Dio!*" he muttered, as he started to unbutton his sodden shirt.

Gina handed him a towel. She continued to try and reassure Anna, who sat watching her with her inscrutable child's dark eyes.

"*Tutto va bene, carissima*. Nota to worry."

She casually moved over to where the girl sat and gently brushed the back of Anna's hand with her own as she passed the chair.

"You sleepa and in the morning, there isa no . . . storm and again there is sun coming."

Anna, on a sudden impulse, got up and caught hold of Gina's hand.

"I like being here with you and Alfredo. It makes me feel safe."

* * *

It took a long time for Anna to go to sleep. She lay, curled into a ball, with a pillow tucked around her ears. Eventually, she fell into an uneasy slumber, slipping from one troubled dream to another, half aware of the noise of the storm, which seemed to surround her.

She dreamed of a man whom she thought was her father but he was walking away from her and she could not see his face. She dreamed of a white unicorn, half-hidden by shifting mist that made the animal seem close to her one minute and distant the next.

At some point during the night, she thought she heard the sound of a bell ringing and hurried footsteps and raised voices but was too confused and sleep-heavy to know if she were still dreaming or not.

* * *

Morning came and with it, as Gina had predicted, the sun. It shone on the town and on the washed, pink roofs of the houses, on the overfull river swirling muddily under the arches of the weakened bridges and on the storm-damaged gardens and parks.

It shone too on the bright red remains of a once

beautiful Lancia, lying on its side with its sleek nose buried in a stone wall. The sun's rays struck the scattered shards of broken glass and glinted on the buckled bumper that had been ripped from the car on its last, crazed ride as it plunged from the road above, ricocheting off an outcrop of rock, demolishing a young tree, careering through the long grass until stopped short by the intransigent, two-hundred-year-old wall. A man's white silk scarf lay twisted on the muddy earth.

* * *

Anna woke with a start. There had been a sound of some sort. Someone was in the bedroom. Blearily, she struggled to sit up.

The Contessa stood, looking down at her without speaking. Her face was the colour of old parchment and her knuckles were white from gripping the rail at the foot of the bed. Anna knew immediately that something was dreadfully wrong but was afraid to ask anything of this terrible-looking old woman. Mutely they stared at one another until finally the Contessa spoke.

"There has been an accident. Your mother is in hospital. They say she will live." Her voice made Anna feel suddenly cold. "Get dressed."

Without another glance in her direction, the Contessa turned and walked stiffly from the room. As the girl scrambled into her clothes, she tried to work out why the old woman had seemed so angry. A door slammed somewhere in the house and she thought she heard the sound of weeping in one of the bedrooms nearby.

Increasingly frightened, she stumbled down the stairs and along the passage to find Gina. She would know what had happened. She would explain everything.

The usually tidy kitchen was in chaos. Unwashed china was stacked in crooked piles by the sink. Anna noticed that the leaves and debris that had blown in during the storm still lay in drifts on the floor. But what made her stop in her tracks was the sight of Paola, sobbing in Gina's arms.

Gina's own eyes were red and her hair dishevelled, as if she had not slept.

"Gina! What is it? The Contessa said my mother will be all right. Why is Paola crying?"

Slowly, Gina let go of Paola and turned to face the girl who stood, looking bewildered, in the middle of the room. Her mind raced. How to tell her? She thought how young and vulnerable the child looked in her short red and white check dress, her cheeks flushed by the sun.

"*Anna, è molto difficile dire* . . ." She gently took the girl's arm, guiding her over to a chair and sat down beside her.

Anna had a sinking feeling in the pit of her stomach. Something worse had happened than just her mother being hurt and in hospital.

"What's the matter? Gina, please tell me."

"La Contessa, she tell you your mamma she isa in 'ospital?"

"Yes, she did."

Anna stared at Gina, willing her to continue, to explain.

"*Cara, Signor Carlo è morto, anche Signor Gianni.*"

Gina could hardly get out the words.

"I don't understand, Gina."Anna's voice rose hysterically. "What about Carlo and Gianni? Say it in English."

"They are . . . dead."

The words fell like blunt hammer-blows to Anna's head.

"Dead!" She stared at Gina, incredulous. "They can't be. How can they be dead?"

In broken English, Gina told her the little she knew of what had happened. After the party at the Leopardi's, Carlo's car had not started. Roberto and Frederica had already left and so he had gone with Gianni, Chiara and Rosalind. For some reason, Rosalind had been driving. The Lancia was seen travelling at high speed along the still partially flooded road back to Pisa. It had apparently swerved violently to avoid an oncoming lorry, loaded with fruit for the early morning market. The car had gone into a skid and plunged off the road.

Carlo and Gianni had been killed instantly and Rosalind had to be cut out of the wreckage. She was to be operated on later that day. Signorina Chiara was bruised and cut but not too badly hurt.

Anna gazed at her, wide-eyed. Carlo, who loved tennis and dancing and picnics, who teased her about her Italian and played tricks on her, was dead. Gianni too. Her head spun with unanswered questions. What would poor Chiara do now? She and Gianni were to have been married in two months' time. Why had her mother been driving the car?

One thing only was clear in Anna's mind. She knew now why the Contessa had been so strange and had looked at her in the way she had. Her mother was to blame for their deaths.

* * *

41

To Gina, the day seemed to go on forever. She was exhausted and beside herself with worry for the Contessa, who had shut herself away in the study, having given orders that she was not to be disturbed. The shutters were closed and the blinds lowered.

Gina knew that the woman had loved her younger son deeply although she had not often shown her affection. She also knew that a brilliant future had been anticipated for the charming boy who had been so uncannily like his dead father. Earlier that morning, she had accidentally caught sight of the Contessa kneeling by her dead son's empty bed. The look of anguish on her face had been unbearable to see. The young woman longed to go to her, to offer her some comfort but she knew only too well that the Contessa's grieving would be done in private.

She went in search of Anna, who had been missing for several hours. The girl had looked like a ghost when she heard what had happened. She had fled from the room without speaking and Gina thought it best to leave her to herself for a while. But now it was getting late and she was becoming concerned. She guessed that Anna was probably hidden away somewhere in the garden.

"*Anna, cara, vieni.* Come to Gina," she called softly as she hunted for some sign of the girl.

There was no answer. She felt angry with herself for not having looked sooner.

* * *

Anna was locked away in a world of her own making. A world in which there were no car crashes, where no one got hurt or killed and where her father was always present, smiling and making the silly jokes that only she and he thought funny. A different world where there was a powerful magic that protected everyone from evil and where unicorns existed because people believed in them. She crept away to a corner of the old garden and sat with her knees drawn up under her chin, her arms held tightly around them. She was almost completely hidden under a canopy of fig leaves that formed a protective shelter of green hands encircling her. Her eyes were open but unseeing.

After a long search, Gina eventually found her. She pushed back the branches of the fig and squatted down beside the girl.

"Anna! Anna?" she said gently, worried by the distant look on the child's face. She touched her shoulder. Anna did not move.

"Anna, *cara*, Gina make nice-a food. Come!"

There was not a flicker of response. The woman was at a loss as to what to do. When she had been a child, people cried or screamed or shouted when they were upset and then they got on with their lives, doing the things that needed doing. They did not become deaf and dumb, especially not the children. She tried again.

"Isa getting late, *cara*."

She unclasped one of Anna's fists and pulled her slowly to her feet. The child stood quietly in front of her, expressionless. Gina leaned down and looked into the blank eyes.

"Anna, you listen to Gina," she said, with some force. "You come with me now."

43

Without further delay, she took the girl's unresponsive hand and led her through the trees, towards the house.

Once inside, Anna allowed herself to be guided towards a chair and a bowl of chicken broth. Gina sat beside her, not saying very much but from time to time encouraging her to eat.

A silent Alfredo also joined them at the table. He had only worked for the Contessa for just over a year and was more concerned by Gina's distress than the family's. He had never seen her so upset. He personally considered the Contessa cold and distant and thought of her simply as his employer, who inhabited a different world with different values. He was sorry that her son had died, sorry too that Signorina Chiara had lost her fiancé. But these things happened from time to time. Life was sometimes cruel.

It was a shame that Signor Roberto had not provided his mother with a grandchild to dote on. There was no doubt in his mind that these well-bred types weren't as fertile as his people. One day, he would marry Gina and he knew God would bless them with an abundance of babies. He was jolted from his thoughts by Gina.

"*Alfredo! La Contessa mi chiama.*" She gave a slight nod in Anna's direction. "*La piccola.*"

He nodded in response. Gina hurriedly left the room, summoned by the study bell.

For a moment, Alfredo studied the child opposite him. Suddenly he picked up Anna's undrunk glass of lemonade. She watched listlessly as he took it over to the sink and emptied out the contents. He proceeded to take two wine glasses from the dresser and a jug, which he placed on the table. Without saying anything, he half filled both glasses with wine and pushed one of them towards her. He raised his own in a toast.

"*Salute!*"

Anna hesitated and then picked up the glass and sipped the red liquid tentatively. She had never been allowed it before and supposed that she had been given some now because today was unlike any other day she had ever known. She liked the fruity smell and the rich, red colour of it but was unsure of the taste.

She glanced over to Alfredo, who drank with gusto – full, man-size gulps until his glass was empty. He wiped his mouth with the back of his hand and looked inquiringly at her.

"*Ti piace il vino? È buono, no?*"

"*Molto buono,*" she said, in a quiet voice.

Just then, Gina came back into the kitchen and sat down wearily at the table.

"Anna, La Contessa say tomorrow Signor Roberto take you to see your mamma."

The recently returned colour drained from Anna's face and her eyes took on a closed look, as if blinds had been pulled down.

"I won't go," she said, in an ominously low voice.

"*Tesoro,* isa your mamma. She need to see her leetle girl."

"I don't care!" Anna shouted. "I won't go – and you can't make me." She pushed back her chair in a frenzy, knocking over her wine glass and ran towards the door leading to the passage. "I don't want to see her. It's her fault Gianni and Carlo are dead. It wouldn't have happened if Daddy was here. I hate her!"

"Anna!"

Gina sounded shocked and alarmed by this violent reaction.

The door slammed shut. She made an attempt to follow Anna but Alfredo pulled her towards him, putting his arms around her. After an initial movement to break free, she let herself be held and comforted.

The spilt wine dripped onto the floor, making a spreading pool of dark red, staining the stone flags.

Chapter Five

"Anna! Roberto will take you to see your mother. You can sit in the front of the car with him," cajoled Frederica the next day.

"No, thank you. I will stay with Gina."

"But, Anna . . ."

"How is Chiara? I haven't seen her."

Frederica sighed in frustration. "She is at home with her parents."

Anna looked up at her. "Is she very sad?"

"Yes, Anna. She is very sad. We all are sad."

"Can I see her?"

"No, I am sorry. That is not possible."

Anna turned away from her, her face impassive. They were angry with her for what her mother had done. She was sure of it. Otherwise, they would let her go and see Chiara so that she could tell her how sorry she was.

* * *

During the days that followed, Anna remained adamant on the subject of visiting her mother. Each time she was asked, she refused with the same, closed look that had first appeared on the day of the accident. She would not talk about her mother and she avoided contact with the Contessa whenever possible. The child had glimpsed her once or twice from her bedroom window as the woman climbed slowly into the waiting car, accompanied by Frederica. Since her son's death, she wore only black and the girl thought she looked like a tall, thin, black bird in her expensive mourning clothes. Her pallor seemed to emphasise her dark eyes and when their paths did cross, Anna was only too aware of the suppressed anger that burned in those eyes.

* * *

One week after the accident, Roberto spoke to David on the telephone. There was a shocked silence from Anna's father as he listened to the brief description of the events of the previous seven days.

Roberto explained that Rosalind's operation had not been as successful as they had hoped and she might never walk again. He did not tell David that she had only agreed to him being contacted when she was told that she would need to be looked after and would have to return home, back to the rejected husband whom she despised so much.

"I . . . How soon will she be able to travel?" David sounded understandably confused on the other end of the line.

"Not for some weeks, I think. What do you want to do about Anna?"

"Oh, my God! Anna! Is she all right?"

There was a slight hesitation before Roberto replied. "Yes, but I think it would be a good thing for her to be with you as soon as possible."

"Of course. I'm sorry. It must have been very difficult for you having her there with all the . . ."

"Yes."

"Could you put her on a plane tomorrow, or the day after?"

"I will arrange for Anna to take the plane. I will ring you again when I have the details."

"That's very kind of you." There was an embarrassed pause. "Roberto, why was my wife driving?"

Another hesitation.

"I think that is something you have to ask her yourself."

Roberto's voice was coolly formal as he said goodbye.

* * *

Gina helped Anna to pack. She watched as the child carefully folded a nightdress into a neat square and thought how, in only a few days, she seemed to have lost weight and become frail and somehow smaller.

When everything was neatly stowed into the suitcase, she delved into the pocket of her apron and produced a rag doll with a straw hat and a small bunch of dried flowers sewn into one of the cloth hands.

"*Cara*, this isa for you. What name you like for her?"

"I don't know." Anna gave the woman a small smile, trying her best to look grateful.

"There are many beautiful Italian names . . ."

"I really don't know."

"Francesca, Caterina, Alda . . . Gabriella, Maria . . ."

"Maria. Maria would be nice."

"*D'accordo!* We call her Maria. Isa good name." Gina tucked the doll into the crook of Anna's arm and smiled. "When you are in *Inghilterra,* you tell everything to Maria. Like Gina, she listen. She also your friend."

"Will you come to see me in England, Gina?"

The note of hope in Anna's voice made it difficult for the woman to reply.

"*Tesoro,* isa not possible. I have to looka after La Contessa. She need me now very much." She stopped suddenly. How to explain to this poor young thing that Anna must go home and she must stay? Gina so wanted to give her some crumb of consolation. "We have hada gooda time – you and Gina, no? I always will think of you, Anna." She lifted Anna's chin with gentle fingers. "Cara, life is nota always so bad, you know."

Anna turned away. Gina too didn't really want her any more. She wished she were already gone. The process of leaving was too painful. She had a lump in her throat that felt like a rock and she wanted to cry but she didn't seem to have any tears to shed.

Anna had felt the same way earlier that morning when, unknown to Gina, Alfredo had also given her an unexpected parting gift. It was a little grey mouse with long whiskers.

"Wise mouse. *Topo Saggio,*" he said, shyly.

As though he had never given anyone a present before, thought Anna.

The man clumsily patted her on the head as he smiled down at her.

"*Forse, un giorno, tu vieni ancora in Italia trovarci.*"

He slipped the mouse into Anna's hand and, unable to think of anything else to do or say to cheer her up, he muttered, "*Ciao, piccola signorina!*" and went back to his work in the garden, feeling uneasy.

* * *

A few hours later, Anna sat looking out of the window as the aircraft climbed and the patterned, warm, brown land of Italy receded into the heat haze below.

Tomorrow, they would be burying Carlo and Gianni and she would not be there to say goodbye to them and put flowers on their graves. Frederica had told her it would be better not to stay for the funeral, that her father must be missing her. To Anna, it was further evidence of their anger. Her head ached. She had tried so hard not to show her feelings, but when she got into Roberto's car, she had looked back at Gina, who stood, smiling bravely, waving to her, and Anna knew then that she would never see her again. She had cried silent tears all the way to the airport.

She stared at the wisps of cloud and thought of seeing her father again. Would he also blame her for what had happened? Or would he be happy that she was going home to him?

Anna wondered if he would remember that today was her ninth birthday. She had almost forgotten about it herself.

Chapter Six

"Anna, I told you to put that damned cat *out*."

Anna scooped up the fluffy, white bundle and carried it out of the room, hooking the door behind her with her foot.

No one seemed to have time for poor Minou, she thought. Especially not her mother. Since her return from Italy in September, she had been even more short-tempered than before. Anna could see that she found life difficult in a wheelchair but every time the girl started to feel sorry for her, she would remember Gianni and Carlo and the spark of sympathy would be instantly smothered.

The cat had been a present from her father, in an attempt to make her less withdrawn, to give her a companion and give him more time to concentrate on Rosalind's demands.

Rosalind was not the only one who disliked Minou. The Beastly Bat, as Anna had secretly named the latest addition to the household, openly detested the animal. Mrs

Battersby came to clean and cook each weekday and Anna seemed to spend most of her time trying to keep out of her way. She thought the woman was evil, with her thin lips that looked to Anna as though they had been drawn by a sharp knife in uncooked pastry. Nor did she like her small eyes, which missed nothing and seemed to look at everything and everyone with sour disapproval.

Edna Battersby was in her mid-sixties, without a shred of humour and deeply disillusioned with life. Her husband, whom she had never liked, had died several years earlier after letting his life insurance lapse the month before his death. She felt that he had done it on purpose. Her only son emigrated to Australia, as soon as he had scraped together the necessary funds. He never wrote and she was not sure whether he was living in Melbourne or Perth and did not much care. He had been a troublesome boy and, although she would never admit it to anyone, she had been relieved to see the back of him.

There were two things in life of which she was certain. One was the uselessness of the male of the species. The other was that children were to be tolerated as a necessary evil for the propagation of the human race but were to be avoided like the plague.

As Anna came into the kitchen with Minou in her arms, she was greeted by the Beastly Bat's indignant voice.

"You're not giving that thing any more to eat. It gets fed better than wot we do," she shrilled. "It's a disgrace."

Anna wanted to tell her that if Minou's diet was better than theirs it was because the Bat was a lousy cook and it was the food she dished up that was the disgrace.

"She only gets left-overs."

"Don't you be smart!" Edna Battersby pointed a nicotine-stained finger at her. "There's people wot live in 'ot places as wot would jump at the chance of eating as well as that moth-eaten thing."

Anna opened her mouth to protest and then thought better of it. The Bat always made sure she had the last word. Anyway, she decided, what was the point in arguing with someone who knew they were always right? She thought longingly of Gina's happy smile and the noisy peal of laughter she gave when something amused her. She remembered the mouth-watering meals that had been prepared in the large, friendly kitchen in Pisa. If only . . .

"I 'eard your mother say she wanted it put outside."

Anna ignored her and continued on her way to the small, freezing scullery with her chin resting on the back of Minou's soft head as she walked. She put her gently down beside a saucer of milk and watched the pink tongue, which she thought looked like a tiny piece of ham, flick in and out as the cat drank. Then, reluctantly, she opened the back door to let her out into the unwelcoming, wintry garden.

However, Minou had other ideas and made a determined dash back towards the sitting-room, where she knew a fire burned.

"I'll swing for that useless lump of an animal, I will," howled Mrs Battesby.

She grabbed hold of a broom and set off in hot pursuit.

Anna stood to one side and watched, rather enjoying the situation because the cat usually got the better of the woman. Minou would hide under the furniture and then, when the Bat got too close for comfort, leap onto the nearest windowsill and claw her way up the curtains. At the top, she would peer smugly down at the infuriated woman.

Today, the cat made for Anna's bedroom and the tall wardrobe, on top of which she knew she would be well out of reach of the Bat and her broom. But the door was closed and she was cornered on the lower of the two landings.

"Gotcha!"

The woman struck out and Minou hurtled back down the stairs, hissing and wailing, leaving long strands of white fur behind on the dark green stair-carpet.

Anna was waiting by the open front door when the angry animal shot outside and Minou was halfway down the front garden with the door closed behind her before she realised that it had begun to rain sleety rain down on her quivering body. She slunk under the thick beech hedge, her tail lashing from side to side as she stared malevolently back towards the house.

"Anna!" The sound of her mother's querulous voice came from the sitting-room.

The child went into the room, unwillingly.

"Yes?"

"What was all that racket about? Did you put Minou out?"

"Yes," said Anna in a resigned voice, "but it's very cold outside."

"Perhaps that will teach her a lesson. I accidentally ran over the tip of her tail and the animal went berserk and turned around and spat at me."

"You probably hurt her."

"Rubbish! That animal is all fur and no nerve endings – she certainly doesn't have any brains."

The Bat listened to the exchange, her chest heaving. There was a bright pink spot of anger in each cheek.

"It's nothing but trouble, that . . . cat is."

She had been going to say 'that bloody cat', but she liked to think that she was every bit as much of a lady as Rosalind. She told herself that she was only helping the poor thing out. If circumstances had been different and she hadn't made such a disastrous marriage, then it might have been Edna Battersby sitting by a roaring fire giving the orders.

Anna watched as the woman sidled up to Rosalind, hands clasped tightly together against her flat chest.

"I don't think it should be allowed in at all. It would make my life a lot more easy if I didn't have to keep trailing after it sweepin' up cat fluff." A gleam appeared in her eye as a thought occurred to her and she added triumphantly, "I saw it scratching itself yesterday. Wot if it brings fleas into the 'ouse? Wot would we do about that, then?"

Anna rounded on her. "Minou does *not* have fleas!"

The pink in Mrs Battersby's cheeks became even more fiery.

"That's quite enough! Anna, go and make some tea, please." Rosalind's voice was sharp.

She was irritated by both of them but she especially resented Mrs Battersby's gratuitous interruptions. Why couldn't the woman just get on with her work and leave her to read her book in peace? Still, Rosalind thought, she was a useful ally every now and then – even if she was dreadful.

Rosalind had decided that if she were going to have to spend her time stuck in a wheelchair, she rather fancied the idea of holding literary evenings. After all, Cambridge was brimming over with the witty and the wise. She imagined handsome, eager undergraduates clustered around her and on the carpet at her feet, swapping quotes and sounding knowledgeable on literary matters.

In order to fill in a few of the gaps in her education, she had been doing some serious reading. At the moment, she was in the middle of ploughing through *Madame Bovary* in French – and was finding it rather heavy going. She had come to the conclusion that what Madame B needed was a good walk in the rain with the dogs to clear her neurotic, Gallic brain.

* * *

Anna banged cups down onto the kitchen table, with enough force to make a rebellious statement but not quite enough to shatter them. As she waited for the water to boil, she leaned against the rail of the Aga and thought for the hundredth time of Gina. She realised sadly that she could no longer see her face clearly, however hard she tried. But she could still remember the way Gina spoke. Anna imagined her stroking Minou and saying, "Isa nice pussy cat." She quickly rubbed her eyes with the back of her hand and picked up the heavy, boiling kettle.

As she carried the tray out of the kitchen, she found herself wondering what Gina would make of the Bat. She reckoned that the Italian woman wouldn't feel much like calling *her* nice.

* * *

Since Rosalind's return, David had tried hard to narrow the gulf between himself and his wife. He had been unexpectedly patient when she had become depressed. But she either ignored him or taunted him with how inadequate he was and how intemperate.

He begged the doctors treating his wife not to leave her without any hope that she would some day walk again. In spite of the regular physiotherapy, it seemed to him that Rosalind was not making any progress.

David guessed that his wife disliked Mrs Battersby almost as much as he did but since she had come on the scene, the two women seemed to have joined forces against him. Although he felt guilty at leaving Anna to face them on her own, he escaped to his club as often as he could, to drink too many glasses of Scotch and then afterwards to seek solace in the arms of understanding girls.

The more bitter Rosalind became, the more David strayed and the more Mrs Battersby was able to fuel the dissatisfaction in the wheelchair-bound woman by reminding her of how difficult things were for her and how all men were lying lechers. She constantly repeated that women were far better off without them. David had overheard her muttering to Rosalind on several occasions and thought it sounded almost like a well-rehearsed mantra.

* * *

Because of the situation at home, Anna had been sent to a new school at the start of September, where she was enrolled as a weekly boarder. At the end of the first week, her father took her to their favourite café, where she sat glumly at the table, ink-stains on her fingers, hair escaping from under her school beret.

"It's awful. The teachers only like you if you're good at the boring stuff like science and maths."

"But, Annie, there are plenty of other subjects you like."

"I like art and drama and they don't count."

"You like music too," he said, cheerfully.

"That doesn't count really either. And you should see the music teacher."

"What's wrong with the poor woman?"

"She's got a mole on her chin with an enormous long black hair sticking out of it. She's like a witch – and she hates me. I know she does. She made me wear my beret in class on Tuesday because she saw me outside the school the other day without it." Anna looked dejected. The sticky bun he had ordered sat untouched on her plate.

"Come on, sweetheart! You've only been there for a week. Give it a chance to work. What about the other girls?"

"They're awful too. *They* only like you if you are good at hockey and can win points for your house. I hate hockey."

David laughed. "I just don't believe it's quite as bad as you're trying to make out."

"Oh, it *is*," said Anna, firmly.

She felt let down. She had counted on his understanding but he didn't seem to be taking it seriously. Anna bit unenthusiastically into the bun. She noticed how two women at another table kept looking in her father's direction. Why? Did they think he was handsome? she wondered. To her, he just looked like a father. He was even starting to get a bald patch on the very top of his head. She'd noticed it for the first time last weekend when he bent down to pick something up. Anna stared at him over the top of her cup of hot chocolate. She thought he looked rather sad – and not really handsome at all. She loved being with him in a way that she never did with her mother.

But things *had* changed since the accident. And her father had changed too. He still told her his silly jokes and made her laugh and he still called her Annie as he used to but she felt that she couldn't get really close to him any more. It was as though he were thinking about something else all the time; as if he were trying to make up his mind about something important. Anna wished he would tell her what it was so that she could help him.

For his part, David did not know what to do about Anna. After she got back from Italy, it had taken several weeks for her to become anything like her old self. When Rosalind returned, she seemed have the effect of making Anna retreat again. It had taken a long while before Anna started to talk to her mother in anything other than monosyllables. She always seemed to be uncomfortable in Rosalind's presence and would invent reasons to leave the room.

As for the new school: he realised that Anna was obviously unhappy there but it was the only reputable one in the area that accepted weekly boarders. He'd hoped that she would settle in and make some friends and it worried him to see her so uninterested in everything. When had he last seen her really laugh he wondered.

He knew it would be a waste of time to try and talk over his worries about Anna with his wife. Rosalind didn't appear to be interested in whether her daughter was happy at school or not. She also seemed to want to undermine him in any way she could. He had seen the way she and Mrs Battersby contrived to make life difficult. Sometimes, if he came home earlier than usual, the two of them would be in a huddle in the front sitting-room. He felt that he had intruded into a witches' coven and interrupted them in the middle of weaving unpleasant spells. All that was missing was the cauldron. He wouldn't have been surprised to find an image of himself being used as a pincushion.

He would look at Rosalind in amazement after a particularly vicious, verbal attack and wonder what had happened to the lovely, fun-loving creature he had married ten years earlier. She had always been cool and rather selfish but at the beginning it hadn't seemed to matter. Occasionally, she would still make some comment that was wittily apt and would make him laugh, but usually at the expense of someone else and only when she had been buoyed up after an attentive visit by one of his male colleagues from the office. Even then, there was often a barbed edge to her laughter that made him feel uncomfortable.

She absolutely refused to talk to him about the car crash.

Frustrated by her angry silence on the subject, he had rung the house in Pisa and insisted on knowing why his wife had been driving on the night of the accident. An embarrassed Roberto had finally told him that Rosalind had flirted with Gianni so blatantly during the evening that Chiara had lost her temper and told her, in front of the assembled guests, that her behaviour was unacceptable and that it would be better if she concentrated on looking after her own husband, instead of trying to steal another woman's fiancé. Rosalind had been humiliated and after drinking too much, had somehow got hold of the car keys and insisted on driving home. Rather than make another unpleasant scene, Gianni had reluctantly given in. From the way she had driven, Roberto seemed to think that she had intended to frighten Chiara. Gianni had apparently tried to force her to stop shortly before the accident had happened.

What Roberto did not tell David was that, since Carlo's death, his seemingly indomitable mother had become frail and ill and they feared she too would die before the end of the year. Nor did he mention the fact that none of them had seen Chiara since the funerals and that she was suffering from a severe form of depression that had her parents in despair.

Looking across the table at his daughter's pale, serious face, David wondered how much Anna knew or guessed. He felt guilty that he didn't seem able to give her the stability she needed. After all, if it hadn't been for his drinking, Rosalind would not have stormed off to Pisa the way she had and none of this would have happened. In spite of admitting his part in it all, he found himself longing for a drink in the quiet, well-upholstered comfort of his club.

Chapter Seven

It was after midnight and the fire had burned low. Rosalind irritably dropped her book onto the table at her side. David was still not back from the office Christmas party. She lay back in her chair and wondered dispiritedly where he was. How nice, she thought, to be able to come and go as you pleased without having to rely on other people to ferry you around like a parcel.

Grimly, she exercised her feet and massaged the muscles in her calves. One thing dominated her waking hours now: the certainty that one day she would be able to walk. She thought of being able to dance again. One of the greatest pleasures she had shared with her husband had been dancing. At Hunt Balls and May Balls, people had often stopped to admire the handsome couple, wishing they had a partner who could glide around the floor as effortlessly.

She thought morosely of the week ahead, leading up to her thirty-fifth birthday on Christmas Eve and wondered if anyone would bother to come to the small party they were to give. Perhaps she had been foolish in the past in not taking the trouble to have women friends. Rosalind had always been too occupied with enjoying the company of men to bother about cultivating female companionship. She was certainly regretting that now. If she'd only married the right man, then it wouldn't have mattered. But as things stood at the moment, she was feeling stranded. Bloody silly woman, she mused, with a wry smile.

* * *

"Thank you, Anna! It's lovely," said Rosalind, giving a quick glance at the drawing of a rather sombre snowman amidst a flock of surprisingly exotic birds that her daughter had given her as a birthday present.

"Daddy says he will get a frame for it if you like," Anna said, smiling over to where David hovered uncertainly at the foot of his wife's bed.

The child thought he looked as though he wished he were somewhere else and it was obvious that her mother wasn't trying too hard to make him feel welcome.

"Mm, sounds like a good idea."

Rosalind was busy ripping off the wrapping from a small, square-shaped package. Anna noticed that her drawing was in danger of getting crumpled where it lay on her mother's counterpane. She decided against trying to retrieve it. That would only irritate her mother. A velvet box was impatiently opened to reveal a pair of diamond earrings. Anna thought they were quite beautiful. They looked to her like large, sparkling teardrops, glinting against the background of cream satin. She studied her mother's impassive face, waiting for her reaction.

"Thank you, David."

The lid snapped shut. Why didn't her mother take them out to look at them properly? Anna wondered.

"I thought you would like them. You always said diamonds were the only stones worth wearing," said David quietly.

Rosalind gave her husband a direct glance, which he correctly interpreted as, 'Don't think this excuses *your* behaviour the other evening. I haven't forgotten or forgiven'.

Anna wasn't to know that he had returned from the office party at one in the morning the previous day, a little drunk and smelling of perfume and that her mother had been waiting for him, claws unsheathed.

David turned away from his wife and, with an assumed cheerfulness, smiled at Anna.

"Shall we go and get the birthday breakfast ready, then?"

Together they went downstairs, Anna only too glad to get away from the claustrophobic atmosphere of her mother's room.

* * *

That night, at the party, it was Rosalind who became inebriated. Only a handful of people turned up and that annoyed her. She was behaving in an artificially bright way: talking a little too loudly and spilling her drink as she gestured, well aware that she was making her husband uncomfortable.

'Good!' she thought. 'Serves him right. Let him squirm. Give him a bit of his own medicine.'

She propelled herself across the room and cornered their unsuspecting next-door neighbour between the window and the revolving bookcase. She looked up at him archly.

"Desmond! Tell me, why do I never get to see you these days? It's ridiculous! Living beside each other and not a glimpse for months at a time."

The man shifted uncomfortably, trapped in her over-direct gaze. David's wife was very attractive but, well, not the sort of woman to make a man feel at ease. There was something predatory and dissatisfied about her. He also didn't like the way she talked in such a loud voice. People were watching them while pretending not to, distracted from their own conversations.

"Well, I'm not around very much really. In fact, I'm going back later tonight."

"Oh, I see! Have we a little friend tucked away in a pied-à-terre in Knightsbridge? That's where your apartment is, isn't it?"

The mild-mannered man found himself blushing as he tried to edge his way unobtrusively out of the corner but Rosalind rolled nearer, almost crushing one of his feet under a wheel.

"Desmond! I do believe you're hiding something. Do tell! I promise not to breathe a word to anyone. Not that I have anyone with whom I can share secrets these days."

She shot a venomous look in her husband's direction.

Desmond carefully ignored the remark.

"Where is your daughter?" he asked quickly, taking a slug of whiskey for moral support.

"Probably lurking upstairs with her familiar." Rosalind's voice lost some of its warmth.

"I beg your pardon?"

"Anna has a cat that spends its time eating and moulting. She seems to prefer its company to mine."

Desmond was not at all surprised. He found himself thrown off balance by this woman whom he hardly knew. She was definitely not his type and he was starting to resent her over-familiar manner more and more. He glanced around, looking for a way to escape.

"She talks to it in bad Italian, you know," continued Rosalind, amused at his discomfort. "And to a ridiculous toy mouse and a tatty doll. She's very odd. She doesn't appear to have any friends." She leaned confidingly towards him. "Do you know, I wanted to have lots of children, especially boys," she lied. "Lovely, tall, handsome sons who would look after me in my old age. It doesn't look as though that will happen now, does it?"

She sighed dramatically, before proceeding to swallow the remains of her glass of whiskey.

Desmond suddenly felt desperately sorry for the child upstairs and for David, whom he thought he rather liked from the few times their paths had crossed. He looked down at the woman in the wheelchair in her expensive dress and extremely beautiful diamond earrings. She was wearing too much makeup for his liking and had been over-generous with her perfume. If he could only get away, he thought, he might find it possible to feel sorry for her as well.

"Is that the time?" he said lamely, looking over at the carriage clock on the mantelpiece.

"Yes, that's the time." Her voice was contemptuous.

"I'm sorry but I really must go. I have some things to sort out before I leave for London."

Rosalind did not budge. She looked him up and down, appraisingly.

"Do you know that you're really rather good-looking? In an understated sort of way."

Desmond managed to catch David's eye. Something of his desperation must have conveyed itself to the other man, who came over and rested his hands on the handles at the back of the wheelchair.

"I was just telling your wife I must be making tracks," Desmond said, gratefully.

He gave a quick glance down at his feet and David began to pull the chair out of the corner, leaving the man enough space to extricate himself.

Rosalind, realising that she was no longer in control of the situation, twisted around like an angry snake and lashed out, catching the back of one of her husband's hands.

The sound was like a pistol shot and seemed to ricochet around the room. People stopped talking, turning in surprise towards the unmoving trio in the corner. For a moment, it looked like a tableau in a waxworks. Then her voice rang out in the uneasy silence.

"How dare you interrupt! I was in the middle of a conversation. Take your hands off my chair at once." David said something to her in a low voice but she turned her head away from him impatiently. "Just leave me alone! Go away and have another drink. You're awfully good at that."

Her eyes blazed and her voice was strident. David backed away from her with a small, embarrassed smile.

There was silence in the room for a few more seconds, as if the stunned onlookers were waiting for the next scene to unfold in front of them. Slowly, stilted conversation got under way again.

Desmond hurriedly slipped away, thanking David and looking apologetic, as though he felt he was to blame for the unpleasant incident that had just taken place. Within ten minutes, the rest of the guests gratefully left, wishing David and Rosalind, 'A very happy Christmas!'.

"Not much bloody hope of that!" Rosalind remarked, before the front door closed behind the last fleeing figure.

David walked slowly back into the room. He looked tired and angry.

Controlling himself with difficulty, he asked in a low voice, "What came over you? What the hell did you think you were doing, pinning that poor chap into the corner like that?"

"You make him sound like a moth. He was just about as exciting."

"You know perfectly well what I'm talking about. You embarrassed the hell out of him. Why?"

"I don't know what you mean. I was having a perfectly civilised, if boring, conversation with the man."

"And why did you attack me in the way you did? There was absolutely no call for that sort of behaviour. It was so . . ." He searched for the appropriate word, running his fingers distractedly through his hair, " . . . unbecoming."

"Oh, I see! My behaviour was unbecoming, was it? And what, may I ask, about *your* behaviour? Your drinking? Your whoring?" Rosalind shouted at him, her face flushed.

"For God's sake! Get a grip on yourself. Anna's upstairs and can probably hear every word."

"I don't care! You should have thought of that before you started behaving like God Almighty, deciding whom I should or shouldn't talk to. Anyway, she knows what you're like. She saw you the other day in the park with your blonde tart. She wanted to know why you had your arm around her. She thought it was one of your clients who was upset about something. Just because I'm stuck in this bloody chair doesn't mean that I don't know what you get up to."

There were unshed tears shining in the corners of Rosalind's eyes as she propelled herself violently towards the fireplace.

David's face was drained of all colour. He had thought that he and Debbie would not be noticed at that time of day. Why on earth had Anna been anywhere near the park during school hours? She must have been playing truant.

He stood, as though rooted to the ground, staring at the back of his wife's head, searching for something to say that might defuse the tension. It was Christmas Eve and their only child was alone in her room upstairs. If only for her sake, he had to try and rescue the situation.

"I'm sorry if I upset you. I didn't mean to," he said in a conciliatory tone. There was no response. "I know I'm to blame for a lot of things, but can we try and make the best of it over Christmas? For Anna, if not for us?"

Rosalind jerked the chair round to face him, her features contorted by anger.

"Damn Anna and damn you! If you care so much about that bizarre brat upstairs, why don't you spend more time being a proper father to her, instead of just a lecherous hypocrite?"

Without thinking, David lifted his hand, as though to hit her. He had never in his life hated his wife as much or been so angry as he was at this moment.

"That's right! I'm a sitting target. Why don't you hit me? That would round the evening off beautifully," she taunted him.

She looked almost pleased at the way the situation had developed.

Slowly, David lowered his arm. He realised that he was trembling.

"What you said just now was dreadful. You can't have meant it . . ."

"Well, you're wrong. I meant it all right. Every bloody word."

David closed his eyes momentarily. He took a deep breath and without saying anything more, turned and left the room.

* * *

Anna's door was closed. Her father opened it as quietly as he could. The room was in darkness and it felt cold.

"Annie? Are you awake?" he whispered.

He moved to the side of the bed. In the reflected light from the landing, he could see her lying, curled up in a ball, with her back to him. Minou watched him, her eyes glowing strangely in the surrounding blackness. A doll and a mouse were propped up against the wall, between the pillow and the cat.

"Annie?"

The child made no sign of having heard him and yet David felt sure she was awake and that she must have heard the bitter exchange between her parents a few minutes earlier.

"I just wanted to say goodnight, poppet," he said quietly, leaning over to kiss the back of her head. Her hair smelt unclean and he realised, with a pang of guilt, that she was expected to look after herself and that she couldn't quite manage it. Suddenly, the whole thing seemed overwhelmingly more than he could cope with.

He laid a hand gently on her shoulder, leaving it there for a few moments, hoping that she would respond. He wanted the chance to explain that the woman she'd seen him with was just a good friend, to make up something to put her mind at rest after what Rosalind had said about Debbie.

Anna heard her father tiptoe out of the room. She held her breath, until she heard the click of the door as he shut it behind him. She listened to his footsteps on the creaking stairs and then the sound of the front door closing.

She reached for Minou in the dark, her whole body shaking with convulsive sobs. It had been difficult not to turn and throw her arms around her father's neck when he leant over her bed and she had nearly given into the temptation but she was feeling too hurt and confused to allow him that comfort.

Anna thought of the pretty blonde woman she had seen in his arms a few days earlier and the things her mother had shouted downstairs. She had not understood some of the words but she knew now that he would rather put his arms around that stranger in the park than be at home with her. She guessed that he had been with her on the night of the office party. Perhaps he'd been with her on all the other nights when he came home so late and that was why her mother had been so especially angry and refused to show any pleasure in his birthday present to her.

Eventually, Anna closed her eyes, resting her cheek on Minou's soft flank.

* * *

Christmas day dawned grey and overcast with a chill wind that blew the top layer of snow into miniature twisters and made the branches of the bare trees sway uneasily.

Anna dressed as quickly as she could, fumbling with cold fingers at the buttons on her clothes. Followed closely by Minou, she made her way warily down the stairs. She wondered if her father had come back during the night. She hadn't heard him.

On her way down the passage, she stopped to listen outside the door of the back sitting-room that had been made into a bedroom for her mother. There was no sound.

The Bat would be coming in soon. Anna had heard the woman telling her father that she was only doing it as a favour for his 'poor wife'. She had given the strong impression that, if it were not for Rosalind, she would gladly have let David and his daughter go without

73

Christmas lunch. Anna doubted that her father would be able to cook it himself – even if she helped. She had only ever seen him make occasional omelettes, full of cheese and herbs. They were golden-brown on the outside and runny in the middle and tasted delicious. She would not have minded living off hot buttered toast and omelettes if it meant getting rid of the Bat, she thought ruefully.

After a hasty breakfast, she let Minou out into the garden. The cat viewed the snow with disgust, its coat looking drab in contrast with the pure white which surrounded them. It dug a hole in a nearby flowerbed, scratching at the cold earth and crouching low to perform, all the while keeping a beady eye on Anna and the half-open back door.

They returned thankfully to the warmth of the kitchen and the Aga. As Anna held her hands over one of the hot plates, Minou groomed herself in a leisurely fashion. The girl watched as the cat casually stuck one leg vertically in the air. She thought that from behind, it looked almost as though the animal were playing a cello.

There was a sudden stamping of feet and a thud as the back door was abruptly thrown open, letting a blast of icy air into the room. The Beastly Bat stood on the threshold, looking irritated as she tried to knock off the snow which clung to her sensible, lined boots. She glared at the cat, which immediately stopped its grooming and got ready to make a dash for the passage.

Anna wondered what it was that made the Bat look so permanently bad-tempered. She looked at the creased, grey face, puckered with the cold, and tried to imagine her as once having been a pink, happy baby. She found it impossible. An impatient voice cut into her daydream.

"Have you 'ad your breakfast then?"

"Happy Christmas, Mrs Battersby."

"Yes, well. 'Ave you?"

"Yes," said Anna, giving up any attempt to bring some Christmas spirit into the proceedings.

"Well, keep out of my way. I've got a lot to do without you cluttering up the place and you can put that creature outside right . . ."

But Anna and the cat were gone.

Mrs Battersby pursed her lips in a familiar grimace, wondering if she would set off in pursuit and then decided against it. Perhaps the girl's father was around and he would be sure to take the child's side and insist the animal be left indoors. Looking as though she had just swallowed a lemon, she reached for her orange and green flower-patterned overall.

* * *

Anna scurried into the front sitting-room, Minou in her arms, and quietly shut the door. The room looked dreary, cluttered with débris from the party of the previous evening. The small Christmas tree that her father had brought home stood, slightly drunkenly, in the corner. He hadn't managed to make the fairy-lights work and the few decorations that Anna had made hung drably from the branches.

Under the tree lay two presents, clumsily wrapped. She knelt down to look. They were both for her. The larger one was from her mother and the smaller, heavier one from her father. The handwriting on both labels was her father's.

Anna opened her mother's first, knowing that she would prefer what her father had chosen. The wrapping fell off to reveal an expensive Laura Ashley corduroy dress covered in small flowers and hastily ordered from a catalogue. She stared at it glumly, holding it up in front of her. She was not surprised. It was just the sort of thing her mother would think suitable. Anna had seen similar garments in some of the fashion magazines, with glossy, model kids simpering into the camera. It was too girlie, too long, too full – too everything. She folded it neatly and placed it on the arm of her father's armchair.

Anna turned her attention to the other parcel. She tore off the wrapping. Inside was the complete set of the *Tales of Narnia* by C.S. Lewis. She turned the pages of one of the books, captivated by the imaginative, graceful drawings. She had borrowed the first one from the Library and had been swept into the realms of knights and castles and talking animals. Anna had found it difficult to emerge back into the real world again. She had sat for long periods, looking at Minou, willing the uninterested animal to talk to her as the animals did in the books. Anna longed to have a mysterious adventure. She had become more and more convinced of the existence of unicorns and the idea that, one day, she would see one. Daydreaming of this, when things seemed particularly hard at home, had a calming effect on her.

Gathering the books carefully together, she carried them upstairs to the upper landing to see if her father was in his room. Minou padded purposefully after her, leaving the odd wisp of white cat fur on the stairs for Mrs Battersby to find later.

The bedroom door was ajar. Anna was aware of the familiar smell of the cologne her father used, as she quietly pushed it open. Perhaps he was still asleep. Her heart sank. He was not there and his bed had not been slept in. A piece of wrapping paper and a pair of scissors lay on his dressing-table beside his comb and silver hairbrushes.

Chapter Eight

It was New Year's Eve and Anna was curled up under her eiderdown. She had just finished reading the second of the Narnia books her father had given her for Christmas and was imagining herself as belonging to that magic land, with a role of her own to play – nothing too important – but part of it all the same. She looked through the window at the falling snow and imagined herself, galloping on a centaur to that place, worlds away from her present surroundings.

Her father had still not come home. All through Christmas, she had willed him to come back. She had finally reached the conclusion that he had decided to spend his Christmas with the fair-haired woman he liked so much. He had stayed away before but at least, in the past, he had always been there for her on Christmas Day.

The child wasn't sure if her mother had made any enquiries. Anna thought not, guessing that she would not like people to suspect that she didn't know where her husband was.

The Bat had come in each day and, as the days went by, she seemed to be taking a more and more important part in the running of the house. From the look of satisfaction on her face, this state of affairs suited her very well. Anna knew that she was revelling in David's absence, never missing an opportunity to say how dreadful it was and making a point of sitting in his armchair whenever she got the chance. It seemed to Anna that the woman was doing everything possible to encourage Rosalind to pretend he didn't exist, to push his memory away, so that if he did return, there would be no place left for him.

In spite of her hurt, the girl longed to hear the sound of his key turning in the front door-lock, to have him bend down and kiss her cheek, to feel his slightly scratchy face against her own with his familiar smell of cologne and whiskey and peppermint. After a whole week's absence, she was beginning to think she might never see him again. She couldn't help being worried that her own behaviour, when he'd come to say goodnight to her after the dreadful evening of the party, had played some part in making him go away. Perhaps he thought she didn't love him any more.

The doorbell rang, making her jump. She heard the Bat's heavy footsteps in the hall and the sound of the front door being opened. Anna crept out of her room, making her way to the top of the stairs where she peered down through the banisters. She could make out two pairs of identical, snow-speckled, black shoes and the bottom half of two lots of navy-blue trousers. A man's voice asked if this was the residence of Mr David Armitage.

Anna tiptoed down the first few steps, in time to see the woman ushering two tall policemen into the front sitting-room.

'Perhaps the Bat has done something really awful and they've come to take her away and they'll lock her up for years and years,' she fantasised happily. She looked at the trail of melting snow lying on the cork tiles and gleefully imagined the grumbles there would be when the Bat discovered the mess they had made on her polished floor.

The policemen did not stay very long. After she had shown them out, Mrs Battersby paused in the hall, watched by the disappointed child. So they had not taken her away after all! Suddenly, it crossed Anna's mind that they might have come to see her mother because they knew where her father was. She started down the stairs.

The Bat turned and looked up at her with a curious expression on her face.

"Your mother will want to speak to you in a little while. So, don't you go doin' one of them vanishing acts you're so good at."

"Why did the policemen come? Was it about Daddy?"

The urgency in Anna's voice was ignored by the woman, who disappeared into the front room again, shutting the door firmly behind her. Edna Battersby was feeling elated. The news she had just heard was more than she could have hoped for. Given a little time to prove how indispensable she was, her position in the house could soon be unassailable.

For what seemed like an eternity, Anna waited patiently on the stairs with a growing certainty that something was terribly wrong. She sat with her arms wrapped around Minou, trying to soak up some of the cat's warmth. She could hear her mother and the Bat talking in low voices from behind the closed door. Then, when the feeble daylight had faded so much that she could barely make out the shape of the big oak chest in the hall, the door was opened with a flourish and the Bat motioned her to go in.

Rosalind was sitting in her wheelchair by the fire, her face lit by a small lamp on the table beside her. She looked strangely remote. Anna waited just inside the doorway with Minou hovering behind her. She was taken by surprise when her mother suddenly held out her arms to her in an uncharacteristically friendly gesture.

"Come over here, darling. I'm afraid I have some bad news."

Her voice sounded strangely husky.

Anna was torn between wanting to know if the news concerned her father and being suspicious of her mother's behaviour. Usually, the term 'darling' was only used when her mother wanted her to do something Anna did not want to do or when Rosalind was trying to get her daughter on her side to annoy her husband.

She made her way tentatively across the room, stopping just out of reach of the proffered hands. The hands were lowered and their eyes met.

"I'm afraid that there's really no way of saying this pleasantly, Anna. Your father has been killed in an accident."

There was a pause and then Rosalind continued to speak but Anna only saw her mother's mouth opening and closing. She could not hear the words because of the roaring sound that filled her head until she though it would burst. First Carlo and Gianni, and now her father. She swayed a little.

"For God's sake, put her in a chair, Mrs Battersby. She's going to faint."

Before the woman could do anything, Anna's legs folded underneath her and a sickening blackness on the edge of her vision grew and engulfed her.

* * *

Anna could hear the Bat repeating her name, as though she were speaking from a great distance. She felt herself being pushed into a sitting position and was aware of the cold edge of a glass as it was pressed against her lips. She opened her eyes, focussing with difficulty on the woman leaning over her, glass of water in her hand. She pushed it away violently, spilling water down the front of her jersey and onto the other's sleeve.

"I feel sick," she mumbled.

Before Mrs Battersby could move, Anna vomited over the woman's shiny, black boots. She gagged again as Mrs Battersby let go of her and leaped backwards with surprising alacrity. The woman angrily thumped the glass down on the table and without a word, went to fetch a cloth and bowl of water. Her previous look of smugness had vanished and her face now showed only disgust and irritation.

Anna lay back in the chair and closed her eyes. She still felt dizzy. She thought that the best thing that could happen would be for her to die as well. Her mother had been responsible for two deaths last summer and Anna was sure that, by being so unkind to him, she had driven her father away and played a part in his death. But if only Anna had told him she loved him when he had come up to say goodnight after that terrible party. Then, he might still be alive now.

Rosalind watched the child's pale face, guessing a little of what was going through her mind. She wanted to say something that would bring her daughter some comfort but she found herself unable to think of anything appropriate.

"Anna, I'm sorry . . . I wish . . ."

The girl turned her head away abruptly, her eyes pressed tightly shut. Her mother would never know or understand how she was feeling. She had never loved him. She remembered all the times she had made fun of him, told him that he was useless, shouted at him to leave her alone, to go back to his club. The angry words tumbled around the child's head. Anna felt she never wanted to speak to her mother again.

The two of them sat, either side of the fire, unspeaking. The sour smell of vomit hung in the air.

* * *

"Sod off!" hissed Mrs Battersby, as Minou scratched at the back door.

She had not been fed and it was freezing outside. The woman hunted in the dresser drawer for a traycloth and spent some time in trying to make Rosalind's unappetising meal look attractive. Anna was upstairs, safely out of the way and, as far as the woman was concerned, after her performance earlier, could do without any supper. The brat might be sick again.

Mrs Battersby had assured an unusually concerned Rosalind that if the child needed anything, she would see that she was looked after. She muttered to herself as she ground the lumpy potatoes with a fork. Her damp boots, that she had done her best to clean, still felt uncomfortable. Bloody child could have waited to be sick in the lavatory – it was almost as if she had done it on purpose. Mrs Battersby made her mind up that whatever happened, she would not mollycoddle the girl and would discourage her mother from letting her get away with things because of what had happened. People died all the time. Children were a lot tougher than was realised. She reminded herself that at least now she wouldn't have that miserable specimen of a man cluttering up the place any more. Edna Battersby almost smiled as she picked up the untidy tray.

* * *

It was the day of her father's funeral and a tearful Anna was glaring at her mother across the room.

"It's wrong! I know it's wrong!"

"Don't be absurd, Anna. I will not have a scene just before we go to the church. Pull yourself together!"

"But Daddy always said he wanted to be buried beside the little church he used to take me to on some of our walks."

"Your father never told me any such thing. Now, be quiet."

"If you let him be burnt, he won't have a grave for me to put his flowers on," Anna insisted, her cheeks red with anger, fresh tears welling up in her eyes. She looked at her mother in disbelief. She seemed so cool and unaffected by the nightmare through which Anna was living. "I won't be able to visit him. Please don't do that to Daddy. Please!"

She moved closer to Rosalind, desperate for her to understand the awfulness of what had been planned for her father. She clutched the sleeve of her mother's soft, mohair coat.

Any sympathy that Rosalind might have felt for her daughter had evaporated some hours earlier. The child's nose needed blowing. She removed the hand from her arm and smoothed out the crushed material with impatient fingers.

"Mrs Battersby, if Anna refuses to behave, she had better go in the other car with you and the aunts."

* * *

The service at the crematorium was short and dismal. Not many people had known of David's death and Rosalind hadn't wanted to advertise the fact that her inebriated husband, after going missing from home for a whole week, had wandered into the path of a speeding taxi and been knocked down.

Fortunately, Anna didn't know the details of her father's sudden death. David had been lifted on to the footpath, a stranger's coat was placed over him and he had died before the ambulance arrived, lying in the muddy, churned-up snow, with the blood draining from his shattered skull.

Neither did the child know that when this happened, he had been on his way home to tell Rosalind that he was leaving her and taking his daughter with him. He had drunk too much in an attempt to bolster his courage before facing the woman whom he knew despised him so much.

In spite of the lack of publicity and the haste with which the cremation had been arranged, a handful of people had shown up at the ugly, redbrick chapel on the outskirts of the town. David's colleagues from work and several acquaintances in the legal profession had come, also some neighbours and a few of his clients. His parents were dead and the only other members of his family Rosalind had seen fit to inform were two aunts who lived nearby and whom she considered to be sufficiently uncritical and harmless.

She glanced over the assembled mourners. She knew most of them but her eye was caught by a blonde in one of the pews at the back of the building. She would have been pretty, if her face had not been blotchy and her eyes pink from crying. The woman looked genuinely upset. Rosalind turned back to face the coffin with its tasteful spray of white tulips, her face grim. One of his women, no doubt. Probably the one Anna had thought was an upset client. What cheek! Realising that she was frowning, she carefully re-arranged her features. Rosalind had taken immense care to give the right impression – grief-stricken but not so as to make her look unattractive. She had used make-up especially chosen for its pallor and had lightly dusted the area under her eyes with blue for added effect.

She gave a small sigh that was noticed by Mrs Battersby, sitting in the front pew, immediately behind her wheelchair. The woman leaned forward and touched her on the shoulder, making her flinch.

"Are you all right, dear?" Her voice dripped with concern.

"Perfectly," hissed Rosalind, through clenched teeth.

She wished now that the wretched woman had stayed behind. Squaring her shoulders, she gazed straight ahead. But an irritating sniffing sound made her turn towards Anna.

The child looked deathly pale and, Rosalind thought, so very unattractive. She sat, huddled in the smart new coat that had been especially purchased for the funeral. Although Anna was next to Mrs Battersby, Rosalind was, for a few seconds, struck by how solitary she looked. The organ wheezed to a discordant stop and the service got under way.

Anna watched with numb fascination as the coffin slid slowly towards the small doors at the end of the conveyor belt. Prayers were intoned in a plummy voice by a bored, tall man whom she had never seen before. He had spoken of her father as if he knew him but the things he'd said seemed to have no relevance, as though he had been talking about someone else.

As the doors closed and she lost sight of the wooden box in which her father lay, Anna tried not to think about what would happen next. If she had hated her mother before, it was nothing compared to the loathing she now felt. Without his occasional interventions on her behalf and the affectionate, if absent-minded, attention he had given her from time to time, Anna could see the future stretching before her in an endless succession of loveless, joyless days with no hope.

At the end of the short service, she followed her mother's wheelchair out of the chapel. As she walked past the handful of mourners, the desolation in her face was noted by the tearful, blonde woman in the back pew.

'Poor, poor kid,' she thought to herself, wondering if the child recognised her from that day in the park. She had looked sad then but nothing compared to the misery that seemed to fill her small face now. It was almost as though the effort of walking out of the building was more than Anna could manage – she looked as if her legs would buckle under her at any minute. One glance at the child's mother confirmed everything she'd suspected. That little girl wouldn't be getting the comfort and love that she needed from that frozen-faced bitch.

* * *

Only a few, handpicked by Rosalind, had been invited back to the house after the funeral. Mrs Battersby was in her element. She graciously offered sandwiches and took charge of the silver teapot she had assiduously cleaned the day before. Rosalind, looking tragic by the fireside, left the woman to it. Let her hang on to her moment of glory, she thought to herself. It would be over soon enough. She had made up her mind that Mrs Battersby's days were numbered.

Rosalind smiled up at Adam Strong, the handsome, competent man who was taking over as head of the firm. Perhaps the future was beginning to look a little less bleak after all.

Unnoticed by any of them, Anna slipped upstairs to her father's room.

It was exactly as he had left it. She went over to the old, blue silk dressing-gown that lay across the back of the chair. Anna picked it up and buried her face in the garment, breathing in the faint smell of his cologne and soap. She stood like this for several minutes before gently laying it down and crossing over to the dressing-table. She could imagine him, standing in front of the window, patting cologne on to his freshly shaved cheeks and brushing back his dark hair, while she sat on the end of his bed and watched his preparations for the day ahead.

"Got to look presentable, Annie. I've a Duchess coming about her Will this morning! You never know, she might have the Duke with her when she arrives in her gold carriage."

Sometimes he had pretended it was a Lord, or even a Princess. He would hand her his clothes brush, stooping so that she could energetically brush away imaginary fluff and hairs from his shoulders.

"Go on! Make me look utterly splendid," he would tease with a mock-serious expression.

She had loved those brief, early-morning chats when they were alone together, before her mother was up and the Bat arrived at nine o'clock.

On a sudden impulse, Anna picked up the bottle of

cologne, one of the two matching silver-backed hairbrushes and the silver photograph frame containing a photo of herself and her father in a punt. She stared down at the photograph. She was leaning back against him. One of his hands rested on her shoulder and she was laughing at something he had said.

She could remember the day clearly. Her mother had refused to come, saying that it was all too complicated. Anna had guessed that she did not want to suffer the indignity of having to be carried from the wheelchair to the punt. Secretly, she had been relieved. So, with the wicker picnic basket full of good things, they had set off by car to meet two friends of her father's.

It had been a lovely, hot day with a slight breeze that rippled the surface of the green-brown river, making the reflections of the overhead willows dance, and cooling them as they drifted along. She remembered thinking how smoothly her father punted, steering the boat skilfully after each long push and twist of the wrist to free the pole from the weedy, muddy river bed. She had thoroughly enjoyed the sight of other, not-so-expert punters as they zigzagged haphazardly across the river, ending up buried in the thick beds of reeds at the edge, or having to ignominiously paddle back for their lost poles, left sticking diagonally out of the water. To her delight, one immaculately dressed undergraduate had lost his balance and fallen in with a satisfactory splash. She and her father had tried hard not to laugh as they watched the seriously irritated young man clamber back on board, where he dripped over an equally unamused and beautifully attired young woman reclining on the leather cushions, a disdainful expression on her face.

She was jolted from her reverie by the sound of people talking in the hall below. Hastily scooping up the dressing-gown from the chair, Anna retreated to her own room, where she knelt down in front of her chest of drawers. One by one, she carefully wrapped all the objects in the dressing-gown and then slid the precious, blue bundle into one of the drawers, taking care to cover it with some of her own clothes.

Suddenly, a loud voice rang out from the hall below.

"Just carry it up to the spare room. Don't leave it there or someone will trip over it and fall flat on their face."

It was a command, not a request. Anna thought the voice was vaguely familiar but she could not remember where or when she had last heard it. She opened her bedroom door, in time to see the angry, red face of the Bat as she stomped along the passage, stopping outside the room opposite Anna's own, where she proceeded to fling open the door and, without any ceremony, deposit a heavy-looking case with a crash on the floor inside. As the woman passed her, she gave Anna a glare.

"You're supposed to be 'elping downstairs, you are."

"Who was that in the hall just now?"

"Your potty aunt from Ireland, that's who. She wasn't expected, nor invited. Your mother will not be best pleased."

"Aunt Pog?" asked Anna, in surprise.

"Yes. That's wot she calls 'erself, I believe. 'Er – *and* I've got better things to do than be a flippin' porter, luggin' her bags around for her ladyship!"

She stamped off down the stairs, muttering ominously.

In spite of her misery, Anna was intrigued. She had been about six when Aunt Pog had last visited them, she thought. She remembered being told that Aunt Pog's real name was Peggy but, for some reason, she had always been called Pog. She had lived in Ireland for a long time, had been married but Anna had never met her husband and she had no children of her own. Anna also remembered her father's youngest aunt as being quite unlike Aunt Chrissie and Aunt Sylvia, downstairs. They were so quiet and well behaved. From what Anna could recall, Aunt Pog had been neither. In fact, she had been rather noisy. She had laughed a lot, smoked a lot, drunk a lot and she and her father had got on famously. Anna also remembered that her mother had not liked Aunt Pog one bit.

* * *

Downstairs, the atmosphere was strained. Rosalind, as Mrs Battersby had suggested, was, 'not best pleased', at the arrival of the least favourite of her dead husband's three aunts.

Aunt Pog strode across to where she sat, looking somewhat limp but interesting and surrounded by a posse of male sympathisers.

"I'm sorry to hear about David. I liked him a lot. A decent chap, but never very good at knowing when to stop, especially when it came to good whiskey. We always had that in common!" The chuckle was husky. "I'm sorry too that you didn't see your way to informing me of his death. Luckily, I rang Chrissie last night and she told me about the accident. Still, I'm here now and I can stay for a few days. I'll do what I can to help." She turned to a stony-faced Mrs Battersby, hovering behind her like some malign spirit. "You weren't around last time I was here. What's your name?"

"Edna Battersby – Mrs," replied the woman sourly, uncomfortably aware that they were the focus of attention and that everyone was watching the latest arrival with amused fascination.

Aunt Pog was certainly a flamboyant figure. She was near to toppling out of her sixties and had decided that she would grow old disgracefully and would enjoy life to the full while she was doing it. She was dressed in flowing emerald-green silk with a mink coat draped around her shoulders, a large blue hat and a thick layer of clumsily applied make-up with a clearly defined orange tidemark along her jaw-line. Around her neck hung three or four heavy gold chains and her fingers were laden with a selection of large and beautiful sapphires and diamonds.

Rosalind had always believed that the woman was too ready to voice her opinions and that she was vulgar and overdressed and today she looked like an over-decorated Christmas tree.

Aunt Pog certainly had more sparkle about her than the pathetic object wilting in its pot in the corner of the overheated room. She stood nearly six feet high; three inches of her impressive stature due to a pair of shiny green shoes with remarkably thin heels. She had once told David that she always wore high heels because walking in flat shoes changed her centre of gravity so that she developed pressure sores on the insides of her knees. David had laughed, amused at this vanity. Rosalind had considered it ridiculous.

"Right, Battersby. I want a large whiskey. None of your ordinary muck. There was always some good stuff in the corner cabinet in the dining-room, if I remember correctly. And no water and absolutely no ice."

Outraged, Mrs Battersby looked towards Rosalind for backup. However, she was disappointed to discover that she was not to get any help from that particular quarter.

"Yes, go and get Mrs Roberts some whiskey, please."

Mrs Battersby had never been called by just her surname and it was a shock. A shock too, that Rosalind had not, in some way, come to her assistance instead of expecting her to run errands for this dreadful woman. Shooting a look of sheer poison in Aunt Pog's direction, she marched out of the room to fetch the whiskey.

Blissfully unaware of the waves of dislike emanating from the departing woman, Pog turned her attention back to Rosalind.

"Where's Anna?"

The question was peremptory.

Rosalind eyed the uninvited guest coolly.

"Probably in her room."

"Has she taken it very badly? How is she?"

"She will be perfectly all right, thank you, Pog."

"I hope so. She and her father were close, were they not?"

"Why don't you go up and see her?" said Rosalind dismissively, turning back to one of the men at her side.

Pog plucked the glass of whiskey from the hand of the advancing Mrs Battersby.

"Good idea!"

Clutching her drink in one hand and a large green handbag in the other, she swept out of the room, in a cloud of 'Wild Musk' tinged with nicotine.

Chapter Nine

Pog Roberts steamed up the stairs with a determined look in her eye. For a woman of sixty-nine, she showed a remarkable turn of speed. Coming to a halt outside the room she remembered as Anna's, she knocked and waited. She was about to knock again when the door was slowly opened.

The child was almost unrecognisable. The last time Pog had seen her, Anna had looked fresh-faced and reasonably sturdy with plenty of energy; although there had been a slightly withdrawn quality about her that her great-aunt had found disconcerting.

She had grown taller – that was to be expected, but she looked so terribly sad. She was thin and pale and there were dark rings under her eyes. It was her eyes that struck Pog most forcibly. They were lack-lustre and devoid of expression as if she had decided to hide her feelings from the world. The woman realised that she would have to be delicate in her handling of this forlorn little creature and that delicacy was perhaps not one of her strong points.

"May I come in, darling?"

Mutely, Anna nodded, cautiously opening the door a little wider. She looked up at the bulky mink-coated figure in front of her. She remembered now how Aunt Pog had always used the word 'darling' a lot. The girl wondered how many small, furry creatures had been killed to make the coat.

"Do you remember me?" asked Pog, stepping into the room. She noticed that it felt chilly.

Anna nodded again. "Yes. You're my great-aunt. You're Daddy's Aunt Pog."

"That's right – the mad one from Ireland. But I think being called a great-aunt is more than I can cope with. Just 'Aunt' will do."

Pog gave Anna a broad smile.

Anna noticed that her aunt's bright red lipstick looked as if it had slipped a bit; as though it had been applied without using a mirror and in a great hurry.

"I've come to see how you are. Your daddy wrote to me a little while ago. He was worried about you, darling. He said he thought you weren't very happy."

Pog could hardly bring herself to look into the blank brown eyes.

She pulled her coat around her and sat down heavily on the bed, gold chains clanking. She narrowly missed squashing Minou who got up, gave the intruder a resentful look and resettled herself at a safe distance.

"Will you come and talk to me? I'm afraid I'm a bit out

of touch with things. Tell me about that Battersby person. She looks rather grim."

Pog shoved her handbag out of the way to make room for Anna and then lit a cigarette.

The girl sat down beside her warily.

"She doesn't like Minou. She chases her and tries to hit her with the broom."

"Good gracious me! What does Minou do?"

"She jumps up onto the wardrobe and spits at her."

"Good for Minou!" Pog chuckled. "And what about you? Is she nice to you?"

Anna considered her answer carefully. If she told the truth, would it then be repeated to her mother? She gave a sideways glance at the woman beside her. She remembered how her father had liked his aunt and how her mother had not. Anna decided to take a risk.

"She hates cats and she hates children."

"I see. She doesn't chase you with a broom, I hope?"

For the first time, Anna smiled. "No, but I think she'd like to. She says I'm a pest and I'm always in the way." She paused. "I have a special name for her which only Daddy knew."

"What is it? Wicked Witch of the West?"

"I call her the Beastly Bat."

Pog laughed. "And a very good name too but a little unkind to bats, don't you think?"

Anna shook her head.

"Not the ones that suck blood," she replied firmly.

For a long time they talked. Anna gave a description of life at school, which was sufficiently vivid to bring back unpleasant memories to Pog of her own schooldays. The child was amazed to hear that her great-aunt had been expelled from one school at the age of six because she had been so wild and badly behaved.

All the time Anna was speaking, Pog watched and listened carefully. The child talked a lot about books, especially the books her father had given her for Christmas. Pog never read anything more taxing than the odd magazine article, the local rag and the *Radio Times* and had never heard of C S Lewis. But she thought she could understand the attraction for Anna of escaping from reality into that other magical world. She reckoned that life with the uncosy Rosalind and the Beastly Bat would be enough to make the strongest character want to do a runner.

By the end of the conversation, Pog felt that she had a pretty clear picture of what had been going on in the house, both before and after her nephew's death. She glanced around the small bedroom, ash cascading down her ample bosom and onto her lap. Brushing it off absent-mindedly, she took in the doll and the mouse on Anna's pillow, the clumsily hand-sewn cushion on the end of the bed, painstakingly embroidered with the cat's name and the drifts of white cat fur lying along the not-so-clean skirting board. Several crayon drawings of flying dragons and other strange animals were stuck on the walls but, on the whole, she thought the room looked drab and cheerless.

She looked back at the child who was stroking the cat, with a distant expression on her face. Pog felt ashamed.

Why hadn't she made more of an effort to keep in touch with them? She had seen how bad things had been two years ago. At least then, David had been around some of the time for his daughter. How much worse it must have been for Anna since the accident. Well, she was here now and better late than never, she thought grimly.

* * *

After an awkward supper that evening, Rosalind sat, staring morosely into the fire while Mrs Battersby crashed pots and pans in the kitchen as a protest against the continued misuse of her name by 'that woman'.

Anna had been sent upstairs to bed by her mother, after the girl had more or less refused to eat any supper. She'd looked wretched, not wanting to be drawn into conversation by her aunt. The woman noticed how Rosalind's daughter never looked at her mother when she was spoken to. It was hard to think of them as mother and daughter. They seemed so very far apart from one another.

Pog sat comfortably, smoking and taking the occasional gulp of whiskey.

She watched the silent figure in the wheelchair for some time before quietly asking, "Will you miss David?"

Rosalind looked momentarily startled.

After an awkward pause, she replied, "As a wage-earner, yes. As a husband, quite frankly, no, I won't."

"That's very honest, darling. You loved him once though, didn't you?"

"At the very beginning, yes . . . I suppose I did but I

made a mistake." Her voice sounded tired. "I don't feel in the mood for revelations, if you don't mind, Pog."

"What about Anna?"

Pog's eyes were glued to the other's face.

"What about her?"

There was a long silence. Then Pog stubbed out her cigarette in her coffee-cup saucer and got clumsily to her feet. She looked down at Rosalind.

"I thought you might have something to say about that poor child upstairs. After all, she has been through the mill, what with your accident and now her father's death."

"'That poor child,' as you call her, will survive. One always does."

"Rosalind! What's the matter with you? You sound as though you couldn't care less if she survived or not."

"Look, Pog! I have enough on my plate without getting upset about Anna. She refuses to talk to me. She's always made it patently clear that she loved her father not me and she disappears upstairs whenever possible rather than spending time in my company. She seems to get on perfectly well without me."

Pog moved over to the wheelchair.

"But, darling, she's a *child*. You are the adult. Surely *you* are the one who has to work at making some sort of a bond between the two of you – before it's too late."

Rosalind raised her head slowly and looked up at her. Her voice lost some of its habitual coldness.

"I'm afraid there never was a bond between us. It was David who wanted children, not me. Her conception was an accident and when I was pregnant with her, every day was like a prison sentence. And when she was born, I didn't know what to do with her. She was bottle-fed because the idea of breast-feeding repelled me. I'm not a monster, you know. I can't help it! I'm just not the maternal sort and I don't know how to handle her. I wish to God I did."

Pog was surprised by the genuine emotion in Rosalind's face.

She patted her encouragingly on the shoulder and said briskly, "Didn't mean to upset you, darling. Don't worry – you'll be all right. At least you're tough and your type doesn't usually go under."

"Thank you so much that vote of confidence," Rosalind replied, with a wintry smile.

* * *

Pog found it hard to sleep that night. She had gone to check on Anna before going to bed herself. The child's cheeks were wet and her eyes swollen but she pretended that she had not been crying. Pog found it difficult to find words that might cheer her up a little.

"I wanted to come up and say goodnight," she said, in a matter-of-fact voice.

Anna was barely able to smother a sob and turned abruptly away from her.

Unsure what to say next, Pog moved over to the bedside.

"Darling! I didn't want to upset you. I just thought you might like me to tuck you in, that's all. I'm afraid that I'm not very good at this sort of thing."

She could barely make out the sudden jumble of words that poured out of the child in the untidy bed.

"Daddy . . . he came and he thought I was asleep. . . I wasn't. . . I wanted him to hug me. . . but I was cross . . . I wanted to hurt him. . . he went away . . . he called me Annie. . . I won't see him ever again. . ."

Anna pressed her face into the damp pillow.

Pog leaned over and uncertainly stroked the back of one of Anna's hands.

"Darling, I've come to help. Things will get better. I promise."

She waited until the sobbing died down and finally ceased.

"I'm OK, Aunt Pog."

"I'll stay as long as you'd like me to," said Pog as she gently eased one cramped foot from under the bed. She had pins and needles in her leg and was feeling cold.

"No, I'm really OK. Please go."

Pog had left the room, feeling as though she should have done or said something more but not knowing exactly what. And now, she was tossing and turning in her own bed, unable to stop her mind from leap-frogging from one worry to the next. Usually, she never worried, leaving that to other people to do for her. Worrying was a waste of time and energy as far as she was concerned. She consoled herself with the thought that she had David's letter and, unknown to Rosalind, a copy of the Will safe in her handbag and tomorrow the Will would be read.

* * *

Adam Strong glanced over to Rosalind to see her reaction to the Will he had just finished reading to her and David's

103

three aunts. It was difficult not to let his eyes drift in her direction all the time. She was certainly one of the most attractive women he'd come across in a long while – even if she were in a wheelchair. Her face was impassive and it was impossible to know what she was thinking. He had been careful not to look at her while he gave details of various bequests, including a generous sum of money to one Debbie Parker. But, on the whole, she should be feeling relieved, he thought to himself. In his eyes, David had been over-insured.

If Rosalind complied with the request her husband had made, backed up by the letter he had written to his aunt, she would become a very wealthy woman indeed. Even if she did not agree, she would still be very comfortably off.

After the solicitor left and Aunt Chrissie and Aunt Sylvia had been got rid of, Rosalind turned to Pog.

"Well, no wonder you made sure you turned up for that little piece of theatre."

Pog had tipped the contents of her handbag out onto the couch and was rooting through a pile of assorted objects for her cigarette lighter and did not answer. "Why didn't you tell me that David wanted you to look after Anna?"

Pog looked up and gave her a beaming smile.

"Because I knew it would make you cross, darling."

"What makes you think for one minute that you would be suitable . . . or that I would dream of letting her go and live with you in Ireland?"

"I think you will let her come and live with me because it will make your life an awful lot easier and you will be able to concentrate on getting better. I know I don't have children of my own but the big difference between us is that you never wanted children and I did, desperately, but was unable to have any."

Rosalind gave a derisive snort. "But you know nothing about children. You hardly know Anna at all. The whole idea is ludicrous."

"If Anna would be prepared to give it a try, I can only say that I will do my best. If things don't work out and she wants to come back to Cambridge, then we will have a re-think . . . and you will still have all the benefits of having fulfilled David's request." Pog gave her a direct look. "But at least we will have tried."

She could see that Rosalind was looking interested, in spite of herself, although her pride was hurt.

"How could she possibly fit into your bridge-playing lifestyle?" Rosalind's voice was scornful. "And what about her education?"

"She will fit in beautifully. Ballynacarrig is a lovely place with plenty of fresh air and children around – and the local school is excellent." Pog had given quite a bit of thought to the subject of how to shoot down any objections Rosalind might fire at her. "The standard of education in Ireland is extremely high," she added knowledgeably.

In fact, she hadn't the slightest idea what the standard was like; only that the children she came across in the village seemed perfectly happy to go to the small, two-teacher school half a mile down the road from where she lived.

"I will have to think about it."

"Of course you will, darling. But don't take too long. I have booked tickets on the ferry for the day after tomorrow."

"You seem to have been pretty sure that I would agree."

"Why don't I talk to Anna and see what she feels about the idea?" said Pog evenly, as she made her way towards the door.

Rosalind felt a mixture of shame and elation. To let Anna go would be an admission of her failure as a mother and yet, with no child around, as Pog had cleverly pointed out, life would be a lot less complicated. Also she had a card up her sleeve. She had hidden the fact that she was now able to stand and even take a few, faltering steps. Rosalind was not quite sure why she hadn't told anyone. Perhaps because she hated the thought of being observed as she struggled to walk again. She had been more shaken by David's death than she admitted to herself and she needed time to adjust. Even so, she found herself half hoping that Anna would dig in her toes and refuse to go.

* * *

Anna listened to Aunt Pog's appropriately edited version of her dead father's letter and the request he had made that if anything should happen to him, he would like her to go and live with his aunt.

"What about Minou?" she asked anxiously, peering through the haze of cigarette smoke.

"Oh, the mog can come too if you want, darling. And you can bring Maria and Topo Whatsit and anything else you like with you."

"But, will there be room for me?"

"Masses, oodles, positively acres, darling. After that husband of mine buggered off ten years ago, I got Kathleen to clear out all his clutter from the den in the loft and it will make a beautiful bedroom for you. We will put your bed by the window and you will be able to see the lake and the mountains from it. You can make a cosy nest for the mog up there too!"

Pog smiled at Anna encouragingly.

"Who's Kathleen?"

"She comes to help in the house, like the Bat, but she's the complete opposite of that malignant specimen downstairs, I assure you. She's great fun; you'll like her. She's got a sister about the same age as you."

"Will my mother be all right?"

Anna was still looking worried.

Bless the child! thought Pog.

"She'll be fine. I think she wants to get rid of the Bat and find someone better to look after her, and Mr Strong says he knows the very person for the job and he will keep an eye on your mother and make sure she is all right. So you need have no worries on that front."

Pog had noticed the care which the good-looking Adam Strong had taken over Rosalind, making sure she understood the detailed Will. He had been both reassuring and supportive. It seemed to her experienced eye that he had more than just a professional interest in David's widow.

Anna gazed unseeingly out of the window into the empty garden and spoke in a quiet voice, "Well, if she doesn't mind, then I would like to come and live with you."

Pog looked pleased. She was also secretly extremely relieved. God knows how it would turn out but anything was better than leaving Anna here in this loveless atmosphere.

"I'm delighted, darling. We will have a lot of fun, you and I!"

Anna looked non-committal. So far, life had not contained an awful lot of that commodity. She didn't hold out any great hopes that things would improve but she didn't much care where she lived now that her father wasn't there. The thought of being away from the Bat's clutches and her mother's critical eye was appealing. And she also realised that, by moving away, perhaps she wouldn't keep being reminded of her father all the time.

Chapter Ten

The bright yellow Renault bumped along between the leafless hawthorn hedges, splashing muddy water onto the grass verges as it bucked in and out of the potholes. Kathleen had hardly paused for breath since she had collected them from Ballina station.

"We had terrible, high winds last week and the old cowshed roof fell in and all the cows were after charging off down to the beach and Da had the divil's own job to get them back." She laughed at the memory. "And poor old Mick Mulhall passed away on Tuesday. It was quiet enough at the end and a merciful release. Oh, and Mrs Roberts, didn't that Mary Comerford give birth to a fine baby boy. That'll put a stop to her cavorting. She won't know what hit her! That one thinks that children are like puppies – give them the odd bit of food every now and then and they'll rear themselves!" The lively blue eyes smiled at Pog in the rear-view mirror. "Is the child still asleep?"

Pog nodded.

"Flat out."

She looked down at the exhausted Anna, who had slipped sideways in the seat, her head lolling forwards as she slept. The overnight crossing to Dun Laoghaire had been a nightmare, with a high sea running and everyone feeling sick. Anna had not once complained. She had remained stoically silent throughout the voyage, her colour fading from pale to white with a greenish tinge. Pog had been very thankful when they had finally stumbled off the heaving ship. She had to concentrate hard not to trip in her high heels as they set off for the customs shed and felt sure the ground under her was moving. The woman wondered if she had downed too many nautical gins or was it just tiredness and the total lack of sea legs that made walking such an effort?

The cat basket on the seat beside Kathleen creaked as an angry Minou tried to chew her way to freedom.

As they bounced along, Pog looked out at the familiar, small, stone-walled fields with a stab of misgiving. Perhaps she was being foolish and her miserable sisters had been right. They had listened in incredulous silence when she told them that she would be taking Anna back to Ireland. She stubbornly refused to take any notice of their objections and, as she had always done in the past, stuck determinedly to her own plan of action. She wanted so much to make David's young daughter happy. Pog sighed. Well, there was only one way to find out if she had made the right decision or not and that was by giving it a bloody good try. She felt happy to be going home and hoped that Anna would grow to love the place as much as she did.

"Darling, wake up! We're there!"

Anna dragged herself out of her deep sleep and rubbed her eyes with her knuckles. She turned her head stiffly to look out of the car window, blinking, unprepared for the sight in front of her. She saw a pretty, white-walled house with gable windows nestling into the grey, slate roof. It was surrounded by shrubs and trees and a gravel drive led up to the bright red front door. To the right of the house lay a small, sandy beach with a rocky island a little way out in the lake's choppy water. In the distance, as a backdrop to the beach and lake, softly rounded mountains reared upwards into the racing clouds. The wind that had made their crossing of the Irish Sea so uncomfortable was still blowing hard and bars of sunlight blazed down onto the grey lake, making it momentarily deep blue, before vanishing as another thick bank of cloud scudded across the sky, killing the fierce, golden light.

"It's beautiful," Anna whispered, drinking in the view of the majestic Mayo mountains and the sweeping curve of golden beach.

She hadn't guessed that it would be like this. She was amazed at the differentness of it all after the flat Cambridgeshire countryside where the sky seemed to go on forever. She stared up at the gulls, driven in from the sea by storms, as they wheeled and tumbled, calling to each other in the windy air. Something within her leapt as she watched and listened to them. 'They sound so wild . . . and sad,' she thought.

"So, what do you think?" Pog's husky voice broke into her thoughts. "Is it what you expected it to be like, darling?"

Anna turned slowly towards her, eyes wide.

"I didn't know it was going to be so beautiful," she said quietly.

Smiling to herself, Kathleen restarted the engine and they rolled over the gravel, up to the front door.

"Wait 'til you see it in the fine weather, Anna. It'd take the sight out of your eyes, when there isn't a breath of wind and the gorse is in flower all around," she said, giving a warm smile over her shoulder to the sad-eyed child.

Anna climbed out onto the thick gravel, which crunched delightfully under foot. Rather unsteadily, she made her way around to the front of the car to the cat basket.

"You'd better not let that animal out 'til we're inside or it might make a run for it," Kathleen warned as Anna picked it up.

"Come on, darling! Welcome to Sandy Bay House." Pog pushed open the cheerful red door and stood back to let Anna in first.

A red-tiled hall led into a large-sitting room where a fire crackled and blazed in an enormous fireplace. Comfortable-looking couches, piled with cushions, stood on either side of the fire. The whole room was decorated in warm golds and browns with a coffee-coloured carpet underfoot. The child could feel its velvety softness under her feet.

Anna took in the small tables scattered around, covered in ashtrays and bric-à-brac, the paintings in ornate gold frames that decorated the walls, and the sideboard and mantelpiece loaded down with silver ornaments. Silver candlesticks, silver picture frames, silver figures of nymphs and shepherdesses, all jostled for space. She had never seen a room so full of *things*. She wondered if Kathleen minded dusting and polishing it all and how long it took to keep everything looking so beautifully shiny. Pog and Kathleen watched as she absent mindedly put the basket down, her fascinated eyes travelling from one object to the next. The room was warm and welcoming and had a feeling of being well lived in. Anna decided that it was very nice, even though there was a smell of stale cigarette-smoke lingering in the air. It was much cosier than her mother's house.

"Kathleen will show you your room, darling. The stairs are a bit steep and I'm dying for a ciggie, so I'll wait for you down here. Take the mog up too and settle her in."

While she warmed her hands in front of the fire, Pog watched as Anna picked up the basket and obediently followed Kathleen through into the conservatory at the far end of the sitting-room. Then the woman kicked off her shoes and sank thankfully into the soft-cushioned couch by the fire. 'So far, so good,' she said to herself, as she ripped open a new pack of cigarettes with a brightly painted fingernail.

* * *

Kathleen had done her best to make the large study in the attic into a suitable bedroom for a nine-year-old child. It had once been used by Desmond Roberts before he had disappeared out of Pog's life one September afternoon ten years earlier.

His method of going had been particularly cruel. He had given his wife no hint of warning. After an apparently contented morning together, when they had sat over cups of coffee and finished *The Times* crossword puzzle, he had gone down to the village to post a letter, while Pog tackled her first gin of the day. He never returned. Sightings were reported in Ballina and later, in London. He neither wrote nor telephoned to explain the reason for his leaving.

At first, Pog was worried that he had suffered some sort of nervous breakdown but, from what she heard from mutual friends in England, this was obviously not the case. No one witnessed the tears she shed as she sat, hour after hour, unable to sleep, night after night, nursing a glass of gin and a cigarette, with the radio on for company.

Then her hurt slowly changed to anger. She made the decision to get on with her life without him. If she ever made any reference to her missing husband, it was usually as 'that bugger Roberts'. It never occurred to her that perhaps her fondness for the gin bottle might have been a contributory factor in his eagerness to get away.

Kathleen had been told by her employer that no expense was to be spared in making the place as comfortable and as welcoming as possible for Anna. She knew very little about the child's background, only that it had been unsettled and often unhappy and that Anna was now without a father. So she had set about the preparations with enthusiasm.

Kathleen Nolan was twenty-five, short and stocky and, as her father often remarked, 'with a good, sensible head on her'. She had enjoyed a happy, busy childhood and was the oldest of three. Her parents, Gem and Bridie Nolan, ran a small farm a little way up the winding track that led back to the narrow road to Ballynacarrig, a mile away. Kathleen had unlimited energy and a fierce loyalty to Pog Roberts. Nothing was too much trouble to her. She would work tirelessly all day in the house and large kitchen garden that lay at the rear, sheltered from the storms that often swept across the lake by a thick belt of trees. Her coming to work for Pog, five years after Desmond Roberts' disappearance, had given both women a lot of pleasure.

Pog disliked driving, partly because her eyesight was poor and she had severe problems trying to tell the difference between a parked car and a grazing cow and partly because she could never remember where she had left her glasses. It had got to the point when even she admitted that she was an extremely bad driver. She had, on a few occasions and, 'with a fair bit of drink taken', as the locals would say, landed in the bog. Her car, known to most of the inhabitants of County Mayo as the 'Yellow Peril', would have to be pulled out by Gem's tractor the next day.

Most of the villagers had a story to tell concerning Mrs Roberts and her exploits behind the wheel. Everyone had got to hear about the night a few months back when she had been stopped by the new, young and enthusiastic garda.

He had stepped out into the road and waved her down. Politely, he pointed out that her driving was erratic and she was not displaying either a tax or an insurance disc.

Pog, who had been chewing dried tea leaves as she drove, in the mistaken conviction that they would render her breath inoffensively neutral, leaned out of the window and launched into a tirade of abuse. The young man winced as the fumes of many gins hit him in the face.

"Listen to me, darling!" she roared at the bemused figure in blue. "Of course my driving's erratic. Aren't I trying to dodge all the bloody potholes?"

"But, Ma'am, you were travelling at well over the correct speed," Garda Ryan ventured weakly. Not even his girlfriend called him 'darling'.

"That's because I'm in a hurry, you silly man. There wasn't a soul around until you leaped out of the bushes and nearly gave me a heart attack."

Garda Ryan realised that this was not going to be a straightforward affair. He cleared his throat before re-launching the attack.

"I have reason to believe that you have been drinking, Ma'am. Would you please step out of the car?"

"Are you mad? I most certainly will *not* step out of the car," said Pog furiously, holding tightly onto the steering wheel for support.

"And may I ask why not, Ma'am?"

There was a short silence while Pog considered the various reasons why not.

"Because I'm tired, my ankles are swollen, it's getting very late, it's bloody freezing . . . and it's starting to rain – again," she ended triumphantly.

As far as Pog was concerned, that was the end of the conversation. After a couple of failed attempts, she managed to get the car into first gear and revved the engine.

However, Garda Ryan had other ideas. With a determined expression, he reached into his breast pocket for his notebook and pencil.

Pog, realising that he was not going to give up, decided that she'd hung around quite long enough. When she thought about the incident some time afterwards, she was never quite sure whether it was fatigue that clouded her judgement or the large amount of gin swimming in her system. Whichever it was, she proceeded to suffer some form of brainstorm. With a grinding of gears, the car jerked forward like an inebriated kangaroo. Garda Ryan leaped hastily backwards. As the Yellow Peril gathered speed, Pog was heard to shout, "I've had quite enough of this bloody nonsense. So just . . . piss off, darling!" With that parting shot, she had roared off into the night, exhaust pipe belching, leaving behind her a strong smell of oil and rubber.

The amazed man scrambled out of the overflowing ditch. In the pitch dark, he groped for his torch and notebook in the long, wet grass. Never, in all his two years with the force, had he been treated with such contempt. 'Wait until the Sergeant hears about this,' he thought grimly as he gingerly pulled pieces of bramble from his muddied, soaking-wet trousers.

Garda Ryan was extremely put out to find that Sergeant Gallagher was not all that sympathetic. He wasn't to have known that his superior officer was a frequent visitor to the house by the lake and had shared many a bottle of gin and whiskey around the fireside with Pog Roberts. The sergeant found her outlook on life refreshing. He sometimes found himself wishing that his own wife had been a little more fun when she had been alive. Still, he thought, the young man had a point and he had to be seen to do something about giving her some sort of a mild reprimand.

He telephoned Pog the next day. He informed her that she was not to tell any more of his officers to 'piss off'. He suggested that it might be a good idea if she cut down on her consumption of alcohol if she wished to go on driving. She should also do something about obtaining up-to-date tax and insurance discs when she had a free moment.

At the other end of the phone, an unrepentant Pog roared with laughter.

"Darling, I haven't seen you for ages. Come and have a drink soon and tell that idiotic young man of yours not to worry so much. Of *course* I wasn't drunk – just a little merry, that's all. Such a fuss about nothing!"

"But you'll deal with the insurance and tax, won't you, Pog?"

"Yes, yes! Don't be a big bully! Soon as I have a moment, I'll see to it. Don't worry, darling!"

Sergeant Gallagher wondered why he didn't feel convinced by her reassurances.

A few weeks later, Pog had an encounter with a cow that put a large dent into the offside front bumper of the Yellow Peril and an even larger one in the flank of the cow. The farmer complained to the gardaí and was placated with difficulty. Shortly after this, Sergeant Gallagher was transferred from nearby Ballina to Castlebar and a younger man with more up-to-date views on policing took his place. Pog wisely decided that, from now on, perhaps it would be a good idea if Kathleen did most of the driving.

* * *

Kathleen led Anna up the steep, wooden stairs to a small

landing at the top. Everything was panelled in honey-coloured wood, from the walls to the ceiling. There were two doors leading off the landing. She pointed to the nearest.

"That's your room, Anna, and the other one is your bathroom."

Anna's eyes widened.

"My bathroom – just for me?" she asked, in pleased surprise.

"Just for you."

Kathleen pushed open the second door and stood back to let the girl enter.

The first impression Anna had was of warm wood and bright light from the three gable windows. Going over to them, she found that she could see the mountains and lake from two of them. The next thing she noticed was how warm and cosy her new bedroom felt. She stood beside the bed, admiring the bright patchwork quilt in blues and greens. Then she noticed that a small, blue armchair stood in a corner of the room, complete with a quilted cushion that matched the bedspread. One wall was lined with blue shelves and a large blue wardrobe. A chest of drawers and table under one of the windows completed the scene. She thought it was possibly the most beautiful bedroom she had ever been in.

"There's a box in the corner there with some books Mrs Dempsey thought you might like. She and Mr Dempsey teach at the school in Ballynacarrig. You'll be going there when term starts next week. Oh, I nearly forgot." Kathleen went to the end of the bed and beckoned Anna over. On the polished wooden floor sat a large blue cushion. "That's for your cat. I hope she likes it."

Anna turned to her, her face glowing with pleasure. Impulsively, she took hold of the other's hand.

"Thank you very much for making it look so lovely."

Kathleen bent down and gave her a quick hug.

"It was fun getting it ready for you. Sure, the only thing I didn't manage to find was a rug for the floor. We'll go into town before school starts and you can choose one."

"I'd like that very much," said Anna, suddenly a little overwhelmed by all this unexpected kindness.

She was beginning to feel that perhaps she really was welcome in this house by the lake in Ireland.

Kathleen helped her open the basket and a tousled-looking Minou emerged with ears well back and tail twitching. Anna picked her up, stroking her gently in an effort to calm her.

"Tomorrow I'll bring you up to the farm and you can meet Ma and Da and Amy and PJ. Tell me, do you like cows, Anna?"

"I don't know," said Anna, solemnly. "I've never met any."

Kathleen laughed.

"Well, I'll be sure you have personal introductions to as many of them as possible!"

It was Anna's turn to laugh.

Chapter Eleven

The next morning was bright and sunny, in sharp contrast to the grey days of freezing weather they had left behind in Cambridge.

"Ireland is like that. One minute it's lashing, the next you could be melting with the heat."

PJ, Kathleen's fourteen-year-old brother and Pog's most willing handyman about the place, was installed at the kitchen counter with a large mug of tea in one hand and a slice of toast in the other.

Anna nodded non committally but said nothing.

While he got on with his second breakfast, she studied him out of the corner of her eye as she ate her cornflakes. She noticed his hands were daubed with, what looked like, some sort of black grease. The ends of his jeans were frayed and he sported a pair of brightly coloured striped socks. His muddy boots lay on their sides by the back door. She thought he smelled of animals and cold fresh air. It mingled pleasantly with the aroma of freshly toasted bread in the warm kitchen. Kathleen's brother was wolfing his food down as though he were starving. Every now and then he would pause and take a gulp of tea. When he caught her eye, he gave her a wide grin. She thought that he looked friendly.

He quickly swallowed the remains of his tea and said, "And it can be so hot in January that you could wear a shirt and then in the summer, it's an overcoat you'd be needing. Did you bring your swimming gear with you?" he teased. "You could take a dip after breakfast. Local custom, you know!"

Anna could see how like his older sister he looked: short, with the same brown hair and pale, freckled skin and a way of laughing with his eyes that Kathleen had.

"PJ! Don't be annoying the poor child." Kathleen gave her brother a dig in the ribs.

Anna watched her as she picked up the coffee pot and filled a large cup to take to Pog, who apparently never appeared before ten in the morning. And then only when she had consumed two or three cups of the pungent brew and made several phone calls.

Pog Roberts ate nothing before lunch, relying on caffeine and nicotine to get her through the first part of the day. Her midday meal usually consisted of a light snack of toasted cheese or pâté – and gin, which she drank with water. No ice, no tonic, no lemon. She would sometimes switch to whiskey if a well-behaved guest had brought along a particularly good brand. Her long-suffering GP fought a losing battle over this regime, pointing out that the emphysema and attacks of bronchitis she suffered would only get worse. Pog responded by telling him not to worry himself into an early grave on her account and that in between attacks she felt just wonderful. She would then ask him to her next party. This suited them both; he enjoyed the party and she had him on the spot if she did overdo things and begin to feel unwell.

* * *

After breakfast, PJ was sent off on his bike by Kathleen to run an errand for Pog, and Anna slipped upstairs to finish her unpacking.

She carefully placed her own books next to the ones that Mrs Dempsey had left for her on the brand new shelves. Topo Saggio and Maria were installed in the armchair beside the radiator. Recovering from the trauma of the previous day, Minou was still asleep on her cushion, snoring gently. The room was full of winter sunshine, pouring in through an east-facing window.

Anna carried the blue silk bundle with its precious contents over to the bed and slowly unfolded it to reveal the silver hairbrush, the bottle of cologne and the framed photograph of herself and her father. One by one, she arranged them on the chest of drawers. She found she could not look at the photograph as she placed it beside the other mementos. Carefully folding the dressing-gown, she put it into the bottom drawer. When I'm tall enough, she thought, I will wear it every single morning and every single evening for the rest of my life. Taking care not to crumple the silk, she slid the drawer shut.

* * *

"Can I take Minou outside now?" she asked Kathleen a little later.

"Sure you can! It's a grand day for a bit of exploring. Just mind Moses!"

Anna looked at her blankly.

"Who is Moses?"

"Moses is Mrs Roberts' goat and, if you don't watch out, he might help you on your way when you're not expecting it! He's not too happy with life at the moment. His mate, Venus, died last summer after eating nearly all the clothes on the washing-line. I think it was the clothes-pegs that did for her."

Anna's expression changed to one of amazement. She hadn't realised that goats ate clothes – or clothes-pegs.

"So . . ." Kathleen continued, "your aunt has decided it would be a great idea to take him up the mountain, where he can stink out the other goats and not be upsetting us any more with his bold ways. Any day now he'll be leaving and then you won't have to worry about him any more."

Kathleen was on her knees on the sitting-room floor, clearing out the remains of the previous day's fire. A stack of firewood was piled neatly to one side of the fireplace. The ashtrays had been emptied and the front windows were open. Anna had heard the girl singing quietly to herself while she worked. As she watched her, the child compared Kathleen's obvious contentment with the very different way the Beastly Bat had tackled housework.

When the Bat had cleaned out the fire, she frowned as she crashed and clattered and dropped the tongs. Although Kathleen was very different from Gina, there was

124

something about the two of them that seemed similar to Anna. She thought that perhaps it was because they didn't mind the lives they had been given and were happy just to be themselves. Neither the Bat nor her mother were at all like that, she decided, as she watched Kathleen neatly sweeping up the last flakes of ash from the grate.

In her warmest jacket and with Minou in her arms, Anna emerged into the garden. Fruit trees, their branches bare in the winter sun, stood to one side of a large vegetable garden. She knew what sprouts and cabbages looked like but she was unsure about some of the other strange plants growing in tidy rows. The Bat would not have known what to make of them either. Anna remembered how she had always referred to any unfamiliar food as, 'that 'orrible foreign muck'.

She felt Minou shift as the cat sniffed the air uneasily. To one side of the orchard, a white goat stood, glaring balefully at both cat and girl. His yellow eyes stared at them without blinking. His jaw moved rhythmically in a grinding motion. Anna had never smelt male goat before. She wrinkled up her nose in disgust. No wonder they wanted to get rid of him! She decided that Moses looked far from friendly and as she tentatively circumnavigated him, she wondered how long the rope was that tethered him to a nearby apple tree.

When the garden had been investigated, Anna carried Minou down to the beach. There was no one about. Small waves lapped the pale, clean sand at her feet. The cat looked at the lake with distaste and struggled to get down. In spite of the sunshine, a cold wind was blowing, which made Anna shiver and her eyes start to water.

She turned back up the beach, pulling her collar up around her and calling to the cat, which followed her warily, glancing around at the wide, open spaces as if expecting something to pounce. The girl noticed several small houses and cottages scattered around the bay. Most were white-walled, with grey, slated roofs like her aunt's. They were half-hidden behind trees and large clumps of gorse and the only sign of life was smoke, streaming from some of the low chimneys. She could smell the unfamiliar scent of their turf fires on the wind as she hurried back to her aunt's cosy house.

Lunch consisted of warm soda bread, fresh from the oven, and delicious potato soup, which Kathleen described as being, 'So thick you can trot a duck across it', while she topped up Anna's bowl with another ladleful. Pog nibbled on a stick of celery and sipped her gin while the other two ate their meal.

After the washing-up was done, Kathleen and Anna set off down the lane to walk the half-mile to Sandy Bay Farm, leaving Pog making the necessary preparations for some serious bridge-playing with three other local addicts.

Anna had never been near a farm before and was unprepared for the smells and sounds that assailed her as they walked into the yard at the back of the neat, whitewashed farmhouse. Two black and white sheepdogs immediately rushed over to them excitedly. She took a step back as they brushed past her legs, barking and tail-wagging. The larger of the dogs jumped up, resting his front paws on Kathleen's jacket.

"Get down, you great eejit," she laughed, firmly pushing

the dog away. She saw the look of uncertainty in Anna's face as the girl watched the excited animals. "Don't worry – they wouldn't hurt a fly." She pointed to the larger of the dogs. "That one's Keavy and the mad one with the white stripe on his nose is Bosco. He's Keavy's pup. She's teaching him how to work the sheep and he's taking to it grand. He has the makings of a good sheepdog in him."

Anna held out a tentative hand, which Bosco licked energetically.

A metal gate on one side of the yard opened onto a large field in which black and white cows placidly stood at round animal feeders. She could see their heavy udders swinging underneath them as they moved and she thought how uncomfortable they looked.

Kathleen called her over to a stable door where an inquisitive chestnut horse watched their every movement with great interest.

"This is PJ's horse. She's called Juno and he thinks she's the best mare in the whole of County Mayo!" Kathleen stroked the soft, whiskered underlip. "He hunts with her when he's able. He says she's more like an eagle than a horse. She fair flies over the stone walls and goes mad with the excitement of it all. Da wants to get her in foal this spring."

Anna reached up and stroked the long neck, breathing in the sweet scent of horse and hay and stable. Juno whickered gently.

"What a lovely sound!"

"That means she likes you. You're honoured! She usually only does that for PJ."

As they walked towards the kitchen door, the horse whickered again as she watched them go.

Bridie Nolan looked up as they came into the room. Dusting the flour off her hands, she moved swiftly over to Anna with a welcoming smile. With her jet-black hair, brown eyes and warm, brown skin, she looked very different from her daughter.

"Well, here you are at last, Anna! Welcome to Ballynacarrig."

Her accent was not like Kathleen's either. Anna later learned that was because Bridie Nolan came, not from Mayo but Donegal. She smiled, looking into the child's face with a friendly directness to which the girl responded immediately. Anna smiled shyly back.

The woman inclined her head towards a figure in the corner of the kitchen.

"The wee girl by the stove is Amy." Anna was aware of two blue eyes watching her over the top of a book. "Kathleen tells me that you like books. Is that so?"

"Yes," Anna replied, nodding vigorously. "I like reading."

"Well then, you're in good company, so you are, because that girl has always got her head in a book and only puts it down when she's remembered a bit of unfinished divilment or her stomach starts to rumble from lack of food. Amy, come over and say hello."

The girl uncurled from the wooden settle, hitched up her jeans and approached, regarding Anna with interest. She looked very much like a small version of Kathleen but with more freckles. She gave the newcomer a conspiratorial grin.

"I've a whole pile of books upstairs. Would you like to see them?"

"Can I go and see Amy's books?"

"Of course you can, chicken!" said Mrs Nolan, moving back to her pastry-making. "Go on up with her and later on there will be some fresh scones for tea." She and Kathleen watched as the two girls left the room and clattered up the stairs. "Typical Amy! She never even managed a hello – just went straight to the point!" she laughed. "How is the wee one doing up at the house?"

"Well enough, I suppose. She's a nice kid but she's a bit on the quiet side. You wouldn't know what was in her mind. I have to do most of the talking."

"Well, you're well able for that, Kathleen! I'm not surprised she's quiet after all she's been through. It would be nice to see some colour in her cheeks. Do you think she'll be all right with Mrs R? The woman's not used to having a young one about the place and she can be mighty forgetful when she has a few drinks in her."

"She'll be fine, Ma. Sure, I'll be around to keep an eye on her," replied her daughter, feeding the big range with sods of hand-cut turf from the rush basket in the corner. "I'm looking forward to making a bit of a fuss of her. From what Mrs Robert's told me, she hasn't had a whole lot of spoiling up 'til now."

* * *

One by one, Anna was shown Amy's treasures: Fin, the one-eared bear, the polished stones in a tin box, the seagull PJ had carved for her on her eighth birthday, the photographs of birds and animals she had cut out from magazines and the collection of beads and buttons her grandmother had given her over the years. As they talked, it became apparent that they not only shared a passion for books but for animals as well.

"I like stories with magic *and* animals best," said Amy, hunting through a heap of books for her favourites. "That's a good one. It's about princesses who are turned into swans by their wicked stepmother. You can borrow it, if you like."

"Are you sure?" Anna enquired uncertainly. She had never lent her Narnia books to anyone.

"Sure I'm sure! I wouldn't have said otherwise."

Anna was shown more books, filled with magical beings, of whom she had never heard. Amy explained at length about a place called *Tír na Óg* where people never grew old. She was told that she must never upset the 'little people' because terrible things would happen to her if she did. They were everywhere and very powerful, Amy assured her.

"The most important thing is, you must never cut down a fairy tree. *They'll* get you if you do." Amy's face was serious.

An hour later, Anna was having banshees explained to her when they were called for tea.

On the way back to Sandy Bay House later, she hardly spoke. She felt somehow empty and lonely, even though Kathleen was walking beside her. Anna had seen how the Nolan family had been together. When Mr Nolan had come in during tea, she couldn't help noticing how pleased they had all been to see him, how everyone had talked and laughed and been like a proper family. Why hadn't *she* ever belonged to a family like that, with a brother and sister and parents who liked each other? She knew it was stupid, but she felt like crying. Why hadn't her mother loved her father and made him happy so that he wouldn't have thought he had to go away from them?

"Are you feeling all right, Anna?" Kathleen asked, at a loss to know what was wrong with the child.

She and Amy seemed to have really hit it off and Amy had certainly liked her. You could always tell – her young sister was never one to be backwards about saying what she felt about someone.

"Yes, thank you," said Anna, turning away quickly to look at the lake.

* * *

That evening, after Anna had gone to bed, having politely refused offers of more food, a concerned Kathleen spoke to Pog.

"How will she manage with the other children at the school next week if she's so . . . different in her ways? With the accent she has, she's going to be teased and if she can't laugh it off, they'll think she's a right stuck-up little article and there's one or two of them who could be giving her a hard time."

Pog waved a cigarette in the air as she swallowed the last of her drink.

"Don't worry, darling. She'll be fine. I know she's had a tough time but she's intelligent and she'll learn to fit in. John and Margaret Dempsey will make sure she's not teased

131

and if there's any trouble, I'll be down at the school in a flash and there will be bloody murder!" She held out her empty glass. "Just top this up, will you, darling?"

Kathleen filled the glass, one-third gin, two-thirds water – the way Mrs R liked it. She didn't feel quite as sanguine as her employer. For one thing, it was only a two-teacher school and, good as they were, the Dempseys couldn't spare the time to give any child all that much individual attention and there were some children there who came from fiercely Republican backgrounds. She handed Pog the drink.

"I think I'll just slip up and see if she needs anything before I go."

Pog was pleasantly engrossed in the evening news on the television. Yet another leading Irish politician had been revealed as having accepted large sums of money from unexpected sources, which had then been paid into a bank account in the Cayman Islands. He had also deceived his wife and defaulted on his taxes and was now getting his come-uppance.

"Why don't they just chuck the bugger into jail and throw away the key? If you or I behaved like that, do you think we'd still be swanning around in a limo, living the good life?" She regarded the reporter speaking on television with approval. "I think investigative journalists are a marvellous breed," she chuckled, puffing contentedly at her cigarette. "Goodnight, darling. See you on Monday."

* * *

Kathleen knocked gently on Anna's door.

"Yes?"

"It's Kathleen. May I come in?"

The child was sitting up in bed, an unopened book on the bedspread in front of her. Minou was curled up on one side of the pillows, Topo Saggio and Maria on the other. It looked to Kathleen as though the girl had been crying.

"Is everything all right, Anna?"

"Yes, thank you."

There was an uncomfortable pause.

"Would you like me to read to you?"

"I . . . if you don't mind I . . ."

Kathleen fought back an impulse to gather her into her arms. 'It's stupid I am,' she told herself. 'She's still grieving for her father, the poor child. How could she be all right?'.

"It's OK," she said cheerfully. "Aren't you well able to read to yourself? I'm off now. I just came up to say goodnight. I hope you have a nice weekend with your aunt. I think she has a few things planned!"

Anna gave her a quick, grateful look.

"I'm just going to read a bit more before I turn the light out," she said, opening up the book.

Kathleen noticed that it was still upside down.

Chapter Twelve

When Anna awoke next morning, the light coming through the dormer windows was chilly and grey. A thick mist hid the surrounding mountains, giving the impression when she looked out of the window that the world had somehow shrunk around the house by the lake. She made her way downstairs in her nightdress with Minou at her heels. The living-room was in darkness. With some difficulty, she managed to pull back the heavy, velvet curtains, to reveal a damp-looking Moses glaring at her from the garden.

He had somehow managed to wrap his tether around two apple trees and had nearly succeeded in throttling himself. His rear end was jammed up against the trunk of a tree and a back leg had become entangled. He had been attempting to chew his way through the thick, nylon rope without much success and was now bleating in an annoyed way.

'Poor Moses,' thought Anna. 'If Aunt Pog isn't up after breakfast, I'll have to do something.' She very much hoped that Aunt Pog would soon be up and that she would deal with the unhappy goat.

The girl turned away from the window and surveyed the room. It was extremely untidy with empty glasses on the tables and squashed cushions scattered on the couches and carpet. The grate held the remains of charred logs and the ashtrays overflowed with lipstick-stained cigarette butts. A card table stood in the centre of the fireside rug with cards strewn across its green baize top. She wrinkled her nose. The air in the room stank of cigarettes. Judging from the chaos, Anna decided that Aunt Pog must have had late-night guests.

In the kitchen, the remains of a meal littered the worktops and draining-boards. Anna could feel breadcrumbs under her bare feet. Leftover pieces of tomato and cucumber lay on the wooden chopping-board. Someone had walked on some butter, which now lay in a smeared blob on the tiled floor that Kathleen had washed the previous day.

Obviously, Aunt Pog didn't bother to clear things up before she went to bed at night. Anna remembered how cross her mother became if her daughter forgot to tidy away her books at the end of the day.

She perched on a stool and ate a bowl of cereal. How quiet it was without Kathleen whisking from one room to another, laughing and talking and stopping in the middle of doing things to tell her about a cranky neighbour or to explain about some local custom or other. The kitchen clock said half past nine. Would Aunt Pog get up soon?

Anna was distracted by a demanding 'meow' from Minou, who had finished her own breakfast and was sitting, looking up at the back-door handle, with a fixed stare.

"If only you could ask me to let you out," said Anna wistfully, as she opened the door.

Immediately, Minou slid off into the bushes, away from the sounds of the protesting Moses.

* * *

"Come here, you idiotic animal! Don't you dare charge me!"

Anna had just finished dressing when she heard Aunt Pog's voice outside.

"Bloody fool! Come here, damn you!"

There was a burst of furious bleating, followed by a shriek from Aunt Pog.

The girl dashed downstairs and into the conservatory. The garden door stood wide open. She stopped in her tracks when she saw what was happening among the fruit-trees.

Her aunt, resplendent in a salmon-pink, silk negligee with cream lace at the neck and cuffs, was sitting in the wet grass with a belligerent-looking Moses, still partly tangled in his tether, eyeing her. He had his head down as though he were about to charge but was unable to do so because of the shortness of the rope. The woman had a cigarette firmly grasped in one hand and was laughing weakly, making futile attempts to get back on her feet. She caught sight of Anna's astonished face.

"Oh, good morning, darling! Come and help me sort out this bugger of a goat, will you, before I'm reduced to stabbing him to death with my nail-scissors?"

Anna made a swift detour around the animal and helped her aunt to stagger to her feet. She noticed that the back of the negligee was sodden and dirty but that Aunt Pog, although a little out of breath, seemed to be unhurt. The woman steadied herself, leaning on Anna's shoulder for support. She had a muddy smudge on one cheek and her very platinum-coloured hair was escaping from its hairpins and starting to fall lopsidedly over an ear. One of her fluffy, high-heeled slippers had come off in the unequal struggle with the angry Moses. She leaned stiffly over and grabbed it. The air reeked of goat.

"You get hold of the rope there and I'll deal with this end," Pog wheezed, giving Moses a couple of hard whacks on the nose with her slipper.

He backed away indignantly. After much puffing and swearing on Pog's part and some deft footwork on Anna's, they managed to give the goat enough slack to enable him to graze without strangling himself.

Pog pushed back her hair with a dirt-streaked hand.

"This is the last bloody straw. That animal is quite out of hand. He'll have to go! I'm not putting it off a moment longer. We'll get him up to the mountain today," she announced in a determined voice, stubbing out her cigarette on a handy tree-trunk.

"Will he be all right up there on the mountain?"

"Of course, darling. He can cavort around with his cousins. They won't even notice how smelly he is because they all stink to high heaven as well! I should have done it ages ago – he's been nothing but a nuisance ever since Venus died. I must have been mad in the head to have got him in the first place. I know you can't cuddle a goldfish but I bet they're a lot less trouble to look after than bloody goats." She tugged her wet slipper over her muddy foot and set off rather unsteadily towards the house. "Come on, darling. Let's go inside, into the warm."

A spasm of violent coughing shook her as she reached the shelter of the conservatory. Pog had to hold on to the door to support herself. Anna waited until the coughing stopped, noticing with alarm that her aunt's face had become a peculiar mauve colour and that her eyes were watering. The woman saw the anxious look on her face and smiled reassuringly.

"It's all right, darling," she croaked. "It happens quite often – nothing to worry about." She pulled the garden door shut behind them. "I'll feel human again when I've had a nice, hot cup of coffee and a ciggie. There's some by the fireplace. Just get them for me, will you?"

Anna dutifully fetched the cigarettes and handed them to her aunt.

"Shouldn't you change your clothes, Aunt Pog? They're awfully wet and you might catch a cold."

"Good Lord, darling! I never catch colds. I'm as strong as a horse. Would you like some coffee?"

"Um, no thank you. Daddy . . . I tried some once and I didn't like the taste very much. Can I have some orange juice, please?"

Anna had a sudden, vivid picture of her father, sitting

opposite her in their favourite Cambridge café, laughing at the expression on her face after she had just tried a mouthful of his extra strong coffee. Her heart gave a lurch.

Her aunt answered her, in between coughs.

"Of course you can. Go and have a look in the fridge and see if there's some."

Pog made a grab at a hairpin as it disappeared into the damp lace around her neck. Still coughing, she lit up her third cigarette of the day.

* * *

It was nearly midday when Anna heard the scatter of gravel and a car pulling up beside the Yellow Peril. There was the sound of heavy footsteps, followed by a loud rap on the front door. She looked inquiringly at Pog.

The woman beamed at her before exhaling a cloud of cigarette smoke in a sudden rush. It made her look rather like a friendly dragon, Anna thought.

"That'll be Jim. Go and let him in, darling, before he demolishes the door," her aunt said, brushing cigarette ash off the front of her suit and cramming her feet back into her stylish high heels. Anna noticed that there was a big hole in the toe of one of Pog's stockings and the beginnings of a wide ladder starting to creep up the side of her foot.

Before she had time to open the front door, there was another burst of impatient rapping and a voice called out, "Are you still in bed, Pog?"

With difficulty, the girl pulled down the stiff handle and pulled the door towards her. She was suddenly confronted by a man who seemed to fill the doorway, his bulk blocking out the garden beyond. Anna didn't think she had ever seen anyone quite as tall. His broad shoulders sported a brilliantly coloured tweed sports jacket and his dark hair was half hidden by a flat cap. She stared up at him mutely. He looked just like the sort of person her father would have referred to as 'a bit of a bounder'.

"Is she up and about?" Anna nodded. "Well, are you going to let me in or treat me like a tinker on the doorstep?"

His voice was loud and sounded falsely cheerful. She recognised the tone. It was the way some people spoke to children when they didn't know how to talk to them properly. She backed away and he stepped into the hall. Like her aunt, he smelled of cigarettes and whiskey but there was another smell that Anna could not make out. She could see he was hiding something wrapped in newspaper behind his back. He gave her a jovial wink but she thought his pale blue eyes were cold and unfriendly.

"I've a present for the lovely lady inside," he said, in a mock-confidential voice.

Without replying, Anna led him into the living-room.

"Hello, darling!" said Pog, tilting her cheek for him to kiss. "Has Anna introduced herself to you?"

The man sat down heavily and settled himself in the couch opposite her, newspaper-wrapped parcel on his lap. He ignored the child standing silently beside Pog's chair.

"I've a present for you," he said, lifting one edge of the newspaper to reveal a plump salmon. "I saw Willie this morning and when I said I was on my way down to see you, he gave me this to bring."

"How lovely! Though I hate to think where he got it, bless him!" Pog looked pleased. She adored fresh salmon. "Darling, will you get some whiskey for Jim? It's on the table over there – and just put the fish in the kitchen for me."

When she had deposited the salmon on the draining-board, Anna went back into the living-room where she went over to the heavy whiskey decanter and, using both hands, carefully poured out the drink and carried it over to the man. He took it from her without saying anything. As he was about to put the glass to his lips, he gave a sudden start. A cushion beside him twitched and a beady, green eye observed him from under one corner.

"Jesus, Mary and Joseph! What in the name of heaven is that?"

"Oh, that's Anna's," chuckled Pog. "It's all right, Jim. She's called Minou and she won't bite!"

"And what class of an animal is it?"

"She's a cat," said Anna, wondering if the man was stupid or just trying to be funny.

"And what sort of a name is Menu for an animal? Are we having it for lunch?"

Anna stared at him. He was definitely stupid and not one bit funny.

"She's called Minou," she enunciated slowly. "It means Puss in French."

"Well, well! What a clever girl you are, to be sure! An English cat with a French name. Whatever next?"

Anna flushed uncomfortably. She hadn't meant to sound as though she was showing off. She looked over to her aunt, hoping Pog would come to her aid but the woman was in the middle of lighting yet another cigarette and seemed unaware of the recent exchange.

Minou didn't seem to like the man any more than Anna did. Emerging from under the cushions, she dropped to the floor and went and sat by the window to watch the birds on the lawn outside.

"So, where do you want to go for lunch?" Jim asked Pog.

"We'll go to O'Hagans. I thought it would be nice for Anna to see a really old-fashioned Irish pub. But before we do anything, Moses has to be taken up the mountain. You know the place, Jim, just above Padraig's farm."

"You're not serious, woman!"

"*Deadly* serious, darling. He very nearly killed me this morning. That animal has outstayed his welcome."

"And how the devil are we going to get him there?"

"Well, I thought he'd fit into the boot of your car. After all, it's only ten minutes away and he won't come to any harm in that short time."

"*He* mightn't but what about the boot of my car? I'm not having that evil-smelling object anywhere near my car."

"Oh, Jim! Don't be awkward. We'll put a bit of newspaper down so the car will be fine."

"No, Pog! I mean it. No!"

Anna remembered being taken to watch a tennis match by her father, as she turned her head in one direction and then the other while the argument bounced back and forth.

Finally, a compromise was reached and it was agreed

that they would take Moses in the Yellow Peril but Jim would do the driving.

* * *

Getting Moses into the back of the car proved even more difficult than had been anticipated. He managed to ram Pog, causing her to flail wildly before she descended ungracefully into the grass for the second time that day. Anna watched with glee as an irritable Jim shoved the goat from behind and she and her aunt pulled on the rope. The man had removed his cap and jacket and tucked his vivid yellow tie into his shirt. In spite of the cold, he was sweating heavily. Just before they managed to cram Moses into the car, the goat decided to relieve himself and the copious donation landed, steaming in the cold air, fair and square on Jim's highly polished shoes.

"The fucking animal's shat on my shoes!" he bellowed, as he slammed the door shut behind the protesting goat, who continued to empty his bowels inside the car from sheer fright.

Jim sounded so outraged that Anna had difficulty smothering her laughter. She thought her aunt too looked as though she was having a problem keeping a straight face. Their eyes met. Pog raised hers expressively skywards. Making a valiant effort to sound sympathetic, she turned to the red-faced Jim.

"Darling, you were magnificent! We couldn't have done it without you."

"No, you bloody couldn't," agreed the man, wiping his brow with a large yellow and green handkerchief.

Apart from Moses making a determined effort to eat Jim's cap on the bumpy journey up the track to Padraig's farm, the ten-minute drive was uneventful, although, even with all the windows open, the stink of goat and fresh goat-droppings were almost more than anyone could stand.

As they jolted past the farm buildings, a couple of young boys who had been playing football in the yard stopped in their tracks and gazed in awe as the strange sight bounced by.

Jim's head touched the roof of the car and after particularly bad bumps, he swore under his breath. His ill temper was ignored by Pog, who was doing her best to stop Moses eating the man's cap. It had fallen off in the battle to get the animal into the car and the goat now seemed hell-bent on getting his own back. He had left several tooth-marks in the tweed. Trying not to breathe too deeply, Anna hung grimly onto Moses' halter.

When the spot was reached that Pog deemed suitable for his liberation, the hobble and halter were untied and the door opened. He didn't waste any time. Like a cork from a bottle, he exploded out of the vehicle, not pausing in his pursuit of freedom. Within seconds, Moses had disappeared behind a clump of gorse and they could hear the sound of his hoofs skittering over the rocks as he scrambled up and away from his persecutors.

* * *

When they arrived back at Sandy Bay House, Pog climbed out of the Yellow Peril, taking care not to stand in Moses' parting gift.

"That was fun, wasn't it, darlings?" she said, licking her finger and rubbing ineffectually at a mark on her smart, cerise-coloured skirt.

"Yes! It was," said Anna, with a broad grin, looking over to where a harassed Jim was trying to brush off some of the mud, weeds and goat-dung clinging to his previously immaculate trousers.

His damaged cap lay on the ground beside him. Moses had managed to bite right through to the lining, Anna noticed with quiet satisfaction.

"Next time you want livestock shifting, Pog, get PJ or Gem to help."

He sounded fed up.

"Yes, darling, of course I will," replied Pog meekly as she stumbled towards the house in her high heels over the churned-up gravel. "What I need is a wash and a stiff gin and then I'll be ready for some lunch."

"At this rate, we'll be lucky to get any," Jim grumbled, staring at the holes in his cap as he walked towards the house.

Anna put a hand up to her mouth to hide her smile. She slowly followed them in and was about to shut the door when a small, furry, white shape shot between her legs and out into the garden.

"Minou! Minou!" she called as the cat disappeared into the bushes.

"First the fucking goat and now that apology for an animal!" she could hear Jim roaring in the kitchen.

Pog appeared in the hallway, looking mildly surprised. Her glance rested first on Anna and then on the figure emerging from the living-room.

"What's all the noise about?" she asked.

Jim was holding the salmon or rather, the remains of a rather chewed-looking salmon. One of its eyes was missing and a large hole had appeared in the middle of its plump side.

"See what that creature is after doing?"

"Oh dear!" said Pog.

"She must have been very hungry," said Anna apologetically to her aunt. "She doesn't usually do things like that."

Jim waved the fish at her.

"I'll give her hungry! If I lay my hands on that thing, it *will* be on the menu."

The girl ignored him. She felt her best option was to maintain a dignified silence. And anyway, why was he roaring like that? It was Aunt Pog's house, not his. If anyone got cross about Minou, it should be her.

"Well, never mind! There's plenty more fish in the sea . . . or in the FitzGeralds' stretch of river, come to that!" said Pog, winking at Anna, as she took the mangled salmon from Jim's shaking hand.

Anna was amazed that Pog seemed to take the whole thing so calmly. She could imagine the drama if it had been her mother or the Bat in the same situation.

* * *

They eventually lunched on smoked salmon and freshly made brown bread at Pog's favourite pub in Ballina. Anna was given her first taste of creamy draught Guinness. O'Hagans was an old-fashioned, crowded pub in the main street. To Anna, it seemed to be crammed with Pog's friends. Her doctor, her solicitor, a circuit-court judge and the master of the hunt – all of them came over to have a word with her aunt. Even Black Sean (so named because of his tangled mass of black hair) who was the head of the local IRA cell, moved to sit beside Pog. He owned several ice-cream vans and was a great admirer of Mrs Roberts. In spite of her having the misfortune of being born British she was, in his eyes, 'a fine woman altogether'. He and she shared a serious love of drink and she had taught him the rudiments of bridge, giving Black Sean an entrée into social circles that would otherwise have been closed to him.

Anna sat quietly on her stool, watching and listening. She thought that everyone seemed to drink a lot without becoming at all drunk. No sooner had they drained a glass, than another one was requested. She noticed that some people didn't wait to finish one glass before they ordered another and had a spare, sitting in front of them. She supposed that was so that no drinking time was wasted. No wonder her father had liked Ireland so much. He'd always said it was a very civilised place where people had their priorities in the right order and knew how to enjoy themselves.

She also noticed that, in one corner of the room, the decibel level had risen to such an extent it became difficult to hear what anyone was saying. People leaned towards one another, eyes fixed on each other's faces, doing their best to lip-read.

She was introduced to Declan O'Hagan himself. He was

large and round with a permanently benign expression and he wore small, round spectacles, perched on the bridge of his shiny, pink nose. The pub had been in his family for generations. He took great pride in the fact that he was the fifth in the line of O'Hagans to offer succour to Ballina's thirsty population. He leant over the bar and shook Anna by the hand.

"You're most welcome, my dear. Let me get you a drink on the house. What will it be?"

Anna hadn't the slightest idea what 'on the house' meant but she decided to order a drink and then see what happened. She looked along the shelves of strangely shaped bottles. Liberal as her aunt appeared to be, Anna didn't think it would be a good idea to order anything alcoholic. In the end, she opted for a fizzy white lemonade with ice and a slice of lemon so that she could pretend she was sipping a gin and tonic.

Concepta, Declan's wife, came to say hello. She was small and thin, with a slightly abstracted look and a gentle manner. Anna thought she looked very tired. She too, made the child feel welcome.

Anna was then introduced to the O'Hagan's overweight Labrador, Horlicks, who seemed to spend most of his life happily hoovering up under the tables and whose waistline imitated his master's. Declan noticed her trying unsuccessfully to stroke the dog, which was intent on reaching a crust of bread that was lodged between the wall and a radiator.

"He has a food fixation. Everything else comes a very poor second! I wouldn't mind him. He won't pay you any attention while there's a morsel of food to be found."

Declan was famous for his unique collection of pipes, home-made snuff and tobacco. It was quite usual to hear an American asking to see the lovingly tended specimens or an Australian, sneezing hard after having sampled one of the aromatic powders. Declan's regulars were proud of his widespread reputation. Anna, having witnessed an explosive sneeze from an overseas visitor who had just taken a good sniff of the best snuff, declined to try it herself with a shy shake of her head and a smile.

As the adults talked, she sat on the tall bar stool, legs dangling and daydreamed of Gina and Alfredo, wondering what they were doing now. She thought of the big, lemon-scented mimosa in the garden in Pisa and suddenly felt an overwhelming yearning for bright colours, sunshine and warmth.

She was shaken out of her reverie by her aunt's voice.

"Darling? Wake up! You were miles away. It's time to go. We're going to visit some friends of mine who own a lovely hotel just outside the town. I think you'll like it – it's full of mad dogs and barmy people – just like me!"

Chapter Thirteen

Anna was woken next morning by the sound of the man's Rover turning out of the driveway. Evidently, Jim was not going to accompany them to church. She was glad, especially when she remembered the conversation she'd overheard between him and her aunt on the previous evening. She had not meant to listen but once she had started, it was impossible to stop.

"Have you really thought all this through, Pog?" he had said. "Having a child about the place is going to complicate things a bit, isn't it?"

"How do you mean, darling?"

"Well, for example, do I stay here tonight or not? What if she suffers from nightmares or whatever nine-year-olds suffer from these days?"

"Don't worry, Jim. She'll be fine. She's a dear child and she's far better off here than with her wretched mother. Of course you can stay the night and if she does suffer from nightmares, I will . . . do something. So, top up my glass, darling, and don't create problems before they happen."

"I was thinking that it might be awkward for you, that's all."

Anna could hear the irritation in his voice. She guessed that the only person for whom it was awkward was Jim. He didn't like her being there. But then, she had known that right from the start.

She turned over in the bed and gazed through the windows at the blue sky. Apart from Jim's presence, yesterday had been fun: letting Moses free on the mountain, going to the pub and then the visit to Mount Charlotte in the afternoon – she had loved that.

Aunt Pog had warned her it would be full of mad dogs and barmy people, which, Anna thought afterwards, had been a bit of an exaggeration. But it *was* certainly different.

As soon as they were through the enormous, wrought-iron gates, she had her first glimpse of the place. Mount Charlotte was turreted and crenellated and looked like a fantasy castle that had been dreamed up by Mervyn Peake or Terry Pratchett. She thought it was marvellous, with its grey stone walls and strangely shaped windows scattered around all over the place and its massive, wooden, arched entrance doors. She found herself staring up at one of the small towers, which had a top like an inverted ice-cream cone. Anna half-expected to see a beautiful woman gazing out forlornly towards the sea. A princess, waiting to be rescued. As they drove along the wide avenue, she thought that, in a way, she too had been rescued – not from any castle – but from the house in Cambridge. And not that

Aunt Pog was exactly a knight on a white horse. She almost giggled out loud at the thought of her aunt, squeezed into a suit of armour aboard a galloping horse. Where would she keep her cigarettes she wondered.

Anna thought the grounds were perfect too, with great clusters of rhododendrons and azaleas dotted around the roughly cut lawns in front of the house and, towering over them, giant cedars, copper beech and weeping ash.

The Misses Jameson were well-bred, charming and rather eccentric, in a way that was particularly Irish. They were elderly now and had been driven to try their hand at running their family home as a hotel because their only brother had gambled away the family fortunes before expiring in a brothel in Bombay.

They ran the establishment in a hit-and-miss fashion that suited a certain sort of visitor perfectly. Lovely old Irish silver, which had belonged to their mother, graced the long refectory table at which everyone dined. The table linen was of heavy, snow-white damask, with silver napkin-rings for each guest, who wrote down what they had drunk in a book in the small pantry, leading off the dining-room. The amount was never questioned and was later added to the bill. The simple food was well prepared, the produce coming from the local rivers and farms. Mount Charlotte had its own stretch of river, and grouse and pheasant were also in plentiful supply. Venison was available from a nearby deer farm.

So, as Aunt Pog said, 'What did a little dirt in the corners and the odd dog-hair in the soup really matter?'

For those with their priorities properly sorted, the place was perfect and they came back again and again.

Half a dozen liver-and-white springer spaniels had the run of the place and the guests were aware, from time to time, of a distinctly doggy odour lingering in the air.

They were ushered into the large wooden-panelled front hall with its black-and-white tiled floor and oak fireplace, in which burned enormous logs. Anna looked admiringly at the double staircase, sweeping gracefully up to the floor above. Dark oil paintings of severe-looking men in military dress lined both sets of stairs and a fine old candelabrum hung on a dusty chain over the centre of the hall. She could imagine herself in a long evening dress, slowly descending the steps, her diamonds sparkling in the candlelight. At the foot of the stairs, her father would be standing, waiting for her.

"We will have tea in the blue sitting-room. The wind is blowing from the east today and so it's warmer in there," said Babs Jameson, leading the way.

Although seventy-eight, she carried herself as straight as a poker and her clear blue eyes had no need of glasses.

Anna wondered why the direction of the wind made a difference in choosing which room you used for tea. Perhaps there were holes in some of the walls. That was all right though; it fitted in perfectly with her idea of ancient castles.

The walls in the blue sitting-room were lined with what appeared to be silk. Anna thought it was like the colour of cornflowers. Another fire crackled and hissed in here too and the girl wondered if the old lady hauled the logs into the grates herself.

As the adults settled themselves, she looked about her

with interest. There were large, glass-fronted bookcases, filled with leather-bound volumes, standing against the cornflower-blue walls. Three comfortable-looking couches surrounded the fireplace and various armchairs and side tables were scattered around the room. Copies of *The Field* and *Country Life* lay on one of the tables under a window. A couple of dogs dozed contentedly in a basket near the brass fender, noses and paws twitching as they dreamed. The daylight was already fading and table-lamps had been switched on, making a golden circle of light around each.

Cecily Jameson, a slightly younger version of her sister, marched into the room with a heavily laden tea tray, followed by a pretty, dark-haired girl bearing another. The girl smiled at Pog.

"Good afternoon, Mrs Roberts. Mr O'Shea."

Anna noticed that the smile she gave was aimed at her aunt and did not include Jim.

Two French fishermen were deep in conversation at one of the tables, occasionally pausing to bite into the floury scones and buttered crumpets piled high on a silver Georgian muffin dish beside them. An expectant dog sat at the foot of one of the men, watching, transfixed, as the food was transferred from plate to mouth.

"Come here, Sasha, and SIT," said Babs Jameson with authority.

With one mournful, backward glance, the dog obeyed, transferring its attentions to Anna who stroked the curly ears and glossy head.

"*Pardon, Monsieur, elle est très méchante,*" apologised Babs, in an atrocious French accent.

The man bowed his head slightly and gave a polite smile. He thought how strange it was that so few of the Irish and English of his acquaintance ever bothered to try and speak his beautiful language well – that was if they made the effort to speak it at all. Usually, when their attempts at conversation had proved incomprehensible, they just repeated themselves more loudly in English while gesticulating foolishly.

The talk was of local goings-on. Anna started to get bored but tried her best not to show it. She fed the odd crumb to the grateful Sasha when she thought no one was looking. Once, she found her eyelids closing and only stopped herself from toppling off the couch with difficulty. She longed to explore the castle but couldn't quite summon up the courage to ask permission. Her aunt seemed to have forgotten all about her.

Eventually, they had left and she'd slept all through the journey back to Ballynacarrig.

* * *

Anna was in the middle of her breakfast when a crumpled Pog appeared in a black, lacy negligée. Her eye make-up was smudged and her hair, tangled. With her hooked nose and general air of dishevelment, Anna thought she looked rather like an untidy, elderly parrot with its feathers in disarray, emerging into the daylight and finding it a little too bright for its liking.

"Hello, darling," Pog croaked, "I'm badly in need of some coffee."

She sounded a little out of breath. Anna wondered if

her aunt had been doing her morning exercises. Aunt Pog had told her that she touched, or tried to touch, her toes twenty times each morning. She watched as her aunt made herself coffee and then absent-mindedly spooned sugar into her cup. Anna knew that she didn't like sugar. The woman sat down on a stool beside her, with the ever-present cigarette in her hand. She peered at Anna over the top of her coffee cup.

"I can't remember, darling. Are you a Catholic?"

"No, I don't think so." Anna was surprised. She'd never given the subject much thought. "I sometimes went to a little church near us in Grange Road. I think it was Church of England."

She omitted to say that she had gone there with her father. It still hurt too much to say his name.

"Good gracious! Well, it really doesn't matter two hoots what you are. The Almighty loves you just the same. Blast! There's sugar in my coffee."

Her aunt stared down at her cup in surprise.

"Are you Catholic, Aunt Pog?"

"Yes, darling. Not a very good one but yes, I am." Pog puffed thoughtfully on her cigarette. "Mind you, I didn't choose to be one. My dear Mama had me baptised as a Catholic when I wasn't in a fit state to have any say in the matter – being only six weeks old." She stared unseeingly out of the window in front of them before continuing in a vague sort of voice. "I think she was in love with the priest at the time. Mind you, it didn't last long. She seemed to have a thing about men of the cloth. She took a fancy to an Anglican clergyman later on. Because of that, my younger sister – that's your father's mother – was probably baptised Church of England and *that's* why you aren't Catholic."

Pog looked satisfied with herself for sorting it all out in her own mind. Anna just looked confused.

"Do you believe in Heaven?" she asked, changing tack.

"I like to."

"And if there's Heaven, do you think that only really good people go there?"

"What do you mean, darling?" said Pog, cautiously.

"The Bat said that Daddy was a bad man and that he did bad things . . . she said he would never go to Heaven."

"If there is a Heaven, then your daddy is definitely up there. He made a few silly mistakes, that's all."

I could throttle that bloody woman. How dare she? Pog thought, furiously. Wasn't it enough of a tragedy that the child's father was dead without consigning him to eternal damnation?

Anna was silent for while.

Then she asked, "Is it very different being one?"

"Being a Catholic, you mean? Oh, there are a few minor details that are different, I suppose, but nothing very important really. Most religions are basically the same. Do your best and try not to upset other people. Don't steal things and never pinch another woman's husband – and don't commit murder, of course. That's an important one. You'll be fairly safe if you stick to those rules."

"I think it's difficult . . . not to upset other people, I mean," said the child, prodding a limp cornflake with the tip of her spoon.

Pog, with an uncharacteristic flash of sensitivity, guessed that she was referring obliquely to the absent Rosalind.

"My darling, it's only human to make mistakes. We all do it, all the time. The secret is not to worry about it and to do your best not to go on making the same mistakes. Most of us spend far too much energy regretting the past or being anxious about the future. I've found that just enjoying the present is a far better way to set about tackling life."

Pog sat, cigarette suspended in mid-air. She thought, fleetingly, of her absent husband. What was the bugger up to these days? As far as she was concerned, he'd have his work cut out for him if he ever wanted to saunter through the pearly gates.

Her great-niece sat thoughtfully beside her. No one had ever explained things to Anna before in such a sunny, straightforward way. She felt strangely comforted by her aunt's refreshingly simple Credo.

* * *

However, Anna did not enjoy Mass at Ballynacarrig church. She felt that people were watching her and she was uncomfortably aware of two girls, in the pew in front of theirs, who kept looking over their shoulders at her, whispering and giggling. The church was cold and the worn, wooden seats uncomfortable. But the priest led the service in a gentle, measured voice, which made Anna feel that he meant every word he said, although some of the men standing at the back of the church seemed restless, as though impatient to be done with the praying. She noticed that they hurriedly left as soon as the blessing had been given.

On the way out, Pog introduced her to Father Mulvey. He was a kindly looking, elderly man, nearing retirement. His face was heavily lined and Anna could see it was covered in tiny red veins that she thought looked like the tributaries of rivers. She also noticed that he had what she and her father had always referred to as smiling lines at the corners of his eyes and mouth. He shook her hand warmly.

"Well now, Anna. It's welcome to the village you are. I hear you will be starting at the school next week. You'll like it there. Mr and Mrs Dempsey are grand people and I'm sure you'll settle in with no problem at all."

Anna wasn't convinced it would be as simple as that, remembering her first, miserable weeks at her Cambridge school but she managed to summon up a confident-looking smile.

Father Mulvey turned to Pog, who was trying her best to avoid the spikes of her high heels from becoming impaled in the decorative grating in the floor of the church porch.

"And how are you finding having a young one about the place, Mrs Roberts?"

"No problem at all, darling. She's fitting in beautifully," replied Pog, nearly overbalancing.

She made a grab for Anna's shoulder.

Father Mulvey winced slightly. Although he had known the woman for over eight years, he still found the 'darlings' a little hard to take. He had realised a long time ago that she was a very individual sort of person, with a good heart, even if her goings-on with that chancer Jim O'Shea shocked his celibate soul. He had tried to warn the woman but she insisted that for all Jim's faults, he was quite all right really. He wondered how someone who was usually such a good judge of character could be so taken in. She must be very fond of him. The priest sighed. He wished she would call him 'Father' like the rest of his parishioners.

"Will you call down to the house for a drink before lunch?" Pog asked, oblivious to the dozen or so members of the congregation stacking up in the aisle behind them. They too wanted a word with Father Mulvey before getting back to their own Sunday lunches.

The priest gently declined, remembering how irate his housekeeper had been last time he had accepted an invitation for a Sunday morning drink at Sandy Bay House. He had lingered over a particularly delicious malt whiskey for too long and it had taken several days of eating humble pie before Mrs Doyle had forgiven him. He also wanted to avoid a possible discussion over a book Pog had been given and which she insisted he read. It apparently told a tale of intrigue and steamy passion involving a high-ranking Cardinal and a curvaceous brunette.

"Things like that happen all the time, darling," she had said, with great authority.

Father Mulvey very much doubted it. Anyway, the book had miraculously disappeared. Perhaps a scandalised Mrs Doyle had done away with it to protect his immortal soul.

Pog climbed into the Yellow Peril, Anna at her side.

This was the one time in the week when she still drove. Reverse gear was engaged with difficulty.

"Tell me if I'm going to hit anything or anyone, darling."

Anna was in the middle of turning around when there was a thump and a crunching sound from behind them. They stopped abruptly and Pog slid open the window and peered out.

A man's cheerful voice called out, "'Tis all right, Mrs Roberts. 'Tis only a bit of fencing next to the bit you hit last time. One more go at it and you'll have it demolished entirely!"

"That's all right then!" said Pog, cheerfully.

Halfway home, the car suddenly swerved and they nearly hit a tree.

"Bugger! Just steer for a moment, will you, darling?"

Without waiting for Anna's reply, Pog let go of the steering wheel, slewed sideways in her seat and started to rummage around on the floor of the car. Anna hung onto the wheel for all she was worth, doing her best to keep the car on the road. After a few seconds, her aunt re-surfaced.

"Bloody shoe! The heel got jammed under the pedal. It's always happening." She surveyed the road ahead. "You're doing very well. You can go on steering if you like, while I press the pedals."

"Er, no thank you."

The child felt it might be safer not to take up the offer. It was nice to be asked though! What *would* her mother and the Bat think if they could see Anna now?

* * *

161

It was very late. Her aunt had been entertaining and Anna could hear the shouted goodbyes and laughter and the sound of cars being driven away over the gravel. She had read for a long time. When her eyelids started to droop and she couldn't stop yawning, she'd switched off the light.

Before falling asleep, Anna lay back on the pillows, thinking, as she so often did, of the talking animals in the book she had just put down. She found that if she concentrated on them, thoughts of her father and Gina did not slip into her mind quite so easily. What she liked to do best was to imagine herself coming face to face with a unicorn. She had found a picture of one once and thought it was the most beautiful animal she had ever seen, with its snowy flanks and long, rippling mane and tail, dark soulful eyes and the sharply pointed horn emerging from the centre of its forehead. It had been standing in front of a young girl, with its neck gracefully curved in submission, so that its soft muzzle rested on her outstretched hand. Anna would have given anything to be that girl. Her father had known how she felt, no one else. Other people thought that unicorns were only to be found in dreams or fairy tales.

She was woken by a car door being slammed shut. She heard a voice, not her aunt's, call from the house. She didn't hear the words but they somehow conveyed a feeling of urgency.

Scrambling to the window, Anna peered down. A man, with what looked like a doctor's bag, was hurrying towards the front door. Anna pulled on a jersey over her nightdress and stumbled onto the landing, still not properly awake.

She made her way silently down the stairs. There was no one in the living-room and the fire had burned low. The door into the hall was wide open and she could hear voices as she crept across the thick carpet. She moved silently into the hall and towards her aunt's room. She felt frightened.

She could hear a man's voice saying, "Now then, Pog. Just breathe slowly. Gently does it. Try and relax."

The bedroom door was half-open and Anna could see into the far side of the room where an ashen-faced Pog was half lying on her big, double bed, propped up on a pile of pillows. Her eyes were wide open and she was gasping for air. She looked very ill. The child could see rosary beads intertwined around her aunt's fingers. The knuckles of her hands were white.

"Oh, God! . . . I can't breathe."

"You'll be fine, woman. Calm down. The injection will start to take effect any time now. Just take it easy. Go on – slow, deep breaths." The doctor's voice was patient as he bent over her, feeling her pulse. "Pog, I've warned you before. You must cut down on the booze and the fags – they're killing you."

"I know. I will . . . I promise," Pog gasped, holding tightly onto his hand. Anna thought she sounded as frightened as she herself felt.

"You're a desperate woman altogether. You say that now but as soon as you're back on your feet, you'll forget all about it and carry on as before, until the next time. I'm getting too old to be dragged out of my bed at two in the morning because Pog Roberts hasn't the sense she was born with!"

Pog's breathing was becoming a little easier. She gave him a weak smile.

"I know, darling. I really will try to be good."

A worried guest, who had stayed late and been present when Pog started to feel unwell, lingered uncomfortably at the foot of the bed. She suddenly caught sight of Anna's alarmed face at the door and hurried over to her.

"You should be in bed, little one," she said, turning the girl gently but firmly away from the scene in the bedroom.

Anna looked up, white-faced, as the flustered woman guided her into the living-room. "Will Aunt Pog die?"

"Of course not! Whatever put that into your head? She needs a good night's sleep – that's all. Upstairs with you now and don't you be worrying about your aunt. Kathleen will be here in the morning."

Anna went back to bed but not to sleep. She waited until she heard the woman leave and then later, the doctor. She retraced her steps, back to her aunt's room. The table-lamp in the hall had been left on and the bedroom door was ajar. She listened. It seemed as though there were no sounds coming from the room.

Perhaps Aunt Pog was dead and the woman had just been pretending that everything was all right, she thought. She forced herself to push open the door a little further. Her eyes adjusted to the darkness and, in the soft light coming from the hall, she could just make out the still figure of her aunt, now in her nightdress and lying under the bed covers.

Anna held her breath as she crept over to the bedside. Summoning up all her courage, she timidly stretched out and touched the back of the heavily veined hand that lay on the counterpane. It felt warm. Then, she realised that her aunt was breathing quietly and evenly. Her relief made her feel weak.

* * *

Anna sat, chin resting on her knees, cushions piled around her on the couch for warmth. The living-room door was wide open – that way she would be close by if her aunt woke and needed her. In spite of her efforts to keep her eyes open, gradually her head sank onto her knees and, fast asleep, she slipped sideways onto a cushion.

Chapter Fourteen

Kathleen found her on the couch next morning, half hidden by cushions. Anna was barely awake and shivering with cold.

"Holy Mother of God! What in Heaven's name are you doing there, Anna?"

She sat down and put an arm around the child's shoulders and listened gravely to the account of the previous night's drama. When she had finished, Anna looked at Kathleen anxiously, her voice becoming distressed.

"I didn't mean to go to sleep. I meant to stay awake here, in case Aunt Pog didn't feel well again." Her eyes widened and she sounded close to tears. "What if she's dead and I didn't know?"

Kathleen gave the tense little body beside her a squeeze.

"Sure she's not dead! Doesn't this sort of a carry-on happen every now and then and when it's all over, your aunt sleeps like a baby and in the morning she's raring to go – there's no stopping her – and the rest of us are in bits! Don't you be upsetting yourself, Anna. She'll be just fine." She smiled down at the girl, "Now, why don't you go and put on some nice, warm clothes and I'll go and see if her Ladyship is ready for her cup of coffee and when you come down, you can see for yourself that she's all in one piece! Right?"

"Right!" said Anna, the tension draining out of her body.

* * *

Kathleen was right.

When Anna knocked on her aunt's bedroom door, she was greeted with a cheerful, "Come in, darling."

There was Aunt Pog, sitting up in bed with a *House and Garden* on her lap and a cup of coffee in her hand. The rosary beads were nowhere to be seen and Anna thought she looked the same as always. Perhaps just a tiny bit more crumpled than she usually was when she first woke.

"Are you really all right, Aunt Pog?" she asked, as she approached the untidy bed.

"Couldn't be better, darling. But what about you? Kathleen tells me that you stayed up all night to keep an eye on me. That was really sweet. I'm a very lucky woman to have such a caring great-niece." Pog looked fondly at Anna's tired face. "It's a good thing that school doesn't start until Wednesday because you look a little the worse for wear! How about a hearty Irish breakfast to put you back on your feet?"

Anna had noticed the delicious smell of frying bacon as she passed the kitchen door and her stomach was feeling decidedly empty.

"Go on, darling! Kathleen is preparing a real feast for you. She thinks you need feeding up. So, go and make her happy and do her cooking justice!"

The girl needed no further encouragement. She sped off in the direction of the kitchen, where she proceeded to eat everything that Kathleen put in front of her. The relief of seeing her aunt looking so normal after the fright of the previous night gave added enjoyment to the meal.

* * *

PJ arrived just as Anna swallowed the last, glorious mouthful. He stared at her clean plate and then looked hopefully at the empty frying-pan sitting on the cooker. Kathleen pushed a mug of tea over to him.

"Would you look at the face on him, Anna?" She laughed. "Anyone would think he hadn't taken a bite of food for weeks. You should have seen what he managed to put away before he left the house this morning."

"That was hours ago. I helped Da with the milking and then I took Juno for a good gallop. All that fresh air gives you an appetite. Could I not have a miserable piece of toast, Kath? My stomach thinks my throat's cut."

"There's no need to look as though you'll faint with the starvation. Ah, go on, have some toast, but don't be long. I've a load of things to be doing and Mrs R had one of her turns last night." Unnoticed by Anna, Kathleen gave her brother a meaningful look. "Oh, and Anna, Amy will be down any minute and she said she would show you around. I asked her to bring some good, strong boots and an anorak for you. She's got feet on her like an elephant and she grows out of shoes and clothes before they've stopped looking like new. She has our mother destroyed trying to keep up with her!"

There was a loud banging at the back door.

"Speak of the devil. That'll be her now."

Anna ran to let Amy in. A pair of Wellington boots was thrust at her through the open door.

"If you wear these, it means we can go down to the other side of the lake, through the brambles and stuff. I've got something to show you," Amy whispered. Then she added in a louder voice: "Are you ready to come out?" The boots and anorak were a perfect fit. "They look grand. Are you coming?" she said, impatiently making for the door.

Just then, Kathleen called from the kitchen. "Amy, come here a moment!"

"We're just go –"

"Amy!"

Amy looked at Anna with a grin, raising her eyes to Heaven, before walking slowly into the kitchen.

"Yes?"

Kathleen looked at her sternly.

"Remember what Ma said about not going near Eddie's place?"

"I know." Amy looked bored. "She's always going on about him. I don't know why she makes such fuss – he's just a bit cracked, that's all."

"That fellow's as crooked as a dog's back leg *and* he's

dangerous when he has drink on him. You are not to go anywhere near the cottage."

"All right! Don't go on. You're getting as bad as Ma. Anyway –" Amy said, innocently, "we've got better things to do than hang around mad Eddie's."

She winked at Anna as they let themselves out of the back door.

"We can get to Eddie's round the back way," Amy announced, as soon as they were out of view from the house.

"But I thought Kathleen said we weren't to go there," Anna said, surprised by her new friend's boldness in the face of adult instruction.

"Ah, don't mind her!" replied Amy, blithely. "Her and Ma are always giving out about something. If you took any notice, you wouldn't have any fun, would you?"

She set off with a purposeful swagger, her hands thrust into her pockets.

Imagining what the Bat's reaction to that inflammatory statement would have been, Anna followed her through the coarse rushes that grew beside the lake.

They had to climb over and around the large stones that littered the shore. Although the air was cold, the bright sunlight seemed to bounce off the water, making Anna screw up her eyes when she looked at it. She noticed that, today, the mountains were misty blue and although it was only January some of the gorse was in flower, its brilliant yellow flowers standing out against the surrounding browns and greys of winter like clusters of small butterflies. She caught the occasional waft of a honey-like scent from them on the breeze.

"What's wrong with Eddie?" Anna was curious to know why Kathleen had been so anxious.

"He does bad things."

"Bad things?"

"All the time," confirmed Amy, nodding her head vigorously so that her curly hair bounced up and down in the sunlight.

"What sort of things?" Anna asked, intrigued.

"Well, he sets snares and Da says that's not allowed – and it's cruel."

"What's a snare?"

"A sort of trap and it hurts anything that gets caught in it something terrible."

Anna was appalled.

"What does get caught in it?"

"Rabbits and hares and sometimes birds. He has big traps too. He hides them in the grass and the teeth on them are so strong they can break a badger's leg. Mrs Ryan's old dog got caught in one of Eddie's traps and he was hurt so bad they had to shoot him."

Anna gave a small shiver. It was as if a dark cloud had suddenly passed over them. The idea of anyone wanting to harm animals made her feel sick. She thought of the unicorn in the picture.

"But that's horrible!"

"I know. I drop stones on them to make them go off if I find any."

Anna looked at her with growing respect.

"What would happen if he caught you doing that? What would he do?"

"Probably kill me," said Amy pragmatically. "But I can run faster than him. He's old – and anyway, he's pissed out of his mind most of the time – so it's not that hard to get away."

"Oh!"

Anna wondered if she really wanted to continue walking in the direction of where this monster lived. She was just about to suggest putting off going there until another day when Amy suddenly turned away from the lakeside and started to push her way through the stunted willow saplings.

"We'd better not talk, except in whispers. He might be around. His boat is over there." She pointed to a flat-bottomed boat, moored to a rusty iron pole in the rushes. "He shoots ducks when he goes out in that. Just before Christmas, I used one of me Ma's kitchen knives and got the bung out of the bottom and threw it away and the boat filled with water. He went *mad* when he found it. Danced a jig, he was so angry. He jumped up and down and said 'Feck' loads of times. I was in the bushes over there. It was great!" Her face lit up at the memory.

Anna could see that the memory was still gloriously fresh in the other's mind. She felt more and more nervous as they approached the forbidden spot. She didn't think that she was in the same league as Amy when it came to being brave and that if they did bump into this dreadful man, she would probably freeze to the spot in terror.

All of a sudden, Amy dropped to a crouching position and looked back over her shoulder at Anna, "I forgot. He carries his gun around with him all the time. Oh, and Eddie has a girlfriend too . . . and he beats her." Anna's face registered disbelief. "He does so!" the other insisted. "I've heard her scream."

The last part of their journey was completed bent double, as they zigzagged from bush to bush until, panting, they reached the end wall of a tumbledown cottage that had once been whitewashed. A thin spiral of turf smoke rose from the chimney. Amy beckoned and then vanished around the side of the cottage. Unwilling to appear afraid, Anna dutifully crept after her. It seemed all the birds had stopped singing and that the day was no longer as bright as it had been.

The tiny windows were dirty and dark. Amy slowly straightened and, standing on tiptoe, peered in. Anna waited, barely able to breathe.

"Perhaps he's not there," she said hopefully in a hoarse whisper, ready to make a run for the safety of the lake.

Amy moved silently to the door where, to Anna's horror, she banged loudly with her fist. There was the sound of falling furniture from inside and the door was flung open with such force that it crashed back onto the wall in front of them. In her fright, Anna did not take in any details of the man in the doorway except that he looked large, dark and threatening.

"Run!" Amy shouted, as she took off at high speed into the trees.

Anna didn't need any encouragement. She ran, hurling herself through the birches, hazels and brambles she had not noticed on the outward journey and which now seemed to loop themselves around her boots, trying to trip her. Small branches lashed her face. She could hear angry roars from behind them.

"You little hoors! I'll teach you'se not to come spying on me, see if I don't."

They ran until they could run no more and the sounds of pursuit had stopped. Amy threw herself, face down, onto a patch of dead bracken fronds that crackled underneath her. Her shoulders shook as she laughed. She continued to laugh until tears streamed down her cheeks. Eventually, she rolled onto her back, looking up at Anna.

"Did you see the look on Eddie's face?" she gasped, as she wiped her eyes with the back of a grubby hand.

"No, I didn't have time."

"He was a sort of purple colour." Amy sounded pleased with life. "Sort of purple-red – *and* his trousers nearly fell down. Wasn't it grand?"

Anna observed her with amazement, her heart still pounding in her ears. There and then, she made up her mind that she would never do anything like that again, even if Amy found it all so enjoyable. She liked the other girl a lot but she couldn't help wondering if she wasn't just a little mad.

Chapter Fifteen

Anna liked Mrs Dempsey at first sight. She was plump and motherly, although obviously not prepared to have any nonsense from some of the wilder boys in the school. Mrs Dempsey mostly took the younger children while her thinner, equally cheerful husband taught the older ones.

Pog's arrival with Anna on the first morning caused plenty of interest among the pupils milling around in the small playground before lessons started for the day. Mrs Roberts was famous in Ballynacarrig – not just for her legendary driving exploits but because she was colourful, friendly and, above all, interestingly different from their own parents. No one could imagine Pog Roberts in a tatty anorak and muddy boots, driving a tractor or bringing the cows in for milking. Someone had once remarked that the Englishwoman must have been born wearing three-inch heels. The thought of her in any other form of footwear was enough to bring on a prolonged attack of hilarity. She didn't let them down this morning either. Wearing what Anna thought of as a kind of orange turban on her head, with her mink coat clutched around her, she swept into the school yard on elegant black patent-leather shoes. They watched in awe as she greeted a couple of girls standing nearby.

"Hello, darlings!" she croaked, oblivious to their fascinated giggles.

Anna had noticed that her aunt's voice didn't work too well first thing in the morning. Later on in the day, after a few drinks, it took on a better-oiled quality.

No sooner had they gone through the school gate than Mrs Dempsey took control.

"Good morning, Mrs Roberts. Good morning, Anna." She gave them both a broad smile. Turning to a panting Amy, who had followed them into the playground at high speed, not wanting to miss their arrival, she instructed her to take care of Anna on her first day. "Make sure you introduce her to the others and show her where everything is." She gave Amy a stern look. "And you'd better explain that punctuality is considered important – although *some* people I know forget to come straight to school because they find other things more interesting to do on the way."

"Sorry," said Amy, not looking the least bit contrite. She grinned at Anna. "Come on! I'll show you around."

At the end of the day, Anna couldn't remember who was Geraldine and who was Bernadette. But on the whole, unlike the Cambridge school, it hadn't been an unpleasant experience. Most of the girls had been eager to make friends. Everyone seemed to like Amy. If Amy liked Anna, then the rest of them were prepared to accept her.

The first time Anna answered a question in front of the class, she was aware that some of the boys were sniggering at the way she spoke.

"Oh, I sa-a-ay!" giggled a dark-haired boy at the back of the class. "Let's all have a fanta-a-astic game of jolly old soccer after school, shall we?"

There were a few muffled explosions of hastily stifled laughter from around him. Mr Dempsey frowned in their direction.

"Would anyone like extra homework today?" There was immediate silence. "I thought not!" said the master, turning back to the blackboard. "Let's concentrate on ending the day a little wiser than when we started it, shall we?"

During break Bernadette Comerford and Moira Lenihan accompanied Anna and Amy out into the playground.

"Don't take any notice of Dessie Hogan. He's a nutter," said Moira with a cheerful grin.

"He'll be a damaged nutter if he goes on saying stupid things like that," scowled Amy, surveying the playground for signs of the offender.

"Ah, leave him alone, Amy. You know what his dad's like."

"Is his dad mad too?" enquired Anna, interested.

"Yeah! He hates the Brits and . . . Ow!"

"Shut up, Moira," Amy interrupted, giving her a sharp dig in the ribs. "Come on. Let's show Anna the horses in the back field."

* * *

"So, do you think you'll like it there, darling?" Pog asked as they settled themselves with trays on their laps in front of a roaring fire.

On her arrival back at the house, she and Kathleen had listened carefully to Anna's description of her first day at the school in the village. From what they could make out, things had gone well. They weren't to know that Anna had omitted to say anything about the boys' teasing. She had concentrated instead on a description of how welcoming Amy's friends and the two teachers had been and the fact that the Irish lesson had left her feeling rather lost.

Picking up her knife and fork, Anna smiled at her aunt. "I think it will be all right, thank you, Aunt Pog."

Unnoticed by Anna, Pog watched her as she ate. She hoped that Kathleen's cooking would result in the child putting on a bit of weight. Her arms and legs were so terribly thin. Still, she told herself as she swallowed a mouthful of stew, it's early days. Give her time.

"Shall we watch something really silly on the telly?" she asked Anna as she fumbled under the cushions with one hand for the remote control. "There's a daft quiz thing on at seven that's sometimes quite funny."

"Yes, please," said Anna politely.

She tried not to look too surprised. Her mother would have had a fit at the thought of sitting around the television with food on your lap. Anna wasn't all that sure she was interested in watching a quiz – they were usually rather boring and she'd much rather read – but the thought of doing two things that would be so disapproved of at home made the prospect rather appealing.

As they watched the programme, Pog's chuckles made Anna smile in turn. It was hard not to. She thought the sound was halfway between an old train letting off steam and rain-water gurgling down a drainpipe.

As soon as her aunt had finished her plate of stew with its baked potato and broccoli from the garden, she put her tray down on the couch beside her and groped for her packet of cigarettes, which had fallen onto the floor at her feet. She lit one and inhaled deeply, leaning back into the cushions with a satisfied sigh.

"That's better! No meal complete without a fag!" She looked over at the small figure sitting on the couch opposite. "I mean for me that is, darling. I advise you never to start smoking. It isn't a good idea. Too bloody expensive for a start. Try and only take pleasure in things that won't end up doing you in."

"You mean, smoking might . . ." Anna hesitated, "might mean that you die?"

Pog gave herself a mental kick on the shins. What was she thinking of? Talking about dying and with David only just in his grave. She'd have to try and be a little more careful what she said.

"Oh, I just meant that it's not the best activity to take up." She had been going to add, 'drinking gin is much better for you', but decided against it. "Gardening or . . . dancing Viennese waltzes would be more healthy."

Anna gave her a funny look.

"Do you dance, Aunt Pog?"

"Quite often," Pog said with a serious expression. "Usually only when I'm gardening, though."

She pulled a face. Anna started to laugh. The idea of her aunt waltzing around the broccoli bed, trowel in one hand, cigarette in the other made her laugh even more.

Pog surveyed her with approval.

"It's lovely to hear you laugh, darling. I want to hear lots more laughter out of you. Best medicine in the world, laughter!"

* * *

Later on that night, laughter was forgotten as Anna woke from a nightmare in which her mother had been driving a car backwards and forwards over her father's limp body, cheered on by Mrs Battersby. He was lying in the middle of the street while Anna, restrained by unseen hands, screamed for her to stop. She was woken by her own screams. She wondered if her aunt's bedroom was too far away for her to have heard the noise.

The room was lit by bright moonlight so that she could see everything clearly. An alarmed Minou crouched on the floor by the door, staring at her with saucer-shaped golden eyes.

For a few moments, Anna sat bolt upright in the bed, trying to force herself to breathe normally. She could feel her heart thumping as though it were trying to escape from her chest. After a few moments, she calmed down enough to climb out of bed and pick up the cat. Then she lay, with her arms around Minou, her chin buried in the fur, staring up through the nearest window at the star-scattered sky. The ache she felt for her father had never been so bad.

During the nights to come, Anna had many more

nightmares. They all seemed to centre around the dead David and she woke each time, breathless and miserable.

If Pog had hoped to see a quick improvement in Anna's colour and appetite, she was disappointed. She confided her worries to Kathleen one morning when Anna was at school.

"I thought she'd be on the mend by now. It's been nearly six weeks since she arrived and, if anything, she looks paler than at the beginning. What am I doing wrong, Kathleen?"

"Well, Mrs R, I was going to tell you what happened last Sunday, only I didn't want to worry you."

Pog lowered her cigarette.

"What? What happened last Sunday?"

Kathleen replaced the iron onto the ironing- board, her face pensive.

"I went down to the lake after lunch for a breath of fresh air and I found Anna." She glanced over to Pog. "She wasn't crying or anything like that, although she looked dead miserable. What got me worried was that when I found her, she was talking."

"Who was with her?" asked Pog.

"Well, that's just it. There was no one with her. She was talking to nobody."

"Perhaps she was just talking to herself," Pog suggested.

"It didn't look like that. So I asked her who she was talking to. At first she didn't want to tell me but then, after a while, she said she was talking to her father." She looked at Pog anxiously. "God, Mrs R, I didn't know what to say to the child."

They looked at each other for a few moments without speaking.

"And I suppose she didn't want you to give her a hug?"

"No, it's like she's not used to being hugged. Curls up like a little hedgehog if she thinks you're going to do that."

"I can't understand why. David must have shown her affection. When I went over last time, I *saw* him cuddling her." Pog frowned worriedly out of the window. Snow was falling, blown by the wind in different directions, making the distant mountains invisible. "Did you manage to cheer her up at all?" she asked, turning back to face Kathleen.

"She was worried that I would think her stupid for pretending he was there with her but I said that if it made her feel close to her father, then it was a good thing. She said that he had always been the only person she could really say what she felt to." She stared across the room at Pog. "That child has a long way to go before she's better. She's suffering badly. I've a feeling it's very patient we'll have to be before we see any change in her."

"So, it's a case of carrying on trying to get her to eat better – and showing her that we care about her and . . . that's all we can do," said Pog.

"I think that's all we can do for the moment," replied Kathleen quietly. Then she suddenly looked more cheerful. "And Amy's good for her. Anna won't fade away from lack of activity when she's around my little sister."

Pog laughed.

"What's needed is a transfusion of some of Amy's rebel high spirits into Anna."

"Yes," Kathleen agreed, smiling. "And some of Anna's gentleness going in the other direction to Amy. That would suit us all just fine! It would be great not to be worrying all the time what the little witch is up to."

* * *

Slowly, as the days and weeks rolled by, Anna started to find that she was beginning to think of Ballynacarrig as home. Correspondence between Cambridge and Mayo was conducted by Rosalind and Pog on a sporadic basis. Pog never suggested Anna write to her mother even when, after six months, she received a letter telling her that Rosalind and Adam Strong had married.

"Why should I tell her to write to the wretched woman?" she blazed one day to Kathleen. "When she can't find the time to send any letters to Anna. It's better the child forgets as much as possible about how miserable she was when she was there."

"But she's Anna's mother," said Kathleen cautiously. "Shouldn't she write a short letter? You never know, the woman might be different now she's married again and happy."

"If she's married again and *if* she has it in her to be happy, then let her write to Anna," replied Pog firmly, jamming her fifteenth cigarette of the day between her lips and feeling in her jacket pocket for her lighter.

Not just Kathleen and Amy but the whole Nolan family had taken the English child to heart. More and more, Anna visited the farm. She no longer flinched when the dogs jumped up at her. She was becoming expert at grooming, cleaning out Juno's stable and making up hay bags for the mare.

By the time the summer holidays arrived, Anna was more often to be found doing jobs around the farm than spending time at her aunt's. She still read avidly and she still spent time down at the lake on her own. Being beside the water, with only the sound of the wind and curlews calling in the sky around her, was important for her peace of mind. She would sit for hours, remembering her father. Repeatedly, Anna went over the details of how he'd looked, the things they'd talked about and the experiences they'd shared. She was determined that he wouldn't slip into the past and become a hazy memory.

She thought too of Gina and Alfredo and the house in Pisa and wondered what had happened to beautiful Chiara. It was difficult not to think of the tragedy that had left her without Gianni. When this happened, her mother would appear in her daydream as she had looked on the night of the car crash: distant, elegant, dressed in silk with the long rope of pearls, blithely unaware of the terrible effect she would have on the lives of the people around her.

But now there was Aunt Pog, Kathleen and Amy and all the Nolans to think about and to enjoy. Although Anna couldn't help wishing that her aunt would smoke and drink a little less. There had been two more occasions when the doctor was summoned in the middle of the night. Occasions that made Anna sick with worry but that had no visible after-effect on Pog.

Towards the end of that first summer in Ballynacarrig, Anna arrived down at the Nolan's farm to find everyone out with the exception of Bridie Nolan.

The dark-haired woman looked up and smiled as Anna let herself into the kitchen.

"There you are, chicken! That's great that you've come. I have a wee present for you." She went over to a table near the fire and picked up a bulky object wrapped in tissue paper. She handed it to Anna. "This is for you, Anna."

The bundle turned out to be a patchwork sleeveless jacket made of quilted multi-coloured squares and with a deep green lining. Anna thought that it was the brightest, most exotic garment she had ever been given. Speechless, she looked at Amy's mother, not knowing how to start thanking her. She wasn't used to presents coming out of the blue like this. She wondered what she had done to merit such a wonderful gift.

"Thank you so much. It's beautiful," she eventually stammered.

Bridie Nolan laughed.

"Slip it on you and we'll see if it fits. Your Aunt Pog gave me an old quilt a long time ago. She knows I like cutting things up and remaking them. I came across it a few months back and I thought I'd make this up for you for when the weather turns. I've made it nice and large so it will fit over a thick sweater." She helped Anna in to it and then stood back to look at the result. "Well now! Although I say it myself, it looks just grand on you, so it does."

Anna pushed both her hands down into the deep pockets.

"It's perfect!"

"Well, that's all right then! You can't get much better than perfect!"

185

"Can I go up and look in Amy's mirror?" Anna asked.

"Of course you can. Go and take a look."

When Amy arrived back from a visit to the nearby donkey sanctuary with her father, she announced enviously that she wanted a jacket too.

"Just like Anna's!"

PJ's reaction was more down-to-earth.

"When you've finished the fashion show, would you come and help me with Bosco, Anna? He's got a tick the size of melon that needs taking off and I can't do it on my own."

"It's *not* the size of a melon. You do exaggerate, PJ," observed Amy scornfully. "Anyway, we were just going to have something to eat. Can't it wait until afterwards?"

"It's all right," said Anna, slipping her arms out of the jacket. "I don't mind."

She loved being asked to help. It made her feel useful and able – qualities she never seemed to have possessed when she was in her mother's house.

Chapter Sixteen

Anna's tenth, eleventh and twelfth birthdays came and went, each marked by generous present-giving from Pog and the Nolans, each going apparently unnoticed by her mother. Rosalind, it seemed, didn't believe in sending birthday greetings. The third time this happened resulted in an infuriated Pog writing to suggest that the woman at least owed her daughter a birthday greeting.

Her letter was answered by a curt note from Rosalind. In it she informed Pog that, as she had the distinct impression that Pog preferred her to keep her distance and not interfere, she was doing just that. This made Anna's aunt even angrier.

"Ah, come on, Mrs R!" cajoled Kathleen after she had found her stomping backwards and forwards in the living-room, Rosalind's letter in her hand. "You can't have your cake and eat it, you know! Didn't you tell the woman she only made Anna unhappy the few times she rang and the child spoke to her?"

"Maybe," said Pog vaguely.

"Well then!"

"Well then, nothing! That woman's a total disaster." She suddenly laughed, her good humour returned. "Look at me! All upset because of Rosalind Armitage – Strong – whatever she calls herself these days, and usually nothing upsets me. I must be in need of a drink."

"I'll get one for you, so," said Kathleen dryly.

* * *

All too soon, Anna was faced with the prospect of moving on to the girls' school on the far side of the lake. She couldn't believe that she had been living in Ballynacarrig for over three years. Although there had been times when she'd felt adrift like a refugee, she knew that, as long as she was living in Ireland with her aunt, she would be loved unconditionally. Nervously, she ticked off the remaining days before her departure. She was immensely cheered by the thought that Amy would be also going. At least she'd have one friend right from the start.

Kilgarry Abbey was an imposing mock-Gothic building, surrounded by banks of rhododendrons, overlooking the lake. The nuns had run it as a boarding-school for the last eighty years and it had a very good reputation both on the academic front and for sports. Pog, although professing to be anti-nun, was secretly pleased that Anna would be going there. She thought that getting the chance to mix with a broader selection of children would be stimulating and fun for her niece. She had conveniently forgotten that she herself had been expelled from two similar establishments as a child because she'd found them unbearably strict and Pog Roberts had never understood what it meant to conform.

Although it wasn't in Amy's nature to be nervous about things, she wasn't mad about the prospect of being away from the farm for weeks at a time.

"God!" she moaned to Anna a couple of days before their departure. "It'll be all rules and prayers and uniforms and *lacrosse!* I mean, who in their right mind wants to play that? It's not a proper game at all."

"Perhaps we can start our own soccer team," suggested Anna with a grin. It was common knowledge that Amy could hold her own against most of the lads on a soccer pitch. Although she was small and solid, she could run like the wind and she was also skilled at knowing when to use her elbows and boots to good effect when the referee was looking in the other direction. Quite a few of the Ballynacarrig boys had the scars to prove it.

"We should be so lucky!" commented her friend with a mournful sigh.

"Well, at least they have a lot of interesting things that we wouldn't have a chance to do if we went to most other schools."

"Like needlework and water-colours, I suppose."

"It might be hard to find a girls' school that did metalwork and deep-sea diving," said Anna, laughing. "Come on, Amy. It'll probably be all right. Once we've got used to it."

Although she was sorry to be leaving Pog and the Nolans, Anna couldn't help feeling relieved that she

wouldn't have to put up with Jim O'Shea's presence in her
new surroundings. She had never grown to like the man,
even though she had tried for her aunt's sake. He had not
made any real effort to like her. When he was in a good
mood, his bonhomie was always superficial. Underneath,
she suspected that her presence in the house was just a
nuisance as far as he was concerned.

The fact that her aunt put up with him had always
puzzled her. She had been a little shocked a few months
before to find, on returning to the house earlier than
planned, Pog's bedroom door closed at four in the
afternoon and a lot of laughter and noise issuing from
behind it. Anna had an uncomfortable feeling that the
noises might have something to do with sex. She and Amy
had discussed the topic of reproduction, with especial
emphasis on how the babies got *into* their mothers' wombs,
in great and ignorant detail. When she told her friend what
she'd heard and her suspicions, Amy had rolled around the
bed in her room, shrieking with laughter.

"Yer great eejit! Everyone knows that sex is only for
people when they're in their twenties. *No one* has sex at Ma
Robert's age. Ah, Anna! She's ancient! Jim's old too but
she's at least ten years older than him."

She had gone into another fit of laughing until her
mother put her head around the door and asked what was
going on.

"Just Anna being an eejit, Ma!" Amy replied, trying
unsuccessfully to keep a straight face.

But Anna suspected that, odd though it might seem,
Aunt Pog put up with Jim O'Shea's moods and silences

because he made her laugh in the bedroom – whatever Amy thought to the contrary.

There was another thing that bothered her. She had noticed him carefully examining some of her aunt's silver when he thought he was alone. Was he going to steal some of the smaller pieces and sell them? Aunt Pog probably wouldn't miss them – there was so much stuff lying around. Or perhaps he hoped that, one day, it would be his? Much as she felt uncomfortable in his presence, if Pog wasn't around, she made it her business to sort-of-accidentally join him in the living-room. The idea of her aunt being taken advantage of by that great lump of a man in his loud-checked suits and garish ties made her feel angry.

* * *

The day before they were due to leave for their new school, Pog announced that she was treating them to a trip to the cinema.

"*High Society* is on in Ballina and it's one of my favourite films. I've always been passionately in love with Louis Armstrong! So put on your glad rags. We're leaving in half-an-hour. Jim's going to chauffeur us!"

Amy dashed back to the farm to change. As she only wore jeans and sweaters, this meant taking off her muddy shoes and putting on a pair of slightly less muddy ones. To her, the worst thing about the new school was having to wear a skirt.

"Can't you get a dispensation or something?" she'd begged her mother. "I'll get frostbite on my knees."

"When you're wearing a skirt, you'll be able to see your

knees properly for the first time in your life. You might even wash your knees for a change instead of hiding them away in jeans," replied her mother unsympathetically.

She reappeared back at Aunt Pog's twenty minutes later.

"Sorry it took so long but Kath was dancing round the gaffe with a hairbrush in her hand. She said I couldn't go out with you until she'd had a go at my hair. Janey Mack! You'd think it's a fashion show we're going to, not a film in that kip of a cinema in Ballina."

Anna couldn't see much difference in Amy's hair. Her gingery curls always looked a bit wind-swept and unruly. Her hair, the mass of freckles across the bridge of her nose and her sharp blue eyes all suited her perfectly the way they were as far as Anna was concerned. She couldn't imagine her looking smart and well-groomed.

Jim O'Shea deposited them outside the cinema. As he helped Pog out of the car, Anna thought he was looking particularly odd in cream-coloured trousers and a navy blue blazer that was a size too small for him. He was wearing a panama, which made him look like something out of a painting by Renoir – only in the pictures she's seen in a book from the library, the men in the paintings looked a lot more cheerful. It was his cream suede desert boots that made Anna look twice. Jim had large feet. She decided he looked rather like a baby elephant – but not as nice.

Pog gave him an absent-minded kiss, her thoughts already with her heart-throb, Louis Armstrong. Anna noticed that she'd left a large red smudge of lipstick on the man's cheek.

"See you later, darling! Be good!" Without waiting, Pog immediately whirled around and started to climb the steps up to the doors of the cinema. "Come on, you two! We want to do this properly and get our money's-worth. We need to buy ice creams and chocolate and something to drink for you."

Pog didn't need to buy something to drink for her. Her flask, full of nearly neat gin, was nestling safely in her handbag.

Anna thoroughly enjoyed the film – almost as much as her aunt, who hummed along with the songs in an off-key way that made a few of the people around them giggle. Amy whispered that it sounded a little like a drowsy blue-bottle. When they emerged from the cinema, Amy could hardly hide her disappointment, although she thanked Aunt Pog for the treat.

"It was great, Mrs R, really!" But while Pog made a trip to the loo, Amy admitted to Anna that she'd been bored out of her mind. "All that swooning around and *singing* made me want to puke. Bunch of crazies, carrying on like that! I mean, if you want to say something important, you don't start *singing*, do you?"

Anna laughed.

"I thought it was nice. Didn't you think Grace Kelly was gorgeous, though?"

"Who's he?"

Amy's mind was elsewhere. She had found what looked like the remains of a Swiss army knife lying on the ground beside a litter bin. She swooped down to take a closer look.

"Amy! He's a she!"

193

Amy looked up from her crouching position, knife in hand.

"Oh, the blonde one in all that floaty gear?" She held her discovery out to Anna. "OK, I s'pose. Look, it's not all broken. There's still a corkscrew and a bottle-opener yoke on it."

Just then Anna spotted Jim rounding the corner in his Rover. He pulled up at the curb beside the two girls and wound down the window.

"Where's herself, then?"

"In the loo," said Amy, slipping the knife into her pocket.

Anna knew she was imagining all the useful things she would be able to do with it. Anything from cleaning out horses' hooves to opening illicit bottles of ginger beer. Amy had discovered ginger beer down in the local pub during the summer holidays and had blackmailed the owner's son to sell her some. She decided that it was the best drink around. "Much nicer than that Guinness stuff," she declared to Anna knowledgeably.

When Pog still hadn't appeared after another five minutes, an impatient Jim sent Anna in to find her.

"She's probably just touching up her make-up," she explained.

He scowled at her.

"Just go and tell her I'm tired of hanging around waiting for her, will you?"

The moment Anna pushed open the door to the Ladies' room, she knew her aunt was in trouble. There was the sound of wheezing from the area of the washbasins. Hurrying over, she found Pog doubled up over one of the basins. Her platinum hair seemed to be strangely crooked. For the first time, it struck Anna that she must be wearing a wig. However, it was Pog's mascara-smudged face, the lipsticked mouth distorted as the woman tried to suck in air and the pallor, apparent under the make-up, that frightened the girl. Holding tightly on to her wrist, Pog motioned to the door.

"Get Jim to take me home," she gasped.

Anna tore out into the foyer, through the doors, almost knocking Jim down.

"Aunt Pog's having one of her attacks. She wants you to go in and get her and take her home."

Jim's expression, already irritated by the delay, now became thunderous, his habitually red face changing to light purple.

"I won't be taking her anywhere. 'Tis an ambulance she needs – no fecking around going back to the house."

With that, he charged up the steps and through the doors. Anna and Amy followed him inside. As they ran to the Ladies' room, he was already on the phone, demanding to be put through to the ambulance service.

Pog was too ill to put up a fight when Anna explained what was happening. The woman wore the same, frightened look as when the girl had seen her having an attack just after she'd first arrived in Ballynacarrig. Anna knew that her aunt hated the idea of being taken to hospital. Hospitals frightened her. She wanted to be cared for in her own home with her own GP, who would tell her off and treat her and leave her to sleep in her own bed, knowing that she'd be herself again the next day.

The girls stayed with her until the ambulance crew

arrived, when Pog was lifted into the vehicle on a stretcher, wrapped up in a blanket with an oxygen mask clamped over her face. Anna couldn't help seeing the fear in her aunt's eyes as the men started to close the doors.

"Can I go with her?" she asked one of them.

Before the man could reply, Jim interrupted. "Don't be wasting their time, Anna. The last thing they want is you getting in the way." He turned to the man. "I'll drop these two home and then follow you in."

Anna was outraged. Who did he think he was? Her aunt needed her.

"But, I want to be with Aunt Pog. She can't go to hospital all on her own."

"She won't be *on* her own if you'd only stop yapping and holding me up. The sooner I drop you back, the sooner I can get in to see her." He opened the rear car door. "Get in, both of you."

Amy threw her friend a look that hinted of mutiny but Anna gave a slight shake of her head and obediently climbed into the back of the car. She had never seen Jim O'Shea being quite so unpleasant. The best thing would be to get home as quickly as possible and enlist Kathleen's help.

* * *

No one was very surprised when Pog discharged herself from hospital on the following morning. She arrived in a taxi, unannounced, just before midday. Anna had not been allowed to see her on the previous day and Kathleen was to have driven her in to the hospital that afternoon to visit her aunt.

"Aunt Pog!" Anna cried, racing over the gravel to the taxi.

She had to wait until Pog had finished giving the driver her special recipe for beef in Guinness with leeks. Anna thought that she still looked extremely pale but her aunt's wig was set fair and square on her head and she'd obviously felt well enough to apply a fresh coat of make-up and lipstick.

"Hello, darling," she said, waving off the taxi driver and dropping her handbag at the same time.

Anna bent down and started to pick up the various objects scattered at her aunt's feet. This done, she stood up and gave back the heavy bag.

"We were so worried, Aunt Pog. They wouldn't let me come and see you yesterday and when Kathleen rang they said no visitors until this afternoon."

"I know! Such a fuss about nothing."

"Jim said I would only be in the way and that he would go in to see you."

"I intend to have a few words with that gentleman. There was no reason to stop you coming in with me in the ambulance," Pog said, her expression grim. "But don't worry. They wouldn't let him in either so he kicked up a fuss and was rude to the Sister – which just meant I hadn't a hope in hell of having a visitor this side of Christmas. The whole thing's just bloody ridiculous!" She put an arm around Anna's shoulders. "Let's get inside. I need a stiff drink and a fag before I pass out. Pity they didn't realise that in hospital. All that messing around with damned oxygen!"

* * *

Anna had thought that her aunt's attack might mean

delaying their setting off to Kilgarry Abbey. Pog wasn't having it.

"Not at all, my darling. The nuns will go into overdrive if you're late for your first day there. PJ is dying to drive you and Amy. So not another word! I'm going down to the Nolans for tea and then I shall have an early night so that tomorrow morning I'll be as right as rain."

PJ had just passed his driving test. The entire Nolan family were tired of him pestering them to do runs for them down to the village or Ballina.

"The question is," said Amy as she climbed into the Nolans' old jeep, "whether we'll survive the journey."

PJ ignored her. His sister had been teasing him mercilessly about the test. Beforehand, she's warned him he hadn't the slightest chance of passing. Now, she kept making him jump by shouting warnings of imaginary drunks weaving over the road or tractors about to charge out of side roads in front of them.

He looked over his shoulder at Anna. She was different from Amy – much more gentle – and so much quieter. She'd changed a lot since her arrival. She had grown taller and stayed slim, whereas Amy was rather short for her age. She just seemed to have got more solid. His sister sometimes reminded him of a small, hyperactive robot, busily beavering away and usually up to no good.

Although there were still times when Anna seemed to be off in a world of her own and sometimes disappeared for long walks by herself, she no longer had that sad look about her. When Minou had died last spring, a victim of her own greed, having choked on a stolen chicken-bone, she'd coped with it well, even though she had been very upset. He'd helped by digging the grave for the cat and had been touched by how grateful she'd been when he picked some wild flowers to leave beside the small wooden marker with Minou's name on it. Her thanks had made him feel flustered and pleased at the same time.

Now he thought how pretty she looked in her blue summer dress, with her long brown hair tied back in a ponytail. She was brown from swimming in the lake over the holiday. Her arms were nearly as brown as his own.

"You all right, Anna?" he asked solicitously.

She smiled at him.

"I'm fine, PJ. Don't take any notice of Amy. I know that we'll get there in one piece."

"I wouldn't be too sure of that," commented the other girl. "He nearly knocked the postman over last week."

"I did *not*!" PJ retorted quickly. "It was his fault anyway. He walked around the side of his van and out into the middle of the road without looking."

"Well, I bet he'll be looking like mad every time he puts a foot outside his van from now on – just in case you're on the horizon!"

"Pity you weren't drowned at birth, Amy!"

Amy giggled, making her eyes squint ferociously as she peered back at him in the mirror.

Anna and Amy waved at the assembled Nolans and Pog, the dogs dancing around their feet, barking. As they drove out of the farm, Anna twisted sideways in her seat to catch a last glimpse of her aunt. She was standing by the gate, still smiling and waving, a cigarette in her other hand.

Chapter Seventeen

During the summer before Anna's thirteenth birthday, Pog received a letter from Rosalind.

"Your mother wants to come and stay for a few days, Anna."

Anna looked at her blankly.

"Why?"

Pog smiled at her.

"Well, perhaps she's just realised that she's missing her daughter and thinks she should come over before she forgets what you look like, darling. I really don't know."

"Does she have to come, Aunt Pog?"

Her aunt was not surprised by her lack of enthusiasm.

"I rather think that she does. She *is* your mother after all." Seeing the glum expression on Anna's face, she added, "You never know, you might get on with each other now that you are more grown up. You'll have things to talk about and –"

"I don't have anything to talk about with my mother," Anna replied quietly. "But if you think she should come, then I'll try to get on with her."

"Good girl! One has to do these things from time to time. It's usually not quite as bad as you think when you get down to it. Concentrate hard on making her visit a good one and the time will fly."

But time did not fly. Not for Anna or her aunt. Rosalind hadn't changed, Pog thought to herself as she watched the woman watching her daughter with a small frown. Elegant as ever in her silk shirt and well-tailored trousers, Rosalind was able to walk but only for short distances. She used a stick to support herself when she moved around outside the house. Pog could see that she was in pain some of the time. Rosalind, however, never complained. If only she would be a little warmer, more human. Pog knew she would have happily put up with a little complaining from the woman if she could just bring herself to be nicer to Anna.

To Rosalind, seeing Anna again after all this time, it re-enforced her feelings of being an inadequate parent. The tall, rather pretty girl with her disconcerting way of looking at you – as though she were trying to work out what you were thinking, made her uncomfortable. Every time she looked into her daughter's face, she saw her dead husband's look of reproach in the dark brown eyes. She knew that Anna would still rather be anywhere except in her mother's company. Rosalind had to admit to herself that, if she were being honest, she couldn't blame her for that.

Anna found it impossible to relax in her mother's company. Suddenly, all the uncomfortable silences and tensions she'd experienced in her life in the Cambridge house returned. It was worse now because Anna was so much more aware. Before, she had been unable to express what she felt to her mother. Now, the frustration of apparently still being viewed as an awkward small girl whenever she put forward an opinion made her want to hide down at the Nolans' farm and not come back until her mother had gone.

The weather was warm but overcast and the swarms of midges living by the lake were making everyone's lives a misery. The cattle and horses constantly swished their tails and shook their heads, trying to rid themselves of the insects. Rosalind, driven outside by the smell of cigarette-smoke in the house, found herself smothered in midges. When she retreated inside, the skin around her eyes was blotched and pink from their bites.

"How can you live in this place, Pog?" she demanded.

"Very easily, darling. You see, they don't like cigarette-smoke."

Point to Aunt Pog, thought Anna with glee. Then, feeling that she shouldn't be spiteful, she tried to explain to her mother the delights of living in the house by the lake.

"They only come out when it's cloudy and there's no wind. It's grand the rest of the time."

"Grand?" queried Rosalind, eyebrows raised.

Stupid woman! Pog smiled at her. "In this part of the world, grand can mean terrific, great, splendid, just what the doctor ordered."

"Oh, really!" Rosalind observed her daughter coolly. "You're becoming quite Irish, aren't you?"

Anna regarded her stonily without answering. If she

202

were, what did it matter? She would rather die than be stuck up and critical like her mother.

Pog smothered a sigh of irritation. Thank God Babs and her sister were coming to tea. The Misses Jameson would give Rosalind something to think about. She'd already made it plain that she thought the rest of Pog's acquaintances were uninteresting country bumpkins.

In fact, tea with the two elderly ladies went very well. Rosalind found them amusing and entertaining. She responded by turning on the charm. Pog had forgotten just what good company she could be when she made the effort. However, the tea party proved to be a solitary oasis in the four-day visit.

Pog didn't know who was the more relieved when Anna's mother eventually left Ballynacarrig – Rosalind, herself or Anna.

When they got back from the small local airport, Pog and Anna stood in the kitchen with their cups of tea.

"You see, she doesn't know anything about what I'm really like. All she wants to do is criticise the way I speak or what I'm wearing. And she hardly bothered to talk to Kathleen, even though she drove us to the airport."

Pog looked at her carefully, searching for signs of incipient tears. But Anna was looking remarkably dry-eyed and resigned.

"It's her way of doing things, darling. Still, we managed not to have any major rows by the skin of our teeth, didn't we?" She chuckled. "Mind you, she was flirting with death when she told me I drank too much. Imagine! In my own house too!"

Anna remembered the incident. It had happened on

Rosalind's second evening. After a couple of glasses of wine and countless gins both before and after the meal, Pog stumbled getting up from the couch. She had been saved from falling into the fire by Anna leaping to her feet and quickly grabbing her from behind.

"Perhaps she thought it was your turn to be criticised," said Anna as cheerfully as she could. Though really, that had been the only time she'd found herself in agreement with her mother during the four long days of her visit. Aunt Pog's drinking seemed to have got worse. Anna had found four empty gin bottles in the dustbin last week. She mentioned the fact to Kathleen.

"It's too late to stop your aunt from drinking, I'm afraid, Anna. It's just part of the way she is and we can't do anything about it."

"But couldn't Dr Treacy say something to her?"

"Oh, Anna. That poor man's driven demented by Mrs R and her smoking and drinking. He's tried to warn her but she just laughs at him. What can he do?"

Anna didn't voice her fear that some harm would come to her aunt because of the way she lived. Perhaps Anna's father would still be alive if he hadn't drunk quite as much. The thought of anything happening to Aunt Pog gave her a cold feeling in the pit of her stomach.

* * *

Before returning to school that summer, both Amy and Anna noticed a change in Kathleen. She seemed unusually abstracted and was spending more time on her appearance than before.

"I think she's in love," said Amy with an expression of distaste. "That Sean Dillon from the farm just before the village. You know, they have a dairy herd."

Anna had seen them together several times. She supposed that, if Kathleen had to fall in love, Sean would be OK. He was rather quiet but, from the way she'd seen him looking at Kathleen, he was definitely mad about her. Bridie and Gem Nolan had had him up to the farm several times for meals and Anna knew that Kathleen had also been down to the Dillon farm for Sunday lunch with Sean and his widowed mother.

When Anna found Kathleen, who was usually busily on the move, standing, gazing out of a window with what Amy would probably have disparagingly referred to as 'a soppy expression on her', she tackled Pog.

"Aunt Pog, I don't think Kathleen's quite with it at the moment. Is there something wrong with her? Amy says she's in love."

Pog chuckled, looking up from the paper and peering at her over the top of her reading glasses.

"Well, I'm sure young Amy thinks that being in love is probably the worst affliction womankind could suffer but it seems to be making our Kathleen happy – a bit absent-minded, but definitely happy. Why do you ask, darling?"

"Oh, it's just that she washed the kitchen floor twice yesterday and, later on, I found her putting the cereal into the fridge instead of back in the cupboard. And sometimes she seems to be miles away and doesn't hear what you're saying to her."

"Sounds like love to me!"

"Aren't you worried?"

"Why should I be worried? Being in love is the best recipe I know for a good complexion. It makes people light up from inside. Even the ugliest of us look passable when we're in love!"

"It's just that, if Kathleen gets married or anything, she won't want to come and work here any more, will she?"

"Don't you worry, darling. Kathleen has no intention of leaving us in the lurch, married or not. She won't abandon us!"

Anna hoped not. Her friendship with Amy's sister was important. She was part of the household and it wouldn't seem right without her around. The girl was torn between being worried at the idea of any change to the happy routine in Aunt Pog's house and wanting Kathleen to be happy.

Amy observed Anna for a moment in silence when Pog's words concerning Kathleen and being in love were repeated to her. Then, she shook her head sadly.

"Kath's mad if she is! I mean, why would she want to move away from home where Ma is there to look after her and she's dead comfortable?"

"I suppose if you love someone, you are happy to give up other things that you like," suggested Anna, her face thoughtful.

"Well, *I'm* never getting married, that's for sure!" replied Amy firmly. She stared suspiciously at her friend. "You wouldn't ever do something like that, sure you wouldn't?"

"I don't know. I think it might be lovely to love

someone so much that all you wanted to do was be with them and make each other happy. It would make you feel sort of safe."

"Right!" Amy pulled an incredulous face. "Let's go and see how Juno's foal is. PJ still hasn't got a name for him."

* * *

One school term followed another in an uneventful way. Anna missed her aunt and Ballynacarrig but she wasn't unhappy at Kilgarry Abbey. She and Amy had plenty of friends and their days were too full to spend much time wondering what was going on in the world outside.

Before going to the school, Anna had been rather in awe at the thought of being taught by nuns. She'd been surprised to find that they were remarkably like other people. Some were patient, some interesting and some not so pleasant. Mother Christopher, the Mother Superior, was cool and distant but Anna had never seen her angry or even raise her voice, although she noticed that pupils and nuns alike treated her with a lot of respect.

What she hadn't expected was that she would find herself so drawn to the little chapel attached to the school. She didn't much like the paintings on the walls of the Stations of the Cross, nor did she like the ivory-coloured Christ, hanging from the cross with bloodstained feet and hands. What she did enjoy was the smell of wax floor polish, candles and incense, the feeling of being in a place that was apart and safe and where nothing changed. Above all, she loved the sound the nuns made when they sang. Their soft voices seemed to fill the chapel and their singing making her feel strangely reassured. Anna felt that no harm could come to you while that sweet sound filled the air. Thoughts of her father, Gina, her mother, faded when she sat on the narrow pew, listening, her eyes closed in an almost trance-like state.

"God! You'll end up as a nun if you're not careful," warned Amy one day after half an hour of hunting for her. "I can just see you in your habit, gliding along, with your little feet working away so you look like you're on wheels!" The idea of slipping into the chapel for a while, when you hadn't actually been told you had to, was a complete mystery to Amy. "What do you do in there? You're not *praying*, are you?"

"No! I'm not!" Anna laughed at the look on her face. "It's just nice there. No one bothers you and it's sort of peaceful. It makes me feel . . . well, happy, I suppose."

"What you mean is, you need to get away from me every now and then because I'm not quiet or peaceful."

"True!" said Anna.

They both laughed.

* * *

When they returned to Ballynacarrig for the Christmas holidays, they heard that Kathleen and Sean were to be married the following summer. Pog seemed so delighted it was easy for Anna to welcome the news too. Amy, on the other hand, looked first appalled and then resigned.

"Well, if she wants to act the maggot, who am I to say anything?"

She then promptly forgot the whole thing and got on

with enjoying being back on the farm. There was another litter of pups and PJ had promised to go out riding with her on the new pony. There was a drag hunt in two weeks' time and visits to the kennels to see the beagles and . . . the list was endless.

For the first time in six years, Anna thought that Aunt Pog was beginning to show signs of wear and tear. Although she still drank and smoked and laughed as much as ever, her cough seemed to bother her more than it had and her face looked thinner. When Anna asked her if she was all right, Pog gave her usual throaty chuckle and denied the possibility of not being well.

"Never felt better, darling!" she assured her niece.

"You've lost weight, Aunt Pog. I'm sure you have," Anna insisted.

"The fact is, my morning toe-touching sessions are finally paying off and I've been walking a lot more than I used to."

Anna was sceptical. Her aunt didn't own walking shoes. The only walking she'd been doing was in three-inch heels around the shops in Ballina or inside the house.

When she asked Kathleen if everything was all right with her aunt, the girl admitted that she was worried.

"I've begged her to go and have a check-up but she won't. You know how stubborn she is, Anna, when she doesn't want to hear what you're saying?" Kathleen hesitated for a moment. "She might be feeling a bit lonely."

"Why?" asked Anna, surprised.

"Well, what with you being away at school and me spending a bit more time at Sean's. Mr O'Shea doesn't call as much as he did either. Mrs R's on her own more than she used to be."

Anna had mixed feelings about Jim O'Shea not being around.

"Why doesn't he come over?"

"I'm not sure. They had some sort of an argument a few weeks back. I don't know what it was about but I do know that your aunt was mighty put out with him."

Anna thought Kathleen was being evasive. She was sure she knew more than she was letting on. Knowing Jim O'Shea's reputation in the village, it crossed her mind that perhaps another woman had been the reason for Aunt Pog becoming upset.

Amy was more enlightening on the subject.

"PJ said he heard them having a fantastic row. Mrs R gave him a right bollocking! He's been having it off with that Sharon one in the pub in Foxford. PJ said she was raging – told him he was a waste of space and she didn't know why she'd put up with him for as long as she had. He said she was spitting bricks – and the language out of her! He said it would make your hair curl. He told me he almost felt sorry for the man."

"Well, I don't," said Anna. "He gives me the creeps with his red face and piggy little eyes. You never know what he's thinking. Aunt Pog's better off without him if you ask me."

Her aunt didn't mention Jim so Anna thought it better to pretend she hadn't noticed his absence. Apart from the constant fog of cigarette-smoke and the nagging worry at the back of her mind that her aunt was not as well as she had been, she loved being back at Sandy Bay House. Aunt Pog insisted that Anna fill her in on what she had been doing at school – with nothing left out. When she felt she was up-to-date on all the news, she, in turn, gave Anna the local gossip.

This included the latest scandal involving Mad Eddie down by the lake.

"You remember, darling, the poor bloke you and Amy used to terrorise at regular intervals a few years ago. Although I suspect it was Amy who did most of the terrorising! Well, the guards came and took him away last month."

"What had he done?"

"I gather the list is pretty spectacular. Apparently he'd been selling drugs to the village kids, amongst other things. It's a good thing the guards got to him before the parents strung him up. But what really got him into trouble was the fact that he beat his girlfriend up so badly the poor girl had to go into hospital and then, of course, questions started to be asked."

"And what's happened to him?"

"I'm afraid he's languishing in jail. But you never know, it might be the making of him – a sort of enforced career break. He'll have time to think about the error of his ways. Perhaps he'll re-emerge full of the milk of human kindness! I'm a firm believer in miracles!"

Anna wondered if God might just possibly prove her aunt right and perform one that would stop her from smoking and drinking quite so much. Being realistic, she doubted there was a powerful enough miracle available to confer instant and total abstinence.

Chapter Eighteen

PJ was now official driver to Aunt Pog, having taken over some of his sister's jobs, including caring for the vegetable garden. Whenever he could be spared from the farm, he was to be found down at Sandy Bay House. Kathleen was true to her word. Even though she was married now, she still went down to Pog Roberts three times a week. It was nearly eighteen months since the wedding – and still she came. Although superficially she seemed unchanged, Pog's experienced eye detected that all was not well. There was an anxious look in the young woman's blue eyes these days. She was worried about something.

Pog ambushed her in the kitchen one morning.

"Come on. Tell me what's wrong, darling! I know there's *something* – so don't try and pretend otherwise. I didn't come down in the last shower of rain. I may look a bit battered on the outside but the old faculties are still more or less intact." Kathleen knew that once Mrs R had an idea in her head, nothing would shake her off until she'd ferreted out the truth. Pog gave her a stern look. "He's treating you well, isn't he, that husband of yours?"

Kathleen nodded and smiled.

"Sean is a lovely man, Mrs R. I have nothing to complain about at all."

"Well, why don't I believe that, I wonder?" retorted Pog.

"It's just that . . . we're both dying to have children and nothing's happened. Sean thought there might be something wrong."

"Good Lord, child! You've only been living together for a blink of an eye! You're still in your twenties and he's not much older. There's plenty of time for children. Right now is the time to enjoy yourselves, really get to know each other, have fun. Soon enough you'll be submerged under a mountain of dirty nappies and one-eyed cuddly toys. Good gracious! I thought there was something really wrong!"

Kathleen couldn't help laughing.

"Perhaps we are being a bit hasty," she conceded.

"Of course you are, darling. I've seen it all before. Once young couples start getting in a tizzy about not being able to start a family, everything goes haywire. What you two need to do is make love anytime you can, anywhere you can and enjoy yourselves to bits while you're doing it!"

Kathleen blushed.

"I'll try and remember that, Mrs R."

Pog noticed that Kathleen was still smiling when she left the house later on in the day. The worried look seemed to have disappeared.

After Kathleen had rattled off down the drive in her car, Pog picked up the list she had been making. Anna would be seventeen in three weeks' time and she wanted to get on with making plans for the occasion. It was going to be a day to remember. It was important that it was special. She sighed to herself, wondering if she would be around for the birthday celebration the following year. If what those damned medics she'd sneaked off to see on a trip to Dublin had said was right, then it was looking doubtful. She reached for a calming cigarette. Bugger them anyway! That lot was rather like the weather forecasts – vague and very often inaccurate.

* * *

PJ leaned down from Juno's back to open the paddock gate. Leading the way through into the field, he waited until Anna's mount ambled up beside him.

"What do you want for your birthday then?"

Anna regarded him with a slight smile.

"Where should I begin? There are so many things I would like."

"Well, I won't know if you don't tell me."

"All right! I would like . . ." She ground to a halt, realising that the things she really wanted were not in PJ's power to give her. Things like good health for her aunt, a mother who loved her, her father alive again – so many impossible things. Out of the blue – she didn't know why – she remembered the drawing of the unicorn. Yes, she would like to see a unicorn. Of course she knew they didn't exist but the idea of something as magical and beautiful *should* be allowed to exist. If she told the down-to-earth PJ that, he would really think she was mad! She made an apologetic face. "I can't think of anything, PJ. Just something small, a surprise."

He shook his head.

"There must be *something* you want. Now, if it were Amy's birthday, there'd be no problem at all."

"I know," Anna laughed. "A tractor would do her nicely!"

As far as Anna could make out, Amy's threat to avoid marriage at all costs looked a serious one. She never wasted any time on men unless they wanted to talk farm machinery or the intricacies of looking after calves suffering from rampant diarrhoea.

The horses stood quietly side by side so that PJ and Anna's legs almost touched. He looked at her as she laughed and, not for the first time, had an overpowering longing to kiss her. She looked so lovely with her long hair around her shoulders, her smooth skin tanned from all the riding and swimming she'd done that summer. He noticed the way her eyes seemed to smile as well as her lips when she laughed. He had always resisted the temptation up until now – after all he was nearly three-and-half years older than she was. Suddenly, unable to stop himself, he leaned over and gave her a quick kiss on her mouth. She instinctively moved away from him, looking surprised.

"PJ! What on earth made you do that?"

She didn't sound angry, just startled.

He coloured slightly and looked down at Juno's mane, concentrating on removing some mud from the mare's neck. "Do you mind?"

She looked at him fondly with her dark eyes. "Come on, PJ! I like you too much to pretend. It was nice of you but I'd prefer it if you didn't do it again. I almost feel part of your family. It's like kissing a brother."

Immediately she'd said it, Anna could see that she had hurt his feelings badly. He clicked his tongue, urging the horse forward and moved away without saying anything. She was about to call after him but something warned her that it would be better to leave him to get over his embarrassment on his own for the time being.

Later, as she removed the saddle and bridle, she thought of the hastily snatched kiss. Had she been unkind? The last thing she wanted to do was upset PJ. But wasn't it better to tell him the truth straight away? She leaned her forehead against the horse's warm neck. The more she thought about it, the more certain she was that she'd done the right thing. After all, if her own mother hadn't pretended to love Anna's father before they married, how different everything might have been.

* * *

Anna's seventeenth birthday party was held at the start of an untypically hot August. She was feeling relaxed and well – more full of energy than she'd ever felt. For weeks, she and Amy had swum and sunbathed until Anna was a deep golden-brown. Amy's freckles had spread so they almost joined up, giving her a strangely mottled look.

She had stared enviously at her friend's even tan.

"It's not fair! You look only gorgeous and I look like something out of one of those medical journal things."

On the day of the party, Anna was banned by Pog from going anywhere near the house until it was time to change for the festivities. Inevitably, Anna made her way down to the Nolans. Kathleen and Amy were both involved in the preparations at Sandy Bay House so she spent most of the day helping PJ and his father around the farm. Amy's brother seemed to have got over his disappointment at Anna's reaction to his kiss. But she was aware that things between them weren't quite as relaxed and easy as they had been before. Every now and then she would catch him watching her. As soon as their eyes met, he would hastily look away. Amy had noticed this happening and was quick to pounce.

"What's up with big brother, then?" she'd asked Anna, head tilted to one side. They were alone in the farm kitchen with only the sleeping cat for company. "Did you two have a fight?"

"No, of course not!" said Anna.

"So why does he go all funny when you come into the room?"

"He *doesn't* go all funny, Amy. You're letting your imagination run away with you."

"Hmm!" Amy snorted. "Well, Ma's noticed it too. So both our imaginations must be doing strange things at the same time. I wonder what the odds are on that happening?"

"Go and . . ."

"Yes?"

"Oh, go and do something useful and leave me in peace."

"Right, so!" said Amy with a wicked grin. Adding

before she left the room. "I only tell it as I see it!" Seeing the look on Anna's face, she said cheerily, "All *right*, I'm going!"

Anna knew that Amy was still suspicious, even though she had been particularly careful not to glance at PJ when there was the slightest chance that he might be looking in her direction.

By six o'clock, she felt she couldn't delay any more. If Aunt Pog, Kathleen and Amy weren't organised for the party by now, they might be glad of an extra helping hand.

She couldn't believe her eyes when she walked in through the gate. Small, white lights hung from the trees around the house and sprays of flowers, tied with white ribbons, decorated the windows. Several trestle tables, covered in white cloths and also decorated with flowers and candles, had been set up on the lawn to one side of the house. When she went into the living-room, Anna saw that there were great vases of roses and lilies in the corners, scenting the air with their perfume. The room had been cleared for dancing with chairs grouped together under the windows.

Suddenly, hands were clapped over her eyes.

"You're not supposed to see any more just yet. Mrs R says you're to go straight upstairs and spend loads of time having a shower and getting yourself ready. Strictest orders!" Amy gave her a shove in the direction of the stairs. "She says she doesn't want to see you a minute before half seven. OK?"

"OK!"

Dutifully, Anna went upstairs without looking back.

She felt excited and rather overwhelmed. How incredible it was to have people around her who wanted to take so much trouble over her birthday.

She and her aunt had gone to Dublin two weeks before to buy Anna a dress.

"Something delicious that will make all the women green and the men swallow their tonsils in admiration. That's what we want," Aunt Pog announced as she sailed through the doors of Brown Thomas and up the marble staircase.

Anna looked doubtful. "Nothing too showy, though."

Her aunt smiled at her.

"Don't worry, darling. I know the sort of thing you like. We'll only buy something you really fall in love with. It's the only way to shop. Unless you're mad about it, leave it on the rail."

After searching through every section of the shop without having any success, they moved across the road to Switzers. An hour later, having drawn a blank there too, Pog admitted that she was running out of steam.

"I think we'll go and have a little drink in The Old Stand."

Glancing down at her aunt's ankles, Anna saw that they were badly swollen.

"We don't *have* to find something. I can always wear the blue dress Bridie made for me. It's lovely and it still fits me."

"You are having something new if it kills me." Seeing the serious look on Anna's face, Pog said, "Don't be such an old worrier! Really, darling, as long as we make regular pitstops so that I can top up with the odd gin to keep me going, I don't mind doing every single shop in Grafton Street until we find something you like."

Luckily for both of them, the perfect garment was hanging in the next place they went into. As soon as Anna put on the dress and looked in the mirror, she knew it was what she wanted. When she came out of the changing room, her aunt gave a small gasp of pleasure.

"My darling, you look simply gorgeous! No other word for it."

Looking at the girl as she turned slowly in front of the mirror, Pog felt a sudden rush of affection. She looked so beautiful in the cream dress with the slim, layered skirt and lightly beaded bodice. Beautiful, unspoilt by life and so – young. If only her mother could see her now! Surely Rosalind would be moved and delighted at the way Anna had turned out.

"Aunt Pog! You look as though you're about to cry! Are you all right?"

Anna's voice was full of concern.

"Right as rain, darling! It's just that you look so splendid, for once I'm lost for words."

Now, as she walked into the living-room, Anna had to admit to herself that she had never felt so assured. It was odd, but somehow, being seventeen *did* make her feel older. Perhaps it was because she had put her hair up and was wearing the pearl earrings the Nolans had given her as a birthday present. Perhaps it was because she was wearing the expensive perfume her aunt had left on her dressing-table, which she'd found when she went upstairs to get ready for the evening. Whatever the reason, Anna felt as though she were walking on air.

A beaming Pog hurried over to greet her. She was resplendent in deep purple with a lattice of gold chains hanging from her neck, making her look like some over-enthusiastic mayoress.

"There you are, darling!" she exclaimed, thrusting a glass of champagne into Anna's hand. "Come outside so you can welcome everybody as they arrive."

It seemed to Anna that the entire village had been invited. By the time she had shaken hands with everyone, her face was stiff from smiling.

It was generally agreed that Pog and Kathleen had really excelled themselves when it came to the evening meal. They all helped themselves from the plates of fresh salmon, spiced beef, casseroles, curries, numerous side salads and dips. Taking their loaded plates, people sat where they wanted at the trestle tables under the lamplit trees. Even the midges stayed away, perhaps overwhelmed by the noise and the dozens of incense coils dotted around the place.

Afterwards, the four-piece band went in action, fortified by large quantities of food and drink, the glasses beside their chairs kept regularly topped up. Anna danced until her feet hurt. She waltzed with Black Sean, who was sweating hard and looking unusually respectable in a dark suit, and did a quickstep with Gem Nolan. She even danced an energetic polka with Babs Jameson, who was obviously having the time of her life. As they spun around, the elderly woman kept poking other dancers in the back and shouting, "Isn't this just splendid fun?" Anna was relieved that Jim

O'Shea hadn't put in an appearance even though Kathleen had told her Pog had sent him an invitation.

Towards the end of the evening, PJ approached her and asked in an embarrassed voice if she would dance with him. He was looking especially smart, Anna noticed. For years he had just been Amy's rather untidily put-together brother with his hair always tangled and his clothes muddy and work-worn. Now, the white shirt and blue slacks made him look like a different person. His clear blue eyes and sunburned face were very attractive, she thought. She saw that he'd even had his hair cut in honour of the occasion.

"I'd love to, PJ," Anna said, happily, "although my feet are starting to feel a bit numb. Don't be surprised if I tread on your toes!"

Dreamily, she rested her chin on his shoulder as they slowly circled the room. He wasn't a bad dancer, she thought with surprise, pleasantly aware of his smell of soap and aftershave and clean sweat. He held her close to him, firmly but not too tightly. Contented and relaxed, Anna realised that she didn't mind. In fact, it was nice.

"Would you mind giving the rest of us lads a chance?" said a voice. "PJ, you're desperate greedy. How about lettin' someone else dance with the girl?"

Anna blinked. She had forgotten that she should be keeping an eye on the guests, making sure that no one was feeling left out. She smiled at the man, whom she recognised as a neighbouring farmer. He took her hand, leading her away from PJ, who seemed reluctant to let her go.

* * *

Lying in bed, re-living the evening, Anna realised that the only thing that had spoiled an otherwise perfect occasion was the fact that Aunt Pog had hardly danced. It was most unlike her. Usually the first on the dance floor and the last to leave it, she had spent a lot of the evening sitting, talking to people. She hadn't even become mildly tipsy – which was also unusual. She'd appeared happy enough with her glass in one hand and a cigarette in the other but Anna had seen how exhausted she looked and how she'd taken her shoes off early in the evening and not put them back on. The girl suspected that the reason was that her aunt's ankles and feet were too swollen and painful.

Chapter Nineteen

"Just think! Only one more term to go and then no more penguins."

Amy lay back on the sofa in Sandy Bay House with a contented smile.

"Poor old nuns," said Anna, laughing. "They're not *that* bad. At least they managed to get you to pass a few exams last year."

Books lay scattered on the table and floor around them. Their final-year exams loomed and they were supposed to be revising.

Pog was having an afternoon sleep. Anna had left her lying on her bed, her wig slightly off kilter, her face smothered in a white face mask, with thick slices of cucumber over each eye. Six months earlier, Dr Treacy had insisted that she rest every day for at least an hour. Anna had been surprised at what little resistance her aunt had made to the suggestion.

"Well, I suppose if a siesta's good enough for all those continental types, why not!" she'd said, with an air of resignation in her gravelly voice.

On her return from school for the Easter holiday, Anna was shocked to see how unwell Pog looked. Kathleen hadn't said much, just shaken her head when the girl tried to find out what was going on.

"Mrs R won't give up her fags or her drinks. The doctor said there's nothing to be done if she won't help herself. I've given up trying to get her to see sense, Anna. Last time I tried, she told me to go home and stop making a nuisance of myself."

"Perhaps she'll listen to me," said Anna, grimly.

But when she brought up the subject of her health with her aunt, Pog, uncharacteristically, snapped at her.

"For God's sake! Not you too!" Then, seeing the hurt look on her niece's face, she quickly relented. "Come here, darling, and give your wicked old aunt a kiss." When they had embraced, she said, "It's too late to do anything about my condition now. Yes, I could go into hospital and have various horrible things done to me, which would leave me feeling quite ghastly. I don't want to feel ghastly. I want to enjoy what time I have left to me." She peered at Anna. "Darling, as long as I have my siesta and take all the goddam pills that bloody medic's prescribed, I don't feel at all bad, you know. I'll be around for a while yet, I promise!"

But Anna didn't feel reassured.

On the days when Kathleen wasn't there, she did her best to cook appetising meals but Pog never seemed to have an appetite, although, the girl noticed that her aunt made sure that the gin bottle was always close to hand.

As they sprawled on the couch, Anna found herself thinking, not of the vagaries of the French subjunctive but of her aunt, lying in her room at the far side of the hall. The day before, she'd talked over her worries with Amy but her friend, pragmatic as ever, hadn't given her any grounds for hope.

"Kath's right! If Mrs R wants to go out with a bang not a whimper, you've just got to respect her wishes, Anna. She won't thank you for making a fuss and you'll make things difficult between you if you try."

"But I don't want her to go – with a bang or a whimper."

"Jesus, Anna! She's not immortal, you know. She can't go on forever. She's seventy-seven after all!"

"That's not *that* old," replied Anna stubbornly, burying her head in her *French Verbs – New Edition*.

Perhaps, now that the weather was improving, her aunt would start to feel better. Anna tried to pretend to herself that things weren't as bad as she feared.

"PJ said he might come down later on," said Amy, casually turning over a page of the book that was propped on her knees.

That was another problem area, thought Anna. The previous August when they'd danced together on the night of her birthday, she'd felt something like attraction for Amy's brother but when they'd seen each other a couple of days later, she realised that the feeling wasn't there any longer. She felt guilty and had made a mess of trying to extricate herself from what PJ obviously believed was the start of something. Since then, he'd tended to avoid being alone with her. So, why was he thinking of calling in this afternoon?

"Do you know why?" she asked Amy.

Her friend gave a chuckle.

"Perhaps he's going to have another go at persuading you to take him seriously."

"I *do* take him seriously. I just don't want him as a boyfriend, that's all."

"What's his problem, anyway?" said Amy, giggling. "As if any girl in her right mind would want to go out with him and his size twelve boots."

"That's not fair, Amy. PJ's sweet."

"Hello? It's his sister you're talking to, remember. *Sweet*, I don't think so! He spends hours in the bathroom squeezing zits – and his ears stick out."

"You're not nice, Amy Nolan."

"I know," replied Amy with a broad grin. "Awful, isn't it?"

* * *

The three-week holiday slipped past so quickly, Anna was surprised to suddenly find there was only one more day to go before the summer term started at Kilgarry Abbey. The fact that it was her last term there didn't excite her as much as Amy. She'd mostly enjoyed her time at the school. Anna had never shone in any subject but had managed to stay in the top third of her class when it came to exams and assessments. She felt reasonably well prepared to do the Leaving and, unlike Amy, hadn't lost any sleep over it.

The weather, which had been cold and unsettled for

days, took a turn for the better. After lunch on the Sunday before she was due to leave, when Pog was lying down and the house was empty and quiet, Anna decided to go down to the lake.

She walked for a long time, strolling aimlessly around the water's edge, stopping every now and then to listen to birds and to watch a heron fishing from a rocky outcrop. The sun felt welcomingly warm on her back. Anna shrugged off her jacket and threw it over one shoulder, hooking her thumb through the loop at the neck. She passed the end of the path that led to Mad Eddie's cottage, remembering Amy lying on the bracken, choking with laughter, after he'd chased them all those years ago. She wondered if he would emerge from prison a wiser and better man, as her aunt had suggested. Had his poor girlfriend found another man who would treat her well? She hoped so. No one should have to put up with violence and unkindness. It was the sort of behaviour that seemed to Anna to be unforgivable, as well as incomprehensible.

Feeling hot, she spread out her jacket and sat down on a patch of reasonably dry gravel. Realising that she felt sleepy after the large Sunday lunch she'd just eaten, Anna lay back and closed her eyes. Almost immediately she fell asleep, lulled by the soothing sound of water lapping gently beside her and the warm sun on her face.

She was woken by rough hands. They seemed to be tugging at her shirt and pulling at the zip on her jeans. Horrified, she started to scream but one of the hands hit her hard on the side of her head, and then clamped itself over her mouth and nose so she found it difficult to breathe. A stranger's face, distorted and sweating, loomed over hers as a blast of whisky-laden breath hit her. Terrified to the point of fainting, she attempted to struggle but the man was now lying on top of her, his unshaven cheek scraping against her neck. It felt as though he were pushing all the air out of her body with his dead weight. She could feel him dragging her jeans down over her thighs with his other hand.

* * *

Anna opened her eyes and slowly lifted her head off the ground. He had gone. She could hear the sound of a car engine, roaring into life somewhere in the trees nearby. She slowly sat up, trembling violently, her breath coming in sobs. Bruised and aching, she felt a dull pain inside her as though she were being burned by fire. She stumbled to her feet and pulled her jeans up, fumbling with the zip. Jamming her torn shirt into her waistband with unsteady hands, she tried to stay upright without falling.

She couldn't and wouldn't let herself think about the horror of what had taken place. No one must ever know what had happened. Especially not her aunt. What would she think? What would it do to her? It might kill her if she found out that Anna had been raped by an unknown man. No one must ever find out.

As quickly as she could, she half-ran, half-staggered back towards the house, her jacket bundled around her, her feet tripping on the stones and tussocks of grass. She was desperately afraid that someone might see her. Every now and then she stopped, her mouth dry, her heart pounding, as she listened, imagining she heard pursuing footsteps, the staccato snap of a twig. Only a short while before, she had listened, with such pleasure, to the birds. Now Anna was deaf to birdsong in this place where, up until now, she had always felt so safe. Suddenly, the lake had become sinister, full of menace. It would never be the same again. Nothing would ever be the same.

* * *

When she'd crept in through the kitchen door, Anna saw that Pog's bridge-playing friends had arrived and, judging from all the talk and laughter, they had already settled down to an enjoyable afternoon of gossip and cards. She knew she wouldn't be missed while Pog was entertaining them. Thankfully, she climbed the stairs up to her room without anyone noticing her.

All she wanted to do was wash herself all over, cleanse her body of the man's stink. She was still shivering when, wrapped in a towel, she climbed into bed and curled up into a ball.

She had never felt so ashamed or dirty. Was it her fault that it had happened? It was the kind of horror story you read about in the paper. It wasn't the sort of thing that happened to you. What would Amy or Kathleen think of her if they knew? Her mind ached.

When she finally dragged herself out of bed, she looked in the mirror. Her clothes had protected her from bad bruising on her arms. The bruises and scratches on her breasts, thighs and stomach would be hidden from the outside world.

There was the sound of footsteps. Aunt Pog called up the stairs.

"Darling? You there?"

Hastily, Anna slipped on the old blue dressing-gown that had belonged to her father. She stuck her head around the bedroom door.

"I was just sorting my things out for school tomorrow and then I thought I'd have an early night."

"Well, if you're sure you don't mind me abandoning you on your last night, some of us are going down to the O'Gorman's for a bite to eat. Sure you don't want to come?"

"Yes, thanks, Aunt Pog. I'll see you in the morning," said Anna, in as steady a voice as she could manage.

She shut the door and leaned against it, feeling sick. At least she'd have until the morning before having to put on an act and pretend that everything was normal – and even then Aunt Pog would be in bed until just before Anna left. She walked slowly into her bathroom and turned on the taps so that she could soak herself in the deep bath. The shower hadn't been enough to stop the feeling of being contaminated. Anna wondered if she would be able to feel really clean ever again.

* * *

She never knew how she managed to get through her last term at Kilgarry Abbey. As the bruises faded, she managed to gradually push what had happened to the back of her mind – but it was always there. Amy noticed how pale and nervous she'd become and put it down to pre-exam jitters.

"So, you're not quite as confident as you like to make

out!" she teased Anna, who was happy to pretend that was the reason for her not being herself.

She was finding it difficult to concentrate and, as the exams drew nearer, she started to wonder if she would be able to get through them. One or two of the nuns took her to task for being inattentive in class and handing in work that was late or not up to her usual standard.

"Now is not the time to start slacking, Anna. Sister Ignatius says that your mind is not on your work and that you seem to be having trouble concentrating. Is there anything bothering you?" Mother Christopher enquired one day after classes had finished.

"No, Mother, I'm just a little worried that my revision isn't going as well as I expected."

"Then, may I suggest that gazing out of windows, with your mind plainly elsewhere, is not the best remedy for success?"

The Mother Superior swept off down the corridor, after giving Anna one last, penetrating look.

The day before the exams started, she received a letter from Kathleen in which her aunt's health was the main reason for her writing. A paragraph at the bottom of the first page made Anna forget her own troubles.

I don't want you to get worried, but you should know that Mrs R has been in hospital for a few days. She had several of her attacks and Dr Treacy persuaded her to go in for a little while. She's back home now and is much better in herself and looking forward to seeing you again soon.

Anna rang that evening and spoke to her aunt.

"How are you, Aunt Pog? Are you really OK?"

There was a brief, chesty laugh from the other end of the line.

"I'm on absolutely tiptop form, darling. Kathleen shouldn't have written. I'm very cross with her for bothering you when you're in the middle of preparing for your exams." When Anna remained silent, Pog added, "I haven't felt as good for a long time. You'll be very proud of me, darling, I've cut the smoking right down."

When Anna told Amy what her aunt had said, she laughed.

"From sixty fags a day to forty-five – *if* we're lucky!"

That was what Anna suspected too. The idea of Aunt Pog without a cigarette in one hand was a rather like trying to imagine a rabbit without its ears.

* * *

PJ seemed to be driving unnecessarily slowly.

"Can't we go a little faster?"

"No, I can't. The road's too full of bends. I'm doing my best," he replied, giving her a reassuring smile.

She looked terrible, he thought. Her face was all blotchy from crying. He didn't know what to say to her. She seemed so devastated. When he'd collected her from the abbey, all PJ wanted to do was put his arms around her and give her a hug but he knew she didn't want him to touch her. When she'd walked out to the car, she looked as though she were in a world of her own, hardly aware of his existence.

The day after the last exam paper, she had been called to Mother Christopher's study and told that she was needed at home. The nun spoke quietly, saying how very sorry she was to have to tell her that her aunt had died earlier that morning.

Now, as they drove along the twisting narrow road, Anna silent, gazing blindly out of the window, she tried to accept the fact that the unthinkable thing she'd always dreaded happening had finally taken place. Aunt Pog was dead! Memories of all the times they'd spent together, very often laughing at something outrageous her aunt had said or done, flooded into her mind. She could imagine the husky voice, roughened by smoke and slightly slurred with gin, the long bouts of terrible coughing, the wicked laugh that was so infectious and that seemed to gurgle up from deep inside the woman's chest. Anna had never managed to keep a straight face when her aunt laughed. What would she do now? Any plans for the future had included Aunt Pog. Not that either of them had the slightest idea what Anna would do after her schooling finished.

"Plenty of time to make up your mind about all that, darling," Pog had said. "I think you should have some fun before you start thinking about what you want to do next. Perhaps we can go on a cruise – or visit Africa. I've always wanted to go there! We've all the time in the world to sort something out."

Anna shut her eyes against the sudden pricking of tears. But there hadn't been all the time in the world, had there? Why, oh, why hadn't her aunt taken more care of herself and allowed the people around her to take care of her too?

When they arrived back at the house, Kathleen was standing at the open front door. Anna could see that she too had been crying. Wordlessly, they hugged each other.

They sat together on stools in the unusually untidy kitchen, sipping their tea while Kathleen filled Anna in on what had happened.

"She was on fantastic form last night. Flying, she was," said Kathleen. "She had a couple of her women friends around and when I left, they were well away. You know, the usual, cards and so on. Her last words to me were, 'Would you mind popping in tomorrow morning if you can spare the time, Kathleen?'" Kathleen shook her head slowly. "It's a good thing I did because when I went through to her room with her cup of coffee, thinking she'd stayed up too late and was having a bit of a lie-in, didn't I find her, sitting up in the bed with her glasses on and a magazine in front of her. I could tell she was gone the moment I looked at her." She put her hand on Anna's, "I wish you could have seen her, Anna. She looked so peaceful, like she'd just drifted off to sleep and not woken up."

"You're not just saying that to make me feel better, are you?" Anna asked. "Only, I had this terrible picture in my mind of her gasping for breath, the way she sometimes did, and being frightened and all on her own." She swallowed hard. "I couldn't bear to think of her like that."

Kathleen gave her a small smile.

"I promise you, she didn't suffer. I *know* she didn't. Just slipped away without any fuss or bother – the way she would have wanted."

Maybe, thought Anna. But if that was true, it wasn't in keeping with the way Aunt Pog had lived her life. She had been noisy, indiscreet, full of affection and a sense of fun that most women half her age never had. Whenever it was time to leave a party, Aunt Pog had to be dragged away, protesting loudly!

* * *

It wasn't until after her aunt's burial that Anna realised, with a sudden shock that she would have to make a decision about what to do next with her life. Everything had been put on hold until now.

The whole of the county appeared to have come to the church on the edge of Ballynacarrig for the funeral. Anna was overcome at the kindness and concern shown to her by so many people, some of whom she had never seen before in her life.

It had been a perfect day as far as the weather was concerned. The sun shone down as the cortège wound its way at a snail's pace to the small cemetery that clung to the lower slopes of the mountain. Everywhere the gorse was in flower. To Anna, it looked as though the countryside was drowning in gold.

She thought that her aunt would probably have enjoyed the scene. Anna could hear her saying, 'How extraordinary, darling! All those people!' She certainly would have approved of the noisy wake that followed the funeral. Her great-niece could imagine her sitting among them, chuckling, as the glasses were emptied and refilled, huge platefuls of sandwiches eaten as the music grew louder and the stories and jokes got more hilarious and graphic as the night wore on.

Fatigue and sadness, and because she was unused to

drinking very much, combined to make her slightly drunk by the end of the night. Anna found she was having difficulty in focussing properly. PJ, watching her from the other side of the room, said something to Kathleen, who immediately went over to where Anna sat. She touched her lightly on the shoulder.

"They'll be gone soon, Anna. You go on up to bed. You look exhausted. I'll lock up and turn off the lights, don't you worry."

Kathleen had been sleeping at Sandy Bay House since Anna's return. It had been a great comfort for Anna to know that she was there when, each morning, the girl was jolted awake by the thought that her aunt had gone – that when she went downstairs, she would never again hear Aunt Pog snoring loudly in her own bed at the other end of the house.

* * *

The appearance of Pog's missing husband, Desmond, at Sandy Bay House two days later, came as a bombshell to everybody, especially Anna.

A large car drew up outside early in the morning. Kathleen had gone back to her own house to check on Sean and his mother, leaving Anna on her own. When Anna looked out of one of the kitchen windows, she saw a short man in a dark suit that looked more suitable for wearing in town than for a trip to the country. He was bald and wore gold-rimmed glasses. As she glimpsed him, it crossed her mind that he could be a solicitor.

She hurried to the front door and opened it just as he

put his hand out to insert a key in the keyhole. Anna looked at him in amazement.

"Hello," she said in an uncertain voice.

"And would I be right in thinking you are Pog's greatniece?" he asked, without greeting her.

She felt he had the sort of voice that could easily turn into a growl. It was somehow threatening. When he pushed past her and walked straight through the hallway and into the living-room, Anna wasn't sure what to do.

"Can I help you?" she asked, following him at a safe distance, at the same time thinking the question sounded inadequate, seeing that the man obviously knew exactly what he was doing.

"Yes, actually, you can." He regarded her puzzled face for a moment before continuing. "I am Desmond Roberts – Pog's husband."

Anna gave an involuntary gasp.

"But . . . you walked out on her nearly twenty years ago. Do you know that she's dead?"

"Of course. That's why I'm here."

Anna stared at him, still puzzled.

He walked slowly over to one of the windows and looked out at the garden. "I suppose you are still living here?"

"Yes, this is my home."

He spun round and held up a small, rather fleshy hand.

"No, my dear girl. This *was* your home. Now that my wife is dead, it is my home and I intend selling it as soon as I can."

"But –"

"I'm afraid there are no buts about it. I've been to our solicitor and, typically, he doesn't have a copy of her Will. But that's irrelevant anyway. By Irish law, this house is now mine and, unfair as it may seem, that means that you will have to find somewhere else to live."

Chapter Twenty

Two weeks after Pog Roberts' death, Anna shocked and disorientated, was on her way to the small airport at Knock. She looked out of the car window at the familiar small fields with their low stone walls and the cloud-patterned mountains that she had grown to love so much. How would she survive in a world that was flat and tamed, a world in which there was no Aunt Pog and no Kathleen? The Nolans would be getting on with their lives without her. Even Minou lay buried under a white rosebush in her aunt's garden.

Anna kept imagining that she heard her aunt's voice. It had also happened at the graveside when she and Kathleen stood close to each other, the last to linger over the cards and scented mounds of flowers. Wanting reassurance, she had asked her if Aunt Pog would have approved of the funeral service. While Kathleen nodded and replied that she was sure Mrs R would have been happy with it, Anna vividly remembered her aunt's voice when she had told them both a few months earlier how they were to behave in the event of her death.

"Which *will* happen at some point, my darlings! Now, when I eventually pop my clogs, no long faces and being miserable. I've had an extremely good innings and, on the whole, enjoyed my life. Just think of me up there, playing bridge with the angels and swigging gin from gold goblets. Mind you, having first had a word with St Peter about that bugger, Roberts. I'll be as happy as Larry, as long as *he's* not allowed through the pearly gates – Roberts, not Larry! So, if you two can't manage to organise a bloody good send-off for me, I'll come back and haunt the pair of you and make your lives a misery. I'll turn all your water into gin! Think what that would do to your cooking!"

Anna wondered what her aunt's reaction would be at the 'Bugger Roberts' turning her niece out and putting her beloved house on the market in the space of a fortnight. She guessed Pog's observations would contain quite a few fruity expletives.

Kathleen was finding it difficult to concentrate on the twisting road ahead. She felt heavy-hearted, unable to console either Anna or Amy – or herself, come to that. The manner of Anna's eviction and now, her leaving them to go to an uncertain future, had hit all of them hard. If only things could be different.

She remained silent, aware that Anna was deep in thought. Glancing over her shoulder at Amy, who was unusually quiet, Kathleen saw that her younger sister looked close to tears. It seemed extraordinary that Anna, who had been so much part of their lives over the last eight years, would no longer be there for their family anniversaries and celebrations in the future. How sad it was that there seemed no way out of her going. She wondered what thoughts filled Anna's mind.

"I don't have to tell you how much I'm going to miss you all," said Anna suddenly, looking over at Kathleen.

"Don't you think we'll miss you too?" the other replied. "I only wish that Mr Roberts had been more understanding. After all, Sandy Bay House has been your home for the last eight years. It's a terrible thing he's after doing." Kathleen sounded as indignant now as when she'd first voiced what they all thought.

Anna gave a small shrug and turned back to the view from the window.

"What's the point in getting upset? Why should I expect him to take any interest in me? I suppose it's natural that he didn't want me around. As he said, it is his house after all, now that Aunt Pog's not there any more." She turned her head and smiled slightly at Kathleen. "And I'll only be living with my mother for a little while and then I'll get a job. You never know, you may see me again sooner than you think!"

Her voice sounded falsely bright.

"Well, I could murder him! What right did he have to come back like that after the way he left Mrs R, without him telling her where he was or why? And I'd like to know who it was spied for him and sent him the news of her death."

Kathleen sounded uncharacteristically fierce.

She had been as stunned as Anna when Desmond Roberts had appeared out of nowhere and casually moved back into the house as if he had been away for a weekend. It was obvious to them all that he was not remotely upset by his wife's death. It was almost as though he was glad she had gone and he couldn't wait to have the place all to himself. The brutal way in which he made it perfectly clear to Anna that she was unwelcome and that she should go back to her mother where she belonged appalled her. To make matters worse, it seemed that Mrs R had left no Will, which put him in an even stronger position. Kathleen knew how fond of Anna her aunt had been and that she had planned to provide for her in some way.

"Must do something about that," Pog had said to her a few weeks before she died. Sadly, it appeared that, somehow, she never had got around to doing anything about it.

Kathleen had seen the look on Anna's face when the girl burst into the Nolans' kitchen with the news of Desmond Roberts' return. There had been tears in her eyes when she repeated what he had said to her.

PJ had to be restrained from rushing off immediately to Sandy Bay House and breaking down the door to confront the man. His family had never seen him so roused.

In the days that had preceded the girl's leaving, Kathleen sometimes had a fleeting glimpse in Anna's dark eyes of the forlorn nine-year-old who had arrived in Ballynacarrig all those years ago with no expectation of being welcomed or wanted.

She had seen her grow, doing her best to adjust to the local school and then later, Kilgarry Abbey. She had coped with any problems that came her way, quietly fitting into the unconventional household at Sandy Bay House, caring for her aunt and gradually, with Amy's enthusiastic assistance, becoming less introverted as she enjoyed learning the ways of country life.

Kathleen knew that there had always been times when Anna seemed to withdraw into her own world. This quality of being apart had caused some problems in the beginning at school with the other children. It reinforced their perception of her as different. She had the capacity to be self-reliant, not seeming to want or need company, often preferring to read or walk by the lake on her own. At first, Kathleen had found it strange that she cut herself off from the rest of them in the way she did. As she drove, she remembered how, for a long time after her arrival, Anna had suffered from nightmares and would be pale and distant the next day, making it impossible for either Kathleen or Mrs Roberts to get near her. In the early days, one or other of them would find her sitting with her doll and mouse, talking to them about someone called Gina or stroking the cat, trying to get it to understand a phrase or a word – like the animals in the books she seemed to love so much. Sometimes, she'd found the child staring at the lake with an expression of such sadness, it had made her catch her breath. She realised now that none of them had known, in those early days, just how much time Anna spent daydreaming of her father or of the weeks she'd spent in Italy and of her friendship with the woman called Gina.

As they drew nearer to the airport, Anna tried to force herself to stop thinking of how much she would miss her aunt. Instead she turned her thoughts to England. Although her mother had seemed genuinely sorry to hear of Aunt Pog's death when her daughter telephoned her, their conversation was stilted. They had communicated so rarely over the past few years that neither of them knew what to say to the other.

"Well, I suppose you'd better come home and we'll sort something out," her mother said, with the hint of a sigh in her voice.

Anna longed to say that Sandy Bay House was home and the last thing she wanted was to go back to live with Rosalind and her second husband. But she'd said nothing. She wondered how she would fit into her mother's new life. Would things be any better than they had been in the Cambridge house? There would be no wheelchair and, more importantly, no Mrs Battersby. Her mother had got rid of her years ago. But what about her mother's new husband, Adam Strong? Anna had a vague memory of him as being tall and rather good-looking. What would his reaction be to her re-appearance on the scene?

During their awkward telephone conversation, Rosalind had told her that she could walk quite well now with the help of a stick and that she and Adam had moved to a large and beautiful house in a pretty village just outside Cambridge.

"You'll like it," she informed Anna.

It had sounded very much like an instruction.

As they neared the small airport, Anna turned towards Kathleen.

"I think I'm going to find it difficult to fit in with my mother's ways after . . . Aunt Pog."

There was a catch in her voice.

Kathleen nodded sympathetically. She couldn't think of anything to say that might bring comfort to the girl. She was pretty sure that Anna was not exaggerating. She'd met the woman during her brief visit when Anna had been thirteen. What was it Kathleen's mother had said after her own brief encounter with Rosalind? She remembered now. The words her mother used to describe her had been, 'busy thinking about herself'. It had struck her at the time as being an accurate description.

"Don't worry, Anna. You'll be all right."

A hand appeared over the back of the seat and Amy gave Anna's shoulder a little squeeze.

"I just wish PJ had come with us. He'd say something stupid and make us all laugh."

PJ had stayed behind with his father, supposedly to deal with a difficult calving. But Amy and Kathleen both knew how devastated he was at Anna's leaving. They knew that he couldn't face having to see her off at the airport. It had been his anger at Desmond Roberts that had made Kathleen realise just how strong his feeling were towards Anna. It had always been PJ who had offered to show her how to do things on the farm when she'd first arrived and wanted to join in and give them a hand. He had spent long hours teaching her to ride Juno. No one else had ever been allowed up on the mare, especially not a novice. When they had a second horse, it was usually PJ who made sure he had the time to ride out with her. Like the rest of the family, he had watched her growing confidence with pleasure and it was he who took on the job of teaching her to drive the tractor, bring in the cattle at milking time, extract sheep ticks from the dogs' faces – and a hundred other small things. Ever since he had heard that she was leaving them, he had been unlike himself, moody and silent. He had refused to make himself available to do any more jobs at Sandy Bay House even though Mrs R's husband had offered to pay him well.

"I won't set foot in the place while that miserable bastard is there," he'd said and Kathleen knew he meant it.

At the departure gate, Anna hugged Amy, who was openly crying now.

"I'll write. I promise," she said in a choked voice.

"I know you won't," teased Anna, gently. "You're allergic to letter-writing, Amy Nolan. Perhaps you could ring me sometimes though."

"I *will* and I'll get PJ to do the writing bit."

"You will not! He's even worse with a pen than you are!"

Anna quickly kissed Kathleen's cheek. She looked into the blue eyes that had always been so full of life and fun but which now looked strained. Anna knew that she and her husband were eager to have a family and, so far, this had not happened and time was passing.

"I hope so much that everything works out for you and Sean."

"Well, don't you know the Nolans are all born optimists, Anna?"

"Of course I do. Otherwise they couldn't have put up with me and my weird ways all these years!" Anna said, doing her best to sound light-hearted. "Thank you for all you've done for me, Kathleen. I won't forget."

"Rubbish! What did I ever do except throw a bit of food in your direction from time to time and help try and keep your aunt on the straight and narrow? Though, sometimes, that was easier said than done!"

They smiled at each other.

Suddenly, the whole scene was more than Anna could bear. Thank God she had already said her farewells to Bridie Nolan, who, like her son, thought it best not to accompany Anna to the airport.

"It's enough of us you'll have with Kathleen and Amy. But I'll say a prayer for you, Anna, for a safe journey," she'd said, giving Anna a hug and then snatching up a cloth to wipe flour off the girl's clothes. "The first time you saw me, wasn't it with a rolling pin in my hand?" she laughed, doing her best to encourage Anna to laugh as well.

Now, Anna looked at Kathleen and Amy, standing close to her, as they all tried to find the appropriate words to make things look a little less bleak.

"I'll have to go or I shall cry – and with Amy already making puddles of tears on the floor, between us we'll flood the place."

She turned away from them as she showed her boarding pass and hurried through the doorway without looking back.

Looking at her, Kathleen thought how lovely Anna was with her oval face and large, dark eyes – even though she was miserable and on the point of tears. She saw several people turn to look at the tall slim girl, wondering who she was and why she seemed so upset.

Chapter Twenty-one

On her arrival at Stansted airport, Anna collected her luggage and boarded the coach for Cambridge. As they sped along the motorway, she thought how boringly flat the countryside looked and how enormous the fields of harvested corn were. Giant rolls of it, encased in ugly, black plastic, lay scattered around. She remembered the old-fashioned stooks that used to stand in tidy lines, like miniature wigwams, when her father had taken her to one of the villages when she was small, for a marvellously unhealthy cream-filled tea. She looked at the vast expanse of sky and longed for the Mayo mountains.

When the coach drew into the terminus, there was no sign of her mother. As she wondered what to do, a silver Volvo estate drew up at the kerbside in front of her and a man got out.

She had forgotten just how good-looking Adam Strong was, although, as he walked towards her, she noticed that he was greying at the temples. Probably the result of living with my mother, she thought. He looked tanned and athletic and very . . . successful was the word that sprang into her mind. And he seemed to exude an aura of satisfaction.

"Anna?"

She picked up her cases.

"Yes. Hello. What do I call you?"

"Adam will do fine. Is this the lot?" He opened up the back of the car and took the luggage from her. "No cat? I seem to remember a white, fluffy thing that followed you around all the time."

"Minou's dead."

"Oh, sorry to hear about that. Still, perhaps it's just as well. Your mother has a dog."

Adam opened the passenger door for her and watched as she folded herself with an unconsciously graceful movement into the front seat. He hadn't been expecting her to be so tall and slim and so very attractive. She had her mother's elegance, although he suspected Anna was unaware of it. He could see that she had also inherited Rosalind's long, slim body and legs and her father's dark eyes. Her clothes were simple and inexpensive and her hair was thick and lay on her shoulders in a glossy, dark-brown curtain. He wondered what his wife's reaction would be when she saw her. He started up the engine and swung the car into the busy traffic.

"Have you ever been to Little Melford?" he asked, pleasantly.

"No, I haven't. I know roughly where it is but I don't think I've ever been there."

Anna glanced at him. He seemed to be making an effort to be nice. She wondered what he really felt about her arrival.

"How is my mother?" she asked, diffidently.

The man smiled slightly.

"In her element. Living the life of the Lady of the Manor and loving every moment."

"Can she really walk now?"

"Yes, she can, pretty well. She's fought hard to get back on her feet. She's a courageous woman, your mother."

Anna supposed she was. It couldn't have been easy for her but then, if she hadn't sent me away, perhaps I could have helped her, she thought.

"How do you feel about coming back to this part of the world?"

The girl hesitated. She could hardly tell him that she was already missing Ireland and that the loss of her aunt lay like a heavy weight on her. How could she explain to him that the idea of seeing her mother again filled her with dread? What would she say if she found out what had happened to Anna by the lake? Would it fill her with disgust that her daughter was no longer a virgin? That state the nuns had hinted at as being more precious than rubies. There was a silence. "Don't worry! If you are your mother's daughter, you'll cope."

She felt herself flush with annoyance. If she was anyone's daughter, she was her father's. As far as Anna was concerned, her mother may have unwillingly given birth to her but that was the end of any real maternal involvement. She felt a surge of panic as she remembered the tone of voice her mother had regularly used when speaking to her and the look of irritation that had so often been present when her daughter did not perform in what Rosalind considered to be an appropriate manner.

"If you really want to know, I don't feel as though I belong here. I expect you both would have preferred it if I'd stayed in Ireland, out of the way."

The palms of her hands felt sweaty. Her mouth was uncomfortably dry.

"My dear girl," he replied coolly, "what I feel about the situation is neither here nor there. We have plenty of space and it will be up to you to fit in."

He accelerated into the faster moving traffic, his face expressionless.

For the remainder of the drive, there was little conversation. Anna could feel the tension mounting in her body. She wanted to shout at him to stop the car so she could get out and run; anywhere – except in the direction of Little Melford.

After a while, they turned off the motorway and she tried to concentrate on the passing countryside. She had forgotten how pretty most of the Cambridgeshire country villages were with their village greens, thatched cottages and old brick houses. There was a different charm about the scenery through which they travelled that caught her eye. Tunnels of leafy trees and lush verges, laced with cow parsley, wild campion and willow herb, flashed past as they drove along the smooth-surfaced roads. She couldn't help thinking with affection of the pot-holed, narrow laneways of Ballynacarrig and of the quirky letters of complaint her aunt wrote from time to time when she thought the council needed another gentle reminder. She shut her eyes and tried not to think.

"Right!" said Adam. "This is it!"

He turned the car into a wide driveway that curved gently so that the house was not on view from the road. As they turned the corner, she saw an expanse of well-tended lawn, half hidden by a copper beech hedge and on the other side, a large orchard. The house was a pale, icing-sugar pink with white doors and windows and was partially covered in clematis and roses. It looked, she thought, like a photo from a women's magazine, incredibly expensive and over-manicured to her eyes, used to the gentle chaos of that other house and garden in far away Ballynacarrig.

"It's known in the village as The Pink House – understandably," said Adam, switching off the engine. There was a burst of frantic barking and a long-haired dachshund hurtled around the end of the house, its feathery coat gleaming in the sunlight. "That's Ruffles. Ignore him at your peril. Oh, I forgot! You like animals, don't you?" The man's tone was quietly sardonic.

Anna climbed out of the car and bent to greet the excited dog. Adam took no notice of the animal as he started to walk towards the flight of steps that led up to the front door.

The girl hesitated, then asked nervously, "What about my cases? Shall I bring them in?"

"No, George will take them up to your room. Come inside and we'll find your mother."

She took a deep breath and followed him into the house.

Inside, she got an impression of cream walls and reflected light from windows and mirrors. Expensive-looking rugs lay on the highly polished wooden floor.

"Well, here she is, safe and sound!" the man said as he walked into the spacious drawing-room, where Rosalind sat reading in front of open French doors. "I'll leave you two to get re-acquainted. I have some work to do before dinner."

As Adam withdrew, Rosalind's green eyes stared at the figure by the door. What a change since she'd last seen her! She found it hard to believe that this tall creature was her daughter. She still had the same rather exaggerated look of reserve about her. But there was something else that hinted of . . . Rosalind wasn't sure what of – but she certainly looked a lot more adult than she'd expected.

Aware of her mother's careful scrutiny, Anna slowly crossed the room, each step an effort.

"Come and sit down beside me," said Rosalind. Still the same way of talking to me, as though I were a naughty six-year-old, thought Anna. She sat down gingerly on the edge of the chaise longue. Her mother's gaze was unwavering. "You've certainly grown!"

She even managed to make that sound like a criticism.

"It's hardly surprising really," Anna replied, carefully. "You haven't seen me since I was thirteen when you came to stay in Ballynacarrig."

She remembered how Aunt Pog had summed up the occasion afterwards as, "Quite ghastly. Best forgotten, darling."

"Did you have a good trip?"

"Yes, thank you."

Plucking up her courage, Anna returned Rosalind's gaze. She took in the beautifully lacquered nails, the elegantly simple, cream summer dress and the light tan. There were fine lines now around the woman's eyes and forehead. In spite of them, her mother was still beautiful. She also noticed a silver-topped cane lying on the floor to one side of the chaise longue.

Ruffles chose that moment to make an entrance. Seeing Anna, he trotted over to her and put his paws up on her knee.

"Good gracious! I see you've made a conquest already. Get down, you silly dog," Rosalind said, sharply.

Ruffles ignored her, looking up expectantly at the newcomer.

"How long have you had him? He's gorgeous!" Anna said, stroking the soft ears and head. She wanted to say something that might diffuse the uncomfortable atmosphere, if she could.

"Three years. There's a woman in the village who breeds them. He's got a pedigree as long as your arm."

Of course! He would have, Anna thought, suddenly amused in spite of the awkwardness. Otherwise her mother wouldn't have considered buying him. She reckoned that if Aunt Pog had had a dog, no doubt it would have been a lunatic mongrel with no manners. She patted Ruffles on the back and he immediately tried to jump up beside her.

"Is he allowed up?" she asked.

"No, he is not."

The girl searched for something to say. What could they talk about? They had nothing in common. Anna felt as though her brain had stopped functioning. Rosalind made a sudden effort to seem interested in her daughter, although she too was finding their meeting more difficult than she had anticipated.

"I was sorry to hear about Pog. I know we never got on but your father was very fond of her." Anna's expression was guarded. Rosalind continued, "I expect you miss her."

Anna could see that her mother was doing her best but she had no intention of discussing dear, mad Aunt Pog with her. She would never understand what she had meant to Anna. She got hastily to her feet.

"Do you think I could go and have a wash? I feel a bit dusty after all the travelling."

Good Lord! I think I've been snubbed, Rosalind remarked to herself with surprise.

"Of course. Push the bell to the right of the fireplace. Mrs Pender will show you to your room. We'll talk later on." As Anna walked over to the far side of the room and pressed the bell, she was aware of her mother's continued scrutiny. "Do you have many clothes with you?"

The woman's tone was deceptively casual. If the girl were going to be around for long, something would have to be done about her wardrobe. She looks a real country bumpkin in that horrible denim skirt, Rosalind thought to herself.

"I've brought everything I have."

"Good! We might need to get a few more things for you though. I suspect that Cambridge in winter is a lot colder than in the West of Ireland."

Before Anna could answer, a plump, grey-haired woman

came into the room. Her face lit up when she saw the girl. She gave a welcoming smile.

"This is Mrs P," said Rosalind. "She will take you up to your room, Anna, and make sure you have everything you need. Dinner is at seven. So you have a couple of hours to unpack and sort yourself out. Please be down by half past six."

She picked up her book.

* * *

"My husband has put your things in your room, Miss Armitage. Your mother said you should have the bedroom at the end of the landing. It looks out over the pool – it's ever so pretty." The woman's voice was cheerful and her speech had a West County lilt to it that Anna liked. At the top of the broad staircase, Mrs P led Anna to the room at the far end of the bright landing and opened the door wide for her to enter. She smiled at the girl again and asked, "Would you like me to bring up a cuppa? You must be hot and tired after your journey."

"No, thank you. I'm not thirsty. I'll unpack and lie down for a while. I do feel a little tired. What is your real name or do you prefer to be called Mrs P?"

What a nice girl, thought the woman. Not at all like her mother in her way of talking – more gently spoken, polite.

"It's Pender, dear, but Mrs P suits me just fine. Even George – he's my husband, calls me that. Odd really, 'cos he never gets called Mr P. It's always been George with him. Still, there you are! Funny things, names!" She laughed. "Are you sure you don't need nothing? It's no trouble."

"Quite sure, thank you," repeated Anna, picking up one of the heavy suitcases and manoeuvring it onto the bed.

"Then I'll leave you in peace, dear."

Mrs P scuttled out of the room, closing the door quietly behind her. She wanted to find George. She couldn't wait to tell him about this girl, who had never been mentioned in all the three years they had worked for the Strongs. She was sure that no photo of her existed anywhere in the house – just like there was no picture of Mrs Strong's first husband to be seen about the place either. She thought the whole thing was very odd. Why would anyone want to make a secret of having a lovely girl like that for a daughter? She tutted to herself quietly as she hurried down the stairs.

Anna unlocked her case, musing on the cheery Mrs P. She was a definite improvement on the Bat! She delved into the middle of her hastily packed clothes and extracted a bundle wrapped in a faded, blue, silk dressing-gown. Kneeling beside the bed, she unwrapped the silver photograph frame, the hairbrush and the bottle of now scentless cologne.

As she walked over to the chest of drawers, Anna glanced out into the garden below. Flowering shrubs dotted the back lawn where herbaceous borders and roses were carefully laid out in gracefully curving beds. A swimming pool glinted attractively in the afternoon sun. Mock Grecian urns spilled cascades of white and pink geraniums down their sides. She sighed. Everything was so tasteful, so tidy. Even the plants had been made to toe the line.

Anna knew that Aunt Pog would have hated it all.

She wondered what sort of a relationship her mother had with her second husband. He didn't look to her like the sort of person who would allow himself to be organised.

* * *

She was woken by the sound of someone knocking on her door. For a few seconds, the girl could not remember where she was. She felt sticky and hot.

"It's Mrs P, dear. Your mother was wondering where you were."

Anna sat up quickly, brushing her hair from her face. She looked at the square, blue-faced watch her aunt had given her for her seventeenth birthday. It was nearly a quarter to seven. With a sinking feeling, she remembered her mother's instructions to be downstairs by half past six.

"I'll be down in a minute, thank you, Mrs P," she called, as she hastily dragged her crumpled shirt over her head and stumbled into the bathroom to splash cold water on her face.

This is a good start, she thought. She had wanted to appear looking tidy and on time – now she would be late. Hastily donning the least creased of her summer dresses, Anna picked up a comb and slipped her feet into sandals as she tugged at the tangled knots. She gave a quick look in the dressing-table mirror. 'Oh Lord!' she said to herself. 'This will just have to do.' She raced down the stairs, pausing in the hall to regain her composure before going into the elegant room that overlooked the terrace.

Conversation stopped as she entered. Rosalind and Adam both turned to look at her. Anna was sure they had been talking about her. Her mother made no comment at her belated appearance, but the girl could feel her irritation like cold waves washing against her skin. Adam rose as she made her way across the room.

Watching her cautious approach, he thought she looked incredibly attractive, her face smooth and rested. The pale yellow dress accentuated the deep brown of her skin and the fact that it was a little short for her made her look long and leggy. He rather liked that look.

What struck Rosalind was the fact that the dress looked home-made and was creased – and the material looked cheap.

Adam smiled at Anna.

"Come and sit down, Anna. What would you like to drink? There's sherry, gin, whiskey, martini, soft drinks if you'd prefer?"

"What about an orange juice?" intervened Rosalind.

Anna smiled back at Adam.

"I would love a gin and tonic."

"One gin and tonic coming up. Make yourself comfortable. We've plenty of time before dinner is ready."

Anna sat down and turned to her mother.

"I'm sorry I was late. I lay on the bed for a few minutes and the next thing I knew, Mrs P was knocking on the door."

"We'll have to get you an alarm clock," Rosalind replied, sipping her sherry. "Tell me, when did you start to drink alcohol?"

"When I was about fourteen, I think."

Rosalind's well-shaped eyebrows rose. "I suppose I

should be thankful you aren't a full-blown alcoholic like Pog."

Anna frowned. "Aunt Pog said it was a good idea to get used to having the odd drink." Her voice was defensive.

"A pity your aunt didn't stick to the idea of having the odd drink."

The girl did not answer her. There had been an unpleasant edge to the way the remark had been made. It reminded her of the distant past and how her mother had so often spoken to Anna's father. Taking the glass from Adam, she took a mouthful of the cool drink, inhaling the scent of lemon. Her aunt had been unable to persuade her that her own preferred tipple of gin and water was anything but disgusting and since Anna had been allowed to have the occasional drink, they had agreed to amicably disagree on the subject.

"Do you play tennis, Anna?" asked Adam, coming to the rescue.

"Sort of. I played at school but I wasn't good enough to get into the school team or anything like that."

"Well, we have a reasonably good hard court here. Perhaps you will give me a game at the weekend."

Anna looked vague. She could imagine that Adam played well and that he played to win. He wouldn't be used to the wildly erratic sort of tennis that she and Amy used to play on the abandoned court belonging to old Mrs Henry near Ballynacarrig. She knew with certainty that he would be completely out of her league. But at least he wasn't giving her the cold shoulder.

* * *

After dinner, Anna made her excuses and slipped out into the garden, closely followed by Ruffles. The food had been delicious but the formal atmosphere and conversation about places and people unknown to her had made her feel stifled. She was used to supper trays on knees, in front of the telly, often with her aunt cheerfully hurling abuse at some politician, who was in the process of being interviewed.

The smell of night-scented stock and lilies drifted over the garden. It was mid-July – summer at its height. The evening air was heavy with residual heat from the day. She sat on a wooden seat at the far end of the lawn and looked back at the house with its windows lit up invitingly. Anna could see her mother, leaning slightly on her cane as she moved across the drawing-room. She watched Adam, as he took his wife's arm and walked with her to the door at the far side of the room, matching his pace to hers. It suddenly struck her that, from as far back as she could remember, she had never seen her look so content. She had certainly never been like that with Anna's father. She felt surprised. Contentment was not the sort of word she would have used in relation to her mother. Anna couldn't help thinking of her only in terms of dissatisfied, uncompromising and, sometimes, rather cruel. Perhaps she loved her second husband. Was that why she was so different with him?

As she walked slowly back to the house, Anna went over the uncomfortable conversation that had taken place during the after-dinner cup of coffee. She had admitted to them that she had not been an ideal pupil during her last term at Kilgarry Abbey and had probably failed most of her final school exams. Anna promised herself that they would never find out why she had not been in a fit state either to study or to sit exams.

"Well, you're obviously not university material then," her mother had said. "Perhaps you're underestimating yourself and you will be pleasantly surprised when the results come out."

"I don't think so," said Anna.

Her mother gave a small sigh.

"Well, perhaps we can get you into the Tech to do some sort of a course or other."

She sounded disappointed.

"Do you have any idea what you might like to study?" Adam asked.

Anna shook her head. "Not really. I don't think I want to study anything at the moment."

Aunt Pog had told her not to worry about the future, that something would crop up that would catch her interest when the time was right. Until then, she mustn't worry. She was fine.

The nuns had disagreed. In her end-of-term report, they commented on Anna's lack of stamina, her lack of concentration, her lack of attention to detail and her lack of devotion. Even given her aunt's illness, during the final term, they felt that she had not really tried. She had not shone in any area of the school curriculum and in their eyes she had let herself, and them, down.

Her aunt had always understood when Anna explained why she was not prepared to play netball or hockey with the deadly concentration and ferocity that was apparently required.

"It's not like I'm doing something really important when we have games. When I start hurting, then I stop!"

"Very sensible, my darling. Bloody silly way to carry on! All that winning – whatever the cost. It was just the same when I was at school. It was the ones with the hairy legs and the flat chests who got most excited by all that sport thing."

Anna stared up into the star-studded sky. As far as she was concerned, if things started hurting then it was foolish to go on taking part in whatever it was that was causing the hurt. It didn't matter whether it was a hockey match or a relationship. Surely, she thought, it was better to withdraw, rather than be made to look a fool or worse still, end up by being badly hurt. That was why she wanted to find some way out of having to stay any longer than was necessary in this expensive, well-ordered house where she knew she didn't belong.

Chapter Twenty-two

The following day, Rosalind made her first move to remedy
what she saw as a complete lack of suitable clothing in
Anna's wardrobe. She stood, looking down at the sorry
collection of garments spread out on her daughter's bed.
Gingerly picking up a pair of jeans with patched knees, she
held the garment in front of her with her fingertips.

"I don't think they would take these in the Oxfam shop."

"That's all right – I like them," said Anna.

The patches had come from an old jacket of Aunt Pog's.

"And what about this extraordinary thing?"

"Bridie Nolan made that waistcoat for me. It's lovely
and warm," countered her daughter, steadily.

She realised that her mother wouldn't be interested in
knowing that it had been made out of pieces from a quilt
that Pog had once used.

Rosalind picked up, then discarded several more items
of clothing.

"I can't see anything that would be suitable for a drinks party. I presume that, as you drink gin and tonic, you do go to drinks parties?" she asked, dryly.

"Sometimes. It was never a problem – what I wore, I mean," replied Anna, thinking how it had never seemed to matter how she had been dressed when she and her aunt had entertained or been entertained.

Aunt Pog had always worked on a system of the later in the day the event was taking place, the higher her heels became and the more glitter she wore, because that was how she liked it. She had not once criticised anything Anna had chosen to wear and had more often than not encouraged her to be daring, to do her own thing and wear whatever seemed right to her at the time. Now, Anna was quietly determined that not one item of clothing would be given away to Oxfam, or anywhere else, by her mother.

"I think the best thing to do is make a clean sweep and start again." Rosalind's voice was firm.

"No!"

"I beg your pardon, Anna?"

"I said no. I like my clothes. Some of them were bought for me by Aunt Pog and some things Kathleen helped me make."

Rosalind stared at her daughter, genuinely bewildered. Surely the girl could see that most of the clothes were just tat. Perhaps a little gentle persuasion would make her come to her senses.

"Anna, I know you've only just arrived but don't you think it would be a good idea to get yourself organised?" She hunted for the right words. "Life in Cambridge is very different from life in rural Ireland. I just want you to have the right sort of things to wear. I would enjoy helping you choose some new clothes."

Rosalind's encouraging tone made Anna feel ungracious.

"Yes, I know. Thank you. But I'm not getting rid of any of my clothes."

"All right! You don't have to." Her mother gave a quick smile to hide her frustration. "But I think we'll do a little shopping this afternoon." She noticed the stubborn glint in Anna's eyes. "Just to fill in some of the gaps in your . . . collection."

On her way out of the bedroom, Rosalind gave a slight start. Hanging on the back of the door was an old, blue, silk dressing-gown.

"Was that your . . ."

"Yes, that was Daddy's," said Anna, in a dangerously quiet voice. "So, we don't need to buy a dressing-gown."

Leaning on her stick, Rosalind observed her daughter coldly.

"Lunch is at one. We'll go shopping straight afterwards. I will expect you to be ready."

"OK."

Anna's tone was resigned.

After her mother left the room, Anna went over to the bedside table and opened the drawer. She extracted a moth-eaten mouse and a small doll that had once held dried flowers in one of its cloth hands. What a long time ago it was when Gina and Alfredo had given her those gifts. What were they doing now? Had they married and had lots of children? Had Chiara found another husband?

She sat down on the bed, holding them in her lap and wept silent, salty tears.

* * *

George had driven the Mercedes coupé around to the front steps for Rosalind, who was now sitting in the driver's seat waiting for Anna. She had been there for a full two minutes and she was tired of being delayed. She gave a prolonged blast on the car horn. Anna appeared in the doorway, Ruffles dancing at her feet.

"Can we bring him?" she called out, thinking that the dog might provide a little light relief from the grind of shopping with her mother.

"Of course not! He'll only leave dog's hairs all over the car. Come on, Anna! Do get in."

She watched as the girl bent down to give Ruffles a farewell pat. He responded by licking her hand.

'Good Lord!' thought Rosalind. 'Not only is she wearing that awful denim thing but now she's covered in dog-drool as well'. She sighed impatiently, tapping the steering wheel with her perfect nails.

* * *

Anna and her mother emerged from the smart little boutique at the far end of the village, Rosalind looking furious. She glared at her sullen daughter, who was disdainfully dangling three glossy green and gold carrier bags as though they contained something unpleasant.

Anna had felt intimidated by the chic saleswoman and

had disliked the way she and her mother had discussed her as though she were invisible. She had slipped into a daydream, remembering how her aunt had believed in trying to bargain for anything she fancied, even in the smart Dublin shops, on one of her rare visits away from the peace of Ballynacarrig. She had never let uppity sales staff intimidate *her*. Anna could hear her saying in that gravelly voice she missed so much, 'They forget they're there to help you, not tell you what you should be wearing. Cheeky so-and-sos', as she laughingly lit up a cigarette, blissfully unaware of the 'No Smoking' sign immediately above her head.

"What on earth do you think you were playing at in there?" Rosalind demanded, as soon as they were back in the car.

"What do you mean?"

"You know perfectly well what I mean! You made no effort whatsoever to be helpful. Helen showed you dozens of lovely things and the best you could manage was to say that they were 'OK', but not what you needed. Did you have to be so uncooperative?"

"I just don't see what's wrong with the clothes I've got. I felt silly in those things."

"But you even made a fuss over the underwear, for God's sake!"

"I've never worn a bra. Aunt Pog said I didn't need one."

"Oh, Anna!" Rosalind was becoming more and more exasperated and she was finding her daughter's slight Irish accent increasingly irritating. "Pog was not the best person to hold forth on the subject of good taste, especially in the area of clothes, I seem to remember."

Suddenly, Anna turned on her, her face distorted with anger.

"Maybe not! But I loved her and she loved me for what I was – am, and that's more than you've *ever* done. That matters to me a thousand times more than wearing the right frocks. She didn't care what people thought. She said you had to be yourself and if other people didn't like the way you were, then that was their problem, not yours. You have absolutely no right to criticise her."

She slumped back in her seat, shaken by her own outburst and fighting back angry tears.

There was an awkward silence. Rosalind sat, staring through the windscreen, her hands gripping the wheel.

Then she turned towards her daughter and said, in a measured voice, "Yes, you are probably right, Anna. I shouldn't make fun of her and I'm glad that she was able to give you what I seemed to be incapable of giving."

Anna was instantly contrite.

"I'm sorry. I shouldn't have spoken to you like that. I'm really sorry."

She desperately regretted being responsible for that unexpected, anguished look she had glimpsed on her mother's face a few moments earlier.

As they sat, unspeaking, in the glare of the afternoon sun, a young man and woman who looked as though they were in their late teens or early twenties, passed by the open-top, sleek, green car. The girl's hair was bright pink, cut in a shaggy crop that stood up from her skull. She wore large gypsy earrings and torn jeans and it was obvious that she didn't believe in wearing a bra either.

Her companion looked as though he had slept in his crumpled T-shirt and tartan trousers. His hair was short and platinum. He had his arm draped around the girl's neck. They stopped a few yards down the street and looked back in the direction of the two silent women in the car. He made a remark to the girl. They both laughed as they strolled on their way.

Neither Anna nor Rosalind noticed them.

* * *

In an attempt to make up for her behaviour that afternoon, Anna put on one of the new silk dresses for dinner. When she joined them in the drawing-room, Adam immediately commented on her appearance.

"You look splendid, Anna." He turned towards his wife. "How clever of you! Your taste is perfect, as always."

Rosalind looked pleased. Anna watched her, as she sipped her drink before dinner. It was as though nothing had happened between them. Her mother's manner towards her seemed unchanged as if Anna's outburst had been completely forgotten. She appeared as cool and self-possessed as always. Anna began to wonder if she had imagined that almost lost look she thought she had seen, briefly, that afternoon in the car. She is as much a stranger to me as Adam, she thought, sadly.

"Have you had any more ideas about the sort of course you might do at the Tech, Anna?"

Adam's voice made her jump. She said the first thing that came into her mind.

"Perhaps I could do a secretarial course."

271

Rosalind seized on the idea.

"Delia Chivers has just done one and she's landed a marvellous job with the fashion editor of *Vogue* in London. Her parents live in the village, Anna. You'll meet them on Sunday. I've invited a few friends in for a drink before lunch. She's a good person to get to know. She's really 'in' with the County set and she could be very useful to you."

Anna wondered what the County set was like. Loud voices, smug expressions, guns and green wellies sprang to mind. She'd seen some of the Anglo-Irish version and hadn't liked much of what she'd seen. She thought it was highly probable that she and Delia Chivers would have little in common.

"I'll get on to the Tech in the morning and see if they have any spare places. I think term starts at the end of August, so it may not be easy to get you in but I'll see what can be managed."

Rosalind's tone was so determined, Anna thought she had better go along with her plans and hoped that it wouldn't be too dreadful. Up until that moment, she had never once thought of becoming a secretary.

* * *

Her mother was as good as her word and an interview was arranged for the following Friday at the Technical College in Cambridge.

"They're sure to take you. I had a word with the Principal."

So that was that! Perhaps it would be useful to be able to type, Anna told herself, doubtfully. During the days that followed, she tried to be pleasant and cheerful. She also did her best to look and sound grateful for all the unwanted garments that were purchased on her behalf. She even gave in to having her long hair cut to a shoulder-length bob. After the deed was done, she secretly rather liked the new look. She was pleasantly surprised to find how much more comfortable it felt, for the weather continued to be unreasonably hot and heavy.

Even Ruffles lost some of his bounce and chose to lie spread-eagled on the cool, tiled floor in the kitchen where he dozed fitfully under the kitchen table.

* * *

As expected, Anna found the Sunday drinks party tedious beyond words. Her nervousness made it difficult for her to remember the names of the people to whom she had been introduced. As soon as she could, she tried to slip out of the crowded room. But before she could make her escape, a pretty, blonde girl came up to her. The stranger held out a hand and said, in an affected voice, "You must be the mysterious Anna! My name's Delia."

"Oh, hello," said Anna, trying not to spill her drink or drop the canapé, whose creamy filling was melting between her fingers, as she shook the other's hand.

Delia Chivers eyed her up and down, taking note of the expensive dress and beautifully cut hair.

"Do you hunt?"

"No."

"Not even drag?"

"No."

273

"What about tennis?"

"I'm afraid I'm not very good at it."

Delia looked a little lost. There was a pause.

"We have a boat in Norfolk. It's splendid fun! Do you sail?"

"I'm afraid not. I get rather seasick. Though I used to go out with the others to check the lobster pots sometimes."

Delia's eyes widened slightly.

"Oh!" She made a final, valiant attempt to find common ground. "Do tell me. What do you like doing?"

"I like reading."

"*House and Garden, Tatler, Vogue?* That sort of thing? Personally, I adore magazines that have horoscopes. Mummy says they're absolute rubbish but she reads them too when she thinks no one is looking! Daddy teases her no end about it!"

Anna became animated for the first time during their conversation.

"Have you read any TH White or Tolkien? I think they are marvellous writers. I've just finished reading the *Alexandrian Quartet* by Durrell. Do you know it?"

It was now Delia's turn to say no. She wondered why on earth her mother had made such a fuss about her making friends with this strange creature, who seemed completely uninterested in anything sensible. She sounds odd too, she thought. If she were Rosalind Strong's daughter, then, she was surprisingly non-U.

She drifted over to talk to Anita Hollingsworth, with whom she felt completely at home. They compared notes and came to the conclusion that Anna, despite her acceptable clothes and hairstyle, was hardly the sort of person they would want to include in their inner circle.

The two girls' mothers were also discussing the newcomer. With the same old faces always turning up at these local drinks parties, it was nice to have something new to talk about.

"It's really rather strange, her turning up like this out of the blue. Did Rosalind ever mention to you the fact that she had a daughter?" asked Mrs Chivers.

"Not a word! She's very pretty. Why on earth would she want to keep her a secret?" said Mrs Hollingsworth.

"Perhaps Anna is a love child."

"Rosalind have a love child? I think not! She's far too well organised for that."

They both laughed tinkling laughs.

"She was married before, I believe. The girl must be the product of the first marriage. I gather she's been living in the wilds of Ireland. That might explain why she's looking so ill at ease now, poor dear!"

"I think that's what Rosalind said. She hasn't really talked about her that much."

"Good heavens! She has an almost Continental look about her, doesn't she? Her mother will have to break her in and get her used to our ways."

"No better woman for the job, I'd say!" remarked Mrs Chivers, dropping the subject as she noticed a short, blonde woman entering the room on her own. "Oh, do look! There's Dodo, back from the Caribbean. I'm dying to hear all the gossip. Apparently the Gore-Smythes bumped into her while they were there and they said her husband was nowhere to be seen and that she was having a fling with a waiter!"

"No! Really?"

"Really! And he was as black as they come!"

"No! I don't believe it!"

"Oh, you can believe it all right, my dear. Come on! Let's see what she has to say for herself!"

Anna stood by herself in a corner of the room. She was watching her mother as she moved from guest to guest. Although it was hot, she looked composed and cool as she perched on the arm of a chair here and the back of a couch there, so that people forgot she walked with a slight limp and that she had to use her cane from time to time.

Anna wondered if anyone else had ever noticed what she had been quick to spot: that the more annoyed her mother was, the more obviously she leaned on her cane.

Adam too was an excellent host. He looked relaxed, as though he were enjoying himself as he smilingly circulated amongst the guests, making sure that he talked to everyone.

Mrs P appeared at Anna's side. She was obviously finding it hot. Perspiration made her cheerful face look shiny and her cheeks were glowing. She thrust a plate of wafer-thin asparagus rolls at the girl.

"Come on, my dear. Have one of these. I made them myself, so I know they're good!"

Anna took one and bit in. The asparagus slithered out of the far end of the roll and fell, slug-like, onto the carpet.

"Oh dear! Now look what I've done!" she moaned.

"Doesn't matter a bit, dear. It'll all come up in the

hoover after," said Mrs P, with a broad smile. She moved on to offer some to the other guests.

Rosalind was watching Anna, while appearing to give her full attention to the conversation going on around her. Perhaps she'd been unwise and this party was a little premature. The girl would need quite a bit of grooming to make her really presentable. At least now she was decently dressed – that was a start. She smiled brightly at Anita's mother whom she knew perfectly well was dying to know more about this girl who had appeared from nowhere. The wretched woman was making her way over with a determined look on her face. Damn her! Rosalind thought to herself, as she prepared to take evasive action.

Chapter Twenty-three

Anna stood at the bus stop. The sun beat down on her face with an intensity that had been missing in the West of Ireland. She'd only been waiting for ten minutes but was already starting to wilt and feel thirsty. She stepped back on to the grass, into the dappled shade of a tall chestnut tree. It was two o'clock and there seemed to be no one moving around. It was as if the whole of Little Melford had taken to its bed for a most un-English siesta.

She looked down the village street, which appeared to shimmer in the heat, making the whitewashed thatched cottages dance and phantom puddles of water come and go in the glare. Brushing the perspiration off her upper lip with her hand, she wondered how long she would have to wait for the bus. Rosalind had offered her a lift, pointing out that the bus ride would be hot and uncomfortable.

"Why do you want to go into Cambridge on an afternoon like this?" she'd asked, puzzled.

"I just want to have a look around on my own. I've been here for nearly two weeks now and I would like to wander around Cambridge without feeling that I'm holding you up."

"Well, I can take you in. I suppose I can find something to do while you are having a wander."

"No, really. There's no need. Thanks."

Her mother had stared at her for a moment, before turning away.

What Anna wanted most was to go back to some of the old haunts of her father's, quietly and at her own pace. She longed to see the places they had visited together, like the café where he had drunk his coffee and told her his silly jokes while she ate meringues and coffee éclairs. She remembered how he used to wait until her mouth was full and then make her laugh. Anna would cough and splutter while he patted her on the back and threatened to call an ambulance to cart her off to hospital. She wanted to go back to the small church where he and she had gone from time to time and which had a churchyard like a wild garden. If she could face it, she might even take a look at their old house in Grange Road. Perhaps not, she thought. The memories would be altogether too painful there. But wherever she chose to go, she was certain that she did not want her mother's company on this bitter-sweet wander through her past.

To Anna's consternation, Rosalind had successfully talked her way into her daughter being given a place at the Tech. This meant that Anna had three weeks left in which to rediscover and to remember, before term started.

She leaned sleepily against the tree trunk, head resting on the smooth bark, eyelids closed.

"You meditatin' or what?" asked a husky voice beside her.

Anna jumped. She didn't recognise the girl who had passed by the car a few days earlier. Now she looked at her with interest, never having seen spiky pink hair before. It looked as though the other had suffered a substantial electric shock. She was wearing patched jeans and an orange top decorated with the signs of the zodiac. It clashed violently with her hair. Anna also noticed that the girl had extraordinarily long legs and the most amazing light blue eyes.

"No, I was just thinking with my eyes shut," she replied, smiling shyly. "Why? Do you meditate?"

"Nah, not any more. Got tired of mantras. I done all that alternative stuff – the lot. Started wiv TM then I was a Moonie for a bit. Even tried being a Buddhist. That weren't too bad but I don't fancy having to follow rules other people make, so I ended up doing my own fing. Wot about you? My name's Jess, by the way. I come from London 'fore I ended up 'ere."

She stuck out a non-too-clean hand, which Anna shook.

"I'm Anna Armitage. I haven't tried any of those things but I've just come back from living in Ireland with my aunt and she liked to do things her way too. She hardly ever followed rules. She said that, sometimes, you had to make them up for yourself as you went along." Anna's voice became reflective. "She had a lot of fun doing that."

"Sound woman!" said Jess, approvingly. "I thought you sounded a bit Irish. Did she die or somefink? Only you said she *had* lots of fun."

"Yes," replied Anna. "She died." For a horrible moment, she thought she was going to cry. This is ridiculous, she told herself. What is the matter with me? She swallowed hard and said, in a slightly shaky voice, "She was lovely. Aunt Pog didn't care what you did and she never minded me making mistakes, even if it made things difficult for her. She'd just laugh and tell me to try again."

Anna wondered why she had blurted all this out to a complete stranger. Jess reached out impulsively and lightly touched Anna's arm.

"I'm ever so sorry," she said, in a quieter voice. "You sounded real sad just then – you must miss her a lot." She peered with interest into Anna's face and then grinned. "Still, I reckon your parents are loaded and that counts for somefink, even if they are a drag like most of 'em. Them were a nice set of wheels you 'ad the other day," she said, enviously. "Do you live in the one of them posh houses back there?" She jerked her head in the direction of The Pink House.

Anna nodded. She did not want to get into the subject of parents or her family life but she couldn't help liking this Jess with her crazy hair and gypsy earrings and the way she had of looking you straight in the eye, as though she were really taking in what you were saying.

"Do you live with your parents here in Melford?"

"Gawd no!" Jess looked horrified at the idea. "I'm kipping down the other end of the green in a caravan wiv Marv."

"Marv?"

"Yup, If you 'ad been more wiv it the other day, you'd a seen us when we was walking past your mum's car. 'E was the one in the tartan trousers. 'E looks drop-dead gorgeous in them!"

"What's his real name?"

"Marvin. I call 'im Marv for short. 'E thinks that's because 'e's marvellous!" She giggled. "'E's not that great. Still, there's no harm in letting 'im hang on to 'is little illusions. Blokes like to feel looked up to, don't they? Anyway, I quite like 'im." Jess picked her nose thoughtfully with the little finger of her left hand. "You got one then?"

"One what?" asked Anna, cautiously.

"A bloke . . ." Jess broke off as a dusty, red double-decker bus appeared in the heat haze at the other end of the street. " About time! That geezer's always late and I'm just about meltin' here."

Anna did not want to get onto the subject of blokes either.

"Where are you going to, Jess?" she asked, as they climbed on board.

"Oh, I got fings to see to. Stuff to get an' that."

When they were seated, Jess dug into the pocket of her jeans for the fare. She fished out a collection of coins, entangled in a piece of string, together with a broken comb and some fluff. She handed the money to the impatient conductor, who immediately returned one of the coins.

"That one's foreign, miss. As you are no doubt well aware."

Jess gave him an enormous grin. The man looked unimpressed.

"Ooh, I *am* sorry. It's all this travellin' around I do. I get ever so mixed up with me money." She winked at Anna, as he moved off down the bus. "Miserable old git. It worked a treat last week with the other bloke." She yanked open one of the windows and sat down again with a sigh. "Now I'll 'ave to try and 'itch a lift back. Funds are running a little low at the moment. And I'll 'ave to look around for a proper job." She shook her head sadly.

"I can give you the fare." Anna still had some change in her hand.

"Great! Thanks." Jess pocketed the money. "I don't suppose you got any fags on you?"

"No, sorry. I don't smoke. My aunt was always puffing away at a cigarette and I used to get a bit fed up with the smell. It got everywhere and it made her so ill. I suppose that put me off."

"Dead right! Filthy 'abit! I'll scrounge some off me mates in town. I got some gum anyway."

Anna politely declined the packet of gum Jess waved at her. She noticed that the fingers of the girl's right hand were stained orange from past cigarettes. Perhaps that was why her voice sounded so hoarse.

They talked all the way into Cambridge. Jess told her that she and Marv had a street-trader's licence and they made earrings and rings, which they sold in town on Saturdays to supplement their dole money. She had run away from her parents at sixteen and spent three miserable months living in a squat in London, where she had met Marv.

"We've been togever for two years now."

"How did you manage for food when you were in the squat?" Anna asked, intrigued. When Jess elaborated on her life in London, she was appalled at the other's description of the rat-infested squalor in which she had lived.

"Stole stuff mostly. There was soup kitchens but some of them was real dodgy. You know, holy molies. You could tell they was only doing it so's they'd get the chance to convert you. That, or making sure they'd get parking space in Heaven. It wasn't all bad though. Met up wiv a few real characters. There was one old Irish geezer wiv one of them penny whistle fings. 'E couldn't half play that! When he wasn't pissed out of his skull!" Jess gave a hoot of laughter, which made a couple of elderly countrywomen look over their shoulders and stare. She called out cheerfully to them. "Like to join us for a larf, then?"

Affronted, they looked away quickly. Anna felt a little embarrassed by their embarrassment. It appeared that Jess didn't care what people thought of her.

The two girls parted at the bus terminus. Jess hoisted her disintegrating woven bag, decorated with tassels, onto her shoulder and gave Anna a grin.

"See you 'round then! Might pop in for cocktails sometime," she added mischievously. Then seeing the doubtful look on Anna's face, she laughed. "Don't worry! Lager's more our kind of booze. Anyway, Marv wouldn't know wot to do wiv anything fancy like a cocktail!"

Anna watched her as she loped off towards the town centre to rendezvous with her mates. She noticed that a tear in the seat of Jess's jeans opened and closed as she walked, revealing a strip of white buttock.

She set off in what she hoped was the direction of the Copper Kettle where she and her father had spent so many Friday teatimes. She wandered along slowly, taking in her surroundings.

It all seemed so much busier than she remembered. She was astonished at the crowded pavements and the number of new shops. Even the bookshop her father had taken her to had moved and, when she came upon it unexpectedly, she was intrigued by how large and imposing it had become. She hesitated outside, admiring the window display. It wasn't all that far from the Tech. She would be able to visit it after the classes were over, before catching the evening bus back to Little Melford.

Turning a corner, she stopped in her tracks. The market square had been made into a pedestrian precinct. Anna liked the way the stalls looked with their brightly striped awnings and no parked cars cluttering up the place. She picked her way between the fruit and vegetables and racks of Indian cotton blouses and shiny nylon track suits, enjoying the bustle and colour. She listened, fascinated, to the flat, Cambridge accent she had almost forgotten. It sounded strangely unmusical and monotonous after what she was used to in Ireland.

As the university term had not yet started, the flocks of undergraduates, tearing from one lecture to the next on their bicycles, were missing from Anna's remembered picture of the town. She cut through a side alley, past the University Church to King's Parade or KP, as it had always been called.

In front of her, King's College Chapel was bathed in

golden sunlight. The enormous chestnut tree still stood as she remembered on the velvet grass in front of the chapel, its leaves beginning to turn yellow and russet.

For a long time, Anna studied the line of college buildings, which stretched the length of the street on one side. She experienced a sudden, unexpected feeling of having come home. The details had become blurred over the years but, standing there, it all somehow seemed intensely familiar, almost as if she had never been away. For the first time in a while, she thought of Pisa and Gina and Alfredo. If she ever went back there, would she experience the same pang of recognition? Or had it all happened too long ago? She decided it was best not to think of Italy. It brought back so many sad, muddled memories and unanswered questions.

She started to walk briskly along the pavement, scanning the shops to her left. The Copper Kettle, where she and her father had gone after school on Fridays, had vanished. Anna retraced her steps to make sure, wondering if her memory was playing tricks. For some reason, it hadn't crossed her mind that the café would not still be where it had always been and she felt cheated. After some minutes, standing, staring at the smart new dress shop that had usurped the café's place, she found herself wandering along aimlessly, being jostled by shoppers and tourists.

Perhaps this is an omen, Anna found herself thinking. People say you should never go back, especially to places that held happy memories – it would always be a disappointment.

Surely the church would still be where she remembered

it? They could hardly have taken that away! Anna decided she would find it, even if she didn't feel up to going back to the old house.

Turning off the main street, she crossed the river, pausing to gaze down at the punts below. That too brought back vivid memories. As she walked, she felt perspiration trickling down her shoulder blades and between her breasts. 'Please, oh, please let it be there and let it be the same,' she prayed, remembering how her aunt used to mutter a quick prayer to the 'Man upstairs,' as she called Him. At unexpected moments, Aunt Pog would drop into a church – it didn't matter which one – when they had been out shopping, to light a candle and say a quick Hail Mary when something was bothering her particularly. If prayers did not have the desired effect, her aunt could be very forthright in her dealings with the Almighty. As she walked, Anna remembered how she had seen her shake a fist at the heavens and quote St Theresa of Avila: "No wonder You have so few friends, if this is the way you treat them!"

To Anna's relief, the church was there and the garden was as wild as ever she had remembered – perhaps even more overgrown and tangled. She opened the side gate and walked up to the solid, wooden doors. They seemed to be locked. Grasping the iron looped handle, she tried again. How could it be closed? she wondered. The church in Ballynacarrig had been open night and day. There had always been someone praying, lighting a candle or just sitting quietly with their thoughts. A church with closed doors seemed to negate the very reason for its existence, as a place of sanctuary and retreat.

Disappointed, she turned away and wandered along the narrow, gravel path that led towards the churchyard. Most of the tombstones were well over a hundred years old. Several of them leaned slightly as though, like the neglected garden around them, they too had given in to winter gales and the passing of time. Many of the carved names had become illegible, with green moss and orange lichen fanning out over the chiselled script. In one corner, there was an old, wooden seat beside a multi-spired yew.

Anna sat down thankfully and gazed at the wild flowers that flourished side by side with a rambling rose and some half-smothered shrubs. She was aware of the sound of traffic in the street beyond but it was remarkably peaceful there in the small jungle-garden. It was this quality of tranquillity that she remembered so well. Closing her eyes, she let herself slip back into the past. She visualised her father sitting beside her while she, aged six, on that summer's day so long ago, told him about the unicorn she had seen in a picture in the art catalogue belonging to her mother. She remembered how he had listened carefully to her detailed description of the animal with its muzzle resting so lightly in the palm of the young girl's hand. When she had informed him earnestly that she *knew* unicorns existed, he had smiled and said, "Of course they exist, my darling. And dragons and elves and all sorts of other magic things. What is sad is that the grown-ups forget that they are there. They're far too busy trying to earn a living to think about things like that. You have to be a very special, lucky person to ever see a unicorn but perhaps one day you will – even if it is only from a distance. But Annie, you probably won't be able to make anyone believe that you have seen one – and that's sad too."

He'd seemed so full of unspoken regret. His melancholy had touched something in Anna but she had not known what words to use to make him smile again.

She opened her eyes, determined not to think about things that made her sad. Even though the church was closed to her and the churchyard uncared for, it was lovely there in the shade of the ancient yew.

As she looked around her, she felt a sudden rush of heightened awareness. It was almost as if all the colours surrounding her had suddenly become more intense. The cumulus clouds above seemed to have swollen into larger, fatter piles of whiteness and she became aware of all sorts of tiny noises, unnoticed before. The little scrapes and patters and resonances made by hundreds of unseen animals and insects. The sun-bleached grasses rustled and she could almost imagine she heard other dry voices, which rasped and crackled and scratched on the very edge of her hearing. Vaguely, she remembered reading a book by Virginia Woolf, in which the author described that same sense of intensity – as if one were seeing the world properly for the first time ever. She shivered suddenly. What was the point in daydreaming like this? It only made her feel sad and filled with a sense of unreality. Like Amy had said to her once: "Come on, Anna! If you could see the face on you! Anyone would think it was the end of the world. What's the point in worrying about things? I don't. Result: perfect happiness! Well almost!"

Anna got to her feet. She'd better hurry or she'd miss the Little Melford bus.

Chapter Twenty-four

What had seemed like a horrible mistake at the beginning turned into a reasonably enjoyable experience for Anna. She regretted having suggested learning secretarial skills the moment the words had passed her lips on that first evening in the house. She remembered seeing a photo of typing pools with lines of girls, looking like battery hens, pounding away on their typewriters. They were all wearing neat, white blouses and they all looked expressionless. Probably because they were bored out of their minds, she thought ruefully.

She was thankful that it was not as bad as she had feared although she was not really in the mood to concentrate on learning how to become someone's efficient secretary.

On her return from the church, she had felt as though, almost without realising, she'd taken a first step in the direction of making the most of this next chapter in her life – even if it were a chapter in which her aunt would be sorely missed. For the first time in a long while, Anna felt a flutter of hope inside her.

* * *

On one of her rambles with Ruffles, Anna bumped into Jess, emerging from the less smart of the two Melford pubs. She was clutching several cans of lager to her nearly non-existent breasts and looking hot – as though she would like to sit down and drink one. The landlord of The Sitting Duck was not fussy about who drank on his premises as long as they did not ask for anything on the slate. However, Marv had been banned, according to Jess.

"What did he do?" asked Anna, as they walked along the road.

"Got a bit pissed one night an' climbed up on one of them barrels and changed the sign. Put an 'h' in sitting." Jess giggled. "It was ever so well done – the same kind of writing an' all. Old Grumps didn't find out for days. By then, all the locals was using the new name. He really lost his cool and some miserable git told him it was Marv wot done it – so he was banned."

"What about The Queen's Arms? Couldn't you both go in there for a drink?"

"Nah! That's run by a lunatic who plays classical music all the time, real loud *and* his game pies are definitely dodgy. He caught Marv writing 'Bugger the Bournemouth Sinfonietta' on the wall in the bogs an' he weren't too thrilled neither."

"Marv doesn't seem to mind living dangerously, does he?" said Anna.

"Mm. But 'e's really talented, is Marv. You should see the scrolls he done for a shop in town. Copied out poems and fings in lovely lettering. The bloke can't get enough of them. Trouble is, Marv can only do it when 'e's in the mood like. Creative stuff can't be turned out at the drop of an 'at, 'e sez." She turned to Anna, earrings rocking wildly. "Why don't you come down to the van an' meet 'im?"

Anna hesitated.

"What if he's busy? He might not want to be disturbed if he's making something."

"Oh, don't you worry about that!" Jess laughed. "'E's never so creative he can't stop for a can of lager an' a pretty girl. Anyway, 'e likes dogs, does Marv. Says they're much nicer than people."

"He might be right. OK, I can come down for a while but I mustn't be late back."

Jess smiled broadly at Anna. "T'riffic!"

They walked along slowly, past the village green that was more brown than green in the continuing drought, and over the bridge at the far end. The normally full river had shrunk to half its usual size and the leaves of the smaller trees looked dusty and lifeless as they hung limply in the heat. The flock of geese living on the green had taken refuge in the shade and the gander barely acknowledged their presence as they walked past.

"Even 'e's too knackered to chase us today," commented Jess. "All that flapping and 'issing must use up an awful lot of energy. Don't chase Marv, just me. Silly sod!"

Anna thought it was possible the gander didn't like Jess's taste in clothes. Today's colour scheme was particularly eye-catching – a brilliant red shift, edged in emerald green, that reached her ankles. She found herself hoping that they wouldn't have to cross any fields that might contain a bull.

Jess led the way down a winding path beside the river and through a spinney of hazel and alder. On a patch of flattened grass at the side of a field of stubble, stood the caravan. It had once been white but was now partly decorated in swirls of colour. The door and windows were wide open. A rug and some cushions were scattered around outside. A collapsible chair and a table, covered in spools of thread and beads, stood in the shade of some nearby sycamores. Beside the table, a figure, dressed in minimal frayed shorts with a crumpled bush hat pulled down over the eyes, lay snoozing in a deck chair that had seen better days. The stripes in the canvas were so faded they were almost indistinguishable.

"Cor! Look at the Sleeping Beauty!" commented Jess with a grin.

The lanky girl walked over and dropped one of the cold cans of lager onto the bronzed belly. The effect was immediate and dramatic. The figure leaped to its feet, the hat and can of lager falling to the ground.

"Jesus, Jess! Must you?"

He bent over to retrieve the can. As he straightened up, Marv saw Anna. He quickly erased a bad-tempered frown and gave her a crooked smile. She saw that he had a silver stud in his nose and that he was tall and slim. His platinum hair contrasted oddly with his narrow, brown eyes. She smiled back, even though she didn't much like the way he was looking her up and down.

"Wotcha! I'm Marv. I saw you in the Merc the other day." He opened the can and licked off the drink as it fizzed out onto his hand. He flopped back into the deck chair and took a long swig.

"Hey, Marv!" protested Jess. "'Ow about giving Anna the chair?"

Marv threw Anna a winsome look.

"There's nice comfy cushions on the rug over there."

Anna walked over to the tattered rug and sat down, glad to put some distance between them. What was someone nice like Jess doing with a man like him she wondered. Jess handed her a can and flopped down gratefully beside her.

"Blimey! I 'ope this 'eat lets up soon. I couldn't sleep at all last night."

"What's the dog called then?" Marv interrupted.

"Ruffles."

Anna watched the man as he gulped down the cool lager, his Adam's apple dancing in his throat. He lowered the can and lazily patted his thigh.

"Come on, Ruffles! Come 'n see yer Uncle Marv, then!"

Anna unwillingly let go of the lead and the dog trotted obligingly over. He sniffed the man's bare feet with interest. Marv patted him absent-mindedly.

"You're a very handsome dog, you are."

Ruffles wagged his tail.

Jess glanced over at the beads on the table.

"You didn't do any then?"

"Nope," replied Marv, taking another swig from his can.

Ruffles lay down in the shade beside the deck chair, resting his chin on his paws and closing his eyes. Anna waited to see if Jess would ask why Marv hadn't 'done any'. But the girl rolled over onto her side and squinted up at the sky.

"You know we got Sal and Josh comin' tomorra? They said they might get some of the others to come down wiv 'em."

Marv nodded. Jess looked up at Anna.

"Would you like to meet 'em? They're a great bunch. They'll bring some nosh and some bottles 'n we'll 'ave some music. Josh is t'rrific on guitar."

"I don't know. I'd like to but I'll have to make sure it's OK first," said Anna, wondering what the reaction would be if she told her mother where she planned to spend the next evening.

Marv gave her a pitying look.

"Wot are you? Seventeen? Eighteen?"

"I'm nearly eighteen."

"Well then. Shouldn't be no trouble. Just tell them yer goin' out," said Marv, in a bored voice. He leaned back in the deck chair and shut his eyes.

Jess gave Anna's arm a squeeze. "Oh, go on, Anna! We'd love you to come. 'Onest!"

"All right. I will. What time?"

"Nine-ish. Fink you'll be able to get away?"

"I'll manage." Anna sounded more certain then she felt. "I should be off. It's nearly Ruffles' suppertime. Thanks for the drink."

She scrambled to her feet and called the dog. With a wave to Jess, she started off in the direction of the spinney.

The other girl called after her. "See you tomorra, then!"

Marv had apparently gone back to sleep but, as she made her way back through the trees, Anna heard him say to Jess, "Mummy might not want her to come out and play with the peasants."

"Give over, Marv! Anna's all right. She can't 'elp it if her lot are loaded. Wot you want for tea? I got some bangers."

"Christ! We had bleeding bangers yesterday."

Anna could just hear Jess's cheerful response.

"Yeah! 'An you'll 'ave them tomorra an' all if you don't get cracking on some more stuff for the market. You said you 'ad to 'ave the booze. Now there's no more dosh left. So, it's bangers or nuffing."

* * *

Rosalind put down her book and stared at her daughter.

"You are going *where?*"

"I've been invited to a party down by the green and I said I'd go."

"By whom? Who are they?"

"I don't know their surnames but the person who asked me is called Jess. I met her waiting for the bus one day. She's sweet and she has a friend called Marv – he was very good with Ruffles yesterday."

Anna had left it to the last minute to tell her mother about the invitation. That way, there wouldn't be enough time to be subjected to a long interrogation she hoped.

"*Marv?*" Rosalind's eyebrows rose slightly.

"Short for marvellous."

"I see!"

"I won't be long. It's a sort of picnic. I just said I would drop in and meet some of their friends," lied Anna.

"I don't suppose Delia would know them?"

"Probably not." Anna stopped an involuntary smile appearing. She could imagine what Delia would make of Jess and Marv. "Anyway, I'm just going up to change. I'll see you on my way out."

Anna left the room without wasting any more time. As she ran up the stairs, she suddenly had a vivid mental picture of Delia, confronted by Jess and Marv. Would she ask them if they hunted?

* * *

Half an hour later, she stuck her head around the edge of the door. Adam and her mother were both in the room.

"I'm off. I've got my key."

"Just a minute, Anna." Rosalind sounded suspicious. "Would you mind coming in to the room to say goodbye properly?"

Anna took a hesitant step inside the door. She was wearing an old T-shirt and her favourite patched jeans. Her feet were clad in a pair of ancient flip-flops her aunt had given her for going down to the beach.

"What *are* you wearing?" Rosalind stared at her daughter in horror.

"My own clothes. It's going to be very informal." Anna smiled as she backed into the hall. "Goodnight. See you tomorrow."

"Goodnight, Anna," Adam replied, swiftly forestalling his wife's next comment. When Anna had gone he said,

"There's no point in getting upset. She is seventeen, very nearly eighteen, and she's been used to quite a liberal upbringing. You won't change her ways easily. She's no fool, Rosalind. Let her be."

Rosalind's mind was working overtime. She'd have to put a stop to her fraternising with the undesirable element in the village. It was a pity Anna and Delia hadn't hit it off. When she'd suggested to Anna it might be nice to invite some of the young things around for a birthday supper-party celebration, Anna had seemed to panic. Well, if she wanted to stay at home and keep it simple, perhaps it was just as well. The longer Rosalind had to work on her daughter's manners and general behaviour, the better. It wouldn't be a bad idea to keep her under wraps for a while longer – until she'd become a little more presentable and polished. She shuddered, remembering the escaping asparagus during the drinks party they'd held shortly after Anna's arrival. Rosalind smiled at Adam.

"Perhaps you're right. But I don't want her to think that she can get away with doing anything that takes her fancy."

"I'm sure she won't," he replied, with an amused expression in his grey eyes.

* * *

Walking down the drive, Anna realised that she had tensed herself for a confrontation with her mother. She stopped and took some deep breaths. Would she ever be able to relax in her company? She had seen other girls with their mothers, chatting and joking, as though with a good friend. It must be nice to be like that, she thought.

She wasn't completely sure that this evening was a good idea but she decided that, as she had made a stand on going, she would look very silly if she backed out now.

It was getting dark and she could hear Mr Pender watering on the other side of the hedge. She breathed in the smell of hot, wet earth. Anna had only spoken to him on a couple of occasions and had found him dour and unfriendly. She wondered how he was with his wife. Mrs P always gave the impression that she was content but Anna guessed that she was not the sort of woman to waste time on her own worries. She was too interested in other people to do that.

As Anna walked, she thought about marriage. It seemed to her that it was an ill-advised move in most people's cases. It was as though getting married stopped them from being themselves, especially the women. What was it Aunt Pog used to say? "The trouble with couples is, one of the pair always does the kissing and the other one just proffers a cheek." She also remembered her aunt saying, "For me, darling, marriage was an absolute disaster. Desmond was quite a pleasant chap before we tied the knot. But as soon as the deed was done, he just stopped trying and it was quite a shock to find out that he had been pretending not to be jealous. Why should I stop enjoying other men's company, just because I was married? Marriage didn't stop him ogling pretty young things in the village shop and the pub. Double standards, darling! So many of them suffer from it and it's very annoying!"

* * *

As Anna approached the spinney, she could hear laughter and the sound of music. She came to an uncertain halt. 'Oh Lord!' she thought. 'Why do I feel so nervous? They're only a bunch of people my own age. It's not as though they will be like Delia and Anita.'

Her self-confidence had taken a knock at the drinks party. They had all been perfectly pleasant but she knew they considered her a bit of an oddity, in spite of her smart new clothes.

For the hundredth time, a picture of cloud shadows, sliding over distant mountains and skimming over the cobbled surface of a lake came into her mind. Don't be pathetic! she told herself as she walked briskly towards the loud voices.

"Well, look who's here!" drawled Marv as she emerged from the trees.

He was lying in the deck chair. Anna wondered if he had bothered to move since she had last seen him.

"Anna! Great!" Jess came flying towards her with a big smile and even larger earrings than she had worn the previous day. "Come an' meet the others." She turned towards the handful of people scattered around the clearing. "You lot! This is Anna, wot I told you about." She pointed out a tall, lean figure in faded jeans and a blue, cotton shirt. "This is Benny. Into computers big time. Don't get 'im going on the subject!"

Benny stood up and shook Anna's hand lightly.

"Hello, nice to meet you."

He spoke softly and his brown eyes were serious under the fringe of curly, black hair as he looked at her.

"An' this is Maureen," continued Jess, directing Anna's attention to a large, blonde girl, with a quantity of pale flesh rolling over the waistband of her shorts, heavy breasts crammed into a minimal top and a lot of very red lipstick.

Maureen giggled as she greeted Anna, flicking back a curl from her eyes.

"Hi!" she said and immediately went back to her conversation with another girl, sitting on the ground next to her.

Maureen's companion looked slim and supple and had dark, short hair. She was introduced as Sal who, after a quick glance at Anna, ignored her. Jess, busy with introductions, failed to notice this blatant snub and nodded in the direction of a man, standing with his back to the group, gazing at the sky while he urinated into the field.

"That's Sal's bloke, Josh."

She was introduced to four or five others who sat around with cans of lager, smoking self-rolled cigarettes. A radio, its volume turned up so high that the music coming from it was distorted, lay on the ground. Smoke drifted lazily in the air and the smell of charred sausages and scented cigarettes filled Anna's nostrils. She was led over to a rug and installed beside a couple who were too involved in gazing into each other's eyes to notice her.

"Back in a tick! I'll get you a can," said Jess, dashing off in the direction of the caravan, her bracelets jingling as she went.

Anna watched as people moved around the home-made

barbecue, doing a sort of crazy dance to avoid the smoke, poking at the sausages with sticks. Someone had hung up a couple of gas-lamps, one on the corner of the caravan and another from a small tree, where they hissed gently, lighting up the group from above and throwing shadows of the circling moths onto the trampled grass below. She guessed the cigarettes were not ordinary ones. When Jess returned with a can, Anna asked what was in them.

"Grass," said Jess, looking surprised. "Do you fancy one?"

"I don't know. What's it like?"

"Never smoked grass? You 'aven't lived! You're not serious?"

Anna nodded. "Well, we'll 'ave to do somefing about that. I'll get Marv to roll you a joint. 'E's the expert!"

Chapter Twenty-five

A faint breeze moved the half-closed curtains as moonlight flowed into the bedroom, making a pale pool of light on the carpet beside the bed. Anna lay with her eyes shut, feeling confused and dizzy from the after-effects of drink and cannabis. She was too muddled to remember exactly how much she had drunk and smoked. After the first few puffs, her throat had begun to feel sore and her head started to swim, reminding her of the first time she had had too much to drink.

It had been on her aunt's birthday and her glass had been refilled several times without either of them realising. Anna experienced a sensation of floating rather than walking across the room and she had hated the feeling of not being in control of her actions.

Benny had come to sit beside her early on in the evening. She'd enjoyed talking to him. How good it felt to have someone who really seemed interested and who listened to what she said. When she described her aunt and the house in Ballynacarrig and how she had been made to feel so welcome, he seemed to understand perfectly why she had not wanted to leave Ireland.

"Where did you live before you went there?" he asked.

"In Cambridge."

"With your aunt?"

"No. Tell me about you. Have you always lived here?"

Benny took the hint and did not ask any more questions but talked about his work, which he told her he loved. He was an only child and his elderly parents lived in London. They got round to the topic of books and found that they shared a liking for many of the same authors.

The time slipped comfortably by and Anna started to feel she had known this tall man with the gentle brown eyes for years. She noticed how beautiful his bare feet and long-fingered, slim hands were. She found herself looking at the smooth, olive skin of his chest, and surprised herself by suddenly wanting to lean forward and stroke the curve of shoulder and neck when he took off his shirt to cool himself in the nearby stream.

Later in the evening, they stood in the moonlight, up to their ankles in the silently flowing water and listened to Josh singing about unrequited love in such mock-melancholic tones that it made them both smile. Then, Benny took both her hands in his.

"Would you mind if I kissed you?"

Anna looked into the serious face, half shrouded in shadow. It had never been like this before – certainly not where PJ was concerned. She felt troubled, unsure, yet wanting to feel his lips on hers. He waited for her to answer, standing motionless, still holding her hands but without exerting any pressure, feeling her uncertainty and making it easy for her to withdraw if she wished.

"You don't have to if you'd rather not," he said softly, releasing her.

Anna stood on tiptoes, resting her hands on his shoulders.

"But I do. I would very much like you to kiss me," she said, in an almost inaudible voice.

Benny's lips were soft on her own. She felt a sudden great surge of longing well up in her. She wanted him to go on kissing her like this forever. She wanted to be held in his strong arms. She returned his kisses with passionate kisses of her own, breathing him in, holding him tightly.

After a while, he led her to the bank and they lay down on the springy mat of dying grass and moss. He stroked her face and arms, leaning over her, staring intently into her face, his breathing quickening. He moved closer, so that she could feel the weight of his body, pressing down on her. She felt the hardness of his erection through his jeans. One of his hands moved to her waist and then gently upwards under her shirt to her breasts.

Suddenly, Anna could not breathe. She felt as though she was drowning. Panic replaced desire. Terrified, she tried to push his body off hers. It felt as though he were crushing all the air out of her lungs. The memory of that other body smothering her, the smell of stale sweat and alcohol, the rough hands that had pummelled and slapped her, tearing at her clothes, holding her down by her hair.

The hideous, engorged thing that had been thrust into her, again and again, making her cry out with pain. The way he had grunted like an animal when he climaxed, his face ugly with lust, concentrated, oblivious. The only thing she could think of was how the man had left her, lying on her back, barely conscious, too numb to feel the bruises on her thighs and neck, her vagina sticky with his semen and her blood. It all flooded back in vivid detail.

Anna felt she was going to be sick. She wrenched her face away, gasping.

"Don't! Please get off me. Please! I can't breathe." Using every ounce of her strength, she pushed him away from her. "I'm sorry! I'm so sorry!" she cried, as the startled man moved back from her.

Tears stung her eyes as she scrambled to her feet, ramming her shirt into her jeans, violently shoving her hair back from her eyes. She could feel her heart thumping in her chest.

"What's the matter, Anna?" he asked, puzzled. "I thought you liked me. You said I could kiss you."

He slowly got to his feet, arms at his sides, the palms of his hands facing her unthreateningly.

"I know," she said, miserably. "I wanted you to kiss me."

She crumpled back on to the ground and sobbed, her hands covering her face. Benny stood, silently looking down, afraid to touch her. Surely, he thought, her reaction was out of all proportion? She had seemed to fancy him as much as he had her. She'd certainly kissed him as though she wanted him to make love to her. What was the problem? He squatted down beside her, taking care not to go too close.

"Was it me? Did I do something wrong?"

Anna flinched slightly at the sound of his voice. She was overcome with shame. What could she say? Now that her fear had started to fade, she felt deeply embarrassed. He had – considering the circumstances – behaved perfectly. But she could never tell him what had happened on that afternoon by the lakeside. How could she explain to him that the revulsion and panic she had just experienced had not been his fault?

"No, it's not you." Still trembling, Anna shook her head. "Really it's not."

"It must be you then," replied Benny, quietly.

There was a long silence. Taking care not to make any sudden movements, he pulled out a crumpled cigarette and some matches from the pocket of his jeans. He lit up, inhaled deeply and offered it to Anna. She shook her head. The sickly-sweet scent of cannabis hung in the air and she felt another wave of nausea rising in her throat as she dropped her forehead onto her knees.

"Sometimes it helps to talk if you have a problem," prompted Benny gently, leaning back and resting on one elbow.

Anna looked at the glowing end of his cigarette and then up at the night sky, which shimmered in the moonlight above them. Even though she felt unutterably miserable, she noticed that each leaf of the nearby trees shone silver against the black of the surrounding shadows. A battle raged in her mind. It was true that talking often helped and he was nice. She liked him a lot, but how could she tell someone she had only just met about what had happened? He would be disgusted – as disgusted as she felt. Anna knew that she just couldn't do it. The shame she had experienced on the beach that day enveloped her again. Very slowly, she got to her feet.

"I'm very sorry but I really don't want to talk about it," she said, in a low voice. "Anyway, it's late and I should be getting back."

Benny stared at her without moving, saying nothing. She left him there, turning from him and walking as fast as she could, pushing her way through the trees and bushes, avoiding the pools of light and Jess and Marv and their friends, as she made her way as quickly as she could back towards the bridge.

In her haste to get away, Anna stumbled on a stone at the side of the road, grazing her hand as she tried to regain her balance. She stopped under a streetlamp and looked at her watch, sucking the back of her knuckles. Oh, God! A quarter to two. I hope they've gone to bed, Anna thought dizzily. Taking some deep breaths, she continued along the empty road.

A lone black cat slipped silently out of a gap in a hedge. It paused in the middle of the road and turned to look at her briefly, its unblinking, golden eyes shining strangely in the lamplight, before it disappeared without a sound, back into the shadows.

* * *

It was getting late by the time Anna stirred next morning. It was the sound of rain, beating against the windows that woke her. She climbed stiffly out of bed and peered into the garden. For the first time since her arrival, she felt autumn in the air as she watched the heavy drops as they fell on the geraniums and roses, their petals strewn over the lawn and on the surface of the pool. The branches of the trees were whipped by a strong wind, their dry leaves bowling across the soaking grass, sailing past the windows. Water rushed, in miniature torrents, along the drought-baked paths and Anna could hear it gurgling as it tumbled into the overflowing gutters and down the drainpipes.

She watched the splashes of rain on the glass, as they slid slowly downwards, merging into each other as they formed small, transparent rivers of their own. She sat dejectedly, remembering the previous night and wishing that she had not allowed herself to be talked into going by Jess. What if they found out what had happened between her and Benny? That would make Marv despise her all the more. More importantly, what would Jess think of her leaving like that, without even saying goodbye? Anna felt that, given the chance, she and Jess could have been good friends. Her heart sank.

* * *

As she cleaned her teeth, Anna looked at herself in the mirror and wondered, as she so often had, if she would ever be able to truly fit in, to feel she belonged. Dropping the toothbrush into the mug, she gave herself a long stare. Was she abnormal? she asked herself. Aunt Pog had not seemed to think so. But then Aunt Pog had been . . . different. Some people had thought her aunt mad. Not that Pog had cared one bit. "They can think what they like, darling. It's like wrinkles, really. It took me years to become what I am and it was bloody hard work some of the time and I'm not going to pretend to be something or someone I'm not. They'll just have to put up with me the way I am – wrinkles, fads, fancies and all!" she had once said, as she laughingly dismissed some unkind comment an acquaintance had made about her.

Anna looked at her own face with distaste. Perhaps there was something about her that was different. Perhaps her mother's lack of feeling towards her was because she was not really loveable. The brown eyes stared back at her. Had it been her fault, all that had happened, all the bad things? Was it possible she was one of those people who were not meant to have a happy life? She shut her eyes, remembering the puzzled look on Benny's face when she had pushed him away from her. With a shrinking feeling, she remembered too her inability to explain or cope with the situation. What had she done? She'd just run away – like a small, frightened child.

A thought suddenly occurred to her and she opened her eyes again. In just over a year, she would be nineteen and would inherit the money her father had left her. It would mean she would be free in a way she had never been before. Anna wondered why she did not feel more elated by the idea.

As she walked slowly back into the bedroom, her thoughts returned to Benny, staring down at her with that questioning look in his eyes. Would she ever find anyone with whom she could feel relaxed and unthreatened, who would care for her in the way she wanted, someone she could trust? Anna suddenly felt a desperate need to love and be loved and, above all, to feel safe. Even dear Aunt Pog hadn't been able to do that for her.

Chapter Twenty-six

The days that followed her meeting with Benny seemed full of gales and torrential rain falling out of grey skies. The weather matched Anna's own feeling of depression. The passing days were predictable and monotonous. Adam dropped her off at the Tech every morning on his way to work and she caught the bus back to Little Melford in the afternoon, sometimes delaying her return, browsing in one of the many bookshops the town had to offer.

She had not seen Jess since the party and she very much doubted her path would cross Benny's. Anna often thought of him, half-hoping they would meet again, the painful embarrassment forgotten. She wrote long letters to Kathleen and Amy, in which she attempted to sound positive, trying hard not to reveal how desperately she missed their cheerful company. She dutifully attended her classes but found the other students uninteresting and not over-friendly – although it crossed her mind that perhaps she was not giving off very happy vibes, which might make her seem rather unapproachable.

To Anna's surprise, her relationship with Adam proved easier than with her mother, who appeared to have come to the conclusion that her idea of trying to mould her daughter into the sort of creature who would be accepted by the Delia Chiverses and Anita Hollingsworths of the world was perhaps unrealistic. She sometimes got the feeling that her mother wanted to talk to her but that something stopped her, as if it were difficult for her to find the right words. If anything, Anna found her more distant than before but less openly critical. It was as if much of the anger and bitterness that had been so evident when Anna was small had evaporated. Perhaps, she thought, her mother had married the right man second time around.

One afternoon, Anna overheard Rosalind talking to an inquisitive friend on the telephone.

"No, she's not very academic, I'm afraid. Her exam results arrived recently and they were unspectacular to say the least. Well, I suppose it was only to be expected. After all, her mad aunt sent her to a tumbledown ruin of a school run by a bunch of nuns in the middle of a bog."

There was a silence, then she said, "That's really sweet of you. Six o'clock on Friday – we'd love to, but I think it's better if Anna doesn't come with us. She has quite a bit of studying to do if she's going to get anywhere with that course of hers."

Anna smiled wryly to herself. It suited her very well not to have to go and stand around at local drinks parties, confronted by all the same old faces, as she tried to juggle with canapés, handbag and a glass – *and* attempt to make appropriate small talk.

* * *

One Saturday, Adam suggested she accompany them to watch a game of rugby.

"I'm not that keen on rugby," she said, with a smile, remembering the hilarious games of soccer she had seen played on the pitch at Ballynacarrig, where everyone was welcome to join in.

"But rugby is a great English institution," he remonstrated.

"Perhaps that's one of the reasons I'm not all that interested in it."

"What! You're as English as they come!"

"I don't *feel* terribly English. Anyway, I like watching Gaelic football."

"Well, you'd have some difficulty finding a game of that taking place in Cambridge, Anna." Adam sounded amused. "Delia's brother, Simon, is playing and a lot of people you've met recently will be there. It could be fun!"

Anna found that she was getting annoyed.

"You shouldn't be so surprised that the things you and my mother like might not interest me. After all, I have spent over half my life in Ireland."

Adam heard the bitterness in her voice as Anna glanced over to where Rosalind sat, oblivious to the conversation, giving crisp instructions over the telephone to a fellow committee member.

After they had left, Anna remembered comments she had heard in Ballynacarrig about how smug and arrogant the

English were and how superior, especially in their dealings with the Irish. She had known nothing about Irish history when she first went to live with her aunt. In her first term at Ballynacarrig School, some of the older children had taken pleasure in informing her on the subject.

"The Brits starved the Irish, so they did, an' put them in jail or shot them when they tried to get food." Mick Joyce was well informed on the wrongdoings of the English. His father belonged to the IRA and hated them, he told her. "They tried to stop everyone from speaking Irish an' they set fire to their houses *an'* sent them off in coffin ships to America. They kept all the food to themselves – emptied all the barns of grain to send back to England, even though the potatoes were rotten. They didn't care!"

Anna had gone to Pog that evening, horrified by what she had heard.

"It's not true, is it?" she demanded to know.

"I'm afraid it is, darling. They were some good English people who did their best to help, but I think they were in the minority."

"So, why do they let English people live in Ireland after what they did? It's not right! They must hate us!"

"You shouldn't feel guilty, Anna darling. What happened was truly terrible and should not be forgotten but life has to move on and some people have to learn to say 'sorry' – and some people have to learn to forgive. I've been living here for years and I've got lots of lovely Irish friends who are good and kind and have a soft spot in their hearts for a loopy, free spirit like me! What's more, although I was born and brought up in England, I'm a Catholic – and that really confuses them! If you accept them as they are and don't pretend to be anything other than you are, you'll be all right. But remember, darling, however hard you try, you won't get along with everyone. Life is not like that, unfortunately. There will always be people like young Mick, ready to judge you, even when they don't know you. As soon as you open your mouth and say something, just because you don't sound like they do, they want to stick a label on you. Just do your best and don't worry! It would be a sad world if everyone sounded and behaved the same, wouldn't it?"

Pog had then given Anna one of her occasional, clumsy hugs. In doing so, she knocked the large, glass ashtray off the corner of the table. It fell onto the carpet with a thud, covering the place with ash and lipstick-smeared cigarette-ends.

"Oh, bugger! Now look what I've done!" she said, laughing.

* * *

In the late afternoon, three weeks after Jess and Marv's party, Anna plucked up her courage and went down with Ruffles to the site by the river. All she found when she got there was muddy, trampled grass and some crumpled lager cans lying on the ground. There were deep ruts: two parallel gashes that looked as though they had been made recently in the wet soil. She guessed they must have had difficulty towing the caravan back to the road. She wondered who had helped them and where they had gone. It had been wrong not to search Jess out earlier but Anna couldn't help feeling let down that the girl had gone without letting her know. She turned away from the dank, unwelcoming clearing and called to the dog, which was frantically digging out an imaginary animal from the base of a beech tree. Its leaves had changed from green to gold and copper and glowed, unnoticed by the girl in the grey October twilight.

* * *

It was at the end of November when Anna saw Benny in the poetry section of Heffer's Bookshop, where she had retreated after a particularly dismal day at the Tech. It was snowing in a desultory way, tiny flakes, flying hither and thither in the icy wind that blew unhindered across the fens of East Anglia.

She had not recognised him at first. His slim body was camouflaged by layers of warm clothing inside a large duffle coat. Anna stopped dead in her tracks, her face suddenly suffused with colour. She was just on the point of retreating, when he looked up.

"Hello!"

He seemed genuinely pleased to see her and was apparently unaware of her blush and acute discomfort.

"Hello," she replied, a little diffidently.

She stood, looking at him, not knowing what to do or say next.

"Finally!"

"Finally what?"

"Well, you said you loved bookshops. So for the past three weeks, when I haven't been working late, I've been visiting each one in turn hoping to find you. Jess warned me that I might not be welcome up at your house. And now, here you are!"

They both laughed. Anna felt herself relax and the colour start to fade from her face. Benny shut the book he was holding.

"Do you know where Jess is?" Anna asked.

"No! Those two come and go! She'll resurface sometime. She's great fun, is Jess. I can't say I'm all that mad about Marv though."

Anna had hoped Benny would know how she could make contact with the girl but, like him, she didn't mind if she never saw Jess's boyfriend ever again.

"You're looking frozen. Would you like to come and have a cup of hot chocolate to warm you up?"

"I'd love to."

Anna had to stop herself from sneaking glances at him as they walked along. She was so happy to see him again that she forgot how bitingly cold the air was. It was difficult to make sensible conversation. What did he feel about her? she wondered. Was it possible he hadn't been put off by what had happened that night on the riverbank?

* * *

In the weeks coming up to Christmas, both Rosalind and Adam noticed that Anna seemed to be enjoying life. Neither of them spent much time wondering what had brought about the change in her. He was busy with his work. She was in the throes of preparations for Christmas parties and shopping for expensive presents. To judge by the sour expression on George Pender's face, he had already had quite enough of chauffeuring her around in the busy pre-Christmas traffic that clogged the narrow streets of

Cambridge. Looking at him, Anna wondered what it would take to get him into the Christmas spirit.

Only Mrs P guessed that the girl might have met a fellow and delightedly shared her suspicions with her husband, who grunted and went back to his crossword puzzle. As far as he was concerned, the lives of the family for whom he worked were of no interest. As long as he was paid what was due to him, that was all that mattered. His wife could amuse herself by picking up scraps of information here and there if it kept her happy but he didn't want to know.

Mrs P looked at her rapidly balding spouse and sighed. Why had she married him? It was a real shame he wasn't more imaginative or romantic. She thought briefly of the handsome young soldier she had once loved and who now lay somewhere in an unmarked grave in Flanders. He had been so romantic – nothing showy – just in the way he treated her and the things he said. He'd always made her feel sort of special. When she waved him off on the train, so many years ago, she'd felt as though her heart would break. But George thought romance was for the idle rich, not for the likes of him and her. She sighed again and went back to wondering who the young man was that had put a sparkle into Anna's eyes and taken away the unhappy look that had been so evident for the first couple of weeks after her arrival. I hope he's good to her. That girl deserves to have someone kind taking an interest in her. Wouldn't it be nice if she felt able to confide in me, she thought, wistfully.

Mrs P knew that was unlikely. She had seen how quiet and distant Anna could be. She had such nice manners, whatever her mother thought, and that lovely, wide smile she gave you when she thanked you for something you'd done – it made you want to give her a hug. It made you want to do things for her.

Even though she was not privy to Anna's thoughts, the woman had become very fond of the tall, reserved girl with the slight hint of Irish in the way she spoke. She had heard Anna's mother correcting her daughter's pronunciation on several occasions and had seen the rebellious look in the other's eyes. There had been an argument the other day after Anna had called the airing cupboard 'the hot press'. Mrs Strong had been very irritated and critical. Why couldn't she just enjoy her lovely daughter Mrs P wondered. She would have given anything to have had a child like that of her own. She'd always tried not to mind her and George not having children but she sometimes found it difficult not to feel resentful when she remembered how the doctor had said that the problem didn't lie with her. Her husband had refused point blank to have any tests done.

"If we don't have any kids, we don't have any. So there's no use in making a fuss about it," he'd said, looking at her angrily as if she were the one being thoroughly unreasonable.

* * *

One week before Christmas, on the last day of the autumn term, Anna and Benny spent the afternoon together in his small flat. He was leaving the next day to spend the holiday with his parents in London. They listened to Brahms and Bach on his portable stereo and talked of books, authors, poetry, music – everything and anything.

Up until then, Benny had been careful not to be intimate, feeling that any move in that direction would have to be initiated by Anna. He was sure that she liked him and found him attractive and he very much wanted to get her into bed with him. He was finding it increasingly difficult not to reach out to her.

He watched her as she bent over a book, her glossy hair half covering her face. She was kneeling on the rug in front of the inadequate electric fire, clutching a mug of coffee with both hands. She became aware of his gaze and looked up at him.

"What?"

"I was just looking at you. You are rather nice to look at! Or hasn't anyone told you that before?"

Anna laughed.

"Of course they have! Aunt Pog used to say that she and I were both 'altogether gorgeous' when we were dressed up in our glad rags, ready to go out on the town. Mind you, she was famous for exaggerating – she suffered from what she called hyper-bowl."

"She suffered from *what*?"

"Hyperbole."

"But of course. How slow of me!" He was aware that she had cleverly sidestepped the topic of her attractiveness. Benny tried again. "Anna, do you find me at all attractive?"

He held his breath. Something truly awful must have happened to make her so afraid of physical intimacy. He knew that she was passionate. He had felt it that first evening when they kissed, standing in the stream in the moonlight. But something, some memory, had come

321

between them, making it impossible for her to let things take their natural course.

"Yes, I do," she replied, looking down at the book.

"Can you look at me when you say that? I want to see your face."

Anna raised her head slowly, her eyes anxious.

Benny paused, searching for the right words. "Anna, I think you are lovely, quite the most lovely girl I have ever known and I've thought of almost nothing but you since we first met. The last thing I want to do is frighten you away. Can you help me understand what the problem is? Please? I'm a very good listener."

"I can't," she said quickly, looking away again, her voice distressed.

"Whatever the problem is, did your Aunt Pog know about it?"

"No, she didn't know."

He could hardly hear her reply.

"Would she have approved of you being miserable, bottling everything up and refusing to let anyone help you?"

There was a long silence and then Anna said, in a muffled voice, "No! She would have thought I was being idiotic."

"So, she only wanted what was best for you. Am I right?" Anna nodded. Benny leaned forward and took one of her hands in his. "Well then, tell me what the matter is and together we'll lay the ghost of whatever it is that frightens you so," he pleaded.

There were tears in her eyes as she looked at him.

"You won't like me any more, if I tell you what happened."

"You're wrong Anna. Whatever it is, I know it won't change the way I feel about you."

"But I'm frightened to talk about it, to remember. I've tried so hard to forget."

He crouched down beside her and put both his arms around her.

"But you haven't succeeded in forgetting, have you? Surely you see that the only way you will be able to forget is to talk about what happened. Then you can really start to live again and it will be truly behind you."

* * *

An hour later, Anna lay, exhausted, slumped in the armchair. Benny knelt beside her, his head resting against her cheek. He too felt drained, appalled by the brutality of what she had told him. Very gently he stroked her temples and forehead with his long, sensitive fingers. After a while, she fell into a deep sleep, not stirring as he carried her through to the bedroom and carefully covered her with blankets. Taking care not to wake her, Benny stretched out on the bed as well, pulling the eiderdown over himself in an effort to keep warm in the freezingly cold room. He meant to rest for a while and then wake Anna in time for her to catch the late bus home. But he too fell into an equally profound sleep.

Chapter Twenty-seven

Christmas came and went. It was a Christmas holiday made bearable for Anna by the knowledge that she could escape from time to time to spend precious hours with Benny. He told her that he had missed her so much he had cut short his visit to London, coming back to Cambridge two days after Christmas Day.

She realised that she had grown to love him and the way he could tune in to her needs. It seemed that he instinctively knew when she wanted to talk or just be with him in silent companionship. He never doled out advice, unlike her mother, and so she asked his opinion on a wide variety of things, listening to him carefully before making up her own mind.

Benny, by being patient, had eventually managed to show her that it was possible for a man to make love in a way that was tender and gentle. Anna feared his lovemaking would never completely erase what had happened before but at least now she no longer felt unclean. She started to dare to believe it when he said she was lovely and that what they shared was neither wrong nor shameful. For the first time, Anna felt he made it possible for all the pent-up love inside her to come bubbling to the surface and find expression in a physical, as well as an emotional, way. Love that had been denied her in the past was forgotten.

At twenty-five, Benny considered himself quite an expert when it came to women but he had to admit to himself that Anna's uninhibited and honest approach to all aspects of their relationship both amazed and delighted him. At the start, he had thought he would be the one in charge. In fact, he realised that his past amorous adventures seemed shallow and unsatisfactory when compared to his relationship with this extraordinary girl who had shown herself to him without any pretensions; playing none of the games that the women he had known before had played. He had suspected that, once he succeeded in getting her into his bed, she would soon lose her attraction. This had not happened and he was pleasantly surprised and intrigued.

In spite of Benny's assurances that keeping their relationship secret was the only way to conduct the affair, it weighed on Anna's mind. Although she did not want to share the knowledge of his existence with anyone else, especially not her mother or Adam, she wished she could be more truthful about the situation. Subterfuge had never been necessary when she was living with Aunt Pog – until the afternoon at the lake that had tainted everything –

making her watch what she said in case she let slip something that might cause worry or questions.

However, Anna could not deceive Mrs P. The middle-aged woman was sure that something was going on. Although denied romance in her own life, she knew in her bones that Anna was seeing a man and guessed, from the spring in the girl's step and her blossoming self-confidence, that she was involved in more than mere conversation and the occasional kiss with this unknown lover. She wished she could talk to her. Anna was so young and, Mrs P was sure, inexperienced in the ways of the world. She guessed that it was most unlikely that the girl would confide in her mother. The woman was worried. She would hate to see Anna hurt but, regretfully decided that the girl, for all her good manners, would resent any intrusion from someone who was not only from a different generation but not even one of the family.

The housekeeper took to staying up later than usual, finding excuses to busy herself in the kitchen, making sure that she had a reason to slip up from the flat in the basement so that she was around when the last bus arrived from Cambridge. That way, if a sympathetic, listening ear were ever needed, she would be there.

* * *

Term re-started, making it possible for Benny and Anna to easily meet two or three times a week. Now more happy in herself, Anna found that she was quite enjoying her classes at the Tech and, to her surprise, discovered that she had a flair for office management. What had seemed tedious at the start had become quite interesting. Anna's teachers were gratified by her change of attitude. The head tutor let the girl know that if she kept up her present progress, he would certainly put a good word in for her when it came to job-hunting at the end of the summer. After he had patted her metaphorically over the head, he nodded approvingly and sailed off self-importantly down the long corridor, leaving Anna smiling to herself.

"What do you think about that then, Auntie? Aren't you proud of your efficient, well-organised great-niece? I'm the one you once accused of being more disorganised and untidy than even you!" she whispered.

Anna suddenly realised, with guilty remorse, that she had not thought of her dead aunt for days. Then she remembered that Aunt Pog had not been one to indulge in sentimentality and would have been only too delighted to see her great-niece happily getting on with her life at last.

"Life is for living, darling and the older you get, the better you should be at it. I consider myself a pretty good example but there are still an awful lot of things I haven't quite sorted out in my mind. There are also a good few things I haven't got around to having a crack at yet," she had commented on the eve of her seventy-eighth birthday, with a wicked twinkle in her eye.

Anna vividly remembered how disappointed her aunt had been that her hints of, 'what fun it would be to try a spot of hang-gliding before the summer ends', had fallen on deaf ears.

For the first time since Pog's death, she found that she was able to think of her without the usual, dull pain – a pain that she had described to Benny as, 'like having really bad toothache but in the heart'.

* * *

Halfway through a snow-filled February, Anna's precious, newly found self-confidence began to crumble. With a jolt, she realised she had not had a period since early December. Every night, she went to bed telling herself that tomorrow all would be well and every morning she awoke to discover that nothing had changed. A black cloud seemed to hang over her.

She thought of Benny. What would his reaction be? Would he blame her, even though he had always been the one to take the necessary precautions? Anna lay back on her bed, feeling numb and frightened, gazing unseeingly at the ceiling.

Then, she remembered her aunt's husky voice saying, "Well, darling. What are you going to *do* about it? Don't waste time being sorry that you've done something daft. Get on with sorting it out!"

She sat up. She'd do just that, she said to herself, swinging her legs over the side of the bed. The first thing to do was to buy one of those pregnancy-testing kits. Then if she were pregnant, she'd go and see Benny. He would know what to do.

* * *

The young woman in the chemist's handed the packet over with a knowing look and a complacent smile. Anna snatched it from her and retreated into the snowy street.

She had to hold hard onto the handrail as she made her way down the steps of the underground lavatories in the Market Square. The steps were worn and slippery with frozen snow. A few minutes later, she emerged on legs that felt like jelly, her worst fears confirmed. She was definitely pregnant.

She thought back to the scandal in Ballynacarrig the previous year when one of the local girls had succumbed to the charms of a member of a visiting soccer team. As the girl had grown wider and more rotund, Anna had heard and seen how spiteful some of the village people had been, especially one or two of the women. She'd been surprised and disappointed by their reaction. At the baptism, the new parish priest had more or less ignored the young mother. Anna could still see her, a forlorn figure with shopping bags hanging from the handle of the pushchair, as she tried to heave it up the steps of the bus, watched contemptuously by two worthy ladies, both staunch churchgoers, standing nearby, hands folded across their stomachs.

Anna decided the best thing to do was to go straight to Benny's flat and wait. She felt she wouldn't be able to think straight until she had talked to him. It was nearly five o'clock and he should be back from work in the next half an hour.

By the time Benny arrived, her resolve had almost disappeared. He looked in surprise at the frozen girl, huddled against the railings.

"Hi! I thought we weren't seeing each other until tomorrow. This is unexpected!" He kissed her cold cheek. "You're like an icicle! Let's get you inside."

When Anna barely responded, he looked at her sharply as he felt around in his coat pocket for the front-door key. Something was wrong. It was most unlike her not to return his kiss and look pleased to see him. Suddenly, alarm bells started to ring.

He followed her up the dark staircase. Neither of them spoke until he had closed the door of the flat behind them. Slowly, Anna turned round to face him, her eyes wide, pupils dilated in the nearly dark room. The only light came from a street lamp shining through the window.

"Benny, I'm pregnant."

For a moment, he didn't move. Anna could hear the clock on the shelf ticking loudly. She had never noticed it before. She stared at him, willing him to take her in his arms, to speak, to say something, anything that would bring her comfort.

"Are you sure?"

Even as he asked the question, Benny knew that she was telling the truth. He only had to look at the shock and fear written on her face to know it. To Anna, he seemed suddenly stiff and unfriendly.

"I tested myself just now. Yes, I'm sure."

She looked at him in disbelief, ice forming in the pit of her stomach. He wasn't going to take her in his arms and hold her.

"What are you planning to do about it?"

"What do you mean, what am I planning to do?"

"Well, you're the one who's pregnant."

"But, I thought . . ."

"Have you told anyone about this?"

Anna realised with horror that he sounded frightened.

"No! I only found out myself an hour ago. Who would I have told?"

"I don't know. Oh, God! What a mess!" He turned away from her and reached for the lamp switch. "Will you tell your mother?"

Anna stood stock-still in the sudden, unkind light that shone on her tense face. Her nose glowed pink from the cold and she was shaking. It was almost as icy in the room as it had been outside. She felt her stomach muscles go into spasm at the thought of telling her mother.

"I can't," she moaned, sitting down heavily on the arm of the chair.

"Well, you'll have to get rid of it."

"Why are you saying 'it' like that? 'It' is a baby," said Anna, roused to sudden anger.

"Anna! For Christ's sake! Neither you nor I were planning on having a baby. So the 'baby' will have to be got rid of." He refused to look at her, to allow himself to see the hurt in her face. He too was feeling desperate. "It's not the time to start being sentimental. There are bound to be some reliable clinics around. How many weeks is it?"

"Six or seven. I'm not sure," Anna replied, in a quiet voice.

"Good! So that means it's early on and it'll be easy to deal with. There shouldn't be a problem, should there? I can give you the money for it. You don't have to worry about that."

Benny, for the first time since they had arrived in the flat, made a movement towards her. Anna got up hastily and almost ran for the door, wrenching it open.

"What's the matter? Where are you going?" he called after her.

The girl did not look back or answer him as she stumbled down the stairs. When she reached the hall, she was painfully aware that he had not come after her or tried to stop her from leaving.

* * *

Anna was confused and lonely. It was four days since she had last seen Benny and he had neither phoned nor written. The thought that she, and only she, would have to decide what to do terrified her. She had grown up in a country where abortion was considered a mortal sin. On the other hand, Aunt Pog had believed in a religious ethic that was liberal, caring but above all, immensely practical. It was a belief that was far from being in agreement with the dictates of the men in the distant Vatican.

"When that dreary lot stop dressing up in long purple frocks and have all been married and had a few poxy brats of their own, then they'll have the right to hold forth on the subject of unwanted pregnancies and other people's marital problems," she had declared crossly one Sunday after listening to a joyless, carping sermon, delivered by a visiting priest.

A week after telling Benny, unable to face having to go on pretending that all was as it should be, Anna feigned a migraine. She couldn't bear the thought of going in to the Tech and this gave her a couple of days' respite. Mrs P cosseted her, sympathising with her having 'one of them horrible, sick headaches', as she called them. She confided in Anna that she suffered from them herself from time to time but her husband said that was because she allowed her over-fertile imagination free rein and it was her own fault she got them.

As she lay in her darkened bedroom, Anna thought of the hours she and Benny had spent together, of his obvious pleasure and apparent appreciation of her. She remembered sadly how intimate she had been with him, how he had encouraged her not to hide anything. She realised now that he had never really talked about himself. Most of all, she kept thinking of how he had looked when she told him she was pregnant – how stony his face had been. All the tenderness she had thought he felt for her wiped away in a few seconds. At that moment, the only thing Anna was sure of was that, whatever she decided to do, Benny was not going to be part of the equation. He had obviously only pretended to love her. He had used her and had no intention of helping her or being supportive. Slowly, her hurt turned to anger.

Late that night, when she eventually fell asleep, she dreamed of her aunt. The following morning, Anna woke feeling strangely calm and full of resolve, knowing that she would keep the baby growing inside her.

Chapter Twenty-eight

Two weeks later, Anna had still not summoned up the courage to tell her mother. The sensation of calmness she'd experienced after her dream seemed to have evaporated, leaving her tense and anxious. Every night, before going to sleep, she promised herself that she would do it the next day. Then, out of the blue, Rosalind informed her that she and Adam were going to Paris for a week's holiday.

"You'll be fine with Mrs P and Ruffles for company, won't you?"

Anna, trying to hide her relief at this unexpected reprieve, smiled.

"Fine. Won't Paris be rather cold in March, though?"

"Probably," Adam said, dryly, "but cold weather never stopped your mother from spending money!"

They left two days later, Mr Pender carefully negotiating the snow-covered drive in Adam's comfortable Volvo. There had been last-minute worries about delayed flights due to bad weather at Stansted airport. Rosalind had paced back and forth, gripping her walking stick tightly.

"It *can't* snow any more," she exclaimed angrily, looking out of the long drawing-room windows at the wintry garden.

"Don't worry – it won't," laughed Adam. "It wouldn't dare!"

Anna, watching her mother, thought how elegant she looked in her long cape. I will never be like that – so polished and well groomed, she mused. It struck her that Rosalind also looked very happy, almost excited at the thought of the holiday ahead. She could see Adam responding to the sparkle in his wife's eyes by being extra attentive. He helped her into the car as though she were fragile and might shatter if handled roughly. Anna tried to block out an inner voice, reminding her that 'fragile' was far from the truth when it came to describing her mother. Perhaps what he admired was her mother's resilience and drive. It had certainly helped her through the difficult times in the past. The girl found herself wishing she had inherited more of these qualities.

Mrs P and Anna watched the car disappear behind the trees that sparkled with hoar frost in the afternoon sunlight.

"Well, I only hope George gets back in one piece. It'll be dark by the time he does." Mrs P turned to Anna, "Come on, dear! It's perishing out here. Let's get back inside and make ourselves a nice cuppa."

Anna called to Ruffles, who was busy snuffling in the snow, following the tracks made by unseen nocturnal visitors during the previous night. He reluctantly obeyed and the three of them went back into the warmth of the house. Anna closed the front door, shutting out the cold, white world behind them.

It was warm and cosy in the kitchen. Ruffles dozed in his basket beside the Aga. Mrs P made the tea and carried the heavy teapot to the table. She had come to a decision. She would just have to run the risk of being told to mind her own business. There was definitely something very wrong with the girl and the woman couldn't leave things the way they were any longer. She sat down and methodically arranged the cups and saucers in front of her, poured out a cup and handed it to Anna with a smile.

"Is there something you'd like to talk about, dear?" she asked, her eyes fixed on the other's face.

Instantly, Anna found herself blushing. She tried to meet the woman's gaze but had to look away.

"What do you mean?"

"Well, I may be very wrong but I think you need to talk to someone who will listen to you and not judge you and who'll do everything they can to help. If you don't mind me saying, I think it might be a good idea if you took up the offer. It wasn't easy for me to come out with it and if you don't talk now, it will only get harder as time goes by."

She sounded a little breathless, as though she had steeled herself to deliver a prepared speech and was thankful she had reached the end of it. There was a pause.

"How did you know?"

Mrs P leaned forward and took one of Anna's hands in her own.

"Oh, goodness me, child! It's how you look. I've seen that look on other girls' faces. I didn't have to be told. How far gone are you?"

"Ten weeks, I think."

"I see." Mrs P's usually cheerful face was thoughtful.

Anna looked down at the work-worn hands holding her own and felt a surge of gratitude at the simple acceptance implicit in the other's voice.

The woman spoke again gently. "How can I help you, dear? Is the father going to stand by you?"

"No. I'm afraid he isn't. He's not interested and I don't think there's anything much you can do, Mrs P, but it is good to talk about it. I haven't been able to say anything to my mother yet. She'll kill me when she finds out."

"I don't think so. She may be a stormy lady sometimes, but she won't do that." Mrs P smiled at Anna encouragingly. "It seems to me that the most important thing to find out is if you want to have this baby."

"Yes. I'm going to have the baby. I couldn't have an abortion," Anna said, fiercely.

"Well, maybe there's worse things in the world than having an abortion if the child isn't wanted. There's a lot of suffering caused by children being born when there isn't a loving place waiting there for them."

This was said in a quiet, almost matter-of-fact way. Anna had felt sure that someone like Mrs P would be outraged at the very idea of abortion.

"But . . . if all unwanted children were killed before they were born, then I might not be alive today," she said, bleakly.

Mrs P sprang to her feet, looking upset and spilling her tea. A surprised Ruffles sat up in his basket, startled by the sudden movement and clatter of china.

"I didn't mean that about you, dear child!"

"I know you didn't," said Anna, quickly. "It's all right, Mrs P."

"I'm sure your parents wanted you when you were born. I'm sure they did!"

"My father wanted me – but he died when I was nine."

"Oh, my dear!"

Anna too got up and went round the table to where Mrs P stood. They hugged each other without speaking. The woman held her tightly in her plump, strong arms and stroked her hair with work-roughened fingers. She smelled of Pond's cold cream and of the onions she had been cooking earlier for their supper.

Anna felt comforted. She knew she had a staunch ally in Mrs P, even if there was not all that much the other could do for her. She also knew, with increasing certainty, she wanted this unborn child and that she would do everything possible to ensure that there would be a place waiting and that the baby would be loved.

* * *

Adam and Rosalind returned from their holiday refreshed. Anna waited until her mother was on her own, deciding to break the news of her pregnancy without any further delay. Rosalind had been almost friendly since she got back. She had, at Adam's suggestion, bought her daughter a present: a *Lalique* greyhound, sitting erect with its ears pricked as though listening intently, head slightly angled to one side. Anna thought it was the most lovely thing she had ever been given but it made confessing all the more difficult. She couldn't help thinking how ironic it was that, just as her mother had become more approachable, she was going to have to shatter the improved atmosphere.

When tea was over, Anna slowly folded her napkin and cleared her throat nervously.

"Mother, I have something to tell you."

Her own voice sounded far away to her. Rosalind looked over in surprise. She could not remember her daughter using the word 'mother' since she had come to live with them. She wondered why Anna was looking so strained.

"Well?"

"You aren't going to like it."

"I won't know until you tell me."

Anna cleared her throat again and said quickly, "I'm going to have a baby."

There was a tense silence while she looked down at her empty plate, waiting for the outburst. But when she spoke, her mother's voice was cool and contained.

"When?"

"September. The beginning of September."

She glanced at the other's face, then looked hastily away. She could see no outward expression of the outrage and disgust she felt sure her mother was feeling. Anna gazed into the fire, uncomfortably aware of Rosalind's eyes resting on her.

"Who . . . no! I think we will discuss this further when Adam gets back this evening."

Rosalind waved a hand dismissively in Anna's direction. She needed time to think. Her thoughts were in turmoil. She could imagine what would happen when the good people of Little Melford got to hear about the scandal. The woman could just see the expression of condescending pity on Laura Chivers' face – and on the faces of all the rest of them. She had not been able to bring herself to ask who the father was. What if it were one of their friends? She tried to think back over possible candidates. It was too much! How dare she do this to us? she fumed. The feeling of being relaxed and content after the Paris trip had disappeared.

Anna sat quietly while her mother thought of all the patient wooing she had done since moving into The Pink House. She thought of all the boring residents' meetings attended, the lack-lustre coffee mornings, the fund-raisings for the decaying church with its dwindling number of desiccated, elderly worshippers, the repetitive drinks parties and dinners with the same collection of bland, uninteresting people. I will not allow her to spoil everything and ruin our reputation, she vowed. Controlling the desire to lash out, she spoke coldly, in a voice Anna remembered so well from the past.

"I think you'd better just go to your room."

The girl did not wait to be told twice.

* * *

That evening, she was called to Adam's study by Mrs P.

"It won't be that bad, my love. Try not to upset yourself," she said, as the girl followed her down the stairs.

Anna managed to give her a feeble smile. She was

dreading confronting the two of them together. Making an effort to 'walk tall and confront her demons', as Aunt Pog would have said, she knocked on the study door and went inside.

Adam was sitting at his desk, grim-faced. Her mother was standing by the fire with her back to Anna, Ruffles at her feet. The dog wagged his tail as the girl entered the room.

Her stepfather came straight to the point.

"I hear you have got yourself pregnant. Are you quite sure that it's not a false alarm?"

He sounds almost like Benny, she thought.

"Yes." Her voice was almost a whisper.

"Who is the father?"

"It doesn't matter. It's not important . . . he doesn't want to be involved."

Adam continued to question her in a controlled, merciless grilling but Anna refused to tell them about Benny.

"You realise of course that you will have to have a termination without delay," he said.

"No!"

The reply was almost a shout, which made Rosalind turn quickly. She and Adam exchanged glances and then they both stared at the girl in disbelief.

"But you must!" Rosalind insisted.

"No," said Anna, quietly. "I'm keeping my baby."

"That would be unwise. It's not too late to have the matter dealt with quickly and quietly. It's the only sensible thing to do, Anna." Adam's tone was firm. "Best for you and us and the . . ."

"And the baby? How could it be best for the baby to be killed? I won't have an abortion and you have no right to try and make me."

Anna glared at him.

"You must see that if you continue with this nonsense, it will ruin your life," said Rosalind, icily.

"In the same way as I ruined yours, Mother?"

Anna's eyes blazed. The word 'Mother' was spoken with contempt.

All of a sudden, the air between them seemed charged with a powerful electric current.

"You selfish little bitch!"

"Not a quality I inherited from my father," Anna cried, her eyes never leaving her mother's. She was fully roused now and suddenly didn't care any more what Rosalind thought of her.

The woman was pale with anger.

"How *dare* you!"

Rosalind struck out, slapping Anna's face as hard as she could. Then she turned away. If only the damned girl would agree to an abortion, no one need ever know about the wretched baby!

There was an agitated whimper from behind the couch, where Ruffles had retreated from the tension and raised voices.

"Stop! This is getting us nowhere," commanded Adam.

He had never seen his wife so angry nor had he suspected that Anna would have the necessary strength of character to stand up to her in the way she just had. He was taken aback by the young woman's furious contempt and her certainty that she was in the right. It was perfectly obvious that nothing he or Rosalind said would make her change her mind. But before he could continue, his wife spoke again.

"If that is the way you want to do things, then you will not be welcome any longer in this house."

Again, Adam intervened.

"Anna, I think it would be a good idea if you left your mother and me to talk." He looked at her flushed face with its scarlet finger-marks where her mother had hit her and noticed for the first time that she was trembling. "Please?"

Responding to the appeal in his voice, Anna left the room stiffly, Ruffles trotting at her heels.

* * *

The next morning, there was a letter from Benny in the post. In spite of the way he had behaved, Anna couldn't stop herself from hoping that perhaps he had changed his mind. She crammed it into her coat pocket and set off down the driveway to catch the bus. After last night, she was not going to wait for Adam to give her a lift and she couldn't face the thought of breakfast. To please Mrs P, she had forced herself to swallow a few mouthfuls of sweet tea.

On the bus, she read his letter to her. It was brief. He said he was going back to London to stay with his parents for a while and to also follow up a job offer. He hoped she would make the right decision – she knew what he meant by that – and he was sure she would be fine. He was sorry he hadn't had time to see her before he left but that was probably all for the best after the way in which they had

343

parted. He ended the letter with the word Benny. No 'with love from', she thought, miserably. Still, it was more honest like this. He must never have loved her, so why pretend? Once, she'd thought he had. Anna was beginning to suspect this was because she had so very much wanted him to love her, now that Aunt Pog was not around any more.

Getting off the bus at the terminus, Anna wasn't sure if she could stand a day of classes at the Tech. All she really wanted to do was to curl up in a ball somewhere warm and dark and go to sleep for a long time. She hesitated at the bus stop, hands in her coat pockets, her shoulders hunched against the cold.

"Flaming Nora! If it ain't Anna!"

She was nearly knocked off her feet by a bear hug and an overpowering odour of *BodyShop*.

"Jess!" For the first time in weeks, Anna laughed out loud. "Jess, it's good to see you."

It was the same old Jess, with her outrageous earrings and wearing a few more layers of clothing than when Anna had last seen her. Her hair was now the colour of tropical water on a sunny day. The sight of the brilliant blue strands, all different lengths, cheered Anna enormously.

"Got time for an 'ot drink, then?"

"I'm going to be desperately late for the Tech."

"Well, be a little bit late! Go on, girl! Live dangerously! I bet you don't mitch all that often!"

Anna didn't need persuading.

"There's a little café around the corner. Let's go there."

Jess linked her arm into Anna's and they set off briskly in the direction of the café. Anna glanced at the other's happy face. She was like a breath of summer on that cold winter's morning, she thought. She was glad Jess had made no mention of the party at the caravan.

They sat beside the steamed-up window in the crowded café and sipped their mugs of hot Bovril.

"Where's Marv?"

"Done a runner to Nepal. 'E got into a little bit of trouble and 'ad to flit."

"Oh, I'm sorry," said Anna, untruthfully.

"I'm not! Fings got a bit difficult an' I was quite glad when he pushed off. Silly sod went wiv Sal, and Josh thumped 'im. Josh don't come round no more. Shame really. Then Marv got caught lifting some stuff out of a supermarket and the plods got called." Jess looked thoughtful. "I don't fink I was interesting enough for Marv – 'e wanted someone classy, like Sal. You know?"

Anna thought Jess looked far from grief-stricken, just cheerfully resigned to her boyfriend's disappearance.

"I bet he wouldn't have as much fun with Sal as he did with you, Jess," she said, indignantly.

Jess beamed at her over the top of her mug and chuckled.

"No, I fink you're right there! Can't imagine her 'avin her backside tattooed with a butterfly." In response to Anna's look of enquiry, she giggled. "Yeah, 'ad it done last summer. I'll show you when the weather gets a bit warmer!"

"Are you enjoying being on your own?" asked Anna, curious to know if there was anyone else on the scene.

"'Snot that bad really. I got time to pluck me eyebrows, which I never 'ad when Marv was around! An' I landed a job in the little Indian shop near the Catholic," said Jess, referring to the large Catholic church near the town centre. "The old bag doesn't pay very well but it's enough for the bedsit an' a bit of grub." She squinted at Anna, head tilted to one side. "Wot about you then? You looked a bit peaky when I saw you back there. You OK?"

"I'm going to have a baby, Jess."

"Christ! Really?" Jess's face glowed with enthusiasm. "That's bloody brilliant, that is! You got a name for it, then?"

Her pleasure was infectious. Again, Anna laughed out loud.

"Not yet. I haven't thought that far ahead." Her face became serious again. "My mother has told me to move out. She would be so ashamed if the neighbours found out that her one-and-only daughter was pregnant."

"Wot?" cried Jess, in disbelief. "She should be chuffed as 'ell to know she's going to be a gran!"

"Well, I'm afraid she thinks it's all a horrible nightmare and if I go away, she will wake up and everything will be all right again."

Seeing the look of unhappiness on her face, Jess leaned over the small table and grabbed Anna by the arm and squeezed hard.

"Listen, you! She's plain daft if she don't know how lucky she is. It's the best bit of news I've 'eard in a long time – really great! Is the dad pleased or don't he want to know?"

"He's not interested. He's gone away."

"Then you're better off wivout 'im!" said Jess with finality. "Do I know 'im – the dad?"

"It's Benny."

"Blimey! I 'aven't seen 'im for ages neither."

They talked, Anna filling in some of the details of her first meeting with Benny. She didn't enlarge on the disastrous ending to the party. She also told Jess about Mrs P and how kind she had been to her. Suddenly, the other girl looked up at the clock on the wall and gave an exclamation.

"Oh, Gawd! I'll 'ave to run. Mrs Rao is a bit of a Tartar an' I don't want to lose me job. Give me yer number an' this is where I'm staying."

She scribbled an address on the back of a paper napkin. Anna wrote down her telephone number and gave it to her.

"Thanks!" said Jess. "I lost it last time or I would've given you a bell to let you know where I was. You will keep in touch an' let me know wot's 'appening, won't you?" She got up to leave. Then, she suddenly leaned over and planted a kiss on Anna's cheek. "Take care of yourself, girl!"

As Jess clattered out of the shop door, Anna smiled to herself as she thought of how delighted the other had been over the news of the baby. As far as Jess was concerned, it was 'just brilliant'. She was the only person who had responded in that way. Even dear Mrs P hadn't been sure.

She half-closed her eyes. The warmth of the café made her feel sleepy. Her thoughts changed from Jess to her mother and Adam and the next inevitable 'discussion' scheduled for that evening. Her stomach lurched.

Chapter Twenty-nine

"They're putting her out of the house." Mrs P's voice was shocked.

Her husband raised his head from the open bonnet of the Volvo.

"What do you expect? Carrying on the way she has," he said, gruffly. He picked up the oil can and continued working.

"But, George! She's only a child herself. She may have been foolish but she's not bad. It's not right to treat her like that."

George did not bother to reply. The whole thing bored him. Perhaps when the girl left, life would get back to normal again, he thought. One thing he did know was that her bloody mother had been sheer murder these past few days. Nothing was right for madam.

Mrs P gave him a withering look before turning away.

"I suppose it's stupid of me to expect any sympathy from you. I never got any, so why should she?"

Her husband half-emerged from the car and looked at her retreating back in surprise. It was out of character for his wife to talk to him in that tone of voice. The foolish woman had got herself all worked up over nothing.

May Pender let herself into the welcoming kitchen. As always during cold weather, Ruffles lay in his basket beside the Aga. He opened an eye and greeted her with a half-hearted wag of the tail. Poor dog, she thought. Things hadn't been normal over the past few days for him either. He had been shouted at by Mrs Strong and his favourite person had been either shut in her room or out. No one had taken him for a walk for days.

She lowered herself into a chair beside the kitchen table and picked up a sprout from the basin. Cutting off the stalk with a practised flick of the knife, she sat, staring at the wall opposite her. It was difficult to concentrate on anything at the moment. She seemed to be always thinking about Anna's dilemma, always listening to see if she could get an idea from a snatch of conversation of what was being decided about the girl's fate.

Mrs P wondered what had been said at the second session in Mr Strong's study when Anna had got back from Cambridge to find them both waiting for her. The poor child had emerged a good while later looking very upset. She'd retreated upstairs, where she had remained for the rest of the evening.

Mrs P had asked if she could take her up a tray. A stony-faced Rosalind had given her the strong impression that it would be prudent if she did not interfere.

"I gather Anna has already informed you of her

condition, Mrs P," Rosalind had said, obviously annoyed that her daughter had confided in the woman. "You will on no account speak to anyone about what has happened," she continued, ignoring the angry flush on the other woman's cheeks. "By the time the situation becomes obvious, Anna will not longer be living here." Mrs P was outraged. She opened her mouth to remonstrate but was cut short by a curt, "That will be all. I do not intend discussing this matter further."

Dismissed, the woman had returned to the kitchen. She felt horribly impotent.

Now, as she looked down at the sprout in her hand May Pender shook her head slightly. Fancy me telling the girl that I would do all I could to help. The fact is, I'm no use at all to the poor thing, she thought angrily to herself as she cut vigorously into the base of another sprout. What was Anna doing – all alone up there?

Mrs P had hardly set eyes on Anna for two days.

She gripped the knife tightly and thought of her only sister, Rose. If only she were still alive. She would have listened to the tale of woe and would have understood how she felt, even if she couldn't come up with a solution. Instead, she thought, the only person to talk to was that miserable, dried-up man out there in the garage, who hadn't got an ounce of compassion in him. The only things he cared about were his wages, his vegetables and getting down to The Queen's Arms for a pint or two of best bitter.

Her chest felt constricted at the unfairness of the situation. Suddenly her arms became leaden, as though stuck to the table and a terrible ache of pain seemed to smother her, making it difficult to breathe. With eyes tightly closed, she sat, patiently waiting for it to pass, as it always did after a while.

* * *

The meeting two days earlier with Adam, Rosalind and Anna had begun not so much as a discussion but a monologue from the girl's stepfather. Rosalind did not speak, keeping her eyes on her husband and more or less ignoring her daughter.

Adam waited until Anna sat down. She did so with a horrible feeling of déjà vu.

"Anna, as you are apparently determined to have this baby, alternative living arrangements will have to be made. You must understand that your mother and I are not prepared to tolerate the embarrassment that your staying here would cause – or the disruption to our lives. You will come into your inheritance in less than four months and then you will be more than generously provided for. Until that time, we have decided to loan you the money necessary to buy an apartment. You will repay us as soon as you are in a position to do so." Adam paused, as though mentally checking off a list of points that had to be made. "Of course, it is up to you but we do not advise you to finish your course at the Tech. The situation there might become too . . . tiring for you and awkward."

Anna looked at him steadily. She would finish the course, however awkward, she thought. She was going to get her diploma. At least then, she would have some sort of qualifications, even if they weren't very impressive ones.

Adam continued, "I have arranged for a couple of the larger estate agents in Cambridge to send us out their current lists. I think for all our sakes it is extremely important that there is no delay."

He glanced over to where his wife sat, manicured hands clenched in her lap. She looked very pale. He knew that she had hardly slept during the past couple of nights. Adam found himself wishing that there might have been an alternative course of action they could have chosen but she had been adamant that Anna had to go. He agreed that the girl had been a damned fool and that to go ahead with the pregnancy was lunacy – but Rosalind was her mother. Did she really feel no bond between her daughter and herself ? he wondered uncomfortably. He had become used to having Anna around the place and he rather liked their morning journeys into Cambridge. She had some strange ideas on some subjects but she was like a breath of fresh air. Unexpectedly, he found himself thinking that he was going to miss her.

Anna felt strangely calm. She realised that she was not really surprised that her mother wanted her to leave. She supposed she had already known that would be her way of dealing with a situation she found unpleasant. At least Adam's offer of financial help meant that it would be possible for her to have a place of her own, away from the charged atmosphere that had filled the house since the announcement of her pregnancy.

"Thank you for saying you'll help me," she said to him, in a quiet voice.

He waved aside her thanks, looking again at his wife.

"Is there anything you want to say, Rosalind?" he prompted.

She shook her head. "No, nothing else needs to be said." She got to her feet. "I would like a drink please, Adam."

She left the room without looking in her daughter's direction. Rosalind had no intention of allowing Anna to see the tears of frustration and disappointment in her eyes.

Adam paused on his way out. He put a hand briefly on the girl's shoulder.

"I'm truly sorry that it had to come to this, Anna. But I promise I will help as much as I can over finding you somewhere reasonable to live."

For the first time, Anna was aware of his discomfort.

"I am sorry too," she said, giving him a brief smile.

After he had gone, she sat for a while in the book-lined room. What would have happened if her father had still been alive she wondered. He wouldn't have been angry like her mother but he might not have understood the way things had been with her and Benny. He too might have been disappointed but she knew he would never have allowed her mother to turn her out of the house. And dear Aunt Pog . . . Anna covered her face with her hands. If *only* Aunt Pog could be with her. She would have known what to do. Anna could imagine her saying, "Well, we haven't been terribly clever, have we, darling? Never mind, don't worry. One step at a time and we'll sort it all out beautifully!"

She got up slowly. It's no good thinking 'if only'. I will find somewhere nice to live and I'll think of Aunt Pog and it'll be all right, she tried to reassure herself.

* * *

Rosalind distanced herself from the search for a new home for Anna. She refused to allow anyone to see how uneasy she felt and threw herself into arranging a forthcoming charity luncheon. She avoided, as much as possible, being alone with her daughter, feeling guilty that Anna would soon be leaving and angry that she should feel guilty. After all, the mess they now found themselves in was all her daughter's fault, wasn't it? Rosalind still couldn't understand why Anna had not agreed to an abortion. She lay awake in the early hours of the morning, remembering her own feelings of panic and rejection at the thought of the child growing in her own womb nineteen years earlier.

Adam, however, was as good as his word and vetted the glossy brochures Anna showed him with an experienced eye, uncovering hidden problems and explaining what the fanciful descriptions really meant. He was surprised at how positive she was and how she seemed to know exactly what she wanted, turning down his idea of an apartment in favour of a small house with a garden.

"For the baby," she said, smiling because he had not thought of that himself.

After ten days of tireless hunting and some missed lectures, Anna took him to see the house she had found and with which she had obviously fallen in love. They met in their lunch hour and walked the ten-minute walk to a small tree-lined square near the river, not far from the centre of Cambridge.

"That's the one! Number ten, on the corner," said Anna, her face lit up with enthusiasm.

As they walked towards it, Adam looked critically at

the neat, terraced brick house with its pretty fanlight and empty window boxes. Early eighteen hundreds, he guessed. It seemed all right on the outside and the brickwork and roof looked sound.

The agent was waiting outside, leaning against the side of his car. He watched them as they approached and smiled pleasantly.

"Miss Armitage!"

He shook hands with Anna and Adam, who he took to be her father. He covertly admired the beautifully tailored suit the older man was wearing and the expensive shoes. He smelt money and his hopes rose. Perhaps this was going to be his lucky day, he thought. The girl was certainly a looker. He'd shown her around the day before and she had seemed very keen on the place. Nice to have one's old man cough up for a house. He wondered if she were a student.

"I only have half an hour to spare. Perhaps you could let us in?" Adam suggested, noticing the lingering look of appreciation in the young man's eye as he spoke to Anna.

The estate agent waited for them in the garden while they viewed the property. Anna led Adam up the narrow stairs to the small landing. There were three bedrooms and a small bathroom, which contained an old-fashioned hip-bath with a built-in seat. All the windows looked out onto trees. The best view was from the back bedroom, which overlooked the long garden containing what looked like a giant walnut, a Judas tree and some untidy apple trees at the far end of the unkempt lawn.

Adam had to admit to himself that the house had a nice feel to it and he could see why Anna had taken such a liking to the place. He was shown the spacious study to the left of the front door and the two reception rooms on the other side of the hall with their original folding doors still intact. The kitchen at the back was old-fashioned but sunny and faced south-west. Spring sunlight flooded the room, making patterns on the worn red-tiled floor. A battered cooker with chipped feet stood against one wall opposite an old, rectangular sink shaped like a drinking-trough. Apart from a rickety-looking cupboard, they were the only pieces of furniture in the room.

Anna turned to Adam, expectantly.

"It's just perfect, isn't it?"

He hadn't the heart to say that he thought it needed a considerable amount of work done on it before it could be called perfect.

"You'll have to put in central heating before next winter comes or you'll freeze," he warned her, looking at the badly worn sash window with its single panes of glass.

"But isn't it a beautiful house?" she insisted.

He relented.

"Yes, it's full of promise," he agreed, with a faint smile.

Chapter Thirty

Today was Anna's nineteenth birthday and now, the money her father had left her was truly hers. She had received her diploma from the Tech. – from a disapproving Principal, who clearly thought it disgraceful she hadn't had the decency to hide herself away with her shame. The doctor was pleased with her state of health and her baby was due in eight weeks – and for the past months, she'd felt that there was a reason for her existence.

Anna could feel the child moving inside her. What had been a sensation like a slight flutter, now made her sometimes wince and nearly jump, the movements were so strong. She cradled her stomach with her hands, impatient to see and hold the small, energetic creature that seemed to be attempting to kick its way out into the world. She lay back in the deck chair, relaxed and happy. It was almost as if Aunt Pog were up there, giving the 'Man upstairs' the odd nudge to make sure that all went well with her great-niece. The girl wondered idly if, now her aunt was in heaven, she ever called Him 'darling'. Perhaps, but it would have to be with a very large capital D. Anna smiled to herself at the thought of a white-gowned Pog, surrounded by all her closest friends, playing never-ending games of bridge while drinking 100% proof gin from golden goblets.

The only negative thoughts she seemed to have now concerned either her mother or Benny. At the back of her mind, there lurked the idea that, when the baby was born, Rosalind wouldn't be able to stop herself from becoming involved – even if it weren't in a particularly close or cosy way – because the child would be Anna's responsibility, not hers, and so it would be easier for her to withdraw when she wanted. Anna found herself hoping that the child she carried would act as an icebreaker. Then, with a sigh, she would tell herself that it was just wishful thinking. Her mother would never change.

There had been a brief time, a few months into the pregnancy, when Anna had almost forgotten about Benny. Her hurt and anger had gone and she was left with a feeling of sadness that he had behaved in the way he had. She realised now that the news of her pregnancy had terrified him. He had run away from a situation with which he was unable to cope. However much she reminded herself that she was perfectly able to manage without him, she still missed him. Anna often imagined waking in her sunny bedroom at the back of the house with Benny's brown body lying beside her. He'd always looked beautiful when he slept. There was something about the sensual shape of his mouth and smooth, long limbs and his gentle, even breathing that made her want to fold herself into the crook of his arm and stretch alongside him so that as much of her skin as possible was in contact with his. She wondered if he thought about her or wondered about their child.

"There you are, my dear. A nice, hot cuppa."

Mrs P handed her a steaming cup. She firmly believed that hot cuppas were the best thing to have at any time of the day and however hot the weather. Anna looked up at her contentedly and thought how different she looked these days. It was as though she had only seen her in monochrome before. Since the move, the woman seemed to have taken on a three-dimensional, coloured persona, which suited her.

Mrs P had given them all a bad fright. A few days before Anna left The Pink House, the middle-aged woman suffered a heart attack and had been found by Adam, clinging to the kitchen table, white with pain and unable to speak. After three weeks in hospital in the attentive care of an eminent cardiologist, who happened to be a satisfied client of Adam's, she had emerged, rejuvenated. Her once pale face was now a healthy pink and all the character and humour that had been suppressed before seemed to have found expression.

When Anna had visited her in hospital, she'd been surprised and touched when Mrs P had offered to come and live with her in No.10, Old Square.

"To tell the truth, I could do with the change, dear," she'd said. "But only if you'd like it and only for as long as I'm useful, mind."

She had been gratified by the warmth of Anna's

response. The girl threw her arms around her in an uncharacteristically abandoned way.

"There's nothing in the world I would like more, Mrs P! Thank you!"

So she had joined Anna in the Cambridge house and a puzzled George had been dispatched to live with his miserable sister in Bournemouth, wondering what had got into his once docile wife.

Rosalind, furious at the woman's defection, wasted no time in replacing them with a couple from the Philippines, who were happy to accept far lower wages than their English counterparts.

Mrs P sat down thankfully beside Anna.

"How are you feeling, my dear?"

"Marvellous! Kicked to bits but I feel great!"

"You *look* marvellous, child," the woman said, looking at the girl fondly.

She was right to keep this baby, she thought. A child to give her love to and who will love her back. Mrs P watched her, thinking how happy she looked and yet calm at the same time. She remembered how strained Anna had been before the move. The transformation had taken place slowly, beginning on the day she had arrived to take up residence in the minimally furnished house. The move had been made with Jess and Adam's help. It was almost as if by removing herself from her mother's house it had made it possible for Anna to really be herself and to start to look forward to the birth of her baby. She had visited Mrs P in hospital the day after the move, looking tired but radiant.

"I'll take my time and only buy what's absolutely right

for the house – things which are beautiful as well as useful," Anna had said to Jess, on the first night in her new home as they ate a simple supper, sitting in two deck chairs with their plates balanced on their knees.

"You'll make it perfect," said Jess. "It's already bloody marvellous!"

When Mrs P eventually joined Anna in the house, she too had been thrilled. She was delighted at how happy the girl seemed. She saw the great care Anna had taken with the colour schemes throughout the house, the little touches the girl had made – like the lovely vase of fresh flowers in Mrs P's bedroom with the brand-new bed, covered in pretty sheets and pillows and the softest blanket the woman had ever touched. The place had been painted from top to bottom and each room glowed with fresh paint.

"Are you sure I can't help in the kitchen?" Anna asked, sipping her scalding tea.

"No, you stay where you are and rest. Everything's organised and your birthday dinner wouldn't be a surprise if you came and poked your nose in," replied Mrs P firmly.

Since the early morning, she had been chopping and slicing and cooking; the house filled with mouth-watering aromas. As they sat outside on the uneven grass, scattered with daisies and dandelions, Anna caught the smell of herbs and wine wafting through the open door and windows. It made her feel deliciously hungry.

"What time is that Jess one coming?" said Mrs P, shading her eyes from the hot sun.

She thoroughly approved of the young woman. After the initial surprise at her clothes and hairstyles, she had taken a great liking to the warm-hearted girl who so obviously cared about Anna's welfare and who had shown herself to be a stalwart, if unpunctual, friend. Both Mrs P and Anna often wondered how she managed to hold on to her job with the long-suffering Mrs Rao. Mrs P liked the way Jess had insisted she stay with Anna until she came out of hospital. Jess had even given up smoking because she had read somewhere that it was bad for the unborn baby.

At first, Mrs P was a little shocked by some of the stories Jess told her but she had also giggled like a young thing at the descriptions of her sometimes rather scandalous adventures. She found that they shared a similar sense of humour and Jess treated her like a second mother, which pleased the childless woman.

Anna put her mug down on the grass beside her.

"Jess will be late as usual," she laughed, "but she promised she'd come straight from work. She said she would ask Mrs Rao to let her off a bit early."

She lay back in the deck chair and closed her eyes. Bees buzzed in the old roses that clung in a haphazard way to the decaying trellis, which sagged slightly over the back door and kitchen windows. Mrs P, who knew a thing or two about roses, had told her that one of them was called the Rambling Rector, which had made them both laugh.

"We'll have to make sure he doesn't climb in the windows when we're not looking," Mrs P had said, gazing up admiringly at the great, arching sprays of small, creamy white flowers.

While Anna drifted into sleep, Mrs P thought how good it was to be given this chance to be useful. She realised that, for possibly the first time ever in her life, she felt really needed. George had only missed her when a meal wasn't ready on time because she'd been delayed for some reason. Now that her sister was dead, she suddenly realised that this girl was the only family she needed or wanted. She sat quietly for a while watching Anna sleep before getting up to go and check on how her chicken and almond dish was coming on. It was one of her best recipes and she wanted it to be perfect for the birthday meal that evening.

* * *

The sound of voices woke Anna. It had only been twenty minutes since Mrs P left her but she felt refreshed. She opened her eyes and listened.

One of the voices was Jess's, the other a man's, which she recognised as Adam's. She hadn't been expecting a visit from him today. For a moment, she wondered if her mother was with him. But before she had time to get up from her chair, Jess erupted out of the house, a pink and red lava flow of swirling colour. She flew across the grass to Anna and bent down to give her a hug.

"'Ello you! 'Ow's things?" She didn't wait to be answered. "You're looking just great! 'Ow's the bulge keeping, then?" She laid a hand lightly on Anna's stomach. Her eyes widened. "Blimey! You must be covered in bruises inside. It just has to be a bloke baby – you wait an' see!"

Before Anna could respond to this onslaught, Adam appeared in the doorway, closely shadowed by Mrs P, who had not forgiven him for allowing Anna to be turned out of The Pink House, although she guessed that it was his wife who had insisted. At least *she* hadn't put in an appearance, she thought thankfully.

When Anna saw that her mother was not with him, she felt a mixture of relief and disappointment well up inside her. She remembered her seventeenth and last birthday she'd celebrated in Ireland, when there had been no card from Rosalind. Why haven't I learned not to want her to be here for me she asked herself, as she made a clumsy effort to get to her feet. She noticed, as he walked towards her, that Adam held a small packet in his hand.

"Don't get up, Anna. How are you?" His enquiry sounded genuine.

"I'm fine. How are you?" she replied carefully as she sat back in the deck chair.

How silly these banal formalities are, she thought. She wondered why he had come. Was there a problem with the trust fund? Anna found herself thinking that perhaps her mother had found a way of spoiling her birthday and then felt ashamed at the thought.

"Don't look so worried! I just wanted to give you this." He handed her the packet. "I also wanted to wish you a Happy Birthday!"

He nodded pleasantly to Jess, who beamed back at him.

Anna also smiled, visibly relaxing and Adam thought, not for the first time, what a beautiful young woman she was and how being pregnant had somehow made her even more attractive. He found himself wishing that Rosalind could find it in her heart to accept the fact that she would soon be a grandmother – whether she liked the idea or not.

If only she could, he thought, she might find it easier to connect with her daughter, perhaps even forgive her for all her perceived wrongdoings. He felt that she was losing out badly because of her inability to be part of it all. On his way through the house, Adam had glimpsed the greyhound she had given her daughter after the Paris trip. It was on the mantelpiece in the sitting-room. He hoped Anna didn't have any unrealistic ideas about Rosalind relenting and offering an olive branch.

"Would you like a cup of tea?" Anna asked.

"No, thank you. I mustn't stay. I have a client coming at six. I just wanted to make sure that you had that on your birthday." He nodded towards the packet in her hand. "There's a note inside that explains everything."

Jess and Anna watched as Adam turned away reluctantly.

As he walked slowly back towards the house, he thought how nice it would be to sit in the untidy, wild garden with the three so very different women. He wanted to stay and talk and relax. He realised that he would like to get to know them all properly – to be included in their conversation. He was amazed at the change in Mrs P. He would not have recognised her as the same featureless woman who had worked for them at The Pink House. As for the other one, whom he had bumped into at the front door just now, not having seen her since the day Anna moved in, it was a good thing Rosalind hadn't set eyes on her. He could just imagine her reaction to the pink hair and multi-coloured, flowing robe, not to mention the unhealthy-looking black nail-varnish adorning her toenails, emerging from the plastic sandals.

"'E's not that bad, really," commented Jess, as soon as Adam had gone. "*And* he brought a lovely bottle of bubbly. Mrs P's put it in the fridge for tonight. Wot's in the parcel then? Go on, open it! I'm dying to know what it is."

She flopped down on to the grass beside Anna and stared pointedly at the bulging, brown envelope.

Anna laughed.

"All right! Give me a moment! Let's wait until Mrs P gets back from her escort duties so she can see too."

As soon as the woman re-appeared, Jess called to her.

"Come on, Mrs P! Anna's got a present an' I'm going to burst if she don't open it soon!"

Mrs P hurried over and they watched as Anna tore off the end of the envelope and shook on to her lap a square, leather box and a piece of folded paper. She smoothed the paper flat and read the contents. Then, very slowly, she opened the box. All three women gasped.

Lying on the cream satin was an antique emerald and pearl ring. The pearls glowed with a subtle, milky light that seemed to come from within and the oval-shaped emerald's rich, green facets sparkled with cool fire in the afternoon light.

"This was left to me in my father's Will. I didn't know about it." Anna's voice was hushed. "It belonged to his mother and he wanted me to have it on my nineteenth birthday."

"Wow! I never seen anything like it. It's only *gorgeous!*" exclaimed Jess. "Aren't you going to put it on then?"

She and Mrs P watched Anna, who sat, looking down at the ring and not speaking. They suddenly noticed the tears coursing down her face. Kneeling on either side of her, they looked at her anxiously, wondering what on earth could be wrong.

"Wot's the matter? Don't you like it?" asked Jess in a worried voice.

"It's the most beautiful thing I've ever seen," said Anna, brushing away her tears. "It's just that I suddenly wanted my father to be here so much. I want him to give it to me. He died such a long time ago and I can't remember him properly. I only have one photo of him and it's not enough." She turned to the older woman. "I want him to be here on my birthday," she sobbed.

Mrs P cradled Anna's head against her, fighting to keep her own composure.

"Of course you do, dear. It would be lovely but . . . isn't it nice that he was able to leave you something so special?" She searched for the right words. "So precious. He must have thought the world of you."

She drew back a little and looked down into Anna's anguished face.

"I don't know what he thought of me, Mrs P," replied Anna, softly. "I can't remember any more."

"Of course 'e thought the world of you!" exclaimed Jess. "No one doles out ruddy great rocks like that wot belonged to their ma wivout really wanting to!"

She sounded so indignant that Anna started to laugh. Mrs P threw Jess an approving glance over the top of Anna's head.

"Go on! Put the flaming thing on, or I will. Wot are you waiting for?" Jess insisted, impatiently.

Anna obediently slipped the ring on to the third finger of her right hand. It fitted perfectly. She held it up so they could all admire the effect.

"Brilliant!" said Jess, beaming.

"It's really lovely. Fit for a princess," agreed Mrs P, taking hold of Anna's wrist and gently turning her hand one way and then the other, watching as the gem flashed in the sunlight. "You are a lucky girl to have been left this beautiful thing."

"Yes, I am, aren't I?" Anna agreed, quietly.

* * *

All Mrs P's hard work paid off and the evening meal turned out to be delicious. Jess had decorated the table with as many roses from the garden as she could lay her hands on. Her arms were covered in scratches from her struggles with the Rambling Rector.

"Bastard plant!" she was heard to mutter after tea, while balancing precariously on a rickety garden table, kitchen scissors dangling from one hand, as she tried to suck out a particularly vicious thorn that had imbedded itself in her thumb. She was almost invisible, surrounded by the enfolding prickly arms of the rector.

"I don't think you should call a rector a bastard," admonished Mrs P with a smile.

The roses, spilling out of any spare receptacle capable of holding water, filled the windowsill and table in the sparsely furnished dining-room. Their perfume hung in the air. Candles stood on the table and mantelpiece. The new dinner service Anna had chosen in a rich green and gold, glowed against the background of the old, cream, embroidered tablecloth that was Mrs P's birthday present to her.

"It belonged to my grandmother. She always loved it and kept it wrapped up in tissue paper in a trunk in the attic. It was a shame really not to use it. I hope you will be able to enjoy it often, dear."

Anna had been touched by being given such a special gift.

"We'll use it on the table tonight for my birthday dinner. It will look lovely. Thank you so much, Mrs P!"

The combination of roses and newly painted apple-green walls, the carefully laid table, the candlelight and the windows thrown open to let in the warm summer air, gave a magic quality to the evening that was memorable.

When no one could eat anything more and they sat contentedly, talking over their cups of coffee, Jess got up suddenly and vanished into the hall. She came back with an untidy parcel wrapped in gaudy gold and red paper. It tinkled slightly as she put it down on the table in front of Anna.

"'Appy Birthday to you and the bulge, wiv love from me, an I 'ope to God you like it, cos I can't take it back."

She sat down in a flurry of clattering bangles and eagerly watched Anna, who was trying to break through the criss-cross of sellotape.

"Heavens, Jess! I don't think you want me to open this," Anna laughed, as she struggled with the unyielding bundle.

After having resorted to using a knife, the wrapping fell away to reveal a many-tiered mobile consisting of stars, moons and suns. It was made from some kind of silvery metal that shone in the candlelight and was highly decorated, covered in pieces of mother-of-pearl and mirror fragments.

"I hope you don't mind cos it's really for the bulge but I thought it would look great over 'is cot and 'e can look at it when 'e's bored. That'll keep 'im from crying and that'll mean you'll be able to get some sleep. So, I reckon it is for you too. It comes from India and it was the only one in the shop. I 'ad to battle with that old bat Mrs Rao to get a special price and I know she won't let me take it back. Do you like it?" Jess asked, anxiously.

"I love it, Jess, and I'm sure the bulge will too. Thank you!" Anna looked at the mobile with pleasure as it hung from her raised hand, spinning gently. She liked the tinkling sound it made and thought it sounded like icicles, shaken by the wind in the branches of distant trees. "We'll hang it over the cot tomorrow. I know he or she will love watching and listening to it."

"I told you, it's a bloke-baby. You just wait an' see!" said Jess, with a pleased grin.

As the last light was switched off and silence settled over the house, the moon slid from behind a cloud to reveal a jet-black cat, sitting patiently on the kitchen windowsill, gazing into the shadowed garden with unblinking golden eyes.

* * *

Anna woke next morning feeling at peace with herself and the world around her. For a few minutes, she lay in bed, remembering the meal Mrs P had prepared for her on the previous day and how good it had felt with the three of them sitting around the table. If she could ever persuade Kathleen and Amy to come over to Cambridge, she was sure they would all like each other.

When she went downstairs, she heard Mrs P talking in the kitchen and assumed that Jess was already up and about. She opened the door to find no trace of Jess but Mrs P addressing a very thin black cat that was busy grooming himself at the open back door. As soon as Anna entered the room, he stopped and stared at her.

"I don't know where he comes from but he's made himself quite at home. Isn't he handsome?" said Mrs P. "He's ever so hungry. He drank a whole saucer of milk in no time at all."

With difficulty, Anna bent down and gently stroked the soft fur at the back of the cat's head. He immediately half-closed his eyes and started to purr loudly.

That day, they made enquiries locally but no one seemed to know anything about the cat and so, after a week, he was formally adopted and given the name of Fortune by Jess, who had undergone yet another psychic experience.

"'E was meant to come," she informed them. "I get real solid vibes when 'e's around. It's karma."

"Whatever *that* is," said Mrs P, shaking her head. That young one was a constant source of amazement to her.

What a lot of daft nonsense the girl talked, she thought to herself later as she sat in the shade of the Judas tree, knitting a shawl for the baby with deft movements of her hands. She was glad Fortune was staying though. There was something special about him. Jess was right there. Mrs P could not quite put a finger on it but she sensed that he was a nice, friendly animal. He'd certainly made it perfectly plain that he liked Anna. Mrs P just hoped that no one was frantically searching for him because she too liked having an animal around the place. His presence somehow made the house seem even more homely than ever.

Chapter Thirty-one

The hot, summer weather continued until the end of August. Then welcome rain fell for a week, almost without a break. Anna was grateful for the cooler nights and fresher days. She was beginning to feel tired and with three weeks still to go of her pregnancy, she found herself happy to just sit with Fortune at her side and write long letters to Kathleen.

She had been thrilled to hear the news of the birth of Kathleen and Sean's child one week earlier. In her letter to Anna, Kathleen sounded happy and full of the enthusiasm that seemed to have left her in the early years of her marriage when it had looked as though she would never be able to have children.

'I know you won't be able to come over to the christening, what with the birth of your own baby so near, but we will all miss you very much. I know you'll be with us in spirit and we will drink a toast to you. (By the way, PJ still has a photo of you in his room!)' Kathleen had written.

There had even been a short, semi-illegible scribble from Amy, threatening to come and visit after Anna's baby was born.

* * *

Fortune hardly left Anna's side, following her from room to room and sleeping at the foot of her bed when she went up for an afternoon nap. Only at night did he vanish silently into the darkness after keeping them company for the evening meal. He always returned with the dawn and would wait patiently on the kitchen windowsill for Mrs P to let him in for his breakfast. Then he would seek out Anna and stay with her for the rest of the day. Mrs P confided in Jess that she thought it was almost as if he were guarding the girl from unseen danger.

Jess nodded sagely.

"Wot did I tell ya? It was meant to 'appen – 'im turning up the way 'e did."

"Well, I just hope he doesn't disappear as suddenly as he turned up. She's got really fond of him," said Mrs P.

"Don't you worry, Mrs P!" said Jess laughing. "Wiv all the food an' attention 'e gets, 'e won't do a bunk!"

Over the past months, they had all worked hard to make the house ready for Anna's child. Mrs P happily sewed curtains on her old treadle sewing machine. She made cushions for the new sofa and when she wasn't sewing, she was knitting tiny jackets and leggings so that the child would be warm for its first winter. Jess spent all the free time she had helping them and accompanying Anna on endless sorties to find the right things for the nursery.

"I don't want it to look ordinary," said Anna firmly, when the subject of decorating the room had first arisen. "It has to be something really different and special."

Jess had come up with some ideas of her own that she thought came under the heading of unusual decor, suitable for new-born infants. One plan she favoured involved draping the walls and ceiling in brightly coloured swathes of material to give the impression of a Mogul tent. Her suggested colour scheme of mustard, orange and gold made Anna flinch.

"It sounds lovely, Jess but don't you think it might be difficult to keep clean?" she said diplomatically. "I thought of having animals on the walls."

Jess's face lit up with renewed enthusiasm.

"Yeah! Great! We could make it like a zoo," she said happily, busily imagining brilliantly coloured tigers, giant pythons and flame-coloured parrots balancing on top of coconut palms and emerald green crocodiles, all rampaging over every square inch of paintable surface.

"Not quite," said Anna hastily when she heard the revised plan. "I meant to make it more of a sort of magic room. The kind of place I always dreamed of going to. I want to have a unicorn and the talking animals out of the books I loved when I was little. We'll put your mobile over where the cot will be and we'll make the ceiling like the night sky and paint luminous stars on it."

"OK!" said Jess, game for anything. "But I think we need to get 'old of someone I know to 'elp. You can't risk balancing on a ladder wiv the bulge making like 'e was dancing the cancan! I know just the right chap. 'E's a really nice guy – a bit mad and more than a bit gay but 'e can't 'alf paint!"

They spent days working on the room with the help of Jess's friend, Dominic – an out-of-work artist who lived close by – who was short of cash. It was evident from his thin, down-at-heel appearance that he needed the work but Dominic wasn't going to admit it.

"You're lucky to get me. It just happens that I'm available at the moment," he told her when she phoned him the next day. "It's a bit like in the theatre, ducky. I'm resting between commissions!"

He listened intently to Anna's description of what she wanted and, once he had been shown the illustrations in the Narnia books that she had kept so carefully over the years, he rose to the challenge magnificently.

The result was better than anyone could have imagined. The ceiling was transformed. It was no longer a one-dimensional surface. Anna thought it was now like looking through a telescope into a swirling confusion of distant galaxies, with stars and comets that glowed and a crescent moon, shimmering from behind shreds of scattered clouds.

On the walls, graceful tree ferns parted to reveal the animals. There were centaurs and creatures that were half-tree, half-human and there were spirits of water and air. A magnificent lion gazed benevolently at a gazelle grazing nearby. On the wall in the corner, where the cot would be, there was a snow-white unicorn, standing guard.

When Anna looked at the glorious animal, she heard a voice from the distant past saying, "One day, you may well catch sight of a unicorn – even if it is only from a distance."

When the last, finishing touches had been made, Dominic stood back with a flourish to let Anna and Jess admire the work of art. Both of them stood in awed silence in the middle of the transformed room. Then, Anna took hold of his hand. Jess thought that the look of delight on her face made her appear like a young child herself.

"I don't know what to say. I couldn't have hoped for anything as marvellous as this."

"The pleasure is all mine, dear!" He gently disengaged his hand from Anna's and brushed back a beautifully highlighted lock from his forehead. "Quite frankly, I never realised I was so talented! With this sort of an ambience to stimulate one, there is no excuse for the new arrival not growing up into something divinely special."

"Exactly wot I thought," agreed Jess, tugging at the knots of half-set paint that were embedded in her hair. "Couldn't 'ave put it better myself. You're a bloody genius, Dom!"

Dominic smiled at her and waved a hand limply, in denial of the charge.

"No, sweetie. Not quite – leave it at inspired."

Jess, grinning broadly, turned to Anna after he'd left,

"Didn' I tell ya? Dom's a pouf but 'e's a lovely pouf and 'e's got talent in buckets!"

* * *

Adam had taken to calling in to the house in Old Square once a week. He had become a welcome visitor, even to the protective Mrs P, who could see that he was anxious to help in any way he could. Each time he was there, the sense of happy anticipation that grew as the date for Anna's delivery got nearer and the relaxed atmosphere that pervaded the small house, made him linger, unwilling to leave. It was in sharp contrast to the atmosphere that filled The Pink House these days. Here, in Anna's Cambridge home, he felt it was as if the sunlight outside had spread into every corner of the newly painted rooms and it made his spirits lift each time he stepped into this new world in which she now lived and where he had at first felt out of place. It seemed to him that the house itself gave off an aura of calm. Even the usually noisy Jess had become more gentle, he noticed.

Slow-moving and content, Anna radiated happiness. Adam would find her sitting, gazing into the distance with a faraway look, while she stroked the black cat that had chosen to take up residence with them.

Although Anna's stepfather had thought himself satisfied with his life up until now, more and more he began to see that he had been missing out on something very important. He kept wondering what he could do or say to make Rosalind agree to visit her daughter. He sensed her carefully concealed jealousy and pleaded with her to come with him on one of his visits. She refused angrily. It was as though she were afraid to admit she had been wrong to turn her back on her daughter; that if she changed her mind, she would have to renew her whole attitude to Anna's very existence. He thought it sad that she, who had shown such great strength of character in the past, seemed unable to summon up the courage to do that. He knew Anna would not go back to The Pink House, unless invited by her mother. It was a total impasse as far as Adam could make out.

The rain stopped and the sun returned but the heat was less overpowering now and everything seemed to be refreshed and invigorated. There was an almost tropical lushness in the way the flowers continued to bloom and the roses produced a second, even a third flowering.

It was Friday, with ten days to go before 'D day' as Jess called it. Adam had been invited for lunch and the table was laid under the old Judas tree in the middle of the still damp lawn.

Jess had tracked down an ancient lawnmower and after sprinkling the machine with liberal quantities of olive oil when Mrs P wasn't looking, she'd set to work with grim determination. The sweet scent of newly cut grass hung in the air. The tops of the molehills she had shaved off in her battle to reduce everything to the same level stood out against the green like untidy blisters in the grass.

"It smells heavenly, doesn't it?" Anna said, watching as Adam carefully draped his jacket over the back of a garden chair before sitting down.

"It really does. It's strange how I never noticed it when the grass was being cut at home." There was a companionable silence and then he said, "You know, Anna, I'm really rather looking forward to being a grandfather – well, a stepgrandfather."

Anna looked at him, amused.

"Well, that's a surprise!"

"I'm rather surprised myself, actually. I never thought I would have to take on that particular role. Somehow, it was never on the agenda."

"And now you like the idea?"

"I like it a lot." He leaned back in his chair and stared up into the leafy canopy above them. "I have never been much of a family man in the conventional sense. I was adopted when I was a baby. My mother died and my father couldn't cope with having a small child around the place. It must have been awkward for him, I suppose. So I was farmed out to various aunts, who didn't know what to do with me. Going away to school was quite a relief really!"

Anna was touched by this unexpected confidence. She had somehow taken it for granted that he came from a privileged and secure background.

"Does it make you sad when you look back, Adam?"

He shrugged slightly.

"I'm sorry that I never knew my mother, of course, but I've spent most of my life concentrating on working hard and building up a successful business. I made sure I didn't leave too much spare time to dwell on things that might have been. I found it easier to survive that way and it got less difficult as the years went by." He gave her a wry smile. "A rather different attitude to life compared with the one you have, I think."

Anna smiled back at him.

"Well, you didn't have the benefit of growing up for eight years under the influence of my Aunt Pog. You might have ended up by being a rather different person if you had!"

Adam laughed.

"My God! What a thought!"

"Well, I consider you to be a proper grandfather. I think you will make a very nice one."

"And I'm going to be an honorary gran," added Mrs P as she approached them with a heavily laden tray.

"Then the child is twice blessed in that case, Mrs P," said Adam, courteously as he stood up to take the tray from her.

"Don't forget that Jess is to be godmother," Anna added, watching to see Adam's reaction.

"Oh, really?" he said, casually. "I'm sure she'll make a terrific – and extraordinary one too!" They all laughed. "Where is the lady in question?"

"Jess is at work. She'll be back for supper. She sent you her love, by the way!" Anna teased. "I think she has a bit of a crush on you, Adam!"

He refused to rise to the bait.

"Tell her I'm sorry to have missed her. By the way, Anna, didn't you say that you had asked your friend Kathleen in Ireland to be a godmother too?" He filled a wine glass.

"Yes, she's going to come over for the christening and Amy's going to try and get off college so that she can come too." Anna smiled at the prospect.

"What about a godfather?" Adam asked.

"I haven't chosen one," said Anna. "I don't know anyone who'd be right."

She had briefly thought of asking PJ but Kathleen's hints that he still carried a torch for her had made her decide against it. She wanted to keep her life as simple as possible from now on.

"Well," said Mrs P. "I don't much think it matters as long as there's someone looking out for the child's soul and from what Anna's told me about that Kathleen over there in Ireland, she sounds as though she fits the bill nicely."

Anna smiled.

"Yes, Kathleen for the spiritual side of things and Jess can teach him or her to do the tango!"

She could hardly wait to see Kathleen and her baby. She felt she would like to be surrounded by all the people she loved and secretly wished that Gina would be coming to the christening as well. There had been no contact since she had left Italy and although she could not visualise her face, she vividly remembered the woman's warmth and kindness to her. Perhaps, when her own child was old enough to travel, they would go back and find Gina and Alfredo again. Perhaps even Frederica and Roberto might be pleased to see her. Now that so much time had passed since that awful accident, perhaps even that was possible.

* * *

After lunch, Adam unwillingly left the two women dozing in their chairs in the half-shade. He had to get back to the office to see an important client. He let himself out of the house, trying to marshal his thoughts and switch back into being the efficient solicitor. He was finding it increasingly irksome to go into the office at the moment, he realised. Home life wasn't so good either. Although recently Rosalind had not criticised his frequent visits to Old Square, his increasing closeness to and sympathy for Anna upset her and he'd found her particularly awkward and distant over the past few weeks.

"Why don't you come with me? We don't have to stay

very long. I think Anna would like you to see the house. She's made it really lovely," he had suggested, a few days earlier.

"Let's face it, Adam," she snapped back at him, "I failed her when she was a child. She knows it and I know it. I really can't start playing Happy Families or the doting mother at this point. Too much has happened. I can't help it – I'm sorry!"

"Perhaps when the baby is born you will feel differently."

"No! I know I won't. Please don't ask me again."

She had looked so miserably bleak, he had not repeated the request.

* * *

Anna awoke with a start. She was alone. Mrs P must have slipped inside with the lunch things and left her to sleep, she thought blearily. In spite of her rest, she felt heavy and muddled. She watched as a lone magpie bounced across the grass towards her, its tail feathers bobbing up and down. He looked strangely evil, she thought. It stopped, turning his sleek head to look at her. Fortune slid out from under Anna's chair and stood, tail twitching, daring the intruder to come any closer.

The bird appeared unconcerned by the cat's presence. It was almost as though it was challenging the animal. Anna clapped her hands together loudly. She disliked the marauding magpies. They seemed to her to represent the criminal element among the flying fraternity and she hated their noisy, bullying tactics. With a loud squawk, the bird took to the air and glided over the wall, disappearing into some trees in the neighbouring garden. Anna bent forward and stroked Fortune.

"Horrible things, aren't they, Puss?" she whispered, as the cat rubbed against her hand.

As she straightened up, Anna realised she didn't feel very well. A pain, that had been a dull ache in her back, now seemed to encircle her. She leaned back in her chair and took a deep breath. It receded and she felt better. She wondered if she had over-eaten at lunch.

When it came back, the pain had increased alarmingly and with a sinking feeling, Anna knew that something beyond her control was taking place. For the first time in her pregnancy, she faced the ordeal of going into labour with fear. It's too soon, she thought, fighting against the panic welling up in her. She called out for Mrs P and by the time the woman reached her, Anna's face was white and she was breathing in shallow gasps.

"Dear child! Is it the baby?" The girl could only nod. "Don't you worry, my love. I'll telephone for the ambulance. Everything will be all right," May Pender said breathlessly before half-running, half-stumbling back towards the house.

She reappeared a few minutes later.

"They're on their way. I can't get hold of Jess – the wretched phone seems to be engaged. Shall I ring Mr Strong?" She squatted down beside the frightened girl. Anna reached out and held on to Mrs P's hands tightly, her eyes shut.

"No, don't disturb him – he's busy," she said, faintly.

By the time the ambulance arrived, Anna was using every ounce of her strength to cope with the waves of pain that threatened to overwhelm her. Gently and expertly, she was helped on to a stretcher by the two ambulance men.

"I'm coming with you," Mrs P informed them in a no-nonsense voice when they had slid the stretcher into the ambulance.

"Shouldn't you bring your handbag and shut the front door behind you then, Missus?" one of them suggested, halting the woman in her frantic scramble up the steps after them.

"Well, please wait for me. I'm the child's grandmother," she lied, " and I must be with her."

Mrs P was desperate at the thought of Anna being taken away from her. She returned, clutching her bag, a few moments later. She was trembling and her hair was untidy from pulling off her apron in a hurry. The ambulance drove off with the siren wailing like the soulless crying of a banshee.

Alone in the garden, beside Anna's overturned chair, Fortune waited. An unseen magpie cackled from the depths of a nearby tree.

* * *

At the hospital, things moved so quickly that, before she knew what was happening, a dazed Mrs P found herself firmly relegated to a waiting room by a steely-faced Sister, who was more than a match for the countrywoman, however much she protested her right to stay at Anna's side. It had been discovered that Mrs P was not in fact a relative.

"It's against hospital policy," the Sister said brusquely. "When Mr Wilson says you may see Miss Armitage, then you will be allowed to do so. There is the possibility that he may have to operate. In the meantime, I suggest you have a cup of tea from the canteen downstairs."

She left the room with a crackle of starched apron and a whiff of disinfectant in her wake.

May Pender felt close to tears. How could she leave Anna in the care of that one? She looked as though she had never smiled at anyone in her life, she thought miserably. It wasn't meant to be like this. She and Jess both wanted to be there for Anna when her baby was born. She felt guilty at allowing herself to be made to abandon Anna when the girl most needed her.

The woman blew her nose noisily and tried to compose herself. They had hardly told her anything. All they had said was that there was a problem with the baby's breathing and there might be no time for it to be born naturally. If there was an operation, she knew how disappointed Anna would be. She had wanted to give birth to her baby herself without gases and interference from doctors.

All of a sudden, Mrs P got unsteadily to her feet, her mind made up. She would ring Mr Strong, whether he was busy or not. He wasn't the type to be bossed around by nurses – or doctors – come to that. They'd have to explain things to him or there would be trouble. It all wouldn't seem so bad if he was in charge. She opened the door cautiously and went in search of a telephone.

Chapter Thirty-two

It was nearly eight o'clock that evening when a dishevelled Jess ran up the steps of the hospital. She crashed through the swing doors into the foyer, pushing her way through the crowd of evening visitors with their bunches of unscented carnations and roses and giant boxes of sickly-sweet chocolates.

"Babies! No! Maternity!" she gasped, out of breath, to the porter in reception.

He gave her hurried instructions, thinking that this wild-looking female in her long, voluminous, red dress might be about to give birth at any moment.

"Do you want someone to come with you?" he asked.

But Jess, taking the steps two at a time, was already halfway up the first flight of stairs.

She was shown into the waiting-room off the main maternity ward. Mrs P sat on a metal chair in one corner of the harshly lit room, talking to a severe-looking young nurse. A look of relief crossed her face when she saw Jess.

"Hello, dear. I'm so glad you're here. It's been dreadful waiting on my own. Mr Strong's been gone for ages."

Jess hurried over. Letting her bag drop to the ground, she looked anxiously at Mrs P and the nurse.

"Tell me what's 'appened. Mr Strong didn't say on the phone – just that I was to come and that you was 'ere. Are Anna and the baby OK?"

Mrs P shook her head in a bewildered way. She looked exhausted, almost as though she were too full of emotion to speak. The dark-haired nurse answered for her in a low voice.

"It's been a difficult couple of hours for poor Mrs Pender, I'm afraid. Things didn't go very smoothly for a while." Seeing the anguished expression on Jess's face, she added briskly, "Anna's asleep just now and the baby is going to have to spend a couple of days in an incubator but he'll be just fine." She paused, suddenly seeming to take in the other girl's appearance. "Are you related to Miss Armitage?"

"No, I mean, yes," said Jess. "I'm the godmuver. You know, the baby's. Wot 'appened?"

"Anna couldn't manage to deliver the child on her own and when the baby was born, he was a little distressed and having difficulty breathing for a while but, as I said, he'll be perfectly all right."

"And Anna?" Jess asked impatiently, her eyes not moving from the other's face.

"She's rather tired and sore after the Caesarean but she'll soon get over that," the nurse replied in a matter-of-fact sort of voice that made Jess want to thump her and blow raspberries. "Mr Strong is with the doctor now. He'll be back any minute."

"When can we see them?" asked Mrs P.

"That depends on the doctor, Mrs Pender."

When the door closed behind her, there was silence inside the over-heated, small room. A window rattled in a sudden gust of wind and hurrying feet tapped past in the echoing corridor outside.

"Don't you just 'ate 'ospitals?" said Jess. "They're all on a flamin' power trip in these places." She looked at Mrs P indignantly. "Why won't they let us see Anna and the baby if everyfing's OK? It don't make sense." She subsided untidily into the chair beside Mrs P and reached over for the woman's cold hand, at the same time noticing that the other's complexion looked almost grey in the unkind strip lighting. "You don't think there's somefing they're not tellin' us, do you?"

Mrs P patted Jess's hand.

"I hope not, dear. I'm afraid this is the sort of carry-on that you have to put up with in hospitals. They'll let us see her soon. Mr Strong will see to that."

They weren't sure how long they had been waiting when Adam eventually came into the room. Jess noticed with surprise that he looked much less smart than usual. He had the appearance of someone who hadn't bothered to gather himself together before dashing to the hospital. He wasn't wearing a jacket and his tie was crooked. She also saw that he was looking anxious.

Both women watched him closely as he walked towards them.

He smiled reassuringly as he sat down beside them on one of the uncomfortable metal chairs.

"Well, after a bit of a panic, I've been assured that there's no need for any worry. As a result of a bit of bullying on my part, Sister says you can go and see them both if you'd like." He gave Mrs P a quick glance that Jess didn't see and added in a low voice, "Just as long as it's brief. She's looking exhausted."

"Just try an' stop us!" said Jess, jumping to her feet. "Come on, Mrs P, before that lot change their minds."

As they walked along the corridor, Jess hurrying in front of them, her sandals making a slapping sound on the lino, Mrs P looked up at the tall man beside her. She spoke quietly.

"Is there something wrong, Mr Strong? Only you seem worried."

"I'm not sure, Mrs P. There's something about Anna that bothers me. I can't explain quite what it is but . . ." He gave her a quick smile. "Perhaps it's me being ridiculous. After all, I'm no expert when it comes to young women who've just given birth. When I said something about it to the Sister, she looked at me as though I had two heads and asked me if I'd expected a woman to be bouncing around after a Caesarean and that it was only normal that Anna looked rather the worse for wear."

While Jess and Mrs P peered into the room, Adam waited outside, not wanting to intrude.

Anna was asleep, her dark hair fanned out over her pillow. The older woman was struck by how pale she looked – and how fragile. There were blue circles under her eyes that made her look very vulnerable. She longed to go over to the bed and gather her up in her arms and hug her gently.

Jess stared at the sleeping figure suspiciously. Then she turned to Mrs P, catching hold of her arm.

"Is she really all right, Mrs P? Only she looks a bit . . ." she whispered.

"I'll live to fight another day," said a voice softly from the bed.

Anna was watching them with an amused look. Groggily, she pulled herself up against the pillows.

"Anna!" Jess made a dash for the bed, closely followed by Mrs P.

When they had both kissed and congratulated her, Jess said, "You see! I woz right all along! It *is* a bloke baby."

Anna laughed weakly.

"Yes, you were right, Jess. It is a bloke baby."

"Have you decided on a name yet?" asked Mrs P eagerly.

"I think so. I'm not *quite* sure and I want to think about it a little more." She hesitated, putting her hand up to her head and shutting her eyes briefly. "I'm feeling a bit dizzy at the moment – it's difficult to think straight but I promise, you two will be the first to know when I've made up my mind."

"You know that I fink Alfie would be lovely for a boy," Jess said, turning to Mrs P. "Don't you fink it would be a good name, Mrs P?"

Mrs P put her finger up to her lips. Anna's eyes had flickered shut again.

"We'll just have to wait and see what she decides," she whispered. "Come on, Jess. It's very late. Let's go and have a look at the baby now before we have to leave. We'll come back and see Anna tomorrow."

She gave a last, concerned look in Anna's direction before they tiptoed out of the room, closing the door quietly behind them. Jess held Mrs P's arm as, accompanied by a preoccupied Adam, they walked the short distance to the neo-natal unit.

When they got there, the young nurse allowed them a quick look through the glass screen.

"But I can't see," complained Jess after the small figure in the incubator had been pointed out to them. The nurse pushed the machine closer to the glass. "Blimey!" she exclaimed. "He's not exactly *pretty*, is he? It's like 'e's been in a car crash. Do they always look all wrinkled and sort of squashed-looking?"

Mrs P chuckled. "Well, I've never had any of my own but I think it's quite normal for a new baby to look like that." She gazed thoughtfully at the baby. "He's lovely though, isn't he?"

Jess continued to stare. "P'raps it's coz 'e came out a bit sooner than planned."

"Perhaps," agreed Mrs P, "but you wait, in a few weeks time, he'll be a really bonny child. See if I'm not right!"

Jess grinned. "Well, even if 'e does look a bit squashed, I reckon 'e's fantastic. I'm just going to tell Anna I approve of me godson before we go." When she saw the approaching Sister pursing her lips and looking pointedly at her watch, she added quickly, "I'm only going to tell 'er that 'e looks great and say goodnight, not sit down an' read her a bleeding nighttime story."

Before anyone could try and stop her, Jess set off at high speed in the direction of Anna's room with Mrs P, Adam and the disapproving Sister following closely behind.

No sooner had the door swung shut after her than Jess reappeared, her face shocked. In a voice that was shrill with panic, she called out to the Sister.

"Quick! There's something wrong wiv Anna."

Mrs P would never forget the sight in the small hospital room. Anna stared at them with frightened eyes. Her skin was glistening with sweat and her damp hair stuck to her forehead in dark strands. The Sister moved swiftly over to her and took hold of her wrist, frowning.

"Anna? What's the matter?" she asked briskly.

The girl grasped her arm. She appeared to be having trouble focussing on the woman's face.

"I feel so faint . . . and I think I'm bleeding . . ."

A convulsion seemed to pass through her body and Adam and the two watching women saw her fall back onto the pillows.

"What's happening?" Adam demanded.

But the Sister ignored him. Ringing the bell with one hand, she quickly lifted the bedclothes covering Anna's motionless body. One glance was enough to tell her what was wrong. Jess, nearest to the bed, caught a glimpse of the blood-soaked nightdress and sheets.

Without looking at them and in a tone that brooked no argument, the Sister told them to leave the room immediately.

Horrified, they found themselves again in the corridor, their faces flushed by the red light over the door, as the dark-haired nurse hurried past them into the room. They heard the Sister telling her to fetch the resuscitation trolley. An alarm buzzed in the nurses' station.

A stunned-looking Jess whispered, "I don't understand. They said she was just tired." She turned to Adam. "You don't think she's . . ."

Grim-faced, he replied, "I don't know what's going on but the best thing for us to do is keep out of their way so that they can do their job." Taking hold of each woman by the arm, he led them back in the direction of the waiting-room. "This is one of those times when we have to be patient."

"But . . ." stammered Jess. "There was blood everywhere. We can't just leave her like that . . ."

"Come on, Jess," Adam insisted.

But as they walked back along the corridor, he experienced a sinking feeling in the pit of his stomach. You didn't have to be a genius to know that something was terribly wrong. They heard a clatter of swing doors behind them and the rattle of trolley wheels. Glancing back, he saw two white-coated doctors hurriedly disappearing into Anna's room, one pushing a drip-stand.

Once in the waiting-room, they sat down without speaking, each of them preoccupied with their own individual, unthinkable thoughts. Jess huddled against Mrs P, her face pressed against the older woman's shoulder, her hand resting on the other's cold hand. She could feel it trembling slightly.

A little apart from them, Adam sat, staring blankly at the black squares of window with the reflections of white ceiling and hanging strip lights. Needing the resuscitation trolley could only mean one thing – that Anna's heart had stopped beating. Judging from what Jess had seen, she must have haemorrhaged badly. He shut his eyes. This was too cruel. After all that girl had gone through, she deserved some happiness. He thought of Anna's child, lying like a small laboratory specimen in its plastic box. Was he going to be one of the many, sad children who never knew their mother? Would he be denied all the tenderness and gentle loving that Anna had so joyfully and generously stored up for him? Adam felt impotent. There weren't many situations that he couldn't deal with but now he knew that he was useless to her. A feeling of anger swept through him. Slowly getting to his feet, he looked down at the two women.

Trying to keep the tension out of his voice, he said, "I think I could do with some tea. Can I get some for either of you?"

Mrs P nodded. "That would be nice, Mr Strong, thank you."

"I'll come with you," said Jess quickly.

Adam shook his head.

"Better to stay here and look after Mrs P," he said gently. "I'll be back in a few minutes."

The door closed behind him with a loud click. Sniffing, Jess opened her bag and started to hunt around for a handkerchief without success. She was going to ask Mrs P to lend her hers but, looking at her, she decided not to disturb her. The woman had her eyes shut. Was she praying? Jess wondered. She wiped her own eyes on the back of her sleeve, leaving a black smudge of mascara on each cheek. Leaning back stiffly in her chair she tried not to think about what was happening in the room further down the corridor. But the image of a pale-faced Anna falling back on the bed filled her mind. Why had there been so much blood? It was unthinkable that anything should happen to someone who was so young and who had so much to live for. She stubbornly refused to accept the fact that Anna might be dead. They would make it all right. She was sure of it. That Sister might be rather frighteningly strict but she was the sort of person who didn't allow her patients to die on her.

* * *

When ten minutes had gone by, Jess began to wonder if she shouldn't go looking for Adam. Perhaps he hadn't gone to get himself some tea after all but was trying to find out what was going on. No sooner had she made up her mind to go and look for him but the door opened.

She sprang to her feet as soon as she saw him, her eyes frantically scanning his face for telltale signs. She stared at him mutely, frightened to ask him anything.

Adam went over to her, putting his arm around her bony shoulders.

"It's all right. They managed to resuscitate Anna. But she's lost a lot of blood. She's down in the theatre now."

Mrs P's hand went up to her mouth. When she spoke, her voice shook. "What does that mean, Mr Strong?"

"It means that they will make sure she won't haemorrhage any more. They've started giving her a blood transfusion straight away to replace what was lost."

Jess stared at him, tears glistening at the corners of her eyes. "So, she'll be OK, won't she?"

Adam thought the girl looked like a small, sad clown with her smudged eyes, outrageous hair and gaudy dress. He felt moved – her distress was so palpable. He gave her shoulders a gentle squeeze.

"She'll be fine, Jess."

"*Really?*"

"Really," he replied in a firm voice.

He hoped to God that he was right.

* * *

It was nearly two o'clock in the morning by the time the three of them left the hospital, wearily stepping out into a night that was full of the sound of a wild wind that had sprung up, unnoticed until now.

They made their way silently towards the car park.

At the entrance, Mrs P turned to Adam, her grey hair blowing into her eyes so that she had to put both hands up to push it back in order to see him clearly.

"Mr Strong, will you take me and Jess back to Old Square, please?" she asked. "Only I don't think we want to be on our own tonight." She looked at Jess. "Am I right, Jess?" The other nodded tiredly. Mrs P hesitated and then asked, "I know it's too soon to celebrate, but the worst is over, isn't it?"

Adam smiled at her. "Yes, Mrs P. You heard what the doctor said. It will take time for Anna to get back on her feet but you'll have her home just as soon as she's feeling well again."

As he unlocked the car, he thought of Rosalind alone in The Pink House. She'd been by herself all day. He'd phoned earlier and told her that he'd gone to the hospital and that Anna's son had been born. Her reaction had been minimal. It hadn't surprised him but he couldn't stop himself from feeling disappointed.

The two women talked quietly together in the back of the car as he drove through the empty Cambridge streets. Feeling unusually light-headed and emotional, Adam thought of Anna – the young woman whom he had, over the past few months, come to admire and like so much – the girl who had faced up to the prospect of becoming an unmarried mother at the age of barely nineteen without her own mother's support and love. She had shown a calm, joyful determination that had amazed him. When he'd spoken to her after she had been brought back to her hospital room immediately after the birth, although plainly exhausted, she had looked radiant.

"Have you seen him?" she'd asked him eagerly. When Adam replied that he had, she said, "Isn't he beautiful?"

When he'd looked at the wrinkled little creature that was Anna's child, lying in the incubator in the brightly lit unit, he had been overcome by a feeling of amazement at the whole experience. To his surprise, he realised that he felt excited and moved by what had just happened. As he had turned away, he couldn't help thinking how lucky the child was to have a mother with such a capacity to love and how incredible it was, considering that Anna herself had never received that same sort of unselfish giving from her own mother.

As he drove, he thought how dreadful it was that it had all gone so nearly disastrously wrong. But, judging by what the doctor had said, it did look as though all would now be well. Unconsciously, he gave a grateful sigh as he drew up outside the small redbrick house that was Anna's.

* * *

"I'm going to call him Malachy," Anna announced several days later as she held the baby in her arms, gently stroking the top of his down-covered head. "Malachi is an old Hebrew name but it's quite often used in Ireland. And after all, I spent quite a long time there." Aunt Pog would approve because she'd always been fond of the permanently intoxicated flautist of the same name who holidayed each year in one of the cottages in Sandy Bay. That, and the fact that it was slightly unusual, she thought contentedly. She looked at Adam questioningly. "His second name will be David, after my father. Do you like it?"

"Yes, I think I do, rather," he replied. "Malachy David! As you say, it's a bit different and that's no bad thing these days in a world where the average and unexciting appears to be the norm." He did like the name but Adam was pretty sure that Rosalind wouldn't. He guessed that she would have preferred a Sam or Josh, the sort of names that her friends' grandsons were being given. "I hear that now Malachy has been given the all clear, the two of you are going to be allowed home the day after tomorrow."

Anna smiled. "I can't wait! They've been so nice here but it's not the same as being where you belong." She sighed contentedly. "Adam, I feel so lucky. I have Mrs P

399

and Jess – and you have been absolutely marvellous. Thank you so much for all that you've done for me. I really don't deserve to be treated so well."

"Rubbish! I've enjoyed feeling useful!" said Adam quickly. He gave her a quizzical glance. "Though, mind you, unplanned pregnancy wasn't really on the agenda when you arrived from Ireland – I have to admit that came as a bit of a shock!" His face became serious. "I feel I owe you an apology, Anna. The way your mother and I handled it at the beginning was very wrong. Although I do think that it's perhaps turned out for the best. You seem so happy in that little house of yours. Between the three of you, it's been turned into a really lovely home."

Anna held the sleeping Malachy close to her, breathing in his smell of newborn child and talcum powder. She looked over to where Adam sat.

"Don't feel guilty. What I did was careless and thoughtless. I don't blame you or my mother for the way you reacted." She looked down at Malachy. "But when I see him like this, I *can't* be sorry that it happened. I think it's the most marvellous thing in the world and I have never felt so . . . complete." She pulled a wry face. "Does that sound, what Jess would call, 'a bit drippy' and over the top?"

"Not in the least!" He looked amused. " I can't help thinking that Jess is going to make an interesting godmother for him. I'd say they'll have a lot of fun together. You'll have to be careful she doesn't kidnap him and run off to live with the gypsies!" He stood up. "I'm afraid I'll have to go. The office is in chaos and if I don't make an appearance soon, they'll go on strike." Casually, he put his hand in his pocket and brought out a small blue leather box, which he placed on the locker beside the bed. "Open it when Malachy's back in his cot. It's just a little something to say congratulations and how pleased I am that you've made me a stepgrandfather. I hope you like it."

He leaned forward and kissed Anna lightly on the cheek. Before she could say anything more than 'Goodbye', he was gone.

Carefully, she manoeuvred herself out of bed and placed the baby in his cot. Leaning over, she picked up the dark blue box. She opened the lid and let out a gasp when she saw the pearl and emerald earrings. They were oval and almost identical to the ring her father had left her.

* * *

The day before Anna's return home, Adam called in to the house in Old Square to see Mrs P and Jess. After a few words with the older woman, he asked Jess if she would join them in the sitting-room. The girl had spent most of the morning searching for Anna's cat. Fortune had been missing from the first night of Anna's absence from the house and Jess and Mrs P were starting to fear that something might have happened to the animal. Now, curious to know why Adam wanted to see her, she clattered into the sitting-room in her heavy clogs and sat down beside Mrs P on the couch that was scattered with gaily-coloured cushions. Adam walked over to the fireplace, filled with large white daisies in the blue jug that Anna had found in the dusty antique shop on the opposite side of the square. He turned and gave Jess a searching look.

"Jess, I'll come straight to the point. How would you feel about giving up your job and moving in here with Mrs P to help her look after Anna and Malachy? I've talked it over with Anna and she loved the idea but wasn't sure that you'd want to."

Jess was momentarily stunned. She looked from Adam to Mrs P and back again. She found it incredible that he should consider her fit for the job. She knew perfectly well that he still found her unconventional ways disconcerting.

"Wow! Really?"

"Really!"

Jess looked at Mrs P. "Would that be all right wiv you, Mrs P?"

The woman nodded, smiling broadly. "Yes, dear. I think it would be a shame not to be together. We make a good team, we do."

"Nuffin' I'd like better," said Jess, grinning. "'Specially when it means I can tell that old bat, Mrs Rao, where she can stuff her incense sticks." Seeing Adam's slightly raised eyebrows, she added, "Mind you, I'll tell 'er ever so nicely!"

"I'll take that as a yes, then," said Adam, unable to stop himself from laughing at the ecstatic expression on her face. He turned back to Mrs P. "There are a few other things I would like to discuss."

While Adam and Mrs P talked, Jess wondered what his wife felt about it all, about the change in her husband – for he was very different from when Jess had first met him. She also wondered what the woman felt about Malachy's arrival on the scene. Surely she must be just a little bit curious to know what he was like. Perhaps Mr Strong would be able to persuade her to take an interest. Jess had only glimpsed Rosalind that once in the car and Anna very rarely mentioned her mother.

A few days earlier, when Jess had said something about how nice it would be if Rosalind would change her mind about not wanting to see Malachy, Anna had replied firmly, "You can't have everything you want in life, Jess. I realise now that it's greedy to expect it all to be perfect." She'd smiled at Jess. "Let's just be thankful that it's all as good as it is. I've decided that Aunt Pog got it right. Live for the moment and deal with the future when it happens!"

Well, thought Jess, if Anna's bloody mother couldn't be happy for them, then perhaps it would be better if she stayed away.

* * *

Anna sat on the garden seat under the Rambling Rector, Malachy asleep in her arms and Fortune curled up beside her. Hoverflies and bees buzzed among the flowers and the sunshine was pleasantly warm on her face. She could hear Jess and Mrs P laughing together in the kitchen as they made lunch. Looking out over the sunlit garden, she thought that it didn't get much better than this. Even Fortune had come home the day she'd brought her son back to the house. Mrs P had been worried that the cat would be jealous of the new arrival but the animal seemed so pleased to see Anna, he didn't appear to take any notice of Malachy.

She turned and watched Adam, who sat at her side, relaxed, one arm behind his head as he too gazed out over the garden.

"I don't think I've ever seen you looking so . . . I don't know . . . happy," she remarked.

He smiled. "I can't begin to tell you how happy I am that all is well with you and Malachy. There's only one thing that we have to try and make right now."

"What's that?" asked Anna, surprised. "Do you mean my mother?"

"Yes, Anna, I do. I have tried to give you as much support as possible over the past few months and Rosalind has suffered because of it." Seeing her anxious expression, he added quickly, "It's not your fault! She's . . ." It was obvious that he was choosing his words with care. "I love your mother, Anna, in spite of what has happened. Her own childhood was pretty miserable, reading between the lines – although she's never said all that much about it. You know how she finds it difficult to express emotions and she's never been one to indulge in self-pity. I think her experiences with her mother left a legacy, which made it impossible for her to be compassionate or understanding with you." He paused, absent-mindedly staring out into the garden. "It's very difficult to find the right person with whom you feel you want to spend the rest of your life. I was starting to think that I would remain a sorry bachelor until I met your mother and . . . I had no idea what being part of a family meant. I so want her to share all this." He spread his hands in a sweeping gesture that took in the baby, the house, the garden and Anna.

"Well, if anyone can bring my mother round, it will be you, Adam." Anna laid her hand on his arm. "I'm glad you love her. I think I'm beginning to understand a little better why things have been the way they have between her and me. I can't pretend that it doesn't still hurt and I don't want to start hoping that it will all turn out happily." She smiled wryly at him. "I know that even if things do get better, it will take time." Glancing down at the sleeping child, her face softened as she watched him. "At the moment, I'm just content. Now, all I want is to be able to enjoy Malachy – and being home and alive!"

Watching them through the kitchen window, Jess remarked, "Life's bloody marvellous really – the way fings 'ave turned out."

"Yes," said Mrs P dryly. "It's pre-ordained, Jess, remember. That ka . . . thingummy. What do you call it?"

"Karma!" said Jess, grinning.

"That's the one."

THE END